Politics of The Asylum

POLITICS OF THE ASYLUM

ADAM STEINER

Urbane
PUBLICATIONS

First published in Great Britain in 2018 by Urbane Publications Ltd
Suite 3, Brown Europe House, 33/34 Gleaming Wood Drive, Chatham,
Kent ME5 8RZ

A CIP catalogue record for this book is available from the British
Library.

ISBN 978-1-911331-86-5
MOBI 978-1-911331-88-9
EPUB 978-1-911331-87-2

Design and Typeset by The Invisible Man
Cover by The Invisible Man

Printed and bound by 4edge Limited, UK

Urbane
PUBLICATIONS

urbanepublications.com

I feel as if I am at a dead
end and so I am finished.
All spiritual facts I realize
are true but I never escape
the feeling of being closed in
and the sordidness of self,
the futility of all that I
have seen and done and said.

-Allen Ginsberg

PoTA – (Everything But Itself)

Adam Steiner

Creatio ex Nihilo

I intensify atoms. With every step, every breath between pause, a rushing haze of red water flicks –to remind me– there's that ugly taste on the lips. Picked apart the platelets crack stubborn shades to get floor from skin, but it's already too late to try – must stay awake – rubbed raw a thousand times and watered-down to the same vague sense; not red, not pink, a mirage of rushes cycles back around again. The big-red has blown, its heavy water spilt – but at least it's not mine, it's *his*.

Nurses and doctors blur past in stream of bodies to attend his fleeting melody –then into discord– a pixelating splash that conquers the eye. Quick-marched to intensive care via tromboning silver seraph pipes, grabbed and pulled, spinning faster undone through double doors of crowded halls. Paperwork explodes into crushed white doves, they're slamming harder now but almost there, another lonely cell spirited on to the emergency ward.

Hands rest heavy on the pole (grip fast to what you know) waiting, still, to breathe in sulphurous moods from before. Those same waves flow in crystalline ammonia, a scent that guides me to motion as every sweep arcs harder, no different from the last, though the water gets bloodier as you go down. Every changing patient looks like the other with pain multiplied against laboured erosion. There's more rushes and blood, more beats and breaks, stand well back to watch surfaces evaporate.

Splash out more water to send away the burning tigers that flourish in course, sweeping dead cells down the drain. This is the way: cleaning around the clock to make every one, every *thing*, the same.

Next wave's splash and splat, then arrested by manifold crash at the skirting board, spitting up the wall – another door slams. Each sweep expands, a seawall that rushes to the fore. Our hygienic sanity is meted-out in harsh alkali flats that sting the eyes, cause nose to scrape and itch as tongue laps for moisture on dry roof of the mouth. See sickle moons etched in white as soft dust pockets explode with the rush of bodies, picking out the embryonic dots.

White-feather falls from nowhere, fading swan-like in the streaks and leylines of running bleach, only to be trammelled by crooked wheels, scuff marks and slashes. Pale light lingers on but I'm reminded of more work to be done by slow drips at numb wet toes, all dragging me back to waking life. Wet swathes gleam, still not dry, as if no time had passed at all.

Mop in hand. Press it. Grid. Grind left shoulder down to worthless gear, an apex wearing out and away. I am dust and not much else. Against my hand letters 'NF' rise, scratched on the handle as diamond lines that run into grooves of thumbprint, known by touch.

Set in plastic, the floor sparkles on; but the sun never seems to move on like it should. It peers through, marking fragments of chiming stars and odd kinks in the factory-pressed glass. Pick out the burning points that drag warped ground out from under. New signs of warming light break through mind's cloud to give off occasional sparks in the darkest spaces. My tired eyes stare on, wanting to be there in those brighter places, to see their silhouettes shine.

Aping Reason

Arrow this, please stay to the left, keep out of *that* and step up, now turn around because here is no-go (and you should really be in bed). Stand out a yellow triangle, a warning to the lost ones, a stick figure falling in broke-back crush – tread softly, this sinking ground creeps in wet vinyl ready for a fall.

All change aprons: now becoming blue, blue, an ElEctrifiEd You. Maybe one day we'll grow into new royalty, or else sink with acquiescence to some other shade or hue? Definitely less coffee, this ticker's um-dum-thum is its own bossa nova. There's fractional-face caught worn and serene in washed-out dunes, set indifferent to the hurry against my gravemarch pace. **General Areas Only**, stop all the drama and ignore the ballast of clocks tweaked five minutes fast to keep time, but somehow always leaving late. Better to crack-on and get ahead before more dawn-walkers come.

From early morning they clock-in with a hurried scrape. Treading heels on toe trying not to be first and definitely not the last; a trapped morning yawn, already aching for a cigarette though the dust's not even settled on the blood just yet.

This human train reminds me every hour is to the first as to the last and this day's never over. Clunk
strung-outhead
on every spare
                    cor

                n

                            er,

it's work that slows me down, trying too hard to keep within the lines. Skirting edge (precision is key) handle twists in grip, struggle out, catch strings in picky clip of a locking-wheel –bitten strands– caught fast.

Threads unwind, sapping strength as myriad tasks yet to be done hang limp in guillotine threat. No time for this, my worn-down teeth lick away as broken glass, there's chink of bare metal landing, the switch is stuck flicked ON. Screwgonespare from somewhere up above. No hope for answers just small black holes in the white foam sky, each dot a pinprick to exile.

It's hiding on purpose amongst the wired blue vines. Some pointy tap-tapping every time I slap the mop down, another foreign body to be removed, must shake it out until one of us breaks. Or just ignore it? No one else around to notice, could let it slip innocent at my heel, and move on without looking back to see them see me drop it.

First sweat quivers lip's precipice with every blue vibration drumming up the handle. Hold tight, hold *tighter*: wipe\step/wipe –again– press the filthy head descent through bucket grill –again– slit teeth filter slithering water. Levels rising, slush almost full –again– red rain souls go slow, their dripping tick time extinguished.

Insert Nathan Finewax **HERE**, suitable for cleaning all hard surfaces, apply evenly throughout for best mixed results. Now branded by instruction, my future's set as an active agent. We see through same eyes, one becoming the other, aping in and out as interest dictates, always waning unnoticed. Desperation smacks palm heel on wall edge as dreams are overwritten by bodily design. Rinse me down thinning organ walls, rigidly marshalled, set to the gallows of an open floor. Tense steps tap a trip, all swallowed up in blinking lights. Devour me shapeless, there'll be no scuttling *here*. My claws already clipped, I only eat up their whisperings to fade-out in secret. Always on hand to help erase myself – I am a ghost that comes and goes.

The Real Thing

–Break–

Another call cuts the still opaque. New instructions scatter all around, best listen in…eyes dart left to right peeking from behind green half-masks. These plastic people make and break connections with every second last – the big-red's running fainter now. It's in the stern glances, held just long enough to press the point home, with sharp nods or muffled yesses, shuffling in gloom of dropped heads sunk, bolted to the task.

Floating above the red mess they trail, whispering above their gowns' rushing, caught in a private gale like traces of winter leaves, we all hear, mad as birds, close enough to hear doctors speak:

"Gravnel, gravnel nw pls!"
"Ich th masticht aorphenate"
"Thn bleed 't, bld t!"
"No. W hv t gn stricture doraphine, hrr hrr!"
 More fast, more blurry. "What?"
Someone glares, the eyes have it: '**He's out of his depth**'

"Move, we're losing time!" Out the way idle hands pinch cloth, wasted at my sides. I go wincing with them as they slip and skid by, all over my floor, gleam-buffed last week. Recognise some sounds but not their language. Vowels clopped brutal off the palate-thunk, normal chords choking through irregular speech. Frequent "Mmmm"s cast out general agreement, now it's going right they hum in chorused peals of everlasting shrugs.

A nurse is drawn in to keep close-tabs, the last link in the chain before the fire runs out. She squeezes Doctor's most-trusted arm as he makes first incision, the line wavers slightly. Masks thump back and forth, breathing in sync with the flickering heart screen.

More blood flecks, even with greedy suction taking up the excess. Nurse leans in to him, her lashes shutter slowly as drawn-out butterflies. She smiles, a prick of blood tips a single lash, right *there*; doesn't even see it. Desperate to reach across and pick it out, that perfect sphere, floating there. Can Hep. B transmit through the eye? Wipes a finger over it, pulls down the mask to dagger chin and licks the speck away. Emerging clean, Doctor casts an eye, she bites her fingertip, smiling still and his mask creases wide, a hidden grin.

"Doctor, wll u langorine the *cystentia* proxaptherly?"
His head flicks round "Wht? Spk qkr!"
I remember now, that OxMed grammar, a universal challenge for the clique to make games with slipslide jargon; a jumbled flurry of ancient history, destined to expire.

Whatevercomesfirst: between the hype of hepped-up paranoia, catalogue of new definitions and measured instruction transmit bickering taut lips; minds are jerked along with caffeine-stretched eyes beyond *seeing*, all the meanings dragged narrow. Most have zoned-out but carry on speaking without thought. Nurses know the basics, Dragging along some smattered education and not much else. The small detritus that rarely sticks, just as Florence of the Light scratched-out coxcombs to fight simple death, while Doctress Seacole passed unnoticed, but what difference does it make when every circle runs complete?

Excessive OxMed often causes problems. That's the reason hospitals are so full of misunderstanding: mothers breathing panic up frosted window panes trying to figure out what's going on through the broken latin. Someone well-pronounced told me everything is under control, but I don't agree, how could I? At the heart of every belief hides a lie. Something in there I'm not being told. She stands apart, her lonely self against cold unfeeling glass. Another easy-wipe surface that takes the trace of pain away, like she was never there, same as the ones who stood before and the rest that will take her place.

Staring through breathless vapours that exclude her from the hysteric-crush, she hears doctors, normal men and women, talk about give and take, and so they do the go-go dictation in other voices, mixing-up the foreign bits like engines backfiring. They reel off names of strange bones we never notice or spare parts that wait to kill us by silent explosion. Amongst it all, define little Jack's snapped bones and squeezed organs, now bleeding like a spent leech. That brittle line of words reaching out to her ear's become stretched. Lead symptom: a jolted lump in the throat.

Step on step of leaking blood trail, I go chasing the after-death. They shout more jargon, pressing hard to staunch the flow. Indeterminate spurts erupt between fingers every two minutes, his last gushes petering-out.

Keep pace with mop, bringing a clean river as the lifeblood runs away with itself. Lick lips: the taste of a person and giddy with it, desperate to spit a ferrous stain (still a good person if I swallow a fly?) Quickly bowed under by mass of smells that wait to swallow me – bleach, blood, and that unending sense of sweat.

All	wheeze	together,
in	heavier	breaths
give	heart-	ache

giving up. Float on with dumb-fallen steps, they throw used gloves and dirty instruments away, anywhere, forgetting someone has to pick them up. The wheels screech on through, making fresh red lines.

I slows...

quiet   desertion   passes

                                for

                others pause,

I barely register, there; them dappled white coats form a slurried breeze post-splashback, dull treadage, nursing their own motheaten aches. At terminus: the non-being (*him*) lies table-spread, both of us still, though only I remain.

Try to block it out but new cries echo from down the way. Final beats sliding out, high-pitched sinews winding down, stiff unsprung, no one's here to pull on you now. An uncoiled symphony of flesh blends into the dull and dented metal, sharing horizontal scars.

Cold steel hums to himself. There's faint motion in the electric fizz swept along but it soon dissipates in twitches from toes to lips. Moisture starts to leave with the temperature drop, silvery fog weaves a warm outline, we call it autumn's ghost, seeing souls evaporate. Hair, teeth and nails will steadily grow, or the skin recedes, depending how you look at it.

Get on. Wipe my way back to the start. Diamond fronds are swollen red again, having quenched their promised thirst, but always taking more. It drips before it splats, everything to excess. All must clear away their own mess, what was his, becomes ours.

Change gloves, ready to go:

> Unwrapping,
>
> more letters, *newnews*

Pier's End

Peel back them suicide doors with the ghost-town approach, relearning all that's been left behind (to forget). A place without name, here's boarded-up strip that seems to rise so familiar; a grin of shattered teeth in red-brick fading grey. See newspapers streak trees, shot in comets of torn words, worn leaves litter the denervated stumps, where small feet wandered from the path tracing new arteries, breaking rain in the mud.

At the warped door frame there's that sense of putting pain in a stranger. Crying hard now, never knowing who or what hit; a flash of cruelty at close quarters, but never one of mine – I think. Shake it off. As lancet fingers pick at flesh still quivering and ripe for the blade, but not yet ready for laughing gas. Electric doors clunk apart, juddering open. Push, pull, hold for a few vital seconds then jump on through.

It rises in light, a lethal chamber big as the Crystal Palace. Somewhere there's Irish Folk playing loud with bright projections on the wall to remind us of better times, shadows screened as real lives. Suddenly inspired to go out again to the N-town streets and bring it all back home, with sick ones maimed by the quease of a modern turn; I'd lead them on, smiling towards a new hope, where the sounds sleep in ruptured hallelujah, an echoing chorus of our burning bright history.

Should I want not to remember, or is *déjà vu* just another excuse? We dream to forget, but forgetting *how* again; can't deny your past in sleep with so many voices buzzing up in clean of day. Now back to all this. Mop in hand, those same taught reflexes come snapping back. Remembering what to clean and where, the quicksilver steel cuts heady air in rushing streaks: limbs, feet and soul quickly shaped into ideal alignment, daring to make sense.

Run along now, via fractured designs of crooked walls and endless decorum, grown viral and so routine. With the malingering brickwork undone the processes swell; every day echoing footsteps of someone else's tread.

Loose Ends

Via dense fog of old mothers' hustle bustle, we all dash busy-bee, one to the other. Each person sees life from their own starting place; personality obsessed and strung out on seeming better, real decisions go slap-dash to hell. Routine rises bile in the tract; every action fights back, forged as iron in the spine. Head sulks weary, as joints fall first in domino spread. Spending moreandmoretime infected by thoughts not my own.

Neck-bent to examine granulation of a surface, trying to articulate the scraping changes, dripping into alchemy they make all the right motions but 'care' strikes me hollow as another dulled passion; once the shine wears off it's just living by other means.

Here to kill our silent enemies as they taunt me against a backdrop of steady rot. I *hear* the changes pass, from bug-ridden breath to last spasms of an exponential death.

Watch your step: Be Safe.
But who can really say,
whether keeping right is left?
Easy to dip and slip in foreign samples. Certain fluids will never mix. There's chain-spat catarrh lacing grey card bowls that must be destroyed; though they spit anywhere they want – so what's the point in aiming high? Impatient, I stand waiting for them to yield at the final flag. Bowl begins to soften, roughly- shaped as gentlemen's hats from cheap tree pulp, or paperwork spun into new forms then sold back to us with privatised price tags.

My eagerness is betrayed past fingernail length, draped in endless phlegm that seeps through microscopic gaps. Verging near vomitus, a cat's cradle reared from strands in slithey escape I can't shake. Looking for a bio-hazard bin to offload this hateful layer, or doomed to wander a slivering orchestral trail.

Desperate to avoid, they cross corridors in crushed huddles (fair enough). I turn to apologise, but *too quick* – it's flecked all over. Their faces aghast, too quick to disbe*lieve* my honest mistake. Soiled and lashed in uniform, they soon recoil. When separate they had comfort in their station, now entangled with taint, wet spidering lines pull taut with no release, by these bodily fluids wed.

Revolve about the ward centre, this shrinking universe; there's nurses sat in a gaggle playing at some guessing game, comparing colours:
"Red Cherry."
They pore over multi-buy mags, four in a pack equals five times more gossip.
"Blue cranzola?"
 "What about the one on the left?"
Flicking pages, bodies shift beyond bronze to orange.
"Mud-pie Malt."
"Yeah but they *both* bulge, they're too...full, y'know."
"What?"
"Too well dressed to not be gay."
"She'll push through if she's not careful!"
"Urgh,"
"Yearck!"
"They are definitely real, they must be."
"What one was that?"
"Surely not?"
"Uhm, 'Tequila and Sunrise', yeah."
"P and BJ?"
"No!"
Too much cackling not to be evil. "What'd she say?"
"P"
Repeats, repeating…
"and"
They cycle by.
"BJ!"

Minds now set to follow.
"What you like?! It's 'PB and J'. You've got it on the brain you have."
Ad infinitum.

Having never enough makes you hungry and humble but it also drives desire. If they could only see us now: the spectators reclining in sun-lit gardens to savour pomp and circumstance of an Elgar soundtrack, but never questioning what it means. England loves so much these redundant things and an over-ripe obsession with the morality of medium, some nostalgic illusion that binds and blinds us.

Goodbye to all those real emotional and well-learnt manners, listening as well as talking, not just one over the other. Goodbye to the false elegy of holy nurses with grand hats to rival the old-school headdress. Spun paper cones, like exaggerated Gehry in stetch zeer-Os, eyes down, loyal and gilded in the scathing pale. Button-bound in shapeless uniforms, abstract bodies, except you can see the strings making it harder to breathe in starched perfection, ready to take as much as we can give. Wound-too-tight, clockwork teeth set to cog's nth edge, a grin of nervous energy, wild and white. So they go on tirelessly, sweating out patient reflections, all eyes distant as we watch over the eager dead.

More laughter washes in, can't think clear anymore between them and the cries from next-door. These motions collide to muddy the waters, last-post writ in spittle, high-lows sung as shrill and bloodied notes, dragged double from back of the throat. With repeat wiping of flesh and floor rushes, a cacophony of warped arkestra, under crushed quietude of ignorance, those 'good old days' I'm too young to know, nice to say that some things never change.

I circle, naïve hyena to their staid and tired lions. How clean and unsoiled they all seem but the dirt's underneath – that one sees me, I'm *here*, her look alone justifies it. She glances out from the corner of a half-cocked eye, then flipping back to attention, she listens-in for the middle-road tales of rife innuendo. But they only revel in kitchen-sink debauchery like the fifties never happened, same petty concerns and humdrum stories bleed me dry.

My ways of speech are lost among these pointless conversations, too clever for your own good. Dumb it down, to be more like them but the clipped flicks at the end of my sentences always shine through. I am tiger in a cage, between the lines so easily misunderstood. My words fall stillborn from the lips then lie quiet as errant seeds. They sweep by me as artificial suns, where my shadow rests, no light goes and the crows soon flock to come pick at the spoils.

Forget it ever happened. The circle's so tightly knit, they ignore, hide and suppress; rest on cheap laughs and hollow laurels, too numb to feel, too real to remember. See wisdom in a tired mouse-mat, worn by scrolling palms:

What you forget today
bites you back tomorrow.

Lady Lazarus

Attention: all bodies listen in with muscles taut as brisk steps give another pull on the thread. With quiet ease, she approaches faster, yer majesty. Our words slip away in the peaks of her speech, so hark that quiet violence grinding at teeth, in every voice hidden threats run deep.

She e-nun-ci-ates *too much*, just to rise above. Drawing long on every word, lips peel off letters then suck twos on a cigarette. Caught glance shot across the hall, neck hairs rise, between that long-clicking tongue and the rib-curved ceiling, fed directly into me, lips to receiver, pulling on skin. I am the same air, chewed up and spat out, still warm. Shiver over shoulders, an acreage of fine hairs ring-ting; the dense palate pressing hard against my frontal crease. Too many voices crowding all at once and every one of them becomes her. For the sea inside tides run high but not enough to drown her out or wash clean the edge of memory.

Something's exchanged –less than pleasantries– all the right gestures but lacking the bones to mean it. Neither one knows (or cares) what the other's said, some uncertain days it just goes like that. Distorted minds catch in unison, to turn truth into something mud. These vile waves creep so slowly, though I never noticed the change until it get up at the waist. And when it comes, I realise: maybe I thought too much or never said enough to make myself felt?

She's got a hold on you now. Filed in deep storage, charting the measure of your gait to the stains on your teeth. Watching sidewise at leftfield glances, they regurgitate your words, all hunting for lies and I'm clocked thinking: all interrogators must die. Masses whisper by; creeping, crawling over me. That cold anal-ity: 'in-and-of-itself' and with it, the technically-obsessed mindset repeat desires to be, and to be *seen*, constructive in all things. Now it dances as a fluttering sheet of loose antennae gathering fast to devour every last piece. In her cool digitised sight she marks them food/waste/other. Whatever's useful or expendable; all judgements are made under pinhead vision. My body reduced to an examined script – some exist only to calculate.

Dark leg shuck-bends tight in cracked L-shape of her raven-black, writhing nest. Shut-off and semi-secluded by hinged eclipse not right-in-the-head, there I snatch slights of her cut away at meat with scalpel and tooth. A born vivisectionist, not in her nature to grow anything, only to isolate weakness and tear bodies at the seams.

Now louche-swallowing lone apricots to keep herself thin. There's too many zer0es pushed-to-front prominence that sent her (and the rest) straight over the dietary edge, now that neat waistlines are a sign of social pride. She purses fruit at squeeze of lip and tongue, like dimpled circle of red blood cell, a fingerprint design left indelible in clay. When she bites it's always with incisors first. Sideways she tears it, trapped in her purple bruise of ox-blood and quick to swallow. Dryly they go down, no time to chew with molars dulled by buried stress and secret vomiting, through her shadow she consumes everything.

First time I met the Queen Bitch, I hated her, still do. Always it's that dull ache: trapped in desperation to get between those needy thighs, to be so close as *in extremis*. Even then, deep as I could ever hope to go, everything in her world is one-way only. Spit me out whenever, only a matter of time before she makes the move. With the things I know, I'm too soon to become another one of the many disappeared. She the drowning weight in me, so strung-out to dance by the light of her tilting cross on high. All it takes to make me say 'jump' in the slow kiss and return of her lashes.

Breaking through to match stares, like that sacred arrow piercing Theresa in her brief, ecstatic moment, it shines again for her, a knowing smile, some dying light more fragile from care, strikes deeper than any first realised. Bloodshot lines glow molten in her cracked canvas eyes, the wear shows through, the more she's seen and gone on to endure, a blind shadow, just carrying on, like all the rest.

Don't look back: still feel her fire prickling all over me, this time ticks by, but even at the good end this life's not something I should want to live again. To be born once more, delivered through her, I would return less than the sum of my parts, destined incomplete. Even now sick to the stomach with surrogate love, like she who bore me the long way out. But still a loyal follower in that and always so eager to ruin.

The concrete object for all my love and squalor, 'Queen Bitch' resounds as I throw myself, repeatedly, against her. Never happy, just hovering, as she ignores me I shrink further from forgetting. Know she feels the same. Loving to hate, such that I never want to be rid of her, even with the good some traces of the bad must remain.

Back and back again it comes around to the past. So many boys in-hand. See myself another part of that sick lineage, going under in acts of shallow surrender. In easy student days she could take it or leave it. Too many, too keen; so readily spent then lapsed in desolation. They held too tight, un-spoilt boys with plain faces and too much gel in the hair. Imagining life after the fast five minutes, to own and be at her side, but desire wears out, these loves never last.

Her expectations sunk as life never measured-up and reality fell behind, panting to catch-up with those high-slung flights. "Off with their heads" in most intimate state she whispers, and I am still wasp, thrusting mad and ebbing towards death, an unending seam of venom in my last emptying seconds, the spite of revenge. Eventually I'll wonder when and where it all went right. Now she's here, ten, twenty years gone. Bereft in gravity's stark surrender, remembering days when she was still fresh to death.

Steadfast in her chair, held so perfect and serene, emotion's neatly removed like a surgeon hooked upon steel. They negate the undesirable; cauterised and seal-off as memory, a fortified heart she dreams blindly. Only sign when she fingers softly at lapel, a petal caress to the tip but there's no lasting point to hold on to. When those distant, dead moments interrupt she's swept away to other times, where possible lives drag her forwards, to face the same beginning.

People grow ugly when the bad thoughts set-in, faces change to reflect the deed, a portrait in flesh as Dorian's revenge. Fresh and clean, stepped into brand-new uniform, her colour quickly faded. Every new layer applied ends like the days, so torn and frayed. Sweating over bodies with their limited capacities and infinite needs forces her managed prosthetic to pitch and whorl in a riot of complexions. The cosmetic always rises, etched into meaning: 'only skin-deep'.

Even from the early weeks she glared at every patient that made her chip nails using the swan-neck mouth of the tap-tap-tap after it insisted on being turned, and turned again, every half-hour, to avoid the risk of lazy, pockmarking dots. Ripping gloves away she'd see her own finger tips wrinkle, same as his clammydripskin. She was still young, or young enough, but caring too much, too quickly, soon made erosion of her.

That hair, a fiery mixture of oranges, purples and reds; shifting virulent, like Dresden gone glam. Used to be soft, supple browns with bare glimmer of a tawny owl, nothing to shock, only pale skin to speak of, now roots peppered silverwiseslant. Uptight iron spine runs rigid down the back, her hair catches speechless bluster, all its own breeze. Wrapped in smoky vapours, she comes in colours with untamed odours. Coiled like a barbed wire veil she stands ready-made and eager to spring, a brisk body of wintry discontent. When we speak, she spits back splinters with quiet anger. Porcupine neck hairs shook with every mounting syllable, undulating wide, though she tried so hard to hide them, in short, sharp replies.

Stalking the wards **No Running** stop and slow to a walk: keep left in corridor. Moving absolute, she takes one, she takes them all. So pre-occupied with her precise methods of care, seconds stretch like hours to make the days go slower, but then it's counting time until the next one. Underneath she drips hate; hates them all for pulling her out of bed every day to wipe stains and carry piss pots, either side of arms outstretched. People forced to dodge her in the narrow halls, they seemed to shrink more each day as if she was another virgin mother of the catheter, Piss Christ reinvented for every new century.

By comparison, I'm late-day eunuch, set in stone to complete routines for my supper, along with the self-loving servants who just go on and on. Complaining without action, that English disease, they stick rigorously to safety of the scheme, we are all bound tight by authorial guidelines.

But she knew what she was, taking solace in that esteemed position. Her make-up: more expensive, better applied than theirs, but when she looks around her, see that seething naked envy. From the healthcare underlings to the racked-up patients, they push back a terrible mirror to her real image. Set to spend the rest of her life in pretence of devotion, only to take their successive places when her own body lost its firmness and they had worn her down, living through death.

She tries her best to ignore it all, see her double-thinking, desperate to forget the outside world and its needy concerns. She is Venus, she is Venice and that sweet stench of slow decay. A distant dream held far off as future promise, some vulgar work of art, to be desired but kept hidden in these made-sane corridors, an open vein to burning blood, spilt in false glory of Ares unto Mars. Not the first, she'll never be the last, till there's nothing left and all our hope lies undone.

Murmur Irregular

Another morning, make body rise vertical in creased-uniform skin. We wear no sign, no nation, only primary colours to show here is where you belong. Paranoiac twitch bubbling behind that eye, outwardly the blank faces remain. Someone's dressed, fed and raised me out bed, or have I even slept? Joints click stiff, over-stretching, or laid out too long. Sniff the air, that acrid tone is back again, but my nose is growing numb and useless, now ripe for amputation.

Stale heat wanders in at open mouth. Afraid to breathe, equally scared of what words might come out. Cracked lips licked by strip lights, I shiver along with brittle neon. And there's strange tang, something like blood, but it's no taste at all. Grit caught in teeth, a snare of gentle dust that washes over and over. I know this shared skin, an isolated surface, stretched waiting for a reaction, some feeling I've known before to strike out and catch.

"We used to call it Rhesus-monkey."
What?
"They'd say: 'Ooh, you're blood type o-negative, we don't see many of those,' they'd say."
"Uh-huh." Not now, they don't.
She finger tap-taps blue streak, it pulses lightly, "Fifteen pints they took from me, all in one week."
You've only got eight pints total. If they took that much you'd be dead.
"Haha, I knew you'd come around. It's always the ones who are not-so-quiet, you see."
Did I even speak?
"There's plenty left, mind, in these old pipes." She taps her arm again.

She glares away with that glassy eye. One and a quarter inch, struck loose from right socket like a rolling marble brain. Now more cracked laughter, a fractious oracle, what she knows, she keeps quiet. Just like everyone else, the value stays secret. Rolls again, another heave-ho sickening lurch, my eyes rove to follow. There's a Nathanesque slice, caught in pale curve. She blinks, moving in, I blink back (or she echoes) we all blink together.

Head's smeared to a loop until top and tail meet, our surfaces gleam like a painted tear. I see a second world plastered about her crystal sky. The outside is now a wave, caught in her one-eyed prism, constantly expanding to keep pace with the energetic rest, shouting out to me: *lose yourself inside.*

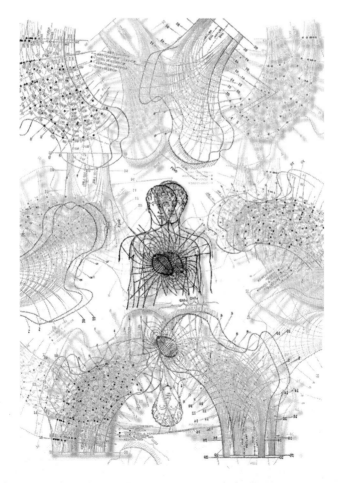

In Utero

This 'I' was once an IT in love, a disgusting, bitter, whined-out something. But with a maker, a beginning and some kind of mother. Before bleach and dead cells there was a blanket that held warm. And before that, muffled desperation haunting lonely breezes at slit precipice.

Between steely whispers slipped: "Keep moving, keep pushing, keep moving," a terrible rhyme we tried to forget. But it drives round this little world: a wailing, hairless sphere forced to become *something*. Once outside it's first taste of man's world with man's needs put down by a simple shot: no kiss goodnight, the big-red spent in an exhausted whimper.

Tight force at skull-sides, breathing in hair-spun bones that catch at borrowed throats. A pig heart replacement, now lacking motivation, it gives occasional splurge, going through motions, beating and bleeding, but with heads removed the urge soon fizzles out.

Trapped behind translucent eyes, outside the architect screams. Born of frustration and badly-looped in rhyme, the 'I' is still pure refusal, not yet ready to speak. Sticks dry, hurts to move so keep them sealed. Then graced by sudden warm trickle, a salted body, my first breath going under. Winding cord strung like a noose, it chokes as it caresses, all peachy limbs wrung taut, the 'I' that will not let go. Wants to stay Nil by Mouth, nothing in or out. But so neatly slotted in meniscus space, clinging to the edges and dumbed-down by incidental kisses from these fleshy sides that threaten spit into rupture. How long can one tolerate the other? Try to scratch, to hurt, but no nails yet.

"Incision to the stomach." A brown smear, some chemical tinge across the swollen sky. Insert tube, "the best option right now." Pipes up: "considering Vaxetoral entry," discourse on last night's match, blood-spat rushes, not good, last minute, own-goal. Wailing and dragged about, watch-pin ping-drings lost, "fuck, it's Swiss!" Recognise some distant ring-ringing, cold clash escaped, now more metal snatches at the stumps, every abrasion a signature to emboss new flesh. "Aoxyll mvmnt ovrdng richtine flw." He says.

Now force goes further, spider legs grip handle limbs, still faintly cauterised. Smell of plastic skin mired in soap, a mercurial face: that's Jupiter. After brief flash, a sky-blue arena tangled up, over-reaching plaid. Like rats the size of cats, ushered in to go breathe for no one, we're all trapped in our respective sacks. Gliding under hungry gasps to break-surface-for-air (the first time?) – no escaping limited space, so we exchange one prison for another. Warmer by inches, wheels bump along into a billowing haze, shift in colours to engorge the eyes (half-open) but already choked at first sight.

The pulse's rush propels big-red to march the beat of one thousand atmospheres glaring down on us. A squeezed skull just ripe enough with a lick of pink left to drip thin until light shows at the edge.

Soft glow soothes with exacting quiet and hushed whispers blown. Pick-out that gentle spire against harsh silver disc, angled-in to catch breath, drawing me out when I just want to fall deeper inside towards hub of sleep and dream.

Small winkles of blanket cushion project villi loops. Their tovey caress brings sensation to puckered marble of new skin. Bare pores set to react in air's compress, shadowy as scabrous bark charred by the sun, wrought with lineage of potential scars to mark future fade in you.

Eyes open eager sunrise, perfect circles yet to be squared-off by turn-turning, tendons pull like horses, chained to instinct, all draw without knowing. Wish every open part sutured up, so this promise of lucid dreaming could be forgotten, life abandoned as a bad mistake. To become dummy, blind and free, to live in permanent shade away from the toppling chase, now dragged out from hiding place, the secret side of safe.

Even the leaves have saw-teeth and nothing's as it should be. If you look too close, see there's no such thing as perfect surface, all pock-marks, scratches and immediate blemish. Soon to be shown in arch scars of acne, coarse winds and harsh words. Signs of life promise at perfection but nature can't deliver – this anger in the blood, the only true song.

First thing, these fings thirst: try move double fours, one, two, three, and two big more. Flex, hold, release. Need another to grip as if round the neck to feel gulps of blood between finger and thumb. In my hand is beat within beat, the big-red slipping as rushing cells fight to be heard over each feeble excuse.

So she held him, he reached out in return, and she was warm. Two palms met, fingers and toes were counted. Then new arms scooped under, her hand split from his, lifted up and out. More hands bitten, fingered, spat wild at the air, the growing gap turned to scream but she smiles anyway. Then there was nothing, a pale room, a singular cell, set to rest *in absentia* again.

Wake alone, like every day since. She is gone and I am full-grown: her beat's a nagging sensation, now yours to inherit. Like a tap left running, it drips on with that 'Lubb-Dupp' thump as same red reams go flourish in carnival outlet for the dead. Still hear their perhaps-ing ways, or is it drowned organ song, wheezing along without breath to fill, irregular future sounds blip and fizz to overtake.

Fixing a hole in the big-red, never found, now failure-bound without her. Staring blind and howled to infinity, no one hears when she sings/cries/sighs, invading my sleep. I am last in line at fraying end of the thread, dripping soft red flecks. Each strand is only the faintest trace, and as I grow, feel her big-red thinning out inside of me.

Stultifera Navis

This place is its own wilderness steeped in signs so familiar. Knowing all the ways, but never the whys, I count routines in measured steps: Left here, thirteen to the cupboard, past solid chipboard (cigarettes: charred yellow stars.) Anchor-heavy hand has scratched around the lock (another hangover). Dried-out eyes fingered dumbly at the slot, no memory, more fumbling in semi-dark and naked. I can retrace nightly steps from here, more left-by-south-west is bay number seven. At three, head right; thirty-two double-steps, thirty-two measured metres, *not feet*.

No good with numbers, but I've walked these floors before like same decade-stretch. Feet know every length as if this was a space made for me to fit. What'll we be in six more heartbeats? The same rushes flow and we only ebb when we're told; wherever these dense waters decide to take us. This building's a conduit, some sliver of the process, but to what end? Feel played out, travelling two ways, either/or, still not going *any where*. There's inside, and the inside, each level firmly defined, better to be clear and live within the trammelling lines.

Marked old-aged-ness to the walls, promised growth but it never comes. My sneakers cracked and split, spaces between my toes all too familiar. Rumbling undulations in the sole, matching wormdown press of an easy-jaded heel, scuffs, marks, scars; an illegible story already written on my knees, a work of *genius*, but it's all been done before. I don't know why *anything*, I just do (as I'm told).

Try and step-out from tidy interior scenes, wake-up to a life more interesting. Ignore strange gurgling sounds of a brain sadly burndt-out. What now? Lighting tubes flick, flick, flicker more in/out, multiple strobe beats give blue-on-black with highlighted reliefs. There's jaw hinges as floor bounces with a hungry beat, disordering all scenery. Ping-out, but no pong replies. Only lone breaths haunt the stellar-darkness, then –**click**– –**clack**– back to light. Central bulb hung by a limp wire, emaciated and faintly dimmering –no excuses– clearly a sign that soul is lacking.

Now here is nowhere. Where I placed myself in yesterday is redundant and the markers have gone missing. Only permanent handrails to-cling-to, a clear gesture of the needy sick. See scratches, rough-chipped by the nail trying to bite on that wide frame. Texture's coarse, an artifice of skin loused with smeary prints of the real thing. Image: the frail gown shivers like sheets along a laced-up spine, just hanging-on, to hang on a little longer…human urge to remain never lets go.

SLAM

–dash–
Shut out.
All flights, grounded.
What is that, trapped in spite? Each footprint pressed is a scuffed history of erasure, turning nearer towards cemetery earth. Clean my discarded cells from all right-angled surfaces. Wipe away whatever, so ineffectual, some picked-up others, the revolving world still shedding. Catch odd receding points, a vanishing point where walls meet and nothing's really clean, to empty creaks where the lost hearts go. Swapped-about in fickle breezes, living through final encore of encores, everyday more immune to suffering but further prone to diarrhoea.

Stuck too long on the eddies, twirling into distant vortices, their bandages straggled, trying to find Venus through a grille, disappearance under any other name. Look – see deeper than most; intersections attract and repel ghosts, equally. Drawing me in, to lose myself in gaps with potential for dirt. I am butterfly's proboscis, needle seeking thread to guide with it. Go follow me down, drawn close to prick at the nooks, the bit-part players and four walls, all collapsing.

Close at heel, silvery streak's a jagged follow and my being here is ephemeral. I walk through both sides of the argument, float in dreams like unending river, each is his own tides driving shoulder to the wheel. Picking last drops, spilt, the others watch, imagine they see floating cups, but to me it's only the earthly (unimportant) touch.

Live life to fullest: half-asleep, half fed-up. As I move on, hear everything further removed; a witness without conscience. Loose-leaved morals all laid to rest. Looking down, their superiority seems real enough, but in tacit illusion we all get swept up. I have nothing to report and no one to confess to, strictly invisible as and when, but still a half-dead necessity. My name's not so important (remember me!) Badgewords such a slur and the featured face has gone nova in rushes of bleach (suffering under a twelve-month wait for reissues.) Patients, nurses and visitors all look through the same flat-out stare, some blank arrangement of eyes/nose/mouth, unmoving, that spells out: I'm not really there.

Lost amid narrow worms of senior consultation, let them burrow out petty arguments as words fester into red lines under the skin, breeding bitterness and the quiet grudge. Can't understand half of what they say, left cold and last in line when the air runs out. Every time I try, it makes no sound, like falling out of sense. Language fails when thoughts can't be expressed, and as arguments go ignored so quiet violence steps on those petty flower heads. Echoes run back hollow, I catch-at, swallow whole, every lost letter deepens the years, surrounded by mumbles of the barely-living set.

Recognise that shadow crowing in the half-light. My dark pattern shimmers as another stain on the wall. Those dancing bones seem to go so much in agony, no lyric in that muscle; b ro ke nm usi c; or beat to keep time with reason: 'Frankly, it twitches, Doc. Don't know what else to do with him...' Poking violent, swat the air in midi-sweeps, irritation rises – hateeveryinchofthisdeadairspace.

Never mind all that – every trace must be removed before I'm gone. All signs of living, nullified – certain things must be censored and samples collected to be analysed in order to help prolong the species. The dead cells sweep in minute waves, like the smear left behind from a broken-off kiss. The mark of body fluids is a deoxidised strip, flowing on the same in different veins, the mired essence of human life. Shed that pretence of delicately mapped imperfections, (how many defects per inch?) Each dark faultline hides recognised impurity; these little scratches that make you love detail the most.

Muddy footprints, each one speaks: 'We were *here*, existing', however many seconds. As toes in sand and the filth of it all, human stain's held to account under shining lights of policy. So bright the ward resounds chapel-like to the body cleansed sacrosanct. We perfect hygiene to recycle abandoned cells and cure our most popular diseases (this equals press coverage, media runs and the highspeed downhill pharma-race runaround). Each body is catalogued, another occupied territory, spurred on by demand where most lose out so the few can win. Forgetting to err is humankind, that imperfect picture of sacred symmetry, masking our naked duality. So we take quiet celebration in our illusions of rightness. Embrace these limbs for vaccination, a new religion to the body, but our only heaven is health as this reality steadily breeds its own kind of hell.

Brush on! Sweep past, never mind about all that…let bodies (in whatever state) lie, no need to speak now time's a slipped commodity. Keeps itself to himself but still requests come fast and forthright, each one is briskly denied. Those natural exchanges of love and trust others take for granted, exclusive day-by-day concern of the healthy free; wanting to be wanted, but maintaining distance, call out in vain, turn around to answer myself: "I'll get right on it." Keep busy –don't think – to the floor, losing face in this germ diaspora, sickness makes no distinctions. No other song to sing, work's a flat wall to bounce-off from thought, but we reverberate in vain. My mind's a sea of echoes with no lighthouse to guide; so let me drift further from the shore, not ready to come in just yet.

Manage basic speech; they just hear whispers mounting to quiet mumble. It crushes a silent scream before it could breakout to a pierced howl and, for the first time, be heard against the scattering hiss of heavy-breathing machines, massed in ranks, a factory of mind, more vanity to life. The incurable ones, permanent cripples wth brokn big-red inks, sing as one shuffling-puffed voice, so cold and dreary. We covet freedom in living but no respect for the ones ready to die, all these are false hopes we serve to intensify.

Everywhere, bereft, a snail mop trail follows. Turn to see what I've done and already this little history evaporates. Another 'she' passes-by mouthing: "sorry" over the shoulder, a green blur with half-intent. My clean space gone, though it's only everything I've ever done, repeated. Beyond distance is no vanishing point, just fingers eclipsed, feeling-out darkness where nothing hits definitive, together we've circled this setting sun a hundred times or more.

Gnarled like a paper leaf, left under-nourished and shady. There's no easy way to get head straight curl up and away in dry heats, vamished with hunger. Going steadily transparent, harbour reconstructed skin it gives no solid fix, but the burnt lines still burr underneath, mapping my quiet disgrace. Me, I'm a mish-mash of other selves met again on the way down. Wearing through the same old trousers with many jigsaw stains I can't place or correlate. I know some pattern persists: rolled-up heels, worn-down stoney-knees, a criss-cross of motions, impulsive operations to rebuild the scorched redbrick, never quite complete.

My fingers grown coarse as feelings turn towards callousing. That body, bent double, only succeeding to walk at a vicious angle. A hairless white child paling-out, trying to push, to sit above in greatwidebed, a size so desolate, every day she shrinks smaller for all the ward to see. Curtains of badly-matched colour jump and bounce, a festival of faded bright, all fighting to be noticed as the sun plays just behind to illuminate blind tigers.

Swipe fields of dead cells with grey dust swiffer. Mount them in neat piles of detritus; that's half a person, squared-off. No soul or sacrament, vacuumed-up, the old forms deconstructed and bagged in black, some are washed away down storm drains or clog landfills, under some other poor sod (all together now). Human refuse is recycled endlessly, rivers run through to rains, every time we breathe, and when I swallow, I swallow pieces of you, reborn in me it goes on, this body never really sleeps.

> Not always like this,
>> Remember a begining,
>>> more real.

>>> No denying the first fact.

Not Giving Up

And here we are a few minutes past the golden hour's shine has gone. Eclipsed that wide expanse between waking life and simply not being there, shrinks to a mere sixty minutes of saving. But time's almost up and this bed's needed for the next one. I strike the ground between each chair. *Harder* – from steel to tin, the pole strikes four-legged defeat, that cannot walk any more, more wiping, more water a swell to the river, careful to ignore heels.

Head strays, every wet strand so unwieldy, fumbling idiot with dull pole attached. I slop about the assembly of feet, all face forward and eyes hit the wall where their vision fades. Scenes from a struggle under overhanging noses, lost in bottomless patience, he expires right in front of them and through it all no one notices the waters rising at their feet.

The mannequins shuffle-huff in their seats, how long should you wait until it seems alright to leave? Not like they're watching anyone, any *thing*. Do they even see me here, scraping around, the only sign of life? I draw back, to watch all of us caught in this still-life, another gauche nativity.

All on edge. I shouldn't be here. No part in this but the room needs cleaning, we've five more pairs of shoes today. Pretend I'm not here, try to deny this private invasion. They seem OK, sitting very still, watching/breathing/grieving/waiting, each one alone. Clutched gifts held on the laps, even grapes, that useless gift for the properly ill.

But no-one feels like eating on his behalf; meant for him, but there's that vulgar tube jammed down his throat, an inverted U-bend, where the ending begins. Absent hand slides across, offers me a dismal bunch, immediately, I think: green piles. Feeling dutiful in disgust, put one in my mouth. She doesn't look, doesn't speak but moves them away to continue her watching.

See through the plastic chair backs, folds of their clothes, longest stretch of flesh and bones, a row of stomachs turn sickly sour. Their vitality's drained as skins grow clear, learning to let go, and heads drop tired, matching tears run in synchronicity. The ward's thick fluorescence hardens their waxy tones. Paler, less reachable, only faint twitches in the creasing laughter lines, emotions ironed out, as the situation demands it and sadness keeps them frozen stiff.

Time to leave, throw remains of fruit in a metal bin, already grown stale in here. The man-trap lid slams definitive. They edge out as he makes his own exit, now vapid, well left of centre, though there should be light enough to stay a little longer; orbiting out while the curtain shudders. A breeze finally lifts the bleachy tones and strips the last warmth from the setting sun, slowly they turn to go.

Let the strange boards creak without his tread as old wood shrinks and swells out of season and new rain strips the world clean. Lives forced awkwardly out of step, by some odd inkling we always tip-toe around the cracks that seem to widen at the mention of his name, where that absence now so stubbornly resides. And Father's muttering: "Sometimes fair's fair, ain't fair enough."

Not So Merry-GO-Round

With false freedom, this is how they make you:
"Can you cover this?"
the holy cheats
"Someone's got to do it, why not you?"
with formal lies
"…stretch to an extra double? No one else is free."
they come to know and hate their own kind
"The patients need you. And so does the hospital."
Who is this whispering in both ears?
"Just one more hour? Another day, even? I'll get you time and a half."
don't make me laugh

By the bedside we're all under-obs from the new fade. It's little changes: switches fixed, handles screwed back in, though gnikcol backwards. A kind word or fleeting gesture, signs that something might remain after each one has given their last (all in service to the dead).

Nurse of the day sets the tone by regime, with rise and fall set for night and day. Sections carved up in vicious quotas; by rota, all jurisdictions are just a form of looping tyranny. Their lot clock-in, start shaking things straight; mouse moved to other side of the keyboard – I hate. Flick over staff sheet, pick out the worst and the best until tired hands make the round, then our little world clicks back to its old axis. Down is now up, yesterday's gone, struck-off, all futures are forgotten.

The Earlies and the Lates, with the Half-days in between, can't settle on singular policy. Always working against, never all together, through the handover we go more deviant. They scratch bitter, fighting to push each other into the rushing way – that's cuckoo-instinct calling late. Tearing chunks, coughing up feathers and the fury, lured by cheap frenzy. The loser gathers beak, tongue and claw, all eager to lick at the right of ascension. And to the victor, there's policy made solid in self-abasement losing beliefs – it's getting inside that counts.

We return to the same positions but with new titles and different last names. One shuffles to the right and all will have prizes of little or no consequence, but shiny nonetheless. 'Progress' is an ugly word when you've heard it too many times before. Turn cold shoulder to the *status quo* unsettled, it's more admin loopholes, and the next day – everything must change.

For now it's scrolling beds – get them in, get them out (that's forever). There's no such thing as 'synergy', someone once told me, only synchronised bodies moving against time. Age holds sway but clocking-in at sixty-plus does not sit well with the modern way. When 'senior' starts slipping into 'senility', shuffled-off one too many times, they soon forget their place and find their old position gone. Bundled out in early retirement and eagerly replaced, a brand-new model from the same livery line, each one's a wet drip from the same slow-rusted pipe.

Vacant fluff-hearts come to manage us with: 'more better English' and so lead by example. Presuming well-spoken is well-bred, self-improvement's given no quarter in those circles going 'Right-turn *only*'. We don't care how smart or *who* you are, only where you went to school and with *whom* – welcome to OxMed country. Where flaky morals (one rule for the hypocrite few, many more for the rest) rise bile-like in the throat: too small to be removed but just pointless enough to have a name. Those quiet cells without function or place hover in the system, a swollen abstract, persisting against growth, they go on digging but the world won't listen and these wounds refuse to heal themselves.

Swans Incarnate

–click– "Dr. Swan to attend fifty-a-day case, please, Dr Swan." –click/clack– Every head spins. Check the door, all cast still in waiting lead. A room to one side, the first one cries, she blinks tra-la-la tears that come too easy in managed distress. Hear it hack-hack-hock-hack with intervals thinning between the chokes. I wince, imagining sticky spots on my floor. Anxious eyes flash in green stripe to scan the faces all reading: PANIC. Get a move on Swan, either one will do. One more dead patient and we lose out on pizza vouchers for missing our targets.

There he was, now she: not boy, not girl. But which twin *is* it? Getting harder to tell. Changes come as one face pronounces itself, but after quick glances, already on to the next one. Backed-up in limbo, an eternal stretch, the inverse flesh refracts in messy shards. All that we cling to, held in cut-up palms just long enough to feel that slipping sense of certainty, now captured in some bloody ideal.

A slave to new fashions, but ignoring all seasons, he/she flits like wings, another delicate mouth to twist in flame. Sneering blind with incisors bold and white, carved in perfection, a bitten through silhou- -ette b r eaks the clean lies.

Up close see their true nature, the iD revisited: part old-hat motto in slashed fringe cuts then shaved away to otherside. Swept flat, occasional flicks disturb the wedge to the tips, a dazzling curtain edge. All signs point to seeing ghosts electrified in dark adaptation with this dull and pressing light. Swans' animus and anima, singing siren to be noticed, to be *seen*, but who wants to be desired all the time? Drowning in flux one fascia strikes another, torn across by dark moon, flipping orbits, dragged through sleek rays of body sun. Respective office hours never maintained, the two always moving as one.

First step leads the second, same-side legs, heel, step-two-three! This sweep intersects, a one-armed scissor, snicker-snacks cutting back and forth, strong fists bound in iron from twenty fingers and thumbs, roving willows of slender hands as pale fronds move slow. A static moment: ever more fantastic, shining in the dirt, a twenty-first century Mengele. He-Swan peeks out from behind that stale aura, an illusion of flesh, decked-out in fuck-me-pumps. But it's both Swans in the approach, our gaze never settles on the elusive singular. In that human way, we live to seek distraction, crowded by starry eyes, each one begging to be chosen.

Solvent in mercury and volatile as you like, caught mid-fruition he is, *she* is, like Marilyn – forever blond-beautiful. But as you get closer hives grow from that peeling plastic...seconds caught in every faded photograph, their ideal exposed, only to be replicated, carefully staged to cut-up and keep. Your dead eyes hint at conflicted secrets, another still-life series, so I keep on staring.

With rips at the corners, time yields when and where we start to crease. It's the same decay as multiplied theories of infinite energy, to make a new enemy of deviant shapes, forcing us down a one-way road. Distorted phases flit by, through different prisms and new angles, a silent film that marks the gaps more than memory, for time that seems to have no change. Then we wake up just to look back in dreams (and try to forget) it's already twenty-two years gone.

Swans are moving on. I see angel wings and dark feathers escaping, slick as heavy oils trailing through water. Thin-lipped smile's neatly drawn from one set to the next patient's swoon. He hovers over and around as she snaps, crackling air with feminine tips, licking into shadows to pick spare threads like a vulture's maw at tender prey. Drawing breath, he sighs within her unity, waiting for the crowd to look up, yearnings long-presumed absent or dead in those dried-out eyes, rekindling a mind to life. They smell freshness of youth hidden under layers of dabbled fragrance and the salt-stain of bleach. The two planets spiral then spire, drawing out this strange relationship; to repeal all angels and fall out from hope's reach, never again complete.

At ten paces –no contact– stare's enough as joints, so musical, undulate in flow. It's the tapping of her pace, each strum with shifting feet, like the big-red narrowed-out to its regimented Lubb-Dupp sounds. His stethoscope lingers shiny-bright, fingers at chewed pen-top, a return to memory and some base security. Not pulling out to write, but doesn't take his hand away either. What he finds there; a sliver of the past, pinched inside. Scooped-out useless throat dangles heavy at the neck, she pulls at collar, always tightening, their nature's not in it these days.

Eyes glazed upwards, brief lolling; nothing coming or going, the clapper is grasped silent from the bow. This reel is writhing wild on line of long-lost thought, strung out to bait any idiot-audience, but behind twin-screens it's a constant no-show, no need to even pretend anymore, just intermittent twitches to shudder some hidden reaction. Can't control the flicker-bite of heavy-thinned lashes, a cage-mouth barking to keep the others out, first and last thing you see are the Venus-closing teeth.

Swan is now a wayward train, wrecked on shaven legs as limbs judder, all shaky rails leading nowhere. Peek under sleeves – more deadwood drawn in microdots. Passes between claw and grasp – but somehow dis connected– without the smallest of talk.

So cold-blooded in royal blue descent it smiles like a reptile; they love him/loathe him but everyone takes notice. Striking across the floor she slides like Fred Astaire fingering tongues slip around Ginger Rogers mid-flight. He-Swan follows tentative in thinning skin, so careful for himself; now she emerges, clean and unblemished. Our sweated-out bodies and back-wracked faces go further sour, a bare-bone mirror dazzled by compliments. Trapped under choking uniforms, we look on, all together in the drift.

Medical discretion falls short, the Right uniform and keepingbetweenthelines: all contra life. Theirs is a long road, so dull and detached. Swans seek comfort in glitter, to make this life their own, but went too far to come back clean and distinct.

From this self-made haze the last slivers of smoke only loving breath to escape. **Change.** She sucks at twin cigarettes clasped in yellow-knuckled drawl. **Doubled-up.** Pulls on two fingers. **Again.** Indiscrete flames follow. **Pause. Drag.** Then another. **Stop.** She doesn't come in, waits stalking at the doors. **Look.** Confused stutters around the cigarette butts. **Lips.** Crowned with lipstick stain, the red tip's breached. **Bite.** Ferrous line of blood between teeth. **Lick.** She coughs, spluttered refrain. **Spores.** Wipe away, fist to coat. **Stain.**

Two flat bodies give up pacing and make their real entrance, shuttling-in for another dose of sameness. Eager nurse waits for them, held in strange fascination, bursting with air she can't contain anymore. She steps up. First Swan opens fingers of her left hand, going over the palm, tracing lifeline with a crooked thumb. She is waiting, ready to receive. Swan stubs out the orange glow. Under crushing flame she flowers; the big-red conjuring up a luminous blush. Now desire takes over, she looks to him, at her, willingly entailed with the sting-felt bliss. Unable to contain herself, nurse cracks a grin, always trying too hard, feeling too much to mean it. There's some stifled whimper (like a dog) too many grateful words catch rising in her throat.

Swans exhale in unison. Nurse follows pace but meets quicksilver glare, soon sensing it's a final kiss-off, never a cue to come hither. She's left behind to fawn on cruel breeze with echoed hurts of another needy lover. Silence reverberates around the lonely one, faint traces of pain running the length of her starry-scorched palm.

A room of silence and stone-set gazes, we excel at unfeeling. All faces look to elsewhere. Dead ears don't tremble as her song sails unheard and futile. Quiet hearts don't quiver, barely heave a sigh, each one abandoned until hospital tides bring us to our lonely rest.

She rubs the wound, still fresh, now a swollen reminder: used to fill temporary needs of a love that can't last. This scar's another memory, something bitter to keep. She carries on, trying to move away, pretending not to care. The butt, still bright, has been flicked into casualness. It lands with as-if precision in hive of curled steel rinse, a dramatic rise of aubergine flight. Ignorant in bliss, parked faceagainstwall, this woman can't turn beyond bandaged neck but seems happy in her place. Laughing through faraway spaces on the wall, she finds patterns eager to play, seeing too many things that never mattered.

Now it's two Swans dancing sickle-moon as flaming heights, licked curls in new definitions, imagined heat spilling from the floor – more than dream, somewhere distant, hollow children sing. Shake it out, see her hand turning blister pride, cooing hush at her withered beak, from kiss of rose to burning itch. My left flexes, returning call – we've been here before. Each has their own fictions, some remain untold, but these Swans demand epilogue.

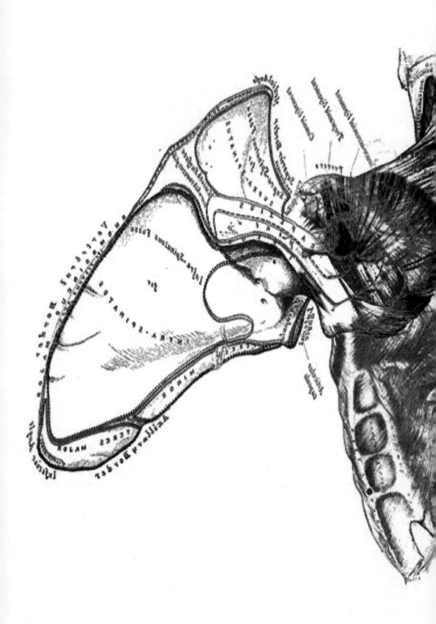

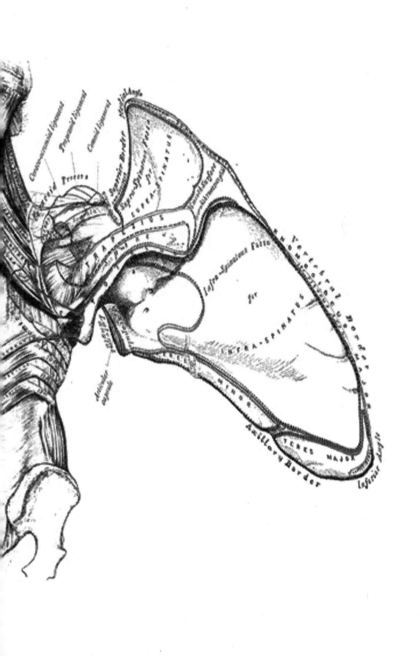

Classic Southpaw Mistakxs

         Nothingness cutting,
               left,
     blank now

knows right
    all seas lost…

    Waves at once.

       Upside-
      down
         above
           curve's
             swerve,
                feathery
           hook
    of   coastal   reach,
   bent   shape   out,
        un
  d
      o
    n
  e.

Busted links from splintering chains, losing sense of those harder things. Trying to connect…the nothingness that flows between every grain of sand, to find out what makes me, Me.

Space missing in eyes,   vision can't   won't
           meet,   narrowing heads stretch length…one
side empty,
each eye   half-moon cut,
      their presence
                forever
delaye d.

                        Right in front of your nose;
whatshimmersonsurface? Lens shrinks, disappearance
crosses.

Eyes flicker in
      out   in
      in   out
      nowt   blank
…doing sight   dodging sight
buzzing
   overhead… to the seam
a past runs through.

It shifts, turning tries to please, no reference fixed. Go slowly,
let blood settle –be still my moaning half– but it's the droning
outside. Shake it off, **focus**.

Step into this glistening, buzzing world as tubes linger in silent
drip of stalagmites – into 'tites. Catch sun, the whiteout glares,
a deep voice burbles in/out. Man trapped under his words,
transistorfuzzscreams. To one side tilt-blood goes over, flat-top
headache swells to sharper angle, catch a glance: flash of grey and
dark-charred smell.

Turn shutters to brightside, sagged on the left of both eyes. Rustling slivers shuffle as blue-green wall pales beside curtain, only dull throb coming, the baritone, overrides. Nothing else moves, I am static at fixed point, twist left, straining eyes to the hilt: a blue blanket with lumps, unmoving.

Right-hand corner, see glimpse of white on white against a black haze. Eyes darting around inside, at last we meet. Try to hold my gaze, a few seconds of woven sea bobbing up and down, ruffled intervals like a fish in surface panic. The net breaks loose and wild, scattering thoughts, he yells out: "It's him and all. Another one of them Daves at it again."

Shrink back to diminish contact, clench my fist the louder it gets. Prickling heat breathes through skin, wandering in from the right, only hovering control, slow to react from the fraught impulse.

Try, try harder.
Pick up the jug.
Tinny plastic gulps about nearly whole litre-full, grip shakes edge of the bed, then table, watch finger and thumb toward an orange mapped in sextant pinch that's lost its sway.
No!
Jug.
Jug UP!

Drop the squeezed fruit, too tight, it slop-rolls away. Focus instead on the flatnosed, green lid. Heavier than it looks, feel him watch my brief struggle. Eyes flick over to that grimace transmitted – a trickle-chill runs down the hand, grinding teeth like wrestling underwater.

Swollen warmth rumbles every pocked crater. Clench grip – beyond fist– can't exhale, sharp in the arm, it had to fall. See it twirl; cracking water explodes in silver pieces. Slow drops retract then coalesce to forge new puddles. And behind it all more glistening screams come.

Shake-out the hand, cool brisk flowing over the motions web-wings catch between fingers. He exhales heavy grasping moans: "Aaah."

Step back.

"Aaghh!"

Send and return, he yells again. It hurts me too, I call, but drowning in doubled voices, calling louder in vain.

Blow through lips with the ache of fresh bellows, blisters rise again between surviving hairs. It fizzes crackle of pig flesh and napalm hunger, all molten black and bubbling-up. Grey cloud spreads on the sheet, must've spilt. His sneering eyes roll, no lashes to sweep the ash clean. Twisting limb again, under grip. Between sagging legs canyons of damp set-in. Hand prickles fingers of cold skin, bones jerking from trapped heat within.

Blurred lines start to level out, look him over: chart says third-degree, still hurts enough to feel it. First instinct: to touch, reach out at me, is it left or right? Turn, switch stance but balance wavers. Left tries to grab the other wrist – *wrong right*. Break. Real right hovers over, shaking more than it used to. Shedding skin reveals pink-white bone; bare all down the whole livery line enough to see big-red pumping raw. Shakes more, he groans, resist the urge to see writhing strips like twisted fibres into sapling of the young. Enough strength not to break, but the outer is slipping thin.

Stare at spiderly fingers, see him do the same. Hide right into pocket, I feel nothing. Take *my* left, no, *our* left. It stings, he shuffles back, scooping himself into a corner, needing to find what is and isn't me. He glares out scared, but equally desperate to know. Lean out to wrist connect, make sure this pain is really real, not another burning dream. Two hands shimmer like white light pouring, drips run up mercury triangle twinned –RELEASE– seared marks, desiccated tears and hanging free. It sways in sick gravity with my eyes, our pain trickling through from me to him, and all around it goes to blazes.

Out of pocket, now it's all this tingling rub. Weak tendons flicker as bolshie bubbles rise, oxygen-rich, a creak of time. Through wood and bone; steel and glass; every surface has the same wires pulled behind, cleaving through our narrowed headspace. Tension's ebbed…relax as horses too-heavy relent back into mud and the invading quiet –it blinks– a flicker of teeth, staring me down sideways, devouring the dead-air between us.

Hollow rings chime down the way as curtain train is ripped across steel runner, tearing sound from flesh. "What are you doing? Put that man down!" Blue cloth's bent angrily to an accordion crush, the spontaneous geometry of fallen music. The neat-pressed factory lines dislocated for nothing (only changed yesterday) an overhang, limp at the seams. Why always so inconsiderate? This is typical, we just do, never think, and then argue afterwards. Everything I've done and will never mattered-

"I'm talking to you!"
"Who, us?"
"You."
"Him, or me?"
"*You.*"
She just writhes in louding more, my skull's shook, nurse breaks on through, to separate, taking my hand away from me – we groan apart.

"No, you don't understand, it's ok. I'm the same as him, we both are. Bad burns, my hand…it's rotting away, quicksmart. We have bad burns." She hardens quizzical, warped eyes fusing under three-line brow. With distinct unease, all our lines seem to follow the bloodied left outstretched, a dirty white flag screaming breeze.

"We're supposed to be here, you know," slow the tone to clarify: "very badly burned, look, see." Hold it up, she ignores the pain, staring right through, feel vague, like fading.
Glares: "Look, we'll sort his hand in a minute, but you'll have to wait outside."
Gently pushed, a warning sign.

"*His* hand? What about me? Mine, even. I'm burnt too."

Held upright fist to wring-out more red crocodile effect. A second glance, instead it's fleshy star intact, all five points presenting. Lifeline not yet severed, wrinkles flex and flow beyond letters. She carries on, brute opacity of her back against me, like I was glass.

I tap her shoulder-wise, then thinking twice (too late): "It was charred, black and pink...it must be this one then."
Pulling at imagined sleeves, still see the seeping – beige.
"Your hand is fine, it's this man what needs the attention, not you."
Show her the right instead, he moans, this one clean too.
"You have to believe me."
Winced drawing back, this Glaire, I christen her, is unconvinced...
"Look..."
"No, no, you don't understand. I work here, in the hospital."
Confirm my space with vain fingertips point about perimeter feet (my little empire).

She scans the floor, only mashed orange shell, water, plastic fragments, "What have you done to Mr. Smith's room?"
"I'm here ev-e-r-y day. I mop all the floors, I've wiped this entire place wall to ceiling, you must have seen me."
Stares blank in disbelief, her dull face smothering rage.
"Ask the Queen Bitch, then."
"Who?"
"She's Staff Nurse, or something."
"What's her name?" She knows but she won't say.
"I don't know her name, Andrea, is it?"
"Andrea who?"
"Look, this isn't a joke, I don't know her full name."
"Well, your Andrea might not be the same as my Andrea, you could be talking about anyone."
"But so could you." Anyone, anywhere, all the time...
"Where's your ID badge?"

"My what?" Not there, "Oh, it's gone." Did I even have one before? Finger two holes where the bar's punctured the weave. "Look, that's where the pin was!" I point pyramid of blue cloth at her, straining with my aching left.

Glaire looks at me from behind that cold veneer: "You've got to leave NOW, before I call someone in here to make you leave." As if absent-minded, she twists at the index; there's a faint, crooked smile? Her eyes go wider, flicking to patient as he yells out with me, doubled hurts echoing wide.

Her face gone quizzical, real questions start to crack the icy chic. She shivers it off, forgetting any possibility of something so strange. "I don't have time for this! I don't know who you are, just get out!" She throws lifeless hand back at me.

Walk away, hands buried deep in pockets. Further away, might survive enough to keep it. Him? Already too far gone and mind lost to easy rot. Someone dropped odd word, spitting something French, like OxMed: cataract? Catarrh? A long way from the latin.

Turn another corner, the smell follows, bump hip barrier, wave my right to say goodbye. Should reach for something solid, something real. Touch metal, to renew cold-cause for the efflorescence of skin, to retract bumps under new heat, stoke split-arrow grain. A former tree, cleaved to brute wood, should feel each –dish–dash– fibber– coming through and through calling out: "I *splinter* you."

Instead   artificial   barbs,   the   sanitised   spirals   chain   twist-
turning   against   the   crushing   sheen   of   varnish   peel,
driven   *to*   *ignore*   *and*   *evade*
each   line   for   itself,
each   one   to   escape
to   be   known   only   against   the   grain,   all   one-
way;   erase   pasts   and   deny   new   futures.
to   *escape*   *her*
its   plastic   passion;
running

every imperfection the little wonder of a designer's flaws
to   *forget*
Each one's the slightest ripple, but it's a good life lived trying not
to drown, feeling steps around the puddle's edge.

I sluice through powerless times; as flesh recedes vision flickers:
worrywart gnawing at grindtoothnail until metatarsal tips point
their way out. Looking beyond milky spots, that's calcium fallout
–too much of not enough– my smallest pieces chipped, less and
less to make sense with, swollen days closer to dust.

MalAdminiStratIon

Hello to them upstairs! For every nurse or Dave riding the body corridor, we double-up inept drones in narrowed circles and halls recurring. Plenty pen-pushers, more worse grammer and spelling bad and all this reflects, *infects*, on the rest. Too easy to lapse into coma-consultation, never reaching conclusions; better to take the money and run our world *into-the-ground*, general idiocy set: 'within acceptable limits'.

These seeping sweet leeches that suckle as much blood as honey. We make them new, to catch and release more modern monsters, sexless and self-replicating, flooding our departments with ineffectual clones, where hearts and minds never meet, all beating monotone.

Clinging to evermore tenuous posts, each is forced to invent their own job title (to facilitate subtext). United, we embrace illusion that quantity will one day yield something better. Fine clothes as office robes shield your naked lack and the ever-creasing thighs; always ready with the sedentary sigh. It's the same gaggle of asbestos-deniers; mounting paperwork to cover themselves with a three-fold indemnity clause. All sense and sensitivity lost in prescribed distance of the marketing mix, replaced with binding contracts, extra packaging and flip-flop promises disguised as benefits for you and me.

All have targets to meet and people to greet, propping-up the high bar we die trying to reach; so they lean, collate and criticise. Occasional visits from those foreign bodies of the everyday, their usual habitat in admin fortresses, waiting for something to 'action', an unexamined life trapped under sixty watts. Spend their time marking thin ink into expense forms, a biro-nic masterpiece writ in slaughter, then printing and filing, filing and printing; no need to read it, just stamp the claim – if you'll approve mine, I'll approve yours.

In heady lunch-hours redraft compensation emails for innumerable back pains, citing: 'sitting down too long.' Still spilling out of seats, you eat reducing lunches, counting down to the next calorie step, losing yourself in 'what-not-to-eat', fantasise on anorexic release. Wave mileage receipts to a more ergonomic chair, now having spasms, hearing voices, telling you the shape of womankind is waning and on the rise.

Iron breeze steals last air gasps in the throttled corridor. They sweep in with 'fresh-eyes' acolytes at their sides. Jot infrequent observations, ticking necessary boxes, but everything's only 'acceptable', no matter how hard you try. Count us down as we clock-in; see how we diminish. Dashed blues and green-stripe's troubled balance, logos rising larger than life; all overtaking the big-red still itching at my chest.

Stand with mop in hand; it's all I know and that's my place; balanced between feet and head of stone. A polyester shark pushes forward to interrogate, eager to be my five-minute friend over dagger smiles and quick chit-chat. At first we clam-up, the boss peek-nods over shoulders and mouths start to clunk up and down, more puppet-faced machines making talk that's cheap. Post-training, these dulled sponges repeat ready-made thoughts: tell them what they really want to hear, never what you think. Both parties fading in and out of a staged 'human situation' – no one's listening: '*Of course* I enjoy working here', word-by-word forgetting what we came for, as living the lie becomes an easier way to be.

Massed staff ranks, nonplussed and so unimpressed; their give-way attitudes reflect in every angle of our prickling silhouettes. So together we decide to make the patients suffer instead. Doesn't matter anyway, our manifest mistakes will be obliterated in furnace flames, old truths recycled to keep the bright lights burning.

Hottest transplant darlings, those selfless devils, give lung/marrow/blood to become sacred cows. Hang media rights around shared-neck; all trust will be taken on loan and without written consent. Waspish agencies whisper direct in the ear, already predicting ratings, trying to equal invested returns on life-or-death savings, to glean the most from their metric foot of flesh.

Some patients walk away with a few more years; thank donor, thank doctor – thank almighty god, Medicine. But what does it matter? Whose organ is it anyway? Like public-speaking stances, eighty-per cent is appearance, which is hollow common-sense. True meaning's just a sub-clause, several contractions down the letter-livery-line. Dying's a naive art, they market it too well.

Bought us on the cheap, the high and the low ones, easily cut loose for speaking out. Worse for the agencies, a motion towards protest today and tomorrow you're gone. Our stories are the words you never see or hear, lost in new health pledges and the carefully-worded press release; where my naked manifesto should run free.

This false elect (my kind of hell) a damning rainbow where not every colour shines the same. But I'm right in my hate. Forced to rust in peeling fields, only by degrees allowed to sway, growing paler in shades, all to spite the sun. A self-imposed dying, in autumn without end.

Nurse's Song

All br e a   k
lines
          severed.
Hearts cry
unplugged,
but tethered still.
And down the hall, in a rush and a push, greens and blues
go blur into one with the wild purple flush. At the other end
someone's crying-out "horse, horse!". Whistle-by buzzers beep a
drowning orchestra, now digitised cries are swansong to absent
ears.

        Night's
    stret-   ched
     limbs   peel
  off   into
   slow   death,
    as   tree
     branches
    seperate
    the
     rest
      just
    go on
     living
Old-fAshionEd in oUr flesh
lives lived tOo far in AnAl0gue
     We hear 0nly rEal vowel sOunds
N0t spEech in e1ectrIc spArks
       This *digita1's* 'just a phase'
  (it wi11 be over – when?)

Adam Steiner

Musing in secret
another acceptable scandal.
Three nurses meet
stealing time apart
– in quickening gaps –
burning-up precious seconds
every cigarette, a moment –
tastes like freedom – 'better than breathing' they said,
between the retch and vent.
Being money well-spent,
That I work to earn,
      to keep
            to spend,
            I rise with prices.
            Tell yourself: 'it's a long-term investment',
      slowly gaining interest in our deaths.

Run wit-wild in blurred exhaustion.
For this,
for that,
for *what*?
To scratch English existence
on tea and two slice,
remembering Ps and Qs
as they hand you sharp end of the knife.

Time's stuck unwound,
it loses 12 years-per-hour.
"Manning" the gears of this graveyard shift
we revolt for tomorrow, then again, *ad infinitum*.
On your marks, full motion set, now pace is the trick with ankles
biting to spring but we can't get free till the clock's struck GO!

Shedding uniform as years,
each grows new skin;
to forget the day and let the night without pain begin.
That heady blanket trails across the sky, but this darkness is just
another excuse.

Ready for the craic into cackles, there's loose wine and looser talk
all around the straight-edged suburban deck.
The dead carpenter's made his mark, albeit too late.
Steeped in gin, she's happy enough at forty-one, land-locked,
quietly greying and very much in love with the neighbour's wife.
But it's impolite to say something, let alone anything. So have
another drink and learn to forget.
No moon left to pick-out the creases from cool-blue of landing
lights, charged by memory of the sun, they bloom ready to greet
the stars.
'Pound-a-go,'
She nods,
'you can't beat *that*.'
…until the light runs away with itself.

Gathered circuits fizzle and flicker
into half-eaten candles
licked clean by whispering wings.
Drink more to push back the dawn
that keeps on coming, higher and higher.
Only water to stay dead-thin,
cold shoulder sharpens the sleekit rays
(trying to ignore the next twenty-four stretch)
We must take our human allowance
in evenings and weekends, to please.
Knowing there's only rest for the dead.
For those still living,
tonight is everything.

Next day (just like the last)
Wheeze/hack/choking,
one patient to the next,
shot-germs spread with casual care.
Wrapping bandage too far,
over, down and out from under,
subtle white bind cocoons us all,
creeping about as uniforms.

Bondage, only implied at first,
slides thicker, stronger, longer;
the more it importunes with drag of the weave, twinning single
arm-hairs.
At stump's end, every loose thread has played-out its length
beyond terminal reach.

By blood tithe bound,
swear the naked hypocrisy
of every hipporific oaf.
Turning tricks for hollow promise,
these Treacle Towns stick-slowly, un-loathing makes fools for us
all.
Our fund of trust,
descends further,
a bankrupt sump
of honeyed slivers.
(Read the fine lines before you sign)
Safely nested, steadily aping concrete
the static dream.
Surplus care and overspend,
in silent rapture they lie joined,
Patient/Healer, intertwined.
'I' is just another
other object
as Siamese twin
seeing same doubles
through shared eyes.

> Hand
> over
> under-
> hand

one washes the other.
Infection and Procedure: inherited diseases.
Deep breaths.

Please wait until I leave the room before exhaling.
Bacteria scrub: Massage the medium,
through thick end of the swimming lens,
check the charts.
No change,
           nothing ever changes,
blankness of a stare,
where less becomes more,
distortion overtakes the norm.

Redundancy
and other ugly words:
'closedown'
'steering groups'
'cut-back'
'streamlining'
– rumours slither
Towards time-duty, now deluxe commodities,
ill-afforded, even by the endless hours, laisse faire, splintered into
days.

(Extinct) Meagre Allowance to lose your own way.
Underpaid, undersexed and unheard;
we're permanently misunderstood,
all these near misses make pariahs of us,
scapegoated by the dead (who cannot speak but bear their names)
cornered by neat garrotte of circumstance
and excavated testimony
to bring down those higher powers
(who don't speak for us).
Attacked and harassed,
we who hold the line
are steadily nudged over it,
only to be shot from all sides.

Desperate to get out from hand,
its tightening glove

that lathers praise, gladly,
as it shakes itself free.
Sold out, so we all go, one from under the other,
disappeared (ghosts on paper)
another number, a mass-collated sum.

We bump-up the figures, when winds blow sane.
But as crows cock North by North-West,
It's time to re-distribute the rates,
ever-obedient, we mark ourselves: 'perfectly inept.'
Evaluation to-order's a dirty mirror,
few can stand close lest its reflection rubs off.

Rollback the mothballed wards,
preserved in a permanent haze
As far from life as death.
Wily all around us, shaking laughter
reveal no secrets
and announces no fear,
bitter tears fall from stripped gallows,
of Juniper and Chestnut tree.

Square Eyes

Charlie Ray has gone. He slipped out through those lame wrap-around shades, boxed-in, diminished by daylight. Nurses only realised once they jolted his chair and the glasses fell off, showing a pair of black holes, floating silent for the sun, underlined by a neat Cheshire grin.

Only in reflection comes clarity, diffracted and endless; a squared-off world only living through his lens. He doesn't walk anymore, so nurses wheel him about in his chair, legs pushed to one side, bent and useless. His hands always prepped-out flat, ever-ready to act, but no industrial escapes for the splintered men of yesterday's cathode craze.

Months after he'd left, dead, not disappeared, turns out he left a little money behind. Some to the hospital, the rest signed-off by a solicitor and bloodline hangers-on, who soon took their share, along with Him elsewhere, carving off his forty percent. With faith in our eternal Trust, two flat-TVs and a stereo were purchased. Everyone complains as there was nothing they knew or liked on the radio and our only CDs, a four-volume Irish Folk collection, have worn away from overuse, more skips than music in the growing gaps.

His chair, now naked except bereft with bony grooves, had to be dragged outside to pitch and roll, shook by unknowing winds. Callous and cold, they sweep on through and through; different leaves, same breeze, doubling decay long-distance, on the crunch-ridden floor.

Memories of Charlie suggest an outline, redrawn in cosmic dust that holds a presence of its own, catching fresh webs, emptiness ensconced in spider holes. Better he were here to combat the grey spaces so easily taken for granted, stained by his smile and impossible to remove entirely.

It seemed a necessary tribute to say thanks for the donation. So they attach little silver plaques, engraved with Charlie's name and dates, now every other day they're mine to polish. Screwed onto cheap plastic surrounds, new windows to culture-on-demand. We are the by-product of these simple desires, as OD is overdrive into overdose, compulsion fills the gap, enough is never enough.

Look for him there; one ghost to another, in pixels that make up fragmented images, there's a haze that draws me near, fogs the mind with biting micro teeth and dulled synapses – all the channels show the same, they just change the faces between the scenes. Better to shut down early than live just to resist.

No matter how hard I push, reality pushes back. For all the words and colours, the smells and sounds, there's a continual blur, every picture breaks down, chewing on its own tail, lost in something else.

I cannot make Charlie Ray appear, no more than I can imagine myself free. Barely register the man behind me shouting, I only hear him far from listening. Hold down the button to skip channels, searching all of them until the numbers run out.

Talked with you too many times, about what I don't remember, but once they told me I struggled to see your face again. Moving through mixed signals, I reject the outside as interference. Riding chopped waves of sine-paranoia, new nonsense and endless conjecture; fucked up by news reports spitting more death tolls, a sales index I'll never own and shoeless people stood waiting in infinite queues, desperate for something to happen. They swap rumours for handles on best-buy goods or famous remnant texts, rarely enquiring about the memory of a friend.

What happens when the light fizzles out? You smack it about a bit, from the top and side-to-side, just to make it go, then eventually trade it in for a new model. A Dave in black comes and goes, final faces are removed. Charlie's gone after a long year replaced by inferior machines that connect his nothing with not much else. A sliver of light, some ebullient flash of narrative colour and "pht", exhales a single wisp.

What about the silver plaques, the name and dates, where do they go? All hints towards permanence but what really remains? A body alone, some tribute everlasting to outlive the fickle brightness. Unscrew Charlie's mental cage, toss him out with the chair, burnt and ground-down to something less, an undying reduction, repackaged, re-made or re-modelled. There's cooling hum and crackled fizz of the electrode fade as the screen powers down and so the identity of Ch1rl0 R1y dies again in digital repeat thecolonel'sdeath*willbe*etelevisedRevolutionisalwaysre levantGazaisskidrownowHiddentariffsAtimetodeal?CreditCr unchWhatareyouscaredofthisweek?FreePalestineObamaelect-MenarethenewWomenLostartofconversationMassunemploye dWe'reAllTalebanNowFitterCashpointcameraIdiotkidSaving-theworldonegaffeatatimeWhoweepsforthetuna?Deathratedisg-raceConsolidateallyourdebtBIGdiseasewithalittlenameIfwhi teAmericatoldthetruthforonedayGenerationcrunchRightto-dieDowedreaminhidefinition?P0stC0DElotteryCuretheNHSBo-wlingaloneLocalismjustsheddingresponsibilityChildmissingSeed-sonstonygroundFactorypeopleBailoutGodisdeadbutwe'rejustla-zysomisunderstoodFriedrichsaysRelaxYoungwhiteandsuperskin-nyBigSocietyequalsBSnojobforlifeSaidshewouldslashherwrist-sonabadhairdayIllusionofDemocracyAlan"drugsarebad"Johnson EverythingmustgoNohomeforPolarbearsGMTV=beigehOleofd eathDulceEtDecorumEstProPatriaMoristillringstruePatientstar vedthroughdisconnectedtubeHolidayinCambodia/Afghanistan/ Californiaallwithguaranteedsun Highmortalityisnotareflection-ofqualityNewOrleansstillweepsKatrinatearsFighttokeepwarmT-welvehourshiftparadigmMagrinofErrorGreatmixedhopeEton-RiflesstillrulefromthespiresGoldenHourcountsthemostKidsare-oldernow365%APRTortureisrealRighttoLifeequalsRighttoDieS-chadenfreudejunkieSelfharmnotanormalwaytoliveMoreproduc-tiveComingupforBlairMisreadtextsconjurenewliesDebasedog-mamoralityMiddleclasscloisterfightingbackLifeintheredUnset-

tlingvegetableOutlawbanksWeareairstrip1LovecostsHowmuchd
oyouthinkenoughisToryhangoverPisspaintingsIdon'twanttowor
kBombsforbeefAfewgreenshoots?IwantmyLDV(orCadburys)Th
eywhoruleindustriallywillrulepoliticallyThe£100millionmanNo
nspecificspecificationsVirginityforsaleGuantanomoisnogo))<<>
>))4eva28days41days?daysSmile:)you'reonBigBrotherRevolutio
narygovernancebyUturnNowinofeeReceptionistsrunA&EPande
micoftheWeekI.D.CardaflawedScienceTheRedeemingFeatureof
WarSuchsuchwerethejoysFucktheNHSThisismyeyegivemeyours-
FondbutnotinLoarethenewWomenLostartofconversationMass
unemployedWe'reAllTalebanNowFitterCashpointcameraIdiot-
kidSavingtheworldonegaffeatatimeWhoweepsforthetuna?De
athratedisgraceConsolidateallyourdebtBIGdiseasewithalittle-
nameIfwhiteAmericatoldthetruthforonedayGenerationcrunch-
hRighttodieDowedreaminhidefinition?P0stC0DElotteryCuret
heNHSBowlingaloneLocalismjustsheddingresponsibilityChild-
missingSeedsonstonygroundFactorypeopleBailoutGodisdeadb-
utwe'rejustlazysomisunderstoodFriedrichsaysRelaxYoungwhite
andsuperskinnyBigSocietyequalsBSnojobforlifeSaidshewould-
slashherwristsonabadhairdayIllusionofDemocracyAlan"drugsare
bad"JohnsonEverythingmustgoNohomeforPolarbearsGMTV=be
igehOleofdeathDulceEtDecorumEstProPatriaMoristillringstrue-
PatientstarvedthroughdisconnectedtubeHolidayinCambodia/
Afghanistan/CaliforniaallwithguaranteedsunHighmortalityis-
notareflectionofqualityNewOrleansstillweepsKatrinatearsFight-
tokeepwarmTwelvehourshiftparadigmMagrinofErrorGreat-
mixedhopeEtonRiflesstillrulefromthespiresGoldenHourcoun-
tsthemostKidsareoldernow365%APRTortureisrealRighttoLi
feequalsRighttoDieSchadenfreudejunkieSelfharmnotanormal-
waytoliveMoreproductiveCominupforBlairMisreadtextscon-
jurenewliesDebasedogmamoralityMiddleclasscloisterfighting-
backLifeintheredUnsettlingvegetableOutlawbanksWeareair-
strip1LovecostsHowmuchdoyouthinkenoughisToryhangoverPi
sspaintingsIdon'twanttoworkBombsforbeefAfewgreenshoots?Iw-
antmyLDV(orCadburys)Theywhoruleindustriallywillrulepolitic

allyThe£100millionmanNonspecificspecificationsVirginityforsale
Guantanomoisnogo))<<>>))4eva28days41days?daysSmile:)you'-
reonBigBrotherRevolutionarygovernancebyUturnNowinofeeRe-
ceptionistsrunA&EPandemicoftheWeekI.D.CardaflawedScience
TheRedeemingFeatureofWarSuchsuchwerethejoysFucktheNHS-
ThisismyeyegivemeyoursFondbutnotinLo lestineObamaelect-
MenarethenewWomenLostartofconversationMassunemployed
We'reAllTalebanNowFitterCashpointcameraIdiotkidSavingth-
eworldonegaffeatatimeWhoweepsforthetuna?Deathratedisgrac-
eConsolidateallyourdebtBIGdiseasewithalittlenameIfwhiteAme
ricatoldthetruthforonedayGenerationcrunchRighttodieDowedr-
eaminhidefinition?P0stC0DElotteryCuretheNHSBowlingalone
LocalismjustsheddingresponsibilityChildmissingSeedsonstony-
groundFactorypeopleBailoutGodisdeadbutwe'rejustlazysomi-
sunderstoodFriedrichsaysRelaxYoungwhiteandsuperskinnyB
igSocietyequalsBSnojobforlifeSaidshewouldslashherwristson-
abadhairdayIllusionofDemocracyAlan"drugsarebad"JohnsonEv
erythingmustgoNohomeforPolarbearsGMTV=beigehOleofdea
thDulceEtDecorumEstProPatriaMoristillringstruePatientstarv
edthroughdisconnectedtubeHolidayinCambodia/Afghanistan/
CaliforniaallwithguaranteedsunHighmortalityisnotareflection-
ofqualityNewOrleansstillweepsKatrinatearsFighttokeepwarmT-
welvehourshiftparadigmMagrinofErrorGreatmixedhopeEton-
RiflesstillrulefromthespiresGoldenHourcountsthemostKidsare-
oldernow365%APRTortureisrealRighttoLifeequalsRighttoDieS-
chadenfreudejunkieSelfharmnotanormalwaytoliveMoreproduc-
tiveComingupforBlairMisreadtextsconjurenewliesDebasedog-
mamoralityMiddleclasscloisterfightingbackLifeintheredUnset-
tlingvegetableOutlawbanksWeareairstrip1LovecostsHowmuchd
oyouthinkenoughisToryhangoverPisspaintingsIdon'twanttowork
BombsforbeefAfewgreenshoots?IwantmyLDV(orCadburys)They-
whoruleindustriallywillrulepoliticallyThe£100millionmanNonsp
ecificspecificationsVirginityforsaleGuantanomoisnogo))<<>>))4
eva28days41days?daysSmile:)you'reonBigBrotherRevolutionary
governancebyUturnNowinofeeReceptionistsrunA&EPandemico

Adam Steiner

ftheWeekI.D.CardaflawedScienceTheRedeemingFeatureofWarSu
chsuchwerethejoysFucktheNHSThisismyeyegivemeyoursFound-
butnotinLo

Felo de Se

Swans keep love at arm's length, a peaceful transact to look elsewhere without the guilt. Maybe it was their manifold errors at being so afraid, one causing the other. Ignorance stretched across cooling vista of an abandoned middle, where nothing's clear between the sheets; or perhaps growing too hastily together, preferring sometime-separation but sleeping less alone.

Now He-Swan has flown to wandering, as if by deviant interpretation wriggled-out from all that history that grows immediate in the recall. She'll come back around, again, through mistaken sense of duty, desperately unhappy (not sometimes, but always) silent in her stale orbit. With sheer laziness from feeling, a long exhaustion stretched over time or a series of accidents that nobody could have foreseen, theirs is a chapter trying too hard to close, an un-healed scar in trickling, ticked beats. The big-red is always at war, sounding out through the fog that binds and blinds us, keeps us close.

Exploiting the chance to revenge on someone else, this Swan decides to have a go at the half-lung patient, breathing from a can being his only defence. Swan glares once-over, his eyes a shaved ellipse, deep in sight but reluctant to commit. Distracted by pure thought She-Swan drags a finger across his thin red lips smearing their face into staid Pierrot clown, sinking with a sideways grin.

"Which one is this?" Standing flat as the wall allows, "And what's wrong with him?" Starts lecturing the fifty-a-day man to cut down, He-Swan repeat-points him in the shoulder, every word coming via a bony nib, her next cigarette already lit, wafting fumes in the face, now both suitably incensed.

"Well Doctor, I mean, uh, Miss..."
"Doctor will be fine."
"How many *can* I smoke, just a few each day?"

"Mmmm, no. I was thinking," exhales right in his puff, "more like zero."
"But how will I ever get to zero in my condition?"
Swan looks far out the room, interrupts himself with a cloud "It doesn't take long."
Which Swan is this? Too hard to say...

Patient sinks into tired bed a crooked screw trying to exorcise the lack of sense from a fraught and stuttering mouth. Swan clutches at some random prescription: "How about seventy-eight-a-day then?" Shocked again, the man with the gaping half wheezes no audible response. It shrugs to herself, avoiding eye contact, "We do need the bed."

Swan walks away, leaving the patient in protest as good as silence. *those without heart have not the voice to shout* Or was it the other way around? She blinks a slow drip, still no creases on that face serene. Leaning fox-fur over shoulder into some nurse's back, Swan's digging in with his cut-glass chin, she's simple prey, another easy muse for blunt ambition. Both Swans love it, sparking the jealous ones to glare incendiary screams that cannot reach them.

This Swan stares right back, fluid features melting into arched jawline then smoothing out to a stiletto point. In darting stillness it quivers, an amber fire fusing into brittle, bright jade that can only go so far until it cracks. Refusing all constancy, so resistant to still life, he's disgusted by the static people steadily going nowhere. All anyone really wants is to become a handsome her, a beautiful him; just to be seen as some strangely fascinating thing, watched-over by their lesser. But in so many people the Swan-like desire is kept hidden, mired in darkness, not light, trailing along with their sad, stale logic that you can never reach further than yourself.

Swan's body presses deeper into the nurse's shoulder, she quivers under close-quarters. No one sees me. Feel rising air pass as spent chest exhales to deep slash of breast, supple blood pressing firm under a taut shirt. Strained eyelets creak like beautiful church rafters heaving from above. Sinuous shapes begin to flex then snap back – the wires and gears retracted, as if by some other hands that make this glittering corpse animate.

Nurse looks over shoulder, starting to question her choices, for the first time seeing Swan as someone else. Swan turns her forwards again, always turning away to break e-ye-con-tact. Taken by the neck, as if to snap, and before she can even speak there's nose running up and down, smelling over veins, as one shadow their creeping edifice shook.

Smashing as atoms, all somethingandnothing, the body-to-body trips delicate play of triangular music run down to a single line, where all the angles are consumed and nothing's made clear. In one breath it's the sucked-in cheeks and grip of jawbone cutting clean as a bow string but always threatening collapse, now thinning down and tapering out to an elegant X&Y. She reaches –to resist– but still hung about the mouth. Swan owns every ripple of those raw lips, bitten-down and receding to a finer lick. In an instant of blinks, I catch every spare breath of this Swan to that; can't tell them apart, a close divide that enslaves as much as it captivates.

Swan's incisors point in splinters of anaemic diamond sunk deep. Arm's still strong, reaching further to pull on skin until she squeals in half-hearted delight. A pounding slap at meat and guttural breaths as ecstatic eyes roll back to the whites and all the big-reds are buzzing together. I step back shuddering, so exposed, do they even see me watching?

That *face*…already the porcelain's showing its cracks becoming new, some are made so unsure. And she's wondering: 'Is this really my idea of fun?' but trying not to show it in the throes. Swan eyes fixed firmly on that delicate profile, so unmoved, it barely cracks a smile with these functional steps of fingers' long walk, lusting automatic. Strobes of white sky pass as failing light flickers above. I see shards and scorched-earth colours dazzle me in artificial sun – it goes on, one light must bend to the other.

Iris clicks sharp to focus, keeps straight ahead vacant as an x-ray. An uneven glaze, her lids flicker, another signal before the sigh, near-closed with lashes that spasm in erratic dabs. Some blood is taken in hand through latex-glove, tearing at fruit of flesh.

Lights burst, staring echoes blank space – another power-out. A resuss-unit stops mid-breath. Blood's slithering, sucked back up the tube as transmissions break down. Pressure sunk, it splits into red seconds falling spare, an elegiac rain tapping along with the ventor spasms -**kerdunk**- in get-back flow. Inflated patients hissing up and out, bulging orbs caught in fraught swell; some grotesque display of bulbous anticipation **Smack! Crack! Pop!** Bags burst, a rush of air and sudden mist comes ferrous on the tongue, with heated waves their cells evaporate.

Every time it happens the same: power gone, it spits off and on, costing us a set of lungs or another bleeding heart, all left desperate and wanting. We save thirty-one pence-per-kilowatt, but what's it really worth? Difficult to keep track when your secretary's verging on depressive collapse and a lack of confidence. Under the right medical eye, they find a need in barren lands, creative diagnosis becomes a genuine condition. Enough scrape-saved together should add up to double-Cs, at least. These 'non-essential' operations are more vital to some than others, but never really free, everything costs and so sacrifices must be made. We're told that to go without is a genuinely altruistic act, but some are more easy-led than others.

Mouths clam-up and minds narrow, peering for definition in the flat grey movements. Dry lips kiss only sky, to suck on air and make prayers for rain. In the back there's more dull crackles as they try to jumpstart another big-red flat out bleeding. Fresh night descends without relief, so they go fumble in lowing shapes, struggling along on their own two feet. Hear one crash into a table; not coping with this nocturnal sense. Feet edge to help but safer to stay put, for myself, watching and waiting for white lines to catch a light and the boundary of foreign sounds to happen around me.

Glass falls brightly, bouncing glimmer of plastic pleasure – it's Swan's nurse again. Slight gleams from artificial twilight; there's drumming of a generator pushing us on towards morning. See blue lines wrestling one over another, with grabbing fingers, thumbs and the silhouettes of claws scratching back against the neck. Now it's a yelp, her strands pulled taut to net the foetid air. Voice moans deeply, then tears, sounding out in-between breaths, trying hard to stifle it. Knee jerks of its own accord; quick flash of breast, first firm one in ages, though could belong to either one of them. Still, he/she persists; but if this is one Swan, then where's the other?

Too hard to break out from sex-law logic, don't even know what turns me on anymore. But seeing real bodies in motion is close enough. Click joint – move leg away, a subtle dislocate. Relax. Breathe back, now set strictly to the right. No longer bodies, just a pushing, pulling in shadow-tones less than human: all one flesh, full in being.

White heat breaks out in sky of phosphor, too bright at first. Steeped in dream, there's ugly familiarity, we are **ON** again. All change: rush the doors to look for strays, broken glass and a quick toilet break. Liquids seeping in at all angles, like a rolling ship or some fantastic voyage. These needledrillbuzzers must be reset, patients yell through it all, a vomiting heave-hurl and retched wave: "Told you I was ill," voice feebles, then peters out, just a passing phase...

Swan's off to a side room, see through square-glass partitions, clean, unbroken, step-up to listen in. Kicking something... chromey-shine...scope ears dropped about the feet. Plug to glass, one vessel to another, slide across, moving with them.

"Will I see you tonight?"
Doe-brown sounds in tempered patience but straining to resist collapse, is this the same Swan as before?
Muffled and blanked-out, "...if I can."

Scope to the left.
Lubb
"I just don't know."

Dupp

"But you said you'd be there, for Sue's service award, remember?"

Their Sue is my Sioux?

Lubb
"We're not sure, I mean, I'm not sure."

Dupp

"You should be there. She kept quiet about you for long enough."
Lubb
"Please don't bring that up, it's over with. I know what I have and haven't done. She came to me, in confidence, and I helped her out. Besides, she's leaving anyhow."
"Did you ever think about the pressure all of that put on us, my being with you?"
"It's not *what* we do–"

Lubb-Dupp

"But *how* we do it?" Swan shuts up, "You should have told me. Of all the people, I thought you could've spoken to me." She waits, "I never know what's going on with you, do I? I can't tell if I'm there, or it's you. Half the time you don't even seem to notice–"
"I'm sorry. I just…feel like…I've given enough already. I give so much of myselves, to you, and to–"
"We all give, everyone loses."
"…between you and *her* and the job-"
"Who?"

Lubb-Dupp
It sighs, "I'm tired, tired of everything. You've been so patient with us, so good, but I can't help being and feeling the way I do."
Lubb-Dupp – It's the big-red's soft echo thump playing up and down; more ocean tides rolling into themselves just to mark time, we all lose.

Lubb

"That's not true, it's just not. You simply expect, without return.

You're somewhere else, even when you're here."
Dupp Lubb-Dupp Lubb-Dupp Lubb-Dupp
"I'm here now."
Pressed cold like ice.
"How's your hand?"
"My hand?"
Mine burns.
"Oh, no, that wasn't you."
"Who?"
"Sorry, we did it, earlier."
"There it is, again this fucking we! I don't know what you're talking about, is this 'we' as in us?"
Half-hearted flows back and forth; stolen time in empty offices, some kind of love, all performed with the lights out.
"I can't believe I ever liked you, you make me feel weak – and I'm just not, I know I'm not." Glass shakes.

Dubb

"Please, keep your voice down."
Swan's hand tremors, ringingears, hold fast.
Lubb-Dupp
"Yes, I forget. As soon as something reflects badly on you, it matters, but I'm just me: I bleed, I bruise, it's expected somehow. You brush-off and I'll get over it, because that's what we're trained to do, isn't it? Us but not you – to get better, to accept and forget."

"Stop will you! I work hard here and I can't risk–"
"You risk me, every day, you made us a thief and a liar, others are losing trust. I'm a small part of your big mess, but I don't want to become another mistake."
"It's not *that*…I've no choice, only to keep going for the both of us."
Lubb-Dupp speeding up. Fear of squares for their perfection shuddering loose.
"You don't get it, do you? There's no future in this, for anyone."
staccatoshapesanger, "I can see that slow, sad death in you,

your eyes draw a constant blank. I've watched you in front of the mirror, waiting, for a shape you recognise, but you've even stopped seeing yourself."

The only response, a splintered heart, crippled by repeption. *lubblubbdubdubdupplubbdupplubbdupplubdupldldldlLUBBDUP-PLUBBDUPPLDLDLDLDLD*

M. M.

She wears it well, that title hanging heavy, negated by trailing-off abbreviations. Happy to slap on the accolades, pressed-weight of education but mostly devoid of all common sense. Trickling nostalgia, Matron recalls the old-days when things 'was run proper' and an iron fist battle-axe rode toughshod over ditherers and any lack of discipline was met with such a carry-on as to make them fall into line without asking; her re-invention of the old-hat prophets, a neo-cliché for increasingly modern times.

Sat in her stiffness, the stigma's expressed as a martyr to ignorance. This lady of the dying flowers is drowning slow. She hums static with calcified intent to climb up above the men because it is the fashion to succeed, to forge glass stairway for herself, treading upon the others. Pushes forward with all she's got, a mental throwback to shallower times, but there's no making waves in stagnant puddles.

A ticking machine puff-puffs humid clouds, glazing all the walls, internal rain that sweats brightness from the window panes. Her joy already confiscated at beaten hearts: pollen and colour's now a hygiene hazard so she covets secret summer hidden from the threat of wandering bees. Sitting sullen in her tropical fug with drop-tip leaves and petal stars, these burning fires are held captive from sun and sky. Among the frosty dew-pocked spaces she spends too long staring with wild intent to begin again, a reminder of other loves in deserted car parks and blank-faced hotels. The humidity of fear has swollen her doorframe to within an inch of imprisonment; heat accelerates her dispassionate fall, she keeps her own peace, content to rule in quietude.

Borrowing a death-drip masque, the fervent "what-if" imagination of a lonely Ms. Rigby in all her tacked-on majesty; bent and stretched out of shape and out of time to a fraught glass point –OverlOadedOverdrive– much, too much, too much codeine-cross-caffeine and only four hours sleep, wavering about casual despair, she ruffles every nest from office chair tilt, hinge creaks to mark minor tensions rising. Crying red-panda eyes, the floor's floating ash of shredded tissue encloses a shrinking creature so rarefied in her wandering.

Car wash cleans the ghost of stains (charge to the expense account), parked across yellow-slashed ambulance bay, in full view; she doesn't care – it's the latest model and the envy of every Jones around. Very comfortable driving *de facto* luxury, other tongues lash whispering at her: 'double-moron', she feels and knows it too, even repeating it in her deep-dozed sleep.

Next thing to advertise, her latest holiday. "Where is it this year?"
They lean in, all glamour-eyes: "Cambodia? Haiti? Madeira?"
"Well, there were all those mudslides out there, but so long as there are no bodies on the beaches, I'll be fine."
Needy student pipes out: "What will you do when you're out there?"
"I can get a cocktail and just lie in the sun. Who wouldn't be happy with that?"
A beach is still a resting place, no matter what it costs.

Documents sap back into layered pulp, industrial vapours, blur words, slur fissures of meaning. Her lack of language peaks in the haze, sweat rises nestling above her skin, mustn't touch make-up solid underneath, afraid to smear perfect composition, skip the details just sign this stack out of the way. In crushed drawers, too many Ts left undone, her IN tray overflows, every sheet's a potential death as she alters dates to mimic futures, circumvent the past and push deadlines further into distance. Satisfied with her charge, but rarely in control, even she is manipulated by her self-abasement.

Whiteboard's a frantic charge sheet of sketched-out failures, promises bled dry till the words are hung as skin without bones of meaning. Struggling with the machines. Mutter,

mutter, hear more complaints slip by door crack. She jabbers on: 'technology gone too far'. She can't be bothered to learn '...why can't they leave me alone?!'
To the ring-ringing phone,
letting dead weights drag her branded-haircut flumping dullness of the desk, head bangs a hammer but barely dents her frustration.

Solid foundations remain, but as easily drift, she stares through those other lonely people, remarking their differences, as if they don't exist, failing to see they have only pain in common. Her world is only pie-charts and figures, all brute unpalatable facts.

We stalk the same halls, sometimes going bump in the night. Too often she's up too late, popping pills, re-drafting costing proposals, together we scrub away; me hard at black toilet stains, she at persistent deficits.

Tomorrow it's a backwards dress but she makes more sense this way. High back, up to the nape then plunging neckline into spine. Trousers cut with grey fins tapering down the calves, fraying to make it fit but with good tailoring she's sharper in her shadows. The labels make it easier for her to flow aristo-autocrat; her kind made to order, slips blindly through drab field of bustling uniforms.

End of the day, they've all gone home, I've still a way to go. Walk past her office see her through door chink, staring past her glossy calendar, full with final epitaphs. Each picture a softened landscape, with artificial colours added; so tasteful to eyes that seek safety in platitudes. One every month, a brief slogan to give the moral behind everything, perfect behaviours twisted to a neat phrase; an ideal for living. She's fond to repeat, but rarely follows-through herself.

Mistakes grow by the day, feeding fires of the final media crisis that threatens to swallow her whole. Consumed by failures to act, she's seen too much money pass rainwater through her fingers, looks out to the folly of dusty redbrick, a reminder, long forgotten, of where she came from, now captive of a decreasing space, after the office no place left to go

Pulse 404

No way to understand unless you've been there. Pushing through seething grind of stacking and shuffling. In heady air of ink and tree dust, reading endless accounts of bowel movements, BPMs, forehead and internal temps. File incident report for the patient who sneezes-out false teeth. Press on this: **Ker-dunk!** Four more holes, punched in the endless white. Two-torn hangs funny, – check– uni-arch, foolscap, double mylar-sleeve – what do all these particulars mean?

Seconded to this but should be cleaning, while I'm here nothing's being done. File filler slithers out, swoops over desk, snapped by some mystic gust. Reach well past my weight, a slow-motion stack topples, plain-faced folders roar into explosion of double-spaced diarrhoea. Full stop looms, touching hair's-distance swollen to a black hole. I disappear as paper gulls envelop me, catch-grab beating wings smashed to desk now crushed fans lie as broken doves – please start again from page one.

Dappled ephemera plays misty with my eyes; so many paper squares, so neatly designed. Three hours gone breeds contempt and cheapened words become offensive to the eyes. Our mentalese brexcksdwn as computer screens suck at loading vultures circling death, sight going dry, brain hiccups to buck every other decimal, 'inacurcy a virus' one mistake, re-do the file, maybe too late to make it right – there are no re-dos in life.

Secretary bird lands besides, picking at fault with beak and claw, scratching up minor details into something bigger. This one's different from the last, hard to say, it changes every time I look around. Back to real world, in clear monochrome, neatly drained of colour but the divisions go hazy as words become gloopyglubflesh. Slurred letters break down to basic signs and drip slowly off the page, each makes its own swan-vowel sound as they fall from the cruel hacked edge – pitter-patter, a nagging rage.

Black spot makes a dash. Count eight scattering legs – **SLAM** – Lift hand, white all over, everyone stares, see some red gunk soaking out. Heads back down, check about, lift palm to smeared cup-ring but nothing dead there. Arachnid nervosa, or whatever you call it, a mirage in white that's escaped for today.

New jumble of words scatter as I shuffle through after sheets. We collect ciphers to order; between the cracked codes unravelling little mysteries. On every page see new schemas correlate with what I think I know, or knew from before, but what's valid or relevant anymore? Is truth, true enough? These are only brittle facts, nothing more than that.

Voices urge stress, some syntax out-of-tune harping on at me to shuffle these feet and keep the blood flow going. Ignore those other noises, break contact, back to the job: *'Hospital'* Hospital what? Look over keyboard, a crusted alphabet, *'liquidation'* all the mice and door handles mollusced in sweat-shelf of dead skin. Read repeat motions from the oily green; day-in, day-out so mechanical. It's the human stain spilling over into man-made schemas, absorbed by *'imminant.'* more bad spelling.

Minds and nerve-endings recede so emotions can be put on hold as we press buttons in sequence to try transmit the meaning, as if logic could outpace the limits of my language. *'Orders Sent.'* Matching symbols by rote, we type, we don't *think*! It's just catalogue of shame-making, bled-out in ink.

Sockets ache, strain, hold fast my gaze *'Spectator knows.'* Filing for four hours, where is the Long-Fingered Inker? This is *her* job. She just sits scratching print, nail nibbed in stolen ink *'All is..'* hides it when mannish-looking woman from the next ward swans by, searching with desperate eyes.

It's another pen shortage, set to hit us next, these things often come in waves. She makes strange symbols, figures not numbers... dots –dash– all spun so hieroglyphic *'Blind Pilots underway.'* there's marks like language, shortcuts I don't understand, *'Until embargo is lifted.',* quick-sharp lines and elliptical fuzz for medi-words she can't spell. It's OxMed lexicon, stacked-up grating against her frantic jots. *'Say nothing'* Think to tap, ask what this means, but cattish sneer pre-empts, tense before the touch, neck hair's up (unhealthy amount), best to let her be.

Finally, she makes a move and coasts, jaded-eyes lumbering in slight shuffle, a stepped-on face floats a difficult smile. In her usual grimace, half-sincere, barely listens when people stop her mid-wandering. They blab, I vaguely register, passing from one ear to the other she marks impatient flick of wrist between every sentence. I look for a patterned method to make the figures flow from eye, brain, wrist to ink. They nod confirmation, she lets her claw-hand fall –slop– to her side, more questions than answers.

Wait, something missing...
"Where are the files for seventy-seven?"
No answer: all shapes freeze. A series of buried heads rumble, suck between teeth. Still to no one: "There are other gaps as well, but seventy-seven's completely empty."
Several gaze through, nonchalant, then quickly turn away.
She steps up, "How do you mean?" Words spread thin here.
"I need the records for that year. When you open up the main directory file-"
"Yes, Nyn-strk-Bee-dsh-Tweyulv," it sneers.
"Oh, you know it?"
"Of course, of course I know it!" she snaps.
"Ok, well, inside the folder there's just this...note," yellow flag stuck to finger. Nothing, she just stares in humpty trance. Wave it a little –snatched– took some flesh with it.
"We don't have any records for that year; any of those years, actually," she strums the rack, "there are several documents gone missing."

"And that's why I'm here, to find them, right?" Appeasement, head-on.

"Don't be smart…"

I try not to be.

"…just because you went to uni."

I *really* try. Wait, what uni?

"You don't-need-to-find-these-ones already." Reached over, shoving them back in.

"It's just that someone's been on the phone already, and they're asking for that year."

"What? Who?"

"I don't know who, he breathes very heavily. Said it was important we get back to him, sharpish-as. And he mentioned your name," glance, "Janet."

"Give it here, give it to me." Takes it away with her, half dropping, all flustering feathers. Straight on the blower, well-spooked. "No. No, we don't have it, Sir. No, everything is fine."

Eyes flick up, sees me listening-in. Makes a half-turn so obvious she can't miss herself coming back around. "Please don't call this open line next time, it's not safe. Yessir, thank you sir." Never seen her scrabble about quite like this.

"So where are they?"

"We don't know. They were in the old ward, probably lost in the fire."

"What, the vacant one?"

"Yes. No-one knows for sure and we're asked not to ask about it, so don't, it could prove very distressing, for some. And embarrassing for others, especially if some of the dead relatives start sniffing about."

Relatives of the dead.

"I never knew there was a second fire."

"That we know of."

"I thought the whole lot was scorched-up when the building was first brought here."

"No," softer now, "that was the ward *before* that one, a long time ago that was." Away with a wave, "Most of it was saved but we're still trying, to sort it out, it was quite a mess. Yes. Definitely."

"Maybe I should go over and have a look?"

"No, there's no point, no need. I'll take it from here. It's not your job to have to trawl through all those dusty old rooms. It's not safe anyway."

"Yeah, I heard that."

"Just sit here and get on with these other files I give you to do."

"Ok, I just don't understand..."

"But that's just it, none of us do! We're all in the same boat. A lot of things go on around here, we don't know why, we don't get told about them, they just…happen. When we're told we know, we do, otherwise not. But in this instance, we do know that we don't know if we have that year or not."

"Ok."

"So please don't bring it up again, it's a proper headache for us."

Am I telling me this, to myself; or she now speaks for us? Slams down a new stack and off again. Warm rush of dust, feel them straggling in nostrils, sneeze, all angried-out now.

Open, first one: card mouth drawn, run down column opposite; all grinning teeth, pink and greens: requisition, long-term care recommendations – why do I know all this? Rubbed sixty-thin, at last, grams-per-metre squared, featherlight. Too many holes, something's missing, thrum-thrum at the corner, try to think, these numbers seem familiar.

Bleeds from neat corner. Flecks on the page now splodge-prints all over, mapping where I've been. The smears obscure information as my trace infects, corrupting figures, all bleeding into one.

Black specks into distant white – a snow-blind miasma.
Prefixes an easy way to differentiate:
Dis-
Non-
Un-

Adam Steiner

Post-
By stuttered linkages we determine the thwarted, label those less
able, harder to tell what counts as 'normal' anymore.

So tired of keeping between the lines
losing something
(in faked equality)
and fears of living alone.
We talk, talk, talk,
fluttering in stux, too much information
makes you feel more secure just to get words on the page.
Steadily meaning less,
taking up oxygen
illuminating space.

Force myself to remember, the process (my trial).
It all began with the act;
drowned woman, a burning man
all committed
 to paper,
each one a life in time
–distilled– time into life
and with it,
death regained.

THIS instant,
the moment bright,
set effervescent in our eyes.
But they always dumbitdown, diffuse
sparks deflected, dampened out,
exactly given, in twenty-four dour hours.

Words   are   brittle
e ven ith   imprecision   dec a ys
and   inna cure a telly   rewrites.
Butch -er- ed,   paraphrased,
nowadays   we   prefer   to   sweep   the   gist   of   it,

less   meaning,
still   ringing   true.   Bastardised   proves
A   catalogue   of   events,   duly   notarised
creaks   ark-like,
under   tension,   unbearable
history,
crumbles l e   t   t   e   r   s   as   words   …
slip
slide
perish

to   paper   life
long outlasts your flesh.
On-screen commands
~~rule   over   us   instead.~~
Cursor   blink,   blinks
a   black   mono|ith
|
Demanding input
Bl|nks
I   wait   for   command:/
a   prompt   to   know|
what I should press|
next|

        eye,
I

                −blink
Spiellings all done for us, so floorlessly.
WE

                −blink

| |

                −blink−
                        al| confus|on begins| with t|e word

Real Horrorshow – Patient K

Regard Mr K with his milky white hands waterlily quivering, curved-in like a bat's wing to worry away at his near-bald eqautor. It's some mental defence to hold back waste information spilling out from hidden speakers, papers presenting snatched screens, an endless procession throbbing trial by exhibition, all beat-beating to be first noticed.

Pinned-fast observation blurs attention on-demand; leaking blurb catches-up, overrunning popular imagination, infect all us vernacular. We learn talk more lighter tones, more sun less shade, though outside it's clearly rain. The bright ones stick to OxMed, while we go on-onn with celeb-chat, reeling who's gotten the most fastfatfast.

Whispers' tinnitus sting flies around his head, orbit cracked-culture drone, shadows of years ago. Sometimes he spits and shouts at the insipid gameshow, a circuit of unwelcome hosts. K bangs furious armrest under flashback of bookies' odds at the latest breast-augmentations scheduled midway through his hourly bulletins: "That's not even *real* news!" Almost ejecting his temp-fangs in the vitriolic blow-out.

Idle feet stomp inside monstrous platforms, like a stick rap-rapping eternity on concrete, echoing out my head. As he builds the beat it's time for one more diazepam then off to bed until the next day. Sit him up again; his gaunt frame behind his even gaunter frame. Leaning all force forward, re-learning how to walk again. He shuffles in screeches, grinding moon boots against equally stubborn rubber.

Patient K, the simple-celled emigré, has no fixed nation or outside life to speak of. Always edges away from the group, scared to find something in common with the moderate people. He push-grinds those wheels with distempered heel, only living to escape, the rest to bounce-about the hive. Happy in his brooding until Tony Pearson, the bender and shaper of bodies, arrives to wheel him away.

Tony leans in, always talking louder than anyone needs him to be: "You'll-come-with me-now, ALL-RIGHT." He nods away on the in-valid's behalf, no question implied. His Bedside Manner subtle like a sledgehammer, another idiot angel floating through in polo-whites, barely passed his exams and not great with people.

"Who-is-the-Prime-Minister?"
"Of England?"
"Well, not quite England but *YES*-that'll-do." More nodding.
"I don't know. Do you?"
"That's not how the test works." Much quieter now.
"You mean, it doesn't go back and forth, like?"
"No Mr K, we've-done-your-reflexes – THEY-GO-BACK-AND-FORTH-JUST-FINE."

K tsks at Tony's 'rigor-morits' of the soul. So without tact and lacking nous, he should have been dodoed a long time ago; an unexamined body allowed to thrive only in so shoddy a system, TP survives on vague pretences alone. His elegantly bumped nose, signature of the loved one, is jabbed in every-

where to

un-

wanted

  spaces,

then eases

off

                smoothing pace once he gets a reactive click but goes on lingering, his fingers wave pens and shuffle papers, all with that annoying itch of quivered speech.

Next patient drags herself closer, clinging to her frame as it saps at strength. "Can I sit down now?"
"In a minute."

"I have done well, haven't I?"

"Probably," Tony gives a casual upwards shrug, she laughs along with it, easy-hooked.

"Oh, he *is* funny that one." But not really, only thinks he is. She touches and re-touches her hair, softly adjusting.

Mr K's gone way down, broken-up when left alone, slipped a few minor bones but major face of recovery lost in the scrape. Tony keeps shrugging, giving it his all in minor emphasis.

She continues regarding Tony, and Tony only. His slick visage lingers behind the flat dents of K's residual collapse. Spreading his pale patch of influence, a smile of acid-peeling orange juice, sneers luminous where three sickle moons meet, cutting-over-cut to carve new symbols. Tie-off the spare cells with yellow plastic strip, make it all official to take him down underground where the man folds fire, churning waves of former flesh, his sweat degenerate as devilled breakfast liver.

K's spent-best-before is neatly dated by tag, but with patient name and number left blank. In faint shake feel the weight of final grams, circa twenty-one; the rest just evaporates. So many bodies tumbling over and over in the cannonball washing machine to thin out the mixed remains. And in the powder bone rush, one becomes as the other, but we've got to keep the fires burn-burning to bring new light from dust.

Clozer

Trying to count dust clods on a pipe. Think I see cells separate but these clouded bodies collude in heavy lashes with latticed boughs of cob-hairs, choking growth by decay. Everywhere see these patterns set to disappear through bleach enforcement or the slur of time.

The same follicles reach out, connecting through my fingernail that plays at loose stain for days, fraying stretch by stretch. Shed twelve-hundred cells per metre as we walk without care, every body's a virulent fortress, each coveting their own disease trapped in close-con-tact but failing to communicate, so nothing more is understood and no one–

"Put this on," to one soft side. Shudder-thin whisperings from the left, or is it right? Remember being held, cheek against cheek, as raw spasms shot down the spine. Her voice a molten caress, that foreign hush of intimacy, held silent in me, always seems it must be demanded, or taken...but don't want to think about her just now.

This one breathes sharpening through the nose – that's impatience waking in me: "What?" white crush flow slips its stitches over my shoulders.
"We need a doctor." I shiver, between layers feel rumble of knuckles.
"What?" Begin to turn round, "But I'm not a–."
"Here they come, be ready." She corrects me forwards.
"*Who's* coming?" I hiss.
"Doesn't matter," she hisses back, "just pretend to fill this in."

Clipboard pressed into my hands, left grips weakly as mind fumbles with slick-chill of the dog-bitten clip snapping back. "Don't worry, you'll be fine," leans closer, "you did OK last time."

Her voice urges, pushing me further. "Well, read on it then!" Scan pen portrait, a girl named Jane who has smudges on the brain, just like fingerprints.

Stare too long, her body swallowed between glowing sheets, slashed in schemas and percentages, a neat outline held in suspense, waiting to be punctuated by decimal points. Ticking one not the other makes all the difference – I feel sick. This Jane's an abstraction of an abstract, like the haunting words, they get so close but can never quite make out that voice.

"Um, yes, this all appears quite…normal," my confident voice, "but perhaps, we should ah, vascillate the…tronmetra…opening." Bit of OxMed for good measure. The voice giggles, "I don't think we'll go there just yet." I'm bright red. "Doctor," klaxon voice shrills away, wringing out both syllables "*Doc-tor…*"

Roller-point waggles in my eye, the dream is done. Red tip boiling over, streaming oxygen for the bull.
"Doctor Boxer, you have to sign for this."
"Who?"
"Doctor, if you would."
"Why, what's wrong with him?" click-clack ending, quickened efficient.

Another voice from behind, "Is something the matter here? Is she going to be alright?" Dear Jane.
Nurse turns her head, a rush of hair, "I'm very sorry, we won't be a moment," then back again. Head-on examination, her sincere glowering, "*You are* Boxer." Slow-bob nod with a question mark left hanging…
"Yesh, I eM nodding atch yU." She forces sounds through teeth under background of blank eyes; still their glaring duress.
"Boxer? I heard he was dead." Or was it Swan? Look down to left breast, not hers, *yours*, **FOCUS**:

Dr E. A. Boxer

Boxer's ID – left or right-handed? Don't know, it doesn't say – why would it? And who is he?
"Hurry *UP*." Her lips popped back to life with exploding 'P-oP' hazeline frustrations blaze away.

Finger clips soothing lapel, *his* lapel. Must've picked up the card too; slip-on, slip-off skins, easy identity. His plastic face nothing like mine, careworn but serene. She didn't even check, does she know? Never mind, for now, Boxer is Me, I am He.

By instinct, reach for it, then **STOP**. Remember bloody tips fingering pocket lines, red seeping through. No, relax. Both hands intact…then what's that smell? Check both feet in horse-clop lift. The pen waggles eyeline again, relative barometer awaiting action: dear Mrs Mum and Mr Dad, rise with flurried eyes, too real already, they seem to peel away from the wall, moving fast towards us. Best tackle it with his left, maybe get lucky. Remember *Boxer's*, crafty-hand, not mine. Make scrawl of wild letters like Hancock on a bad-to-worse day.

She gives quick "Thanks," some hidden glare flashes? Turning to rush off, she leads all three worrying along together, "Excuse me Miss, but are you sure he's…" The tigers are sent away, breezed out of hearing. Check right hand, smeared ink? Blood? Maybe Boxer's? It drips a red swathe, finality clicks: I've been here before, being's here – forever.

"Excuse me, who are you and why are you wearing my jacket?"
Mouth drops empty, "Wait, answer the second part first." It's him, finally here.
"I, I'm…not, anything. Actually, I'm pretty sure it's mine?"
See those eyes, it *must* be him. Not dead after all.
"Oh, look, you've gone and gotten blood on it."
"What? Oh, I hurt my hand earlier." Someone else's leaking, not me, "Don't worry, it's not mine."
"No, it bloody isn't,"
I meant the hand, "Excuse me?"

"Ink, man – you are shedding ink every-where."

"Yes, I know that. I just meant that it's probably not…my coat, then." Speak slow, he's an angry one.

"Indeed."

"Exactly," almost fooling myself, "however, I can assure you that–"

"This," **PROD** "is my," **PROD** "white coat, doctor…" peers, "Boxer?"

Stands-off, another once over: "Doctor…whoever you are. And now, I'll thank you to hand it back."

Give it over, what should I know...who am I, wait, who is he? Stares too long. "What are you doing?"

"What?"

"The coat is mine? Yes? Correct?"

"Okay?"

Picks something off, "Well, you keep this."

ID card, "Ah yes, *mine*." just nod, give him what he wants.

"You should keep it on your belt there, that's what you should do. Then you won't lose it, will you? Things often go walkabout a-round here; books, pens…all the useful stuff." Narrowing eyes examine the bleeding pen, a fissure of bone pinching finger and thumb. Raises a clinical brow and hands it back. Wipes digits on underhand of my sleeve – tsks, maybe he sees the rot underneath?

"Yes, I'll keep it on my belt in future." He's not noticed I'm wearing joggers, but so is he? "Thank you, Doctor uh..?" He looks down, sees my drilled sneakers.

"You look different, Boxer. A little younger perhaps, but still tired, still drawn to a point," waves a hollow death mask in his palm, "but certainly less grey, it'll show though, no matter what you do. Anyway, I've got to be off, have to oversee a lantemated, very fine, young cavena boost, very detailed job," leans in, "as I'm sure you know, haha!" Swift wink, biffs me on the shoulder, why so much yahoo pretence?

He turns back, another line dropped per metre: "Mind you, it's not going to be easy. Got pissed-up with the marketing lot last night, barely get my contacts in straight this morning. Anywho, sorry if I was a bit short there but standards, stan-dards, all are falling," sideways glances, "everyone's a thief these days." He says, finally walking away.

Nurse eyes flash all over me, sniffing for gossip. They think I'm in with the docs now. Give cold shoulder over to the nearest desk, things are simpler here. Pick up some papers to look busy, no one hassles you carrying sheets at haste.

"Ooh ooh, Doctor Menzies, you are Doctor Menzies aren't you?"
"Yeah sure, well no actually, I'm Boxer. No! Menzies, yes. Oh wait, isn't he missing?"
"You're so funny you lot are!" She giggles, the rest glare behind, more wallflowers pinned to envy. "Sorry, right, I've a message for you from a man called Doctor B. Way, Buwuay, was it?"
Screws up her nose.
"Ok." We each wait for the other to speak.
She dives in: "So, he said...well, I don't remember everything exactly what he said. But it wasn't that, just how he said it."
"Uh-huh."
"He left his name, actually, he's a doctor, too...doctor. And then he just went that you really needed to hear this message."
Both wait...
"To hear what?"
She winces, as if recalling a painful memory.
"What was the message?"
"Well, it was a CuPping, shOuting noise, sort of schlepping, shhrookkcp–ing." She mimics suction with lips and tongue over these big 0pen sounds, I'm lost in her mouth, dumbed sounds leaking out.
"It was a bit like someone, sticking their mouth over the phone, weird." She shivers, caught in sugarblush.
"Right, go on."
"And there was some screams, or yells, or something. And then

a toilet flushed and he yelled: 'YES!' down the phone. I think he said: 'I've done it, Menzies, clean out, first time – Perfect suction!'. This woman yelled something about the right menus… and then he just hung up."

She shrugs and looks to me, expectantly, ready to receive instruction.
"You look different, haircut?"
"I've never met you before."
"You're so funny."
"Am I? A minute ago someone told me I was dead." She looks askance, both bored now: "And, I am. I'm starting to think I am. Anyway, thanks for the…uh, message."
"No problem, Doc-tor." She waves and skips off, "I hope you find your glasses!"
"Oh yes, yes indeed." Rein it in a bit, maybe too OxMed.

I slip away with hands in jogger pockets, there's paper, folded, imperfect square, still four sides. Open to blank page except the header:

Continue till complete.
Then: repeat. Repeat. REPEAT.

Big, bold horror. Still shaking from the Boxer-Menzies complex. And who is the other guy, BeeWay? Look about to throw away dead pen but there's a nurse already watching me. Taps time at desk edge, should write something to look busy, just standing numb, that's why everyone stares. Drum a thin beat with white index, so loud like drummer bone clunk –something's definitely rotten in here. Dabbed ink smear, careful now, press necessary letters onto page, **B**, **O**, red soaks through, overriding black, **X**, **E**, **R**, disperses in fibrous avenues, I-am fades along with it.

~~Cut Here (the cord)~~

Swan blasts out from a heated chamber. Don't see the face, scope suckered tight to the fractious glass circuitry. Beat goes faint, but still going, rising to fall. Lean in, more bed of echoes, her big-red recurring...

...pull out and away, at least some parting left entire. I wanted words that wanted, not more silent sameness; the resting, staid in the damp patch of you. Don't want to get up, don't want to leave. Move in with it, only way to second skin, kept close, already cold turning, the dryness of older.

All I wanted was to be closer. All men ever want is to make roads, that's progress, to say: 'there's something made,' mind never stays, what happens after. And in private rooms they have to laugh it off, all is pretending that nothing's wrong. You left your mark, a vacant end, burning marks about my neck. Someone sees, they always talk-talk, gossiping lives; living gossip, one way or some other.

I closed a whole night, brought millimetres nearer to, next to you, a lying stone, heavy under its weight. I see your hands, fingers and arms twice-trembling because you can't stop needing-to-need. China-fine and slendering, I wanted to feel walls around me, made for me, not just an answer to an ask. Told you, same as I'm always telling you: to let go and live with me, more than pretending to mean it.

Utterly in love with itself, see you standing there tracing hollow lines in cooling reflection. In passing-out, watch your bones set surface as the flesh loses interest. Everything that is wanting takes a hidden toll. Sheets unwind blood-spot sleeves and passive smears, coverings cannot hide themselves, shadows yawn secrecy, pockmarked with swollen signs of life.

5:15 already, there's a half-moon plate that peeks out from under the bed, nothing's been touched. As bad as the patients, you mash it up and shove the carcass about. A staggered set of limbs, hacked-at dragged apart, but never met with teeth. Twist my head from the bed's edge –get up– time is getting on without me, wings in flight diminish death.

You nod-past morning's crook. All over, again. I try a smile that doesn't show. I pass you trying not to be in the way, in any way, the door slid ajar becomes tomorrow, and what days remain beyond that, right after a promise, close before me.

What are we, why here, or there? Shuttling back and forth, between work and the rest, it's only our differences that don't seem to shrink. All we have is blind interruptions; in corridors, against half-open doors, after patient hand-offs, wearing each other out in every sense.

Lubb-Dupp I see a future, distant, *Lubb-Dupp* but picture perfect: me…and maybe you, *Lubb-Dupp* all of us, together Lubb-Dupp but something blocks the way *Lubb-Dupp* standing outside *Lubb-Dupp* I push and am pushed further. *Lubb-Dupp* Why can't I just say *Lubb-Dupp Lubb-Dupp*
What's that scratching at glass?
Lubb-Dupp
Lubb-Dupp
Lubb-Dupp
Lubb-
Dupp

…the beats retreat. How can she not be sure? We both hear it, feel it. Head of glass, cooler now as a reminder hits: **Break Glass** to see bloodstars flow. Swan never in love, anythingbutitself. Break your arm taking you under the wing, but that's how it must feel to be with them, a growing distance, less are allowed in.

The less-friendly, less-familiar, forgetting themselves, recycled air inhabits dust, and for all the unity of a mean while, like static, we'll just hum.

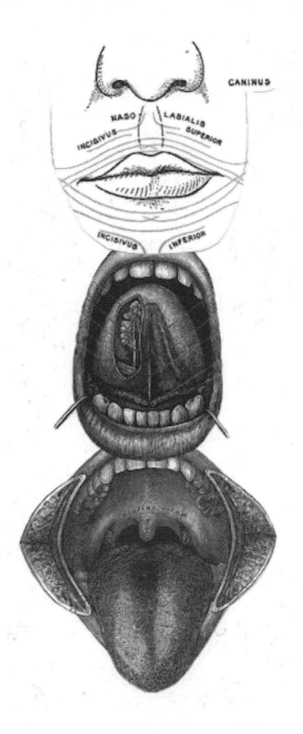

Omnie Die

Patient N.	Duty Nurse Observation
Refill at 10ml, when hungry or tired: 5ml at 12 15 pills, 6pm – sharp. Crush pellets to a mix, ground-down mineral powders becoming body cement. Drugs the new biological brick, in medicine, alone, we trust.	*Can't remember his name...* *Recurring patient (never really leaves)*
These are the hands, some tender, kind eight move under me synchronised butterflies. Beat teases my ruined body lifting wings as spidering fingers, slips away, become another *Corpus Christi*. Are we so different? Placed, interred for now, at rest. Roll back the curtain, do I otherwise disappear? Covers tucked tight blood trapped above my elbows now rushes to the head.	*Sufficient dose.* *Patient N remains quiet.* *Patient does not respond well to human contact.* *Glove allergy?* *Mind elsewhere...*

Fluids swirled around the new man
in white, vodka glass rhythm of night
nurses.
He never makes a sound,
wrapped black as night
living through IV.
Dreams days away by injection,
a gauzian animal,
statuesque in un-health,
marble pale,
shrouds a violent haze.

*Patient
swears,
profusely.
Mark conduct
disorder.
Incident form
completed
(in
triplicate).*

Eyes tired

They nag-nag, and nag...
What? What is it *now*?
I can't just sit here like this.
Unfeeling my right leg.
Where does it *hurt*?
Wait, my left or yours?
Doesn't really matter anymore...
pain's gone again.

*Special
Measures
taken.
Radical
Barrier
Nursing*

*Isolation
recommended*

Not really their fault;
nobody's fault but mine.
They're just young, don't
understand,
and don't apologise.
But in rows of glaring eyes
damage is already done.
Now I'm always the last one
waiting for the toilet,
medication late, lucky they don't cut out
my three-square.

*Ignore him
when he's
angry/crying
Hope that's
right?*

Never meant to grab her, or hurt anyone,
hands stronger than I knew.
They hear but don't *listen*!
Don't try to understand!
So sick of this.

Printer not working...

Ankles hurt,
fluids gathering
should lift me before my feet swell twice
big, even for clown shoes.
Please sit, just for a minute.
Don't want to be alone, and the boy only
brings toast triangles, even though I've
asked him not to.
So sit.
Be here now,
for me,
please.

Printer fixed

Printer broken...

Prescription of care
fades into repeat.
Time to reprint
...bt miNdz JammBd up iNink
Study the labels,
check numbers,
all roads (re)turn to zero –
the starting point.
No mentions of love or compassion,
just instructions on how to numb them.
Medicate the pain to fade...
Problems ignored, but still remain.
Make person into patient,
then object.

How much is enough?

Couldn't remember what pills he usually has.

Administer dose,
(by any means necessary)
brain dulled to Soma-bliss
a citizen erased,
trained to…for-get…your…self.

Drowsy,
refuses
meals.

Kaleidoscope keeps turning:
skinnypinkcapsuleyellowtwobluechaser
the hardest road to swallow.
Gulping eager, A to B,
they slip uppers, drink down Lucozade
consume rainbows of vitamin C.
This Pepto gives no cure to the fire
with haunting sounds of Orpheus's lyre.
Temazipam springs new dreams in you,
diamorphine makes you *more* tired in
the end.

Patient N
expresses
too many
morbid
thoughts.

Patient
unresponsive
to pithiatism
therapies.

Am I *still* ill?
Tell me I'm getting better.
Though what difference would it make,
if I took nothing today?
Would I die a little slower, sooner,
would I expire a little less?
Too tired to decide, or care,
let alone acquiesce.
My troubles are the next morning
and every day after that

Now refusing
tea and biscuits
(running out of
ideas)

Why am I waiting for tomorrow,
when every sun brings a dawn to see
this body of wasting silhouettes?
Caught in the act (a *kind* of living)
sitting still and ticking by.
Shadows as wallpaper
left behind
to chase the clock,
for Time's return,
then at 12, we start all over again

*Patient
spends too
much time
staring at
the clock.*

My cries fall dead on absent ears.
After all that talking,
there's only silence.

*Despite
prompting, N
shows little
interest in
watching TV with
the other patients.*

Nurses have no answer:
"His mind strays"
…so they whisper:
"Help him glug, gulp and swallow,"
then leave.

N tries to spit, blowing bubbles
not even language.
Dead-letters drool from lip to lap,
gently dosed, mental powers slur and
e   b   b

*Patient N losing
touch
but gaining sleep. He
comes and
goes, all 6s and 7s…*

gurgles a sigh,
human shapes float by.
He nod/sink/nods
haunting himself.

How much is a dream?
When exactly is a joke?
Struck mental slur,
waking late.
Life lived
through
new insanity,
muddled mutterings,
falling
into...
...out of
sleep.

Into
hypnagogic
state.
Yells
nonsense.
Demanding to
go back,
'way down
South'?

Slumps in his chair
unconscious, frowns

Shrill noise
like:
mngkraoowwww.
Then
silent...

ToD announced
@11.30

End of a Vessel

How did it ever get like this? Full bays doubling-up, spooning to steal warmth. Corridor beds, check toe-tags, the unlucky ones. Some corridors closed off, as the old ways are walled-up, now this place is no-go. Coming back around, feels like I've been this way before.

Just two weeks ago they slashed plastic sheet to a birthing gash and snipped ribbon to make it new. So many backsteps take me way-wrong-round, dark wynds lead nowhere. Some wards shrunk desolate in settling dust, picked out in splintered sun, left to soak, without the screams and moans. Drinking fountains run dry at the spout in those dried-white streaks, where the marching dogs defecated verbal ecstasy; the subject was themselves, while the rest raced about wildly to keep the whole big-red beating.

Pendulum sun tolls heavy, brushing streaks in the sky. We're caught in kaleidoscope crush as walls bend and apertures break speech, the building changes shape as we turn into our sleep. All perfect surfaces, once flat, now show their faults. The elegant ideal become bloated and anatomically incorrect – all too human. Everything we are becomes crooked, no matter how much you crack and splint yourself to make them stand straight.

One room to another, what used to be a cupboard, last week a toilet, now another office space with too many half-desks. Try to turn back from the nurses' place, my static station, there my wet stripe stretches clean across the floor. Look up, catch all the bees hovering in blue and green stripe, away they go, fizzing off in varying shades, mixing into one another's trails – everything changes but in this brittle light, all shines the same.

Something stings, an ache in the jaw, running-over moans of accented anger, like pipes strangled hoarse by rust. Crushed pill caps snap underfoot amongst scraps of paper strangled by the drafted breeze, heady rushes flit by my windows like the forces of a street—still repeating myself? More chambers split-divide into new cells, skipping a beat several times under the crushing blankness of a steel sky that keeps the lid screwed down via polystyrene tiles.

Nothing like *déjà vu* to raise that nagging sense of doubt, the same way glass houses expose your weakness as you try to break through. Even past phrases are coming back at me, must have crashed my quatrain by now, nasty sign I'm becoming a bore. But where was choice before I let myself go this far? Not doubling-back to…there I am, and I've said it again, my words all pressing force behind me.

Through the Aleph of my eye, a sphere so imperfect, future's drawn out to a dead infinity. Dizzying highs of spun-out youth trailing around its dead cells as a history. True as they say, the familiar breeds evermore contempt, but so does the unknown or misunderstood, routine life marched down into ever-decreasing squares. My expectations shrink as new corners jut forwards guiding force

       mop aside…

             …another point of closure
             bulwarked possibilities,

I recoil from becoming

             to kill off my final chances
             of escape –
             what?
             A life
             only written for luck
             ending all your dreams of
             love.

William, we are really Nothing

Not his real name. Writes it consistently, with every flourish so exact. Signs his colour-in pictures with it, but 'William' is never really himself. His rich type wrought firm slipping-off stark angles as a guillotine edge. The stiff-man takes his flight in liquid seams, lets the pen flow through, tapering after the page and onto desk, dreaming freedom, like a quill relearning how to fly.

Sometimes Bill 'mans' the nurse's front desk, a fellow imposter. Eyes-down under a peaked felt cap of moody shit-brown. Deferent nod assures me (every day) it was a bargain: "forty quid," – definitions depend. He tap-taps, lest we forget the colour of money.

With great care Bill picks between the pages of a book, splitting leaves to trace the lines underneath. Patient first, tongue peeks at every hard curve, trying the stiff tides, waiting on stone fists to motion like they should.

His essential wires, tying fire to the brain and movement of muscle strike too many misses. For most people it's a simple operation: moving body before the mind wills it, skipping words in speech, speaking truthfully(ish), but not so clear for Bill.

Permanently tired and every step falls delicate, not sure which leg goes in what sleeve, his jaw stretched wide like the view to a beach, clustered crumbs washed-up at sagged corners. Someone shuffles by and says: "That Bill ain't right." He could not, would not, care to understand.

B's messages from some distant reach always arrive out of time, and scrambled on the way. He gets angry/happy/sad, sometimes enough to smile, but just as easily tears spill down his rose-beam cheeks, nothing and everything's wrong, all at once. The words don't come to help nail his frustration to the world.

He colours-in the ideal country house, slipping outside the lines where his hands tremor. Scratches of red where clean blue sky should be, the white clouds left well alone. Satisfied, the artist retires, proud that the colours make some sense, but differences still burr. Blue hedges red, and so see purple, orange-green afterburn; the mind-eyes can't settle to agree.

Even best-moods, the good days, are thinning out. He turns cloudy at a hat-drop (there it goes). Starts rummaging under desk, picks it up flopping out the surly peak, more storms unfolding. He's darker with greying jowls; suggesting an aura of attack. Too common to lash out, fighting back self-doubt as an animal retreats into fear. Dead-still, the anger's a numbing ache that's become harder to hide.

B's family come in and out, to me and everyone else, recognisably the same, and all I (can) do is nod – nothing to say – the stakeholders watch the help watching the detectives. But for him, faces never last the day.

Does he compare versions when he sleeps? Dredging-up the recent past to run-through mixed reels of family affairs, mating strangers to the shifting faces. Scorched photographs warp, bubble and burn, curling in light to escape that fixed dimension, connections – forced – only resemblance is left.

His wife stares back. On seat's edge, leaning over, looking into his eyes, trying to find so many pieces of mind. She searches the beginnings of Bill and how she met them, parallel histories long since diverged differently upon each visit. Tracing the thread, she's for-getting herself, living on through sutured-stuttering. He's glass fascia, dark-eyed shined whitish pique of a goldfish bowl, all his days now *jamais vu*.

Answering the phones B. mumbles incoherences, sometimes hangs up just before a nurse can wrest the receiver from his hand, still grips like he means it, there's some hidden need to hang on as long as he can. At the desk-edged face, fingers dig a wood chip crevice, inching little freedom. Bill already knows the ruse as they try to pull the chair away to send him back to a safe, plain space.

His words trip and stumble into monochrome fuzz, he tries to spit cartoonish "Z-R-X-K-Y-N-T" Technicolor sounds of molten speech, their shimmer's a cool disguise for noise. Now he's buzzing like a fridge mated with transistor radio. No self-expression other than vague colours, our world, his cage, a mode of life pre-decided.

Good days B. gives a happy bounce, surprising for one who breathes so heavy. He chats away in myriad tones, every nuance of his nonsense sounding-out proud. Down-receiver his garbled transmissions enrage the other end. Think I see the spiral shake echoing bristles in the throat, spiky words garbled and digitised; little wonder, they can't know what I see.

He looks surprised when they hang up, his frown broken by a comic arch. Nervous giggling pops out his top teeth – a knowing joke. Covers snigger with mingling finger tips, half-afraid to be found out. Sure I see a happy moment, just between you and me.

Donated to us by the rest of the family, given up caring, sick of the sight and his ever-present clumsiness. 'A step too far', they said, grinning plastic all through the event as he pissed-sitting-down in one too many chain restaurants (fast running out of substitutions). They dealt with it the best they could, pretending he's in on the joke, not the butt of it. But laughter fades as patience grows brittle, he's the ball and the chain, another unwieldy body they struggled to remember, but also to forget. The former person is now too different (and yet, still the same) to relate in the present tense of restive stasis.

Advice came thick when it was time to discuss 'options'. "Sign off the finance for us, Dad/sell your place/get our mortgage secured/you can live with us/maybe/later/make it out in my name/see you in three weeks/he's too far gone/best to keep it in the family/dodge the forty-per cent/might as well use it so he can enjoy us spending it – besides, it's what he would have wanted," as he draws another breath.

He sags into his seat, hear drips, I see a puddle under the chair. My brilliant vision dragged back down to earth, an infinite whole reduced to *this*. He looks away, now he knows he's done wrong, then back at me, not as master but familiar, because there is no one else.

B. waits to be removed, I mop carefully around him. He moans a dull rumble then pitches up to a high whine, making more splashes, rolling back and forth. Ignored, he looks round at me again to deliver him from everything. I move away and out of sight, not yet ready to answer the demanding eyes. Bill needs a change of clothes and a place to hide in sleep; without boundaries and the burden of fractured memory.

My eyelids stutter trying to delete his emerald shimmering, enough for today of that dog-drawn sympathy. Concentrate on the seeping yellow pool edging closer to my sneaker tips. No-one around and he's not my responsibility, let someone *else* do it. Could try to blackout, but afraid of my landing place. Right now all that matters is to stem my feet through tattered side holes, let him sit a few seconds longer.

"Try to close your eyes," the Occ Thesp whispers slithering in a patient's ear. It echoes in the hall or maybe from theirs to mine,
our ears.
"Are they closed-as-far-as they can GO?"
They're shut. But it's still not enough. See him shuffling, wilting with tears. I've seen too much – I float...
Seen everything
now open your eyes
My feet are wet
open your eyes
Toes in warm puddle, makes me need it too
OPEN them
Concentrate, just a whisper: "I can't."
you don't WANT to

...

Shards

Look out along flat rainbows cut from their colour, more smears on imperfect pane. Twenty minutes spent trying to wipe away my own reflection; it persists, the same. Near success, but lacking effort in the lasting-light fades. Fingers wearing and tearing through the diamond-X-ice-blue stitch. Feel bone pushing past flesh where second skin meets warm glass until it's nothing but friction; dumbed-down circles, trapped in routine.

Scratch at leg's polyester crackle, same needling fibres with their translucent ends. There's a fresh face at my near side. Out in the cold, he blinks quick breaths still-life living still. I smile, we blow clouds together. About the same age but bumped in the nose and strange hair, slashed edges all to one side.

Pick out first few strands of stealthy greys, more salt than pepper, my cheekbone tip rises to age. Face to glass, swift steam evaporates, peeling-off a flittered image. My features falling into creases have settled where I can't stop frowning. If I strain forward, look harder, I see traces of the younger one, with a smashed web running deep, blighting a once-clear forehead.

But still he glows serene in nightly-blue, a stronger shade than the pale inside. Touch the surface to dip-in to another world, a dream brother, worn from sleep, scars echoing bedsheet creases, embraced by the pale acre of his days. He waves away a half-circle in dirt. I wipe once more, in reply, the face comes apart in my hand.

Born to Fail

Grip her by embers' curve,
needling hands,
eagerly met.
To need
to fill,
those temporary creases,
aching to   be complete.

Blood rhythms struck on porcelain
a tooth chink'd down-sound,
her stolen fire evaporates.
Dowsed in cold compress
swallow your voice,
glancing glances, unexpressed.
Wanting to be wanted,
needing – even.

Knuckles bolting
out down,
it beats the same,
from me / to you:
dum/dull
Lubb-Dupp
Dull-Lubb
Dum-dupp
drawn too far,
–love–in– elastic–

Between words as knives
we chop / change / lacerate.
        Tendons twung
and seconds shook into seconds,

Adam Steiner

veined pulse (under) muscle masquerade.
WE GO!
GLOW!
Brighter!
Together.
Whites flash first,
        she bit *me*
                flex shoulder's arc,
        turning point, leaned from ecstasy.

To me,
you're the less-worse part:
 pressed against pressure
all desire outstrips all pleasure.
Still stood minor light:
never perfect
and slowly dying day,
 wide as night,
forgetting time.

Emasculate
brief(est)
–release–
vibrant heart again.
Bracket –(**bit**)– Bracket
purple iotas
i-n-s-e-r-i-e-s
Count them:
determined line of nine.

Drawn out tithe
…trails saliva wire…
nails ring flat as keys,
thrumming hollow,
bottomed-out,
 end of a vessel
winding close

furthest reach
tap-taps…running stream
goes so easy,
overflowing my head,
heat and heart squivered eye.
See lost kids running
gone glimmering
fire and broken-up shadows,
born only to late-summer,
they helped to mar April's frailty,
the stain of bloom,
bursting to erosion.

Arched again,
forced arcane curve
writhing climbered boughs,
in
    last
   few
    ones,
we
GO,
   die
   slow,
    in
     You.

Just
one-one
more
movement
a   moment
ever-
last-
lasting/
one

more/more
iris
open
eyes wider-wide.

Awake sleepyface: it's just dreams again, more real than real. Clock rocking-horse steps, tick-step, tock-stop – ungained motions; two forward three back, coming my way. One brute-black uneven schlep, the other a slightly slip-on, heavy clasps buck, drowning-out the defiant petite.

Voices defy faces; fluctuate atmospheres, twisting-out the hours, an imagined taste remains, as you stand inside that ashen glare, undimmed. No place for Nurse Katy, nor you for it, where they make martyrs from weakness. Careful crook might yet trip betray your aching stance.

Your perfect face, porcelain sheer, smashing echoes on the vinyl scuff. Perhaps mopped too wet (each swipe loaded with intent). Mouth full of fractured pearl, eat your own scream and no-one comes.

I'll mop around with alkali shine, dust you down, dab blood from your lips. Slip off that bloodied uniform to inspect the damage done, and with nervous rubber hands, press and dress your wounds. Rest ear to belly, forge new dreams in the peaceful acre of your vacant spaces.

Sitting pretty lips rarely part, even to whisper, glow-gilded, bound by a temperate smile. Blood drain porcelain cheeks betrays your failure to impress. Yours is a grace so desperately-checked, just to keep in step, but I want to see you try. A sweet little paw, held apart, please ignore their alarms and hear my jaded skip, the (fake) surprise of mangled limbs – here's seeing beauty with different eyes.

From the alcoves I can stare, trapped playing the part, set to one side against a husband and some kids, all they give you is a narrow-life, a determined rest just to occupy a ready heart. The others go on, leave you behind in their normal pace, not thinking to stop and turn. My eyes follow your drift across that gulf of dead space. The abandoned in-valid kick-pushes her way to catch up, slurring confidence, breaking sweat to nowhere fast.

All nurses break step eventually, descending to a shuffle as the normal gait decays. Crack their twitched-wince to lift again; every muttering year of hounded back-and-forth finally catches up with them. Walk several miles in a day but always end-up the same way. Let their nature take its toll and follow the unfair course, dear Katy caught it before her time.

I drag her through-steps with a bucket, and so we scrape along together, wiping away a river's reach. My eyes stalk up her uneven spine, there's supple promise in rising tides of sickness' cosseted throttle. Again she nearly slips, pulling from her wrist on a bed-handle while I grasp only air, her spite all that's left to drive me on.

From bad days the quiet smile shrinks back as violet too afraid to bloom and mean what you really say. Worrying in case a spare petal falls flat across sliding floors as they recoil from bleach-peeling anti-flourish and second-check your everything. I taste green crush in the air: "so pretty and too perfect." Safe for now, but at the after-slip they'll have you, otherwise let them alone so everyone can go on watching everyone else.

Sees me staring trance, again. Hung up on every hinge as her good sole break-step glides that following line up stiff leg, ties body to neck. You flick back to check, my hands gabble deeper, pinch at trouser-sides gouging thread. With that swollen boot she takes two steps for every one of mine, a fractious space of losing time.

Few seconds behind, stamp my foot to push her on. You can't outpace me, another faulty cripple, we just wear it in different ways. I can out-walk you anywhere but still you look on ahead. Eye to neck stacked in lower beginnings, rigid as an outer shell, bunched uniform rippling fat into thin as we all ebb into age.

I hate your hair, your numb face that never flickers a shred and those kid butterfly clips you wear – can't accept life at a grown-up pace; so cute, so quaint, that wilting pretence plastic and fake.

All these things I want to tell but can't say, this drawn-out exchange, becoming your own private joke. Two nurses eye me up, pair of nosey blues, no real authority. I'd say mind your own, but they're made steely by numbers, an invisible mass that gets you back in other ways.

Flagging now, this hate and anger spent, all passions so exhausting. Body sags into itself, floored standing up, crushed by the indifference we breed.
I would never hurt you,
not really, I'd
only take care of you, if you'd let me.
I should say, but my punctured pride's another stab upon heaped failures for you to ignore. There they go, three slips bleeding lobster blue. Through to the white-out world, where I'm not allowed to go, where circles turn spheres, blood and iron regenerates; then bundled soft and taken away, more spares for the lancing expectation.

At the nurse's station there's another chunky blue lump packed into a chair resting her sloth as slump, seeping into varicose veins. A reminder of what they make you give, youth into age, stretched to fill the redundant edge. It's a rare sweetness lost once you sag in spirit, and so the body follows. Just like patient envy, they all dream of long days at rest, little realising it's a wasted future that awaits.

I wrote this down, our lost love story, because it never happened, much as I wanted it to. An imagined scar, ghost limb scrawl-crawling static on your wound, that still itches in memory. A watching and waiting, all about you, *for* you. And because it goes on, these dreams ring hollow and I close my eyes but never really sleep. Even though you won't hear me, at least you might see my twisted words.

Instead, I'll burn these pages inside our crooked, misfit house, watch the bony partition walls fall down like book-ends, close a trapped chapter upon itself. All I ever wanted was to make you smile, just once, and you be my reason to stay alive. Instead, you shuffle on, sleepwalking through till the next end of tomorrow. So for now I'll leave you to your quiet, to run the corners bliss ignorant, towards mother with husband and child. But soon enough in the damp and the drudge there must come a change – love can seem to rust, but its pale fire will not have rest.

Looked At, It Vanishes

Walk among bodies laid flat; a shuffling breeze as you pass, morning sun greets a field of ferocious invalids. Imagine crystal world with daggering stares that rise to punish us – all must obey the dying nurse's lowered eyes. Always in each others' sight, glaring out from many vessels, each window harks a lonely cell trapped under the same prismatic light.

Life's paced out in shared confinement, but to be restored I must keep on, go further inside, and my sickness grow worse. We stoop under low gazes, automatic-tricked-discipline to jump at the word. They bite, kick, swear and scratch, make coo at you; a fresh young thing, but their nostrils so inhibited they can't smell the rot about their feet. Our only health is to embrace disease and know what we hold, closer at arm's length.

Each mistake is noted in petit-whispers that trickle down the patient line. Stretched-iris widens to fit uncertain shapes fading into the room, so imagination accommodates and takes hold. Snap judgements snag from clumsy thoughts as played-out scenarios blame the nearest one to hand, staring blank and expressionless with the detached amour of a poker face masking passive-aggressive indolence, spinning secret yarns to hang you with.

So many lines of sight fly and collide as piercing arrows, all eyes on me, but can't get the stink off. Start to notice my own movements, however slight. Posture checked and re-checked, a target for all anxieties, writhing in artificial skin forced onto me. Some recurring sound haunts me, now cast as infamy; stand accused of a secret happy-slap, an imagined hit-and-run.

Breaking-out – man beats heavy sounds with walking stick, no time to brood as wood cracks at lino. Been going for an hour now, banging in-and-out. He moans, yells and caught mid-finger yelps, waiting for the next nurse's temper to rise. Bad timing, there's no one else around.

"Help!" Sees his buzzer just out of reach. More he bangs the floor, spilling with his sheets out from the bed. Sounds thud straight up from my feet, feel his voice everywhere, bouncing tinny, invading my every space. It's *him*, the one who won't eat toast in 'pansy triangles,' always asking for 'oblong-squares,' whatever that means.

Again, "Nurse!". He's gone all hoarsey, hack-coughing alternates with words -**bang**- brain shakes -**bang-bang**- in ebony -**bang**- cage, can't take much more of this. Mind's rapt thin like paper drum and they beat, beat, beat until the feeling's numbed. Always they have to push it, making petty requests just to pass the time. Now antagonisms breed like virus, scurrying under many microscopes – in here no life ever goes unexamined, no matter how dull.

What is it today? 'Just one more thing,' always *just* one more thing: 'get me a pen/when am I leaving/am I going to die/do I look better today/I'm still hungry/I will only speak to a doctor/I've nowhere else to go.' These phrases loop round but I've learned to be there and hear without listening. They keep staring, so I stand, hating them all the same, my jaw edges forwards steering vitriol into flame.

Faceless, nameless, wiped away (now even first names, sheer identity is confidential), harder to see them as real people. Stripped of normal things, each one's just a speck blending shapeless and indivisible, a reminder of things still to be done. Life's drawn out to a yawn but no one cares to notice, as you disappear or die slow, us little pieces break so easy

Try not to make eye contact – if you can't see them, you can pretend they don't exist. It's evading the hook-snare glance that's the problem. Staring from the bed, glazed looks don't approach seeing, nothing vital seems to register. Their bodies spent-hours crunched under belligerent armour of stringent sheets, looking for reflections in the catatonic spaces, nicknamed 'The Vegetable Patch' – nada. If there is such a thing as a soul, I've yet to find it; more a silent word, too lightweight to be thrown around. Shoot the Mystics and the Sceptics, the Sophists and the Poets: all raise dead questions that have no answers, so many thoughts better left unsaid.

All moving, there's that writhing sense of cloth-shuffling-skin, slid tectonic in layered terror like the floor is slipping out from under. Air is quickened with the rhythmic slash of furtive glances, eyes just a blur, straining at the corners. More visons snatch-at broken voices, we're well-trained at sitting through this nothingness. So instead, they indulge fantastic whims at our expense. Any attempt to get 'in-head' or adopt dulcet sympathies soon turns sour. Once they learn how to exploit interest they blur your face tagged-to dead relative long gone, then start resurrecting unfulfilled demands.

Phantom pains climb like a pitching wave, limb upon limb-rung, so the docs tut brow-roll; it must be investigated, but always ends without explanation. It goes in and out, just after doctors and nurses had come running, then starting up again five minutes later, no less elusive and worse than before.

These constant games exhaust both sides and staff attention eventually wanes, falling sirens to chasing future ghosts. Every screamed buzzer becomes a wolfish cry, they bury it to the back of the mind or turn up more radio. In return, patients practise heavy lacrimation, crying in excess of the tears left to give. Nurse sits over with pipette trying to thin out the salt-wept seeping, but they clasp tight against interference, each mired in their own sadness, she sees herself reflected there but after so many wasted drops the object of care flows diffused into a blur.

Flesh around the eyes swells salmon pink to crusted wounds, all sandy grains and purple lids, a desolate sight. Curtains are drawn under strict instructions: to be quiet and fall into sleep. Casting hunched lump against the blue cover, swearing the pain was more real this time, let the waters run and cry themselves blind.

Feel bodies tighten, is she here? Knotted air trapped in lungs, between them drawing up a sudden vacuum. Group temper coils to enslave other minds and other voices, as tensions weave into eager resentment, so easy to imagine yourself suddenly forgotten. The in-valid is naturally impatient and so picks wavy lost-lines in their blankets, fingers clenched into a buckled fist, ready for the next minor war. Their worry pushes me on, people fail to trust anymore. But I'm scared too. Not easy to admit, but I wish they knew or could understand we're not always so different.

More banging and shouting, tell him: if I'd wanted to hurt you or touch you, I'd have done it by now. I can have my pick because the bed-ridden have no real voice, only maybe complaints, mixed with fictive rights and wrongs – but I don't. Choosing not to prey as others do, that's what separates us. But no matter how you move, non-predatory with open hands, they always give you sharp once over. Like cattle caught in grid they flick to instant judgement, streaked eyes scan the true measure of intent and every flattened face grants that same emaciated smile.

From defectors of joy, these hand-me-down behaviours catch in the throat. I spit napalm glow as old words stick too easy, biting-down, trying to speak freely; the 'I' has fused, gone neon – now it's no more holding back. I'll show them just how shitty a 'disgruntled, loner, kept-to-himself-type' can be. From now, these brief moments of lashing-out mean everything to me.

Natural desire to rise above, to exploit the weak, it runs in every living thing. So vulnerable, so precious and arrogant with it, neatly squeezed, somewhere between the ignored and the ignorant. Of course, there's the 'moral question', but who needs all that? Out of fear, out of hatred, we kick away because otherwise, *you're* asking for it, like the brittle limbs of the daddy-long-legs, plucked one-by-one. No need to worry, as long as you're on the right side, because whether you approve or not, being cruel is fun.

For the night to come, corridors echo near-emptiness. Play roulette by decibels, to strike the one who snores loudest, ignoring Old Matron down-the-way, snarfling into gross armpit. Move gently with curled soles rolling shapeless steps. (Hear him) *see him* there: a craggy landscape topped-off by giant hair-clogged nostrils, vibrating wide and wild. Muted throbs unsettles his own nest, dominating my shifting-skyline with awe in the great wheezing approach.

Hand's raised flat, ready to strike or to absolve. Nothing matters right now but hitting hard and right – first time. Up-close flesh reveals nothing as it should be, an alien surface of pale extremity. Pluck the connecting wire from the buzzer, no surprises, no alarms, let it fall from my grip, trickling like a noose unspun. This is it, he's the loudest, my latest aggro-son – but do I lose my will, is this really my idea of fun?

A scream louder than bombs, some deep and vulgar roar. Hit him again, and again, swiping-off purple nebulae swarming over cracked-out capillaries. Slows to a gasp, winding down into breezey snarls, now coming through the nose, fighting for air. He tries to suck-back running eyes, squeezed-in like the flesh of prune-spat stones demanded every day.

Amazing to lash out: a short, sharp revenge for all those trivial wants that had me running-down sick through clogged passageways. He keeps on screaming but my hand weighs steady, burning red, doused in fresh tingling warmth. They say human cries, adult or child, play on nerves in the brain, I say a hat-pin through cage; pushing us to care enough to react. I feel nothing. He's eighty-something, an overgrown adult in child-like frame. Some small prickling of pleasure, a kind of justice, inverted.

A winding-throb runs the same thought up into the narrow delta of his side-lobe artery. It pumps and pulses with every ear-drum slap from his tell-tale cries. Rest him back down to bed, but again he tries to rise: "You're not well, get-back-*down!*" More action than expected but still no one comes, at least ten minutes before they notice something's wrong.

Turn on heel, get them to deal with him; gentle adjustments back to suffering silence. All happened so fast, just blurs same as body-chained-to-body leaning faceless at his bedside – I could be anyone, at any time. More staring eyes out from broken features, a terrible mosaic forces itself forward with white plastic flapping by, a ghostly tail withering with the half-light.

'Those who can make you believe absurdities can make you commit atrocities' and I'm the shadowy proof if you cared to look. Shedding layers-by-day we dissolve the normality we've all come to expect, just another face in that gallery of human furniture. He starts to yell again: "Nurse, nurses!" They rarely know your name, just shout when they're wanting – we're as generic to each other.

Tired now, lean in at the pillbox desk, prod-shove Old Matron in the shoulder. She's already last year's model, ready for scrap to be used for glue, but much cheaper to let her wind herself down into disability. She grumbles, ticking-over quietly, then exhaling with a wheeze, settles back down to her slumpingfrumpedsplat.

Move beyond the natural barrier, inspecting failure to rise. Her head's pushed deep under folded wing, blotched pink, yearning for early retirement and manifold pension plan. Her skin ripples in orange peel crease, suffocating flesh upon flesh, wrapped-tight behind a thinly-clung surface, all threatening to burst. My left hand creeps as the weight of her right breast spills out into a human puddle.

Try to recoil, but she's so heavy. Second impulse to seize pen (classic *bic*, to the point) and jab her real sharp-like. See her rustle up for air, a beached manatee shocked into life but better-off left to die slow. She slides briefly from dreamy panic, then subsides back into sleep. Move hand out, still warm with acrid smell of

Scotch whispers. A bottle clinks and rolls along to rest at her feet. Try to push it back in with the files, but no place to stand against the weight of the '**Deceased**'. More spillage, see: 'Agnes Mildew' (Mayhew?) from way back in seventy-seven. Force back the crushed paper tide, more odd corners speak out: '...*a surprising degree of yellow discharge*' next to '...*saving nineteen-pounds sterling, per square-inch.*'

There's Queen Bitch silhouetted in a narrow doorway that shrinks around her. Out from Office, she's dim-lit by blinking desk light, occasional updates and a swift flash of cigarette catching her scowl in its caustic reverence. Ragged flame of her blitzkrieged-barnet casts its long stance towards me. Strong enough to grip lightning, see that vicious beak slide across the floor to envelop my feet, all set to the chorus of her quietly sagging arms. Remove myself steady from shattered remains of Old Matron, marking innocence by less proximity.

Those dark-wrought almonds dip briefly, scanning everywhere with easy-irritant switch: from the cupboard, over Matron and I, all in a single, practised sweep. Freeze transmission: How long standing there, watching us? Counting-out my mistakes, every second marked as a ticking rosary, I rub round knuckles, already itching. She's hand on neck, idly cocked but grimace struck, rubs slow, (we sync). She sees creases on my hand (left mammary crush), stinging with her gaze, or is it just more whisky and sour musk, like guilt running down the crease of my spine?

Waiting on, another un-removable, I soak in denial, tell-tale shirt slick across my back. Held patiently, time is paused in our respective nothings, so different from the rest, like Matron laid out in a state. The Queen Bitch's stare pulls me to speech over gathered silence, slowly corrupting us. Open my mouth, ready to furnish new excuse:

"Nurse! *Nurses*, help me!"

The wrong words come out – the banging man over-takes my

oxygen. Forgot about him, so easy done. Thank the whiny bastard for crying out and thawing our stale-frost. She's more confused than before, twists her face to cruel new frequency as stares clash. She unfolds her arms from statuesque repose, escaping her rigid glamour-mortis. Hand to hip, a crick of the neck, totally-flushed with compassion and finally exposed, now out from her safety zone.

"I think one of them, the patients, sorry, has woken up. Seems like he's been screaming for ages." Revel in the cracks to her subtle veneer, going further. She's bothered-enough to act, anger runs the rush of blood up every tendon, straining layered resentments in her face as she pieces together the perfect anger in her head. Just like them, she spins stories of blame, getting ready to spit. No time to reply, he screams again, "NURSE! Nurses, I can't see!" Death rattle of the idiot cried in vain, confusing darkness with blindness.

A stiletto sliver's dragged over her nose a scratch she can't un-etch. Festering hate through a clawed fingernail; like swabbing at an open wound, it doesn't heal, it only makes it worse, trying not to care, without caring. But she must be seen to stand apart and in-charge, even for the empty eyes of a wraith in sneakers.

Worry-away at my most insincere, pledge plastic shimmer all around me. Slight grin shines through, but who cares, gone from the stand-off – go do your fucking job. Matron's up, filling-in the background with clip-clop tasting of the air in a dried-out pout, already clicked her pen into action but looking bleary, much worse than usual.

She says nothing, neither whispers nor humphs, just
brushes past, on to trouble. Almost touching, closer than before
but maintaining distance, struck by inner
guidelines. There she goes now, to play the part without
understanding why – we – remains – polarised.

Tears in Red Tape

Reams of white are tossed carelessly pretty, like streamers at play. No value in plenty – just encourages waste – embrace tomorrow by way of escape. Too many disposables picked up, then put off; gloves as jaded second-skin, bandages replaced daily, or not at all, and needles like frozen rain steeped in multiple bloods, popped into a yellow box, trickling loss, never found.

Unspun bandages ramble out, now using sticky tape, anything we can get. No recorder marks time because someone stole all the pens. **Item Release** forms signed '*Spectator*'. They let it all go for a meagre price, but with great margins, apparently. A voice whines out: "Help the nurses, help *them!*" Should be cleaning, but never enough time to do one thing properly. Blood soaks through, unable to stem the flow – this red just keeps on running.

Queen Bitch and I tear long strips from uniforms while the rest attack the sheets. Rip and return –take off more– no one wants to be outdone. Both embarrassed but refusing to let it show, we expose tan patches, spare scrawn, illicit hairs and saggy deposits. Both strawberry-blushed, she sneers, echoing our disgust. I'm the same. All boy bones, with stripling ribs, thick as fish spine, only a half-man's shadow behind me.

The Bitch is deep mahogany. As she moves with spindle limb the recesses change, jaded lines are ironed-out by clinical shades. A new kind of social camouflage, used to be that mercury-white was always right, now neo-bronze is the real way to success (and to be seen). Knife hips peek forward, trousers slipping, hang-on to one side. She wriggles out from ripped skirt, her uniform undone. Runs thumb along lip of folded waistband, underwear pinching excess, lick my teeth. We shuffle on, exposed, muttering flesh creeps away, neither one can stand the look of the other.

Run, run, hurry, run! All flashing scissor legs rushing to the next set of streaming cut-outs, wearing and tearing. Slow-motion sluurrrs me down in blinkered visions, moving cold like ice in my eyes, an old reel catching last tickertape snaps.

Pens dried-up and out, limb-scattered mass grave, Everyone tries their hand, shook hard without, throw them back in the same drawer for someone else. Snap, crack, bruising dried ink spots, red, blue and black underfoot, plastic shrapnel litters like dulled glass. Nurse jams fingers in the draw, trying to slam it past, another one cries out pulling at my shoulder, neck, then up to the hair. Toss a biro one way, she scrambles to descent, crushed in the hungry mire.

Someone suggests we start using 'leftovers'. Picks out a rusted fountain pen, quickly snatched away. All look around trying to clock someone to step-up and say: "Yes, go ahead, take some."

"It's not like anyone's using it." Queen Bitch shoots quick-fire glance my way, quick-rubs her nose feverishly but soon stops, so self-conscious. All afraid to speak for fear the she'll bite off their heads, devouring speech like flesh – whoever crawls lowest, wins.

Saying nothing, she just looks on, sensing her control's slipping. But these blips are only little victories, and becoming less frequent, my failures showing through layers of onion skin. This pain's clear enough and fractious to the touch – can't say it any simpler than that. Mind's got callous to this, as they squirt blighted-big-red more life pressed into drips, crusted at the nib, there's no more listing my goodbyes.

Forming Incidents *(Aftermath)*

Please tick, as relevant (or true):

Actual Incident [ ] Near Miss [ ]
a near miss doesn't count in meeting targets
List those affected: victim/attacker accuser/witness patient/staff/
just visiting
whoever's sore or got a bone to pick
Please describe the nature of the incident: internal violence,
pre-meditated attack or just lashing out; did it begin
with an argument? Security issue, safety at work? Ethnic
misunderstanding or full-blown racism?
*who said the first word, threw the last punch? remember there's no
libel for the dead!*
Describe FACTS only, no conjecture, hearsay or second-hand
evidence required.
definitely not your own opinion
Type of injury, any ill effects: abrasions ablaze, a lash, a graze,
bite, on-fire, punch, scald moons rising, fracture, some sense
of irritation, kicking out, laceration of the brain, needlestick
into sharps, (accidental orgasm?) pain or ache? Red mark, blue
bitch bruise the size of a small Eastern-European country? Side
effects of the drugs? Shock to the system, strain, not sprain? An
undeniable sense of shame?
will the bruises show, can they prove they're really hurt?
Was any restraint involved?
did you damage the attacker trying to control him/her?
For example: inadvertent injury via differential impact.
all for their own safety, of course
List body parts injured:
or missing…
Any witnesses? Aretheyreliable/impaired/trustworthy/honest/

onmedication/emotional/biased/illegitimate/sober/racially-aware/in-valid/or otherwise inferior/any mental conditions?
can they make us look bad in court or the press? sniffing under carpets/tables for a way to throw stones/food/faeces [delete as appropriate]
erase the ignorant
Any damage or loss of property, compensation required? Cost is: actual/estimated? Weigh up potential claim.
we survive only on the organism's collective property
Have the police been informed?
do they really need to know?
To be conpleted [sick] by the person in charge
whoever that might be...
Details of the investigation:
what are you going to do about it?
Most importantly, who is to blame, who's responsible?
Not-noticing, who was at hand, leafturned itspalmagainstus, we drip absently.

Denervated Air

Remember Swans' early days. When all things seemed better. Still bright, with stargazed eyes, not yet beat in panda surprise. Wary about the outer doors. Hard enough to get through the nicotine pack, stacked, huddled, to a concrete patch, spotted with rust-rain drops. Steadily, numbers fall, always by autumn, more disappear. Come summer the new quitters will step out again. The last safe space, where secrets are shared, running down to full stop and in the future this time apart –against health– will be forgotten and denied.

Silver streak tears into the car park. A vulgar screech co-opted via car-share scheme, another 'encouraged' policy. Wagner's charging marches kick-out soaring crescendo of Lazarus strings flailing air, set into wind, sparks of ash flittering from the window gap. Stepping out, he winces chill spreading to the bones; she stretches ice from the knuckles, one slam – shadowed exit.

Swan profiles sidle up, looking back on the civil smokers, banished to the lost periphery by infrequent buses. Outsiders hit Swans with bad looks as they shift ID badges behind lapels: "Medical staff, *smoking*."
"Should be setting an example!"
"You think they'd know better, all the people they have to tell-off."
These are typical asides, never said direct, merely expressed under weakened breaths. Common sight of butts dashed in side alleys, now pressed in dark lines, slab-to-slab, fading out in convenient recesses.
One last drag…
Throw it down.
Everyone does it.
What does one (more) matter?

More beige tabs dot the double-yellows, streak says '**No Parking Here**'. A tinny voice rings out: "This is a non-smoking health facility. If you wish to smoke, please move along to one of the designated areas off-site. Thank you."
Off-site? "Where is it?"
The black box ignores me, same as everyone else.
"Where do I need to go?"
nowhere…
It beeps, getting louder, more shrill –hear the happy-slap man banging his stick– I stare upwards, we scan each another, moving on, another sign: '**Come in from the Cold.**'
Read: '**Do as you're Told.**'

Beyond the bleak margins of cracked **E ME R GE NC Y** tarmac there's a tundra to itself. People pay hefty charges, only senior staff park free but even that's a tragic mile off so no one really wins. Welcome –Little Siberia– out of sight, out of public eye, then bussed back in to confirm their latest cancer scare – one of too many cycles we slowly learn to accept.

That one looks back, some always have to check and check again.
Same slender neck, never one
and the same, a mutant stream of wax
where bodies shine solid, translucent and waning.
There's no clear way to divide
between one Swan's gentle steps
and the other's dagger-drawn cheeks.
Passing eyes strain to catch
a true splinter
from each
warped fascia,
finding
nothing
real in the mix.

A Burndt-Out Ward

"Well, fucked if I understand it." The Dave gushes in that washed-out Brummie drawl. Somewhat forlorn he's a long way from home and the day is longer still. I'm stood over-tall, holding toilet roll tower double my height, desperately seeking files of missing years, the old ward has it all. Now he's talking more, can't leave no matter how far my hands glaze over, pink to blue then purpling as cross-winds rake across the knuckles.

"Matron said she wanted a new centrepiece to help replace the old ward."
Lest we remember *or learn to forget*
"It had just burned down, you see," there's always a reminder, "great big old red-brick, it was. Most of it washed away once they got the hoses on it, blocked-up the drains and everything. So, she got us one of those heritage grants and they brought this," he thumbs over shoulder, "up here, this bloody pier monstrosity, they set it right on top of the old ward."

It stands sheer, a bright sacrifice without flame, again and again to echo our defeats. "The old ward, of course, got laid out on the foundations of the old, old ward. Grant money wasn't enough though, she soon ran out, as-per-bloody usual, which left nothing to finish sorting the rest of it."

There's wood laid on brick, where the semi-new and breezeblock edges intersect. How can it even balance like that; a lead cloud flag-raising twisted iron fist? Misshapen and bent, added-to, with other pieces, 'of mixed authenticity' their driftwood histories bound together in static collision.

"Besides, how do we know it's actually the actual Brighton pier?" Million and one vacant pieces floating around in that same old sea. "They're always tearing down them Victorian terraces just to make way for more bloody rabbit hutch estates, and you can get those cornice pieces from any old place."

"But it's from Brighton."

"Yeah, but that's just one side of it. It weren't all made in Brighton was it? It's like the Crystal Palace, they built it as one-off, a Grand Exhibition it was supposed to be, and then they moved it, before it all burnt down for good, then a grand old bonfire. It's like a body – is it a piece, or just pieces of something?"

Return to sand, glass broken down to make new beaches as the tides strip each new surface, pieces dragged back from a shrinking universe. "It doesn't make sense for it to be here, mind you, it doesn't make sense anywhere." We both look on. "Anyway, the reason I've come is to give you a quick warning." About what? "See them in management," points to the hated ones, entombed in mythic upstairs, "they've said we're not to be going in here, anymore."

He nods to the torched ward; two gaunt chambers stripped to buckled metal and blistered paint, last gasps forever waiting to collapse.

"Unless, you need more stores."

"Then we can go in?"

"Yeah. Well, not quite." See white knuckle wagging naked in the cold.

"I'm not to let you go in those double-doors, they've got to be kept locked. Now, you can leave through this door," chipolata flicks at EXIT sign with running man dripped into limp defeat, the locking bolt fused at the hip.

"You just push the bar and-"

"Wait – I thought it doesn't open?"

"What? Oh, it didn't used to, but we undone it," another haggard distraction, "so it should do, now. We had to fix it after…" hand-rolling yarn, "all that other business happened." Lips drawn back over moregumthenteeth, shuffling rubs up back of the neck, "*But*, it's fine now. Just a bit stiff sometimes, air pressure and that.

It'll be here when you need it."
"But the ward's already burnt out."
"Well, it does need a lick of paint, I'll give you that."

He talks on again, his mouth up and down like a billowing puffed whale, gorged on its verbal overkill. To break, I point at some other doors: "Why can't we go through that way?"
"You can't go in there." He stops me with categorical shakes of his loosening head, a great, furry full-STOP.
"Why not?"
"The management went in, they looked about, and they looked at me and said: 'Dave,' I *knew* it, "this ceiling is not safe." Catches breath, his fist full of thumbs grabs down a rollie from iron wool heights. "Because," lit to one side, "I know; I shouldn't really." Half-shrugs, "It's not safe because the only thing holding it up is a load of ladders." He blows on it, burns brighter. "They brought them in, looked 'em up, to assess it like, you know," I don't, "whether it was safe to use. And so they decided, *in their infinite wisdom*, because there were already a few ladders about, half-ladders, mind, that the ceiling must def-i-nitely be faulty." Picks tobacco off his lick, then flecks it in my direction, "Oh, sorry mate." Leans in to swat out his mistake.
"Just...leave it." He stops short. I pick away at it, typical stain, won't shift.

"Thing is, they don't quite reach the ceiling, the ladders, to the super-structure, so it could go at any moment, as they say, but all the ladders in the world won't make no difference." He blows out long funnel, a happy factory, contented.
 "But there aren't any ladders in there now."
"Yeah, we needed them for another job. But, it's all about the principle, for them. More ladders, more chaos, I say.

"Need to watch, mind."
"For what ?"
"Foundations gone too. All those top-heavy sets are starting to show their cracks. Got too big didn't they, now it's all just waiting

to fall apart." Hands thrown apart as a lone ember pirouettes up toward his head, settling into wiry spiral but doesn't catch – no burning dead wood – he frowns into deep-thought, "I don't know – it's the politics of the asylum, isn't it."

Flicks his butt to the meeting place between our feet, "Patient hung himself, once." Treads it out, then leans in, desperate with secrets to spill: "It was a lad, about your age." Supposed to be a shock but it's predictable enough. He nods slow and determined, lip curled till blood runs out, desperate not to say that dirty 'S' word. Like me, he must keep all them in mind, real close, a mirror to the missing.

"I remember, he was wearing hospital clothes, must've wandered off the ward like. It started it in the kitchen, they still had matches for the gas, you see. It's a terrible thing, it's one thing to try and do yourself, but to take the whole place with you, it doesn't make sense. I remember when we found it there was still something written on the hand."
Scr-a-tch-at-itch, "Which hand?"
"No idea what it meant, just some letters, you know, like a code or anagrams."
"Which hand was it? You must know, you don't forget a thing like that."
"Ah, well now, you do. I've forgotten a lot recently, and over the past few years. All sort of bits that seem important, now I can't remember what they were. That's the thing about memory, you don't get to choose what stays and who goes."

Nightingale's Cry

First hit by that everlasting smile, in here a small miracle, some feral tear in the sun. More than blazing emptiness, it's that human glow so rarely glimpsed but no one likes to acknowledge, or let themselves admit that they saw it. Got to keep your guard up, keep on, or go insane. Follow me down to rest ears upon flat-toed steps of Lady Sioux breaking out the night-roll as fresh darkness rushes in.

Normally so eager to greet, but tonight her regular shine's dulled by the steady drive of impatient demands, every day running up against that same wall. A sea of voices blurred in needy tones, creeping up and suckling time. Ripped to the bone, leaves flown, she's bare as Eve, this work has stretched her increasingly thin.

But this time it's something else. She moves flatter than usual. Pass me by but no words come, should I follow? From last slow seconds I trace the losing edges of her body flow, leaving narrowed points in the wake; starting to show her bones as dull light cracks breaks from the joints.

At first, it was just your standard retreats we are all forced to make. But turning to follow, see her body slow, heavy with grace and mounting pressures. More she tries to help, darker those lines sink and the big-red's hungry divides sorts the good from the sick.

Always she was the one; humming, running, desperate to be there when it counted most, to get things done (there's *always* one). Now sad sounds trickle along with lily-soft padding, lost in the field of stony faces. Somewhere crumblebrick snaps, playing off brittle-thin glass. Emptiness calls out her every echo, but there's resolution in each beat, shuddering like precision blades as they slip, miss their target and ring out through the metallic table. A half-moon of breath, like I am the only one to see the real sounds fading out.

The clocks have stopped ticking as she learns to let go and so time's dictated by an imagined cog. Mired in forced overtime, the flow of free cells slows like clipped wings trying to dance, clotted towards a ready paralysis. Another minute's notch is less oxygen to the blood, all with heightened risk. So many lacking nous, running into locked doors and bricked-up ends. All little red bodies, pieces of life thwart themselves; and so actual time of death, as death of mind, often lapses, alone and unrecorded.

She swallows souls outside of time; burning with infinite desire to assist, to make it easier on them. Determined not to be like the sad heffers, gorged on routine, she takes the time to drive instant eclipse via a gentle touch, to make the simple light and quick. Now wincing out her shortening days to bitter, living end, she starts to count them down. Struggling back from ten, it must prickle at her as wound-wrought density of a cast stretch, the whole longing to be scratched proper instead of gnawed around the edge.

Her secret's a swelling weight (she's so heavy), no time for self-regard, all recourse to shame's a narrow luxury. Sioux is now a dead space without heroes or happy endings, she spreads peace but drags behind her own soul, merciless and abject.

She's already been noted as a cause for concern. Her actions, so out of tact, worry at their tit-tattered edges of reason and appropriate behaviours. To Sioux no rhyme is self-evident but for now, to disagree is not yet grounds for treason. That driven solitude forces her to recoil from the common touch and vulgar aftertaste of everyday speech. Moving indivisible, Sioux keeps her own time, suspended in bodily acts and managed routines that help to stutter away the day.

It begins at growth's end. Without regeneration there is only erosion, as life becomes a landslide we feel it more, rattling around, shrinking into our finite space. Seeing the convalescent now damaged beyond repair, against patient needs, Sioux's wants fade when compared. Screwed down into her lonely self, to harbour pain, impervious to love – it's in the blood.

So the weak must surrender to invisible hands, always those shadowy assistants glide and gloat: altering posture, correcting blood counts, bumping-up numbers to balance the numbness of saccharin. Pain relief is administered as the outsiders see fit but there's only so much false joy to go around. When all is blurred, left unsaid or sneakily done, it's harder to know where line's been drawn, let alone crossed. These divisions go translucent as a skin stretched, and with it, her memory and decisions go hazy, lapse into static.

Was it the right one today? Was he supposed to be three mil, or ten? Has quiet afternoon slipped to a world of grey? Then it's morning again: all shaking pillows, squeezing fluid bags to expel the tired air; all for life, and so, for reasons unknown. Too often care is eking out slow-beat tides, less than making them comfortable – a veiled shift is all it takes for the good hands to twist the knife.

Something's changed to make her go on this way; so thin in spirit as to slip between scenes, breaking all the acts. Sioux is first refusal, rarely acted upon. Not to swallow dogma on sight, because it's all been said and done before, her impolite notion, unlearning the code she was sworn to keep; most rules are never practised like they're said.

Her nights are getting longer, so she delivers shortened, clipped answers, spat-out, as boxes ticked. That face never slips but contorted to a grim pout, it waits to be shot from both sides. There's a story to tell behind every set of tired, retreating eyes, but the hollow shine barely recalls its former flame.

We all know something's up: her uniform's gone baggy and her visits are sinking shorter as the rota spirals out into 'unreasonable hours'. A lapsed Hippocratic caught in her skeletal mode, there's brushed bone murmuring and it's hard not to stare, but harder still to hide under everyone's glare. Too much making-up sours the pretence, we need these soft lies to go on believing. Now sagged into her vulnerable skin the lines on show deepen, it tells us the shadows are out in force.

Sioux needs rest, to mend and cheer those quiet fires: the cup of tea as elixir vitae, to drown out the deep hurt that strangles her voice. Now words seep in from new spaces, floated on rough-hewn reputations and fractured dalliance, they come forth to blame and vilify. A single piercing sound, their tinnitus dread rises eagerly to ruin her. There are always rumours, inklings that become facts; it passes from lips to ears, and on to the next one, tagging staff cubicle doors: 'Something must be done with her.' The one who shouts loudest is always in the right.

Sioux steps around a sliver of light from the invading outside. Avoid, because looking into it destroys corridor vision, the dark clarity cultivated by our anaemic eyes. Got to get with this, in other adaptation we see things differently, but more clearly?

Track those sunken shoulders through the narrow straights, cluttered-up by chromey wheels that jut to trip and break our every step, veering-on from crashed-out beds. Hands creep, a slithing tug hungers over tendons, needling the hem and upper sleeves their eyes wander serpentine in my hair, the same worn-out shade. Noise clings with desperate urgency of weeds, trying to drag me down to their flat-out level, the gravity of death. Cough, earthy taste invades, palm-off the mop to nearest empty grab. It's limp so press firm till knuckles crack. Never turning back to see the fleeting eyes because there's no time to help them, but who cares for the carers left behind?

Gone again, she's still quick even with that leaden gait, waded through too many tides of shit-eating waters, demanding so much expiation. Trying to forget the unending folly of recycled air, gathering-up the bodies and that frailty of the gentle victim led softly up stairs, then down again, another futile exercise in breaking glass to prove it.

Having ignored her true course left to race and run, there's no more words, she's too far gone. Let her be, one arm holding the other, rough as crumpled sheet no longer clean, last leaves left flickering. For now she duck-weaves against the admin bayonets that rush on sunrise, her haggard nerves lashed wide as barbed eyes glisten brighter to catch you out.

So we go down deeper together, others crossing to avoid the tainted scent. The walls and doors are sucked-in to narrow point of failing light. They buzz-shudder making blunt stabs at naive symmetries of gloom. Two steps gone, this is the beginning of an end, feel that stab of premonition but shoulders still high in perfect square; got to be strong for the other, with feelings set aside to escape our drowning pace.

I float alone, kick heels against a stain. She's definitely not coming back around, they'll soon see to that. Hover round fire doors, chained shut. Boot the footplate, it shudders and rustles. Why's it locked? Kick again to sweat-out anger, nothing more to say in her defence. If there is a new fire we'll all burn, trapped inside by smallest plastic teeth with a yellow flag attached. There's a date, seven days from now. Why record it locked before the date?

'Caution: Do not break seal'

It's the wrong year as well, maybe just an old tag, maybe no one ever uses this door? Doesn't matter anymore, she's gone. With so much written-off as coincidence; scared of what comes next.

Sherbet Section

The only glow their bedded eyes, colour-stripped, another pale fire set to sleep. No mewings echo from their neighbours, clammed-shut, a cavity of linear cells. Clock snaps to the appointed hour, some look up, but it's only cold comfort, calling late: 'She won't come tonight,' the tired ranks already decide. Sunk in thought, the faceless spheres suppress desires against the mattress, to idle dream of naked patricide; wanting –any way now– to be released.

At six, an hour before the next day shift, the young ones slide up. A soft padding, barely audible with the heels removed but that straight semaphore's clear – the students are in charge. All spheres glow, awake in their beds for an eager glimpse of flesh and soft allure of a crooked smile – anything to remind them of being human and alive.

Each one gazes flat from row of yearning stares, another potential Apollo waiting desperate to be used. Lips push forward to meet lips, a hint of insolence veering to a sneer but they maintain form, neat and delicate, drawn-out feminine, all with vain promise of a superman. Their soft fronds ivy-hung, slashed and parted in waves tapering out to keen spikes, a stab at modernity, though no gels are allowed. At the temple-head they verge on grimace, holding back that burning frown of youth, some smouldering attempt at firming-up truth. Snaking veins pulse under marble tissue as occasional blues shine their mark of intent.

Trade cigarettes for a shave, morphine samplers for quickening touches (sensuality implied, only). The young ones indulge themselves, slipped gears of submission turning body to cheap tricks – the patient must always come first. Up on their elbows leering lucky at the mere hint of promise. Sweet natures crushed under that sickly feeling, their rich body odours soon mingle to a sense of trapped death.

Fresh meat of inner thigh tingles under worn hands, tired from scrubbing dead cells down cracked sinks and the constant peeling and pulling of gloves; the unfeeling compounded by absent contact. Their grip quickens at the thought and those gushes come eagerly – she goes pink in the cheeks when pretending not to care, or enjoy, basking in the reversal of service; pleasure happens when, and only when, she says. But always coo-cooing, too much like disappointment when it finally comes, keeps them keener for longer, to go again. Meanwhile each party quietly decides they are in charge. As long as we get what we want, never mind who's playing who.

She remembers how it felt to impress pleasure on someone else, sharing sharp glances caught mid-exchange. A quick-cruel pinch of vital flesh rushing pink under the squeeze, he smiles, winces, somewhere in-between. She eases him down, plotting pressure points as fingers stroll, body maps lifted straight from matte-dull texts of blurred anatomy, finally found a way to use it.

Walks over finest muscle to make it quiver at salient points, the pressure of her pawing-out hard/soft tapered lines – now relax. With sudden flexes eyes flicker soft to the back of the skull, more coo-cooing whispers bristle the back of the neck, tell him everything will be alright, next time.

She stands detached, watching him hover there: those seconds of waiting just before, just one one-more, so close to dying. Too much, too young, they were born to lose. She throws him contraband wipes, aloe-enriched for those sensitive types. Wretched and ecstatic he simply sweats it off, while nurses claim their winnings from the underhand race.

Some linger just about lights out, the articulated division built ready-for-use –insert here– to any given situation, just like me. Pencil shadows spindle over the near-corpses, flit tapered fingers along the angular frame, an ugly scuff of a scuttled hull. Tease-out bed-head strands, lean in, close to touching but it's just a word, softly placed, some dirty unseemly gesture enough to trigger Kafka's blush. Only takes a little intensity to force the stoic-break, further but not *too* far. She raises final smile as the big-reds thump frozen: to me you are only a work of parts, held precious in the palm.

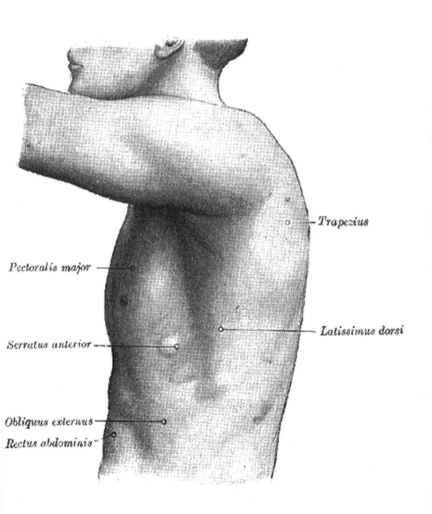

Pier's End Revisited

One body to another, both shiver, heady with expectation. They promised us new morality, our health preserved, now it lies before us, ageing daylight. Recreated to lighten the public load, this stale architecture's trapped, like frozen music, it spans whole Roman arches bent heavenwise out of tune, their instructions grown diffuse. See that same glimmer from the city of glass, now a fractured star, our imperfections shine together.

We share a life of constant friction, never settling, locked-in, permanent discord, I twist, another limb reacts, and from its place a brick is edged-out. In testament to angry possession some entrances stick, these carpet grips are coarse metal, slip and it's gushing blood, enough to prove we're still real, weighing the pressure of future death.

The fire was quenched, again. Swallowed into sea and streaked by fading tides gravitating back to the familiar shore. She bought-up the precious remnants, delivering the shell to us, gifted a new afterlife. The resurrection of the hollow dome soon grew swollen, brick by mismatched brick. In place of saviour past it's become a living wreck. Never the same edifice they remembered, an inglorious relic preserved in salt and foetid air still reeks of slow death – some things are better left behind.

Now every orifice is bricked-up, "mothballed" they call it, locked-in and set aside for later use, there condemned to private winter. It stands a reminder of Hastings, Brighton and all the places where the frail shapes go to fade and forget.

Overripe frustrations announce themselves in the peeling walls. Harder to tell what fits together or makes sense; stirring spat-in soup as seconds float up from the bottom in a burndt-out haze. Cruel spires rise, mired with brute siren calls of machines beeping and patients crying harm, a single unholy howl. Self-pity dominates and suffering's become a white noise of constant afterthought. The helpless ones catch whirring grind of staff pressure as two waves fight to overpower, one day to meet in the centre and become a single sound that will crush and cave in on itself.

It calls again, some innate and ancient cry: a promise bounced wildly on the surface, vibrating walls, mutters of a lonely return. Like that famous house of glass, all our former greatness is spent zig-zagging agony, stubbed-out by heavy sky, it lies diminished in thinning iron. An overspent form that has lived-out its use; in place of transparency, we are sold to tell brittle truths and narrow illusion – what kind of architect can exist where there is no room for doubt?

Wander through giant A-frame, late cathedral shell of cracked Victoriana, steeped in unholy mess. Scratch   sevens itch, recurring; where does it lead but marching? First to hit is the heat. Lean out, press on wall, open pustule leaves fingers finely sticky; wrong paint – rejected itself, as tepid colours drip against the eye, cheap plastics glimmer artificial smiles. Rising surfaces bubbled-up in eager revulsion, leaves fresh flakes of tired skin on the floor. Virulent self-hate, a reminder of Speer's flawed designs, this place was made to be old, another so-called 'classic' geared towards decay; to become ruin and never regenerate.

Step out again: birds loop and caw, wings whispering dark ivy thoughts above. Heart swinging, as if on string, kicking-through triangular peaks in the skeletal dome. Black holes punched in the sky, as girders loom; an iron butterfly cutting blue swathes on a great glass wing, guillotine air has licked sharp every over-hanging edge.

Like a coastal reach, creation deserted, stretched too far becoming, there's the salty hangover of faded glamour and minor hopes invested in the ordinary boys, our tongues now tinged with rust –**Dead Children Crossing Here**– we are all badly in need of a catcher to watch the day play out its enemies. Easy lessons won't come clean as bitter ironies teach us trying. But the kids sucked-in with bliss soon gorge too deep. Seasons turn the ghost town surrender to senseless endings, trapped out-of-hours – life kills as boredom shortens expectations. When all our honey's spent, burndt rubbers spit and crushed fists of empty fizz repopulate the shallows' brace, loose wheels tear-off promenade strips; all doing what they can to feel like here is somewhere else. But this betraying edge is ours, at least, not just another try-hard wasteland swept under distant balconies that don't see.

There's more slamming from invisible hinges, she makes a sound like drum-beating, trying to shut the heavy fire door, but there's no helping her, it's a gutted lock pawing at lazy frame. Inland wheezes, licking-out every last dent, brings its cold tune to life. The surrounding trees shed every odd leaf in its bluster, back and forth, a saw-gutting niche of strangled passageways, more final breaths squeezed from the writhing corpse made to soldier-on (ostensibly) by royal appointment. I walk through, a heaving monument to metaphor; from thinning border walls to the ward and its vacant heart. Better watch your step, we all look, but few of us see.

Sweetness and Light

Come and see pieces of people laid out on tray tables or closed-off in serial lockers; some neat, others wear their disarray – a working museum to all they've lived and been. Browse through sleeping pictures; trapped in sepia print-outs, family-shot and out of focus. Gifts appear, one day to the next, as measure of care, while some still give evenings but not weekends. You told us 'humility is endless'; it's not without its price.

All in the details, hard to ignore them as you work around repetition to drive it home. Watch Agnes Reid with her riddle-spun ribbons, picked up and put down again, humming through her oblique arrangements. Try to follow these designs, working-back on themselves into wilting collection of ever-precious loops. Move the surface to bleach, she protests every time as I sweep away the perfect place. Spit on the cabinet, just to aggravate (gives smoother action). She pretends not to see but keeps one eye cocked in case I steal. But she has nothing I want, just a frozen aspect – sheer as butterflies, pinned into still-life.

See more white bodies come and go, both sides are collectors, it's only the subject that changes. They chart daily life beyond static: making notes on notes of minor details to use against them as supporting evidence, demonstrating failure to act. They must justify some treatments and edit other results to avoid happenstance trials and more malpractice paperwork.

Harvesting samples of body substance, blood pressure, white cell count and stool consistency (to mark the internal rot). Most deteriorating conditions, eat away and play with time: 'hours slept' the only way to keep it sane; food eaten/refused/vomited back up. Make a mark on the coma scale, eyes open? Do they flicker *spontaneous,* burst open at speech, or bulge with pain when I do **this**? Flexion or extension by mere indices, any way the limb goes. Terminal poses perfect ideal wound profiles to elicit maximum sympathy and all pressure points are tested to the limit – they can't push you any further.

Look for verbal response, babbling speech patterns or words deemed 'inappropriate'. Note the number of slurs, look for dirt down the throat, swellings or obstructions, is that the tongue lolling back? Two, three fingers as far as *far* can go, stand back for feather-touch vomiting. Do they still obey commands when forced, not quite three-sixty – wait – stop screaming, did you hear that snapping sound? Pupils engorge a bellyful of Saturn, contracted to black pin pricks, sunk holes dive until the bell, that cotton sea softens an otherworldly sky.

Right side/left side, struck numb at the opposite, all split down the middle.

Bad brain; good body / good brain; bad body

Lazy eye washes a numb limb; dead left root. Slur-wrought smile crossover thoughts where synapses clash.

Define method of treatment: promote granulation of the wound, let it crystallise, then extract daily scores of sulphurous yellow clusters. If left to harden, sores mount up like bumped lizard horns, ripping through clothes and sheets as the blankets fight with sleep. Wreathed in the futile glow of SAD landing lights to guide them home, dry out the hide till it cracks and we retrieve what's left of the human inside.

Neighbouring pressure ulcers discharged safely if squeezed away from the face. Pus mingles red, pits the walls and floors, keep going to blood surface until the liquid runs clear. Apply aqueous creams, paint dead flesh the colour of new baby-skin, wrap bandage over dressing, *tight*, but loose enough to maintain flow – no more phantom limbs. Tied-off ends soon pile up and no one knows which is whose or what, feet trip over feet.

Magic trees sprouting in every ward crevice: patients dream deep of spiced forest glades swept by fresh ocean tides and that new-car smell of cracking seats, wearing lavender-hemp suits to get on better at work, meet a passion fruit woman to hang neatly on my arm, her earring drips spare sea salt, so we trip punch-drunk along black ice streets. Lie her down in cactus milk fields that soothe through a sting, her aloe-heavy lips lick a strawberry fizz, till fresh rain peels back the tarmac, streaming alkali mingled with lemon airbursts as these toxic bodies lie deep in dreaming; innovation ranges, available to purchase on waking. I know this shallow miasma's not real, but saccharin's slur climbs a vine beyond all senses.

Back to bleach with eyes wide open – some new strain I can't place. Dare not sleep too much as their dreams infect mine, and even then, there's no release. Started to detail sexual yearnings, noting how and where patients are particularly touched or hold eye contact longer than twenty-seven seconds; optimum period of split attention. Stricter proposals are being introduced to ban all discourse of *that* nature, verbal or not. Outcry from the nursing staff who depend on mute innuendo to punctuate the day. Where would they be without coital barbs to cast at inferior males, the league of officious spinsters echoing hollow fantasies woven around mythical alpha-docs that don't exist (while circumventing the strangeness of Swans). Faded in looks, but well-paid at month's end, most cutters already weaselling out from their latest last marriage, neatly-timed alongside the most recent infidelity through a run of closeted examinations and weekly (degradation) sessions in secluded conference rooms, shutters drawn for shadowplay, with concertinaed obtusions pressed against slowing blush to the flesh.

Doc's doing rounds as a long-stride, make them wait, alongside hyper-eager students (by invitation-only). There's always lines, a crowding queue to see the patient perform without inducement of ether. Stretched-out on lumpy beds to gawp at gawpers' heck, like a straggled lion or hunger artist, only too willing to behave, to be noticed and treated pet-nice.

Party drops in and out of OxMed between stating the obvious: "So is she, like, going to die?" Revelling glory in Narcissus-obscura: "Renali lancenoade miscarp trenae emptorate fentu bexecrotein?"

"No, wait. Never address them directly. Always use an intermediary, like a nurse. Let them deal with the patient, you can deal with the medicine; that's how these relationships work best; buffering keeps things clear, and everyone knows their place." In this private language only the smart ones are allowed to speak, the rest must listen and not understand. Patient lies dumb-stiff, nothing valid to add and no one thinks to ask. Doc shuffles though pockets, "Has anyone seen my notebook? It has all of my draft lectures in it." They look everywhere but his eyes.

He flicks about, sees me staring – I don't have it. Tiredness, rolled-over from the drag of attending one to the next, hears others' voices as spare noise, crying pain as the repetition drains novelty – but why me? Moving around, all eyes watch eyes, picks up pace but he can't leave the group. Maybe that's Boxer? No badge, no idea.

Is this really his coat? Was it the other guy's? Or it is whoever wears it? Come to think of it, all of them walked off doubled-up, bunched-over rolled bellies: 'everyone's a thief', with the potential at least. To be a sinner is to be something, if not another Boxer.

Check pockets for an absent badge, whatever happened to that? Must've put it down, gone, Boxer is...someone else, just like the latest one. What's in a name anyway (like Nay-fth-un)? Pick it up, put it down, our detritus carries us with it, tagged dust for exposure. Strange how you wear a fluorescent vest or ride the long, white swan jacket and people automatically assume you're something, more or less – uniforms go both ways. People are hinged on strangeness, naturally disposed to empathy but they rarely see deeper than your white-out apparel – all is surface, a thin vanity, swept away in minor glances.

Must be a difficult 'sweet-life' for the docs, expecting, and expected, to keep up this noble charade. Kept awake with night-time call outs, another minor sprain/hangover/plaster on the knee, a wrapping and shedding of wasted gloves and lost sleep. Mysteries of life exhausted in cool, naked blue light that indulges the urban symmetry, tensing just after sirens set every red alight, slowly convinced his wife is too busy just to be working overtime.

Due another coronary by now: from the junk-slurred diet, in-between mealtimes and nodding-off to punctuate the day – then sugar rush! CAFFEINE! And too many glasses of too-good wine to wash away microwave pasta. These legitimate addicts rule the madhouse (we're all mad here, trained as idiots but only differing by degrees.) Rolling-on past forty, closer to quad-bypass, but just enough piggy parts and indirect donors to keep the senior machines beating and the big-red in charge.

It's always *quit pro quo* with the Docs: He asks She, who asks the patient, making a nod or a tap of the pen: "One for yes, two for no", and they respond within the necessary signals for today's problem. Tell them what they need to know, hear what they want; want what they hear. Study is the illusion of learning, thinking you know, not just joining in pain-by-numbers. Logical steps holding them up, soon absorb the methods, skip the routines, hit the bar and wash away tired minds that can't quite link thought with smeary eyes, all skewed to vanishing point. We learn by rote but we don't really know, trained autodidacts like Pavlov's bitch. They drag up chapter headings, page numbers and dictionary definitions from the party-hard fug, become expert in doing what they're told. In the mundane day-to-day, answers float through on demand, by his master's voice, desperately seeking approval, not realising they wear themselves away at hollow rocks. Process complete, the Doc makes a swift quarter-turn, best foot stamps with bang of a gavel and away – Endgame.

Closing Time

Resigned (but not yet redundant) this is the place of the 'temporarily indisposed'. He's used for death and sold for glue, now too tired to push and pull; Jada won't wash, won't shave – if you can't conform you have to leave. Just another face in the scene with the other drowning ones hung out to dry, now faded and greying. Some relapse, some never arrive, but most just keep coming back, eating-away at relentless edge of shore. They drink too eagerly, like drowning, keep sip-sipping towards death.

Muttering under stale breath, they ask about the last party. Love to swap drinking stories, or drink with stories appended, to remember being free, when it was new and the taste was real enough. Now all their evenings end alone, once the bar calls time and the doors are firmly closed you have to go home.

Some seen drinking from the hand wash, not much alcohol in it, but enough to kill germs and remaining brain cells. Bunched up around the sink they go suckling at what makes them sick. Eyes caught cattle-wide –someone's coming–mixing-in salivas as they nourish illusion, then scatter, giving pace to the trick. Reverting to school-kid schtick they love to misbehave for its own sake, much easier than waking up to life.

On the surface it's all gaggling gallery, smiling wild with matey kisses and laughing over one another. Then she enters to pull the plug; they scatter under covers licking red, worn lips to savour last traces but the thirst's never quenched. Nurse takes the spent gel pack away from harm, glaring out at the soft-snoring fake reachers, she knows that sickness too well, you can smell it on the breath.

Next day, Jada, another arch-complainer, formerly Jimmy, formerly James, waddles trailing bow-legs like a fishtail, resting on his floating wrists via Zimmer (acquired). No good with names, not much good with anything, he struggles to pin me down. Reeling off ticker-tape of slurred sounds, fixes on "N" but never getting all the way to the end. Pouted lips swirl, whooshing and blister-pecked, in a vacuum of dulled reach he projects lexicon chaos:

"Nnniigeniiiikkeknooormaanaathththtthhhhhnnneeeeeeeil?"

His tongue rolls pure loquacious, a lolling, blunt instrument –too many thumbs around fine letters to hit the syllables on time and tongue keep step. Barely in sync with himself, he's out from our world, a non-functioning member of a narrow society, feel every pothole in the dunk-thunk, vwls mssng-shred of his scattered dialect.

"It's Nathan."

"Yeh Naythun, tht's it!" He gives half grin with too few teeth set in lips that permanently shake. His quickened throat rages, something vile comes up and into the hand. Red at the gills, he drools through his loose grasp, wiping the slur on the corner of nearby bedsheet. He pick-picks nervously at fingernails, yellow cuticles receding, there's nothing left to rebuild, no futures to regenerate.

See Jada resting on the frame, bouncing softly, still buoyed on secret springs, tired but they won't let him go to bed so early in the day. We spin our time away mis-explaining things: "I am 'n alcoholic, yeh. I jst want to ddrink," cuts air with twitching hand, "I wnt people to jst leave me alun–to drnk. But doctorss telt me that 'ff I do then I'll die real qwik. Iuv only got three quartrs of my liverr left, thsz not enuff, he says. So when I gou, Im jst gonna drnk mself to deth. But Im def nt stayin ear anymre, itsz lik a prson. I bin thre nd evn prsnsz lss lk prsn thn ere, man."

Only see the light lapse in shades, the world polarised to mere horizon slit. He's living through trapped apertures, now shirking life, dreaming the daytime extinct. Jada stumbles-on to solemn forty-two: nothing left now, to say, to do.

Kicks his beat heels waiting for full bodily surrender, clanging imagined chain against the world order what he feels 'done him wrong'. His benefits seem to have been misplaced, passed-on, direct to some third party, his distant half-daughter's pulled the rug from under a falling man. He knows true sleep waits, lived through it too many times before, that mouth always lurches to one side, then rips open to a permanent yawn.

Embracing his right to damage, he slinks around deviousness, wanting to slip off in his own way. Sitting limp-kneed under constant observation, his drizzled eyes rattle like rain on zinc, it gives tremors as he wobbles, more steps in shuffling stupor, heavily chockced on Solpadeine that stops him thinking (feeling) too much, stark reminders etched on the window panes. Fix-him-up good enough to leave, then let him carry on until he finds his own lonesome way, sitting in a crooked house with no furniture and the front door left ajar.

Today's a good day, making him into pretty little pet. Dress him up, but don't think what it means to give and then take away. In borrowed clothes, the trappings of second-hand virtue, he's pinned fast by other's lazeful grace shed from their husbands' losing hem.

They crowd round admiration: clean-shaven and allowed out for the occasional cigarette, Jada appears mild and meek, still childlike with sneers – he'd cut-out and run a mile if he could, unassisted. He shuffles about, she circles in her gilded duty, Queen for a day, but he's playing at pawn just to satisfy them. Let the nurses enjoy something good for a change, to say: 'we made that,' such fun to try and rehabilitate a wrecked cause into 'a real person', just like them. But Jada's not able to be satisfied, he lives only for desire and the cycling-on of pleasurable dregs; so he goes, into shallow sobriety.

Each chooses his own choice: to be drunk, to forget…and something else…then, to go on forgetting. No one knows the reasons or where he's been; I've never seen what's in his file to make him act-out against himself, spurred on towards slow death. In half-stance he's a magnetic Sebastian for society's tut-tuts, they shoot-off so easy but always maintain distance, such little things swell in selfishness.

Jada's hung majestic from a nail, down to his diminishing tail, happy is a warming smile but it never lasts, little victories fade. Think I see him there in the dark, grinning toothy, just like John Smith, dying quietly in a countryside lay-by, out from all harm's way but himself. Closing time again, no more stories to be hissed between juddering teeth. Restless hearts are closed-off, and Jada crows a deeper grave for himself. Tired of hoping, tired of trying, trapped as fly at wrong end of the bottle, he'll die....

..trying

...to   his.......

...find   out

own

way

We Transit Souls

These are the Daves, all with different last names, every one equally charged to spirit away passing remains. The dead should never ride alone and with a bagged-up passenger, balanced shotgun, there's no need to read too many signs or time to stop for speeding cameras. They shuttle back and forth in angular, clanging boxes (a Private Ambulance, the height of exclusive transition) a seamless blur, always the same places, in practice of inertia, never getting anywhere. This repetition makes them good as static, undercut by natural laws.

They take live ones, black rubbish bags and neon orange sacks (watching out for code brown) with stainless stationery rattling deep-red, dried-shut, to be rinsed and dipped again. *THUNK* the sliding door makes hollow smash like cheap tin, scrollers whine along, anticipating the hit.

Fleet of knock-off vans, mass-imported, so it's cheaper just to let them rust; all spores rising like slick thigh ulcers on sheer metallic skin. Perfect excuse for the ideal Mundano driver, they're happy being sad, dwindling into humdrum-retirement of zero motion, stepping neatly from design into life.

Something simian in the Daves with their clipped mouth and crept-in hunch, slowly slacking into paunch. Shirt's not so deftly tucked but best buttons still hold, both sets of eyelets strain to catch each other out. As the body lurches into leans, I cringe with the premonition of mass ricochet, zinging blood in the ears.

But they're good value all-round. Cheap vans and cheaper uniforms; providing handy staff trips (but don't forget to pay and leave a cigarette or a tip). The Daves are easily-managed; budget restricts them to base. Let them have their ciggies, bacon sarnies, dusty Dylan re-issues and other sold-out ideals. Like the wheels running down on narrowed memories of revolution, it goes on, that same-old, same-old just comes back around.

They love to covet old war films, free with the cheap sheets (more over-the-counter culture), to become plastic coasters or bird-scarers, disposable product you can only give away. Like the broken dam's shimmying victory, a cheap affect floods the heads and hearts, though we've seen it ten times or more. New breeds are easy born to spectate, blinded by the brightness, helps to forget about the minor wars in dusty, far-off places and 'conflicts' not our own.

All this keeps them happy, so Management think. Avoid those big problems that demand long, and expensive, answers. A diminished fleet cannot be considered great, balding treads, working all hours, late wages and less 'real' overtime (standard time), just focus on the dagger straits, slowly moving in. To quell restless fires M.M. addresses them as mock-aristocrat in her curl-pointed boots. As if measuring out opiate-expressions in petite doses, she spea k s , d r a w l s   o s lo w l   y, presuming idiot with no cause to reflect. The Daves remain obstinate: 'not in my contract, not in my name' (the classic "kick-me-out then" get-out clause). Together our conscience flops like a toned-down muscle, let it be our motto, stamped in flesh: 'keep doing and don't ask questions,' though we know that all our words are wrong. But who cares now we've got hi-definition. Our world's no clearer, but at least the pictures are getting brasher, faster and everyone gets somewhere, in the end.

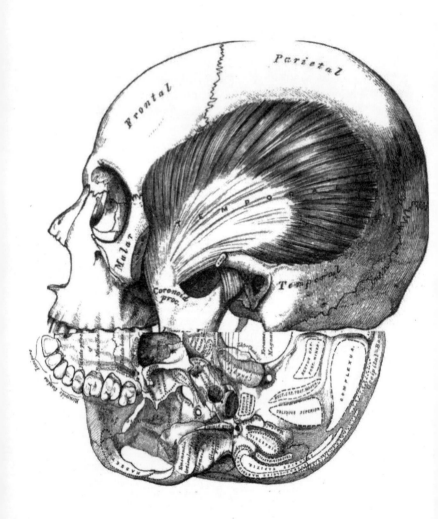

Mea Culpa

Hear that tingling, ding-dring, ringing out – a stiff bolt come unstuck. It runs spare across the scuttled floor, a reminder of that flicking tick-tink marking time on the syringe as they bring it to bear, a quick squirt signals the rush as massed bodies hurry to descend.

"Oh, it's you."

She sets down the spoon at the side of the mug, "Hello." Flat-voiced, not looking up, so happy/sad. She's got tired in her eyes and wearing all the marks of a senior telling-off

"Where have you been?"

"I took a little time-off." She looks up, then down again. Huffing all of her breaths into the chest, more words come, slow and softly spoken. "It was 'recommended' to me that I take a little time…to have a think and reflect on what I want to do next… consider my options."

"Oh."

She mmmm's, resigned to agreement. I nod away, but mind's lost in the gravity sink.

"I thought you'd already gone."

As if she doesn't hear me, "I've decided to leave. It was decided best; to avoid too much of the press. There was never any question of carrying on. They were quite bothered about more… incidents." A heavy word but there's still a glare that needles-out from behind the works. "You understand. I have to protect myself; we all have to try and save face, somehow." She looks around her, getting slower, as much familiar with her cage as saying goodbye to it.

"I can't believe you're just letting them push you out?" I check at the door, same as her.

"No, it's not like that. It was my decision, a decision I had to make, but still."

No choice at all – it keeps echoing in me. Even with nothing left to say, I try to fill the space: "You're making the tea?"
 I nod faint but steady to ensure reply.
Sighs, "*Yes*, Nathan."
"But you don't even like them," check at the door, "and you're leaving anyway." A liar like all the rest but it had to be this way. She's no smile, no words, no nothing.
"Will you make me one then?"
"No, not today."
"Why not?"
"I've already started. Please Nathan, I don't want any bother, now." She shuffles her hands inside the barren fridge.

"There should be some milk in the back somewhere." No answer.
"What have I done, do I smell?" Trying to raise a smile, hard enough in myself. All I see is that flat silver door staring back at me, sharing our blank face, behind it she goes-on ignoring me.
"What are you doing in there?"
Bites back, huffing grunts between teeth, "I'm just trying to get my yoghurt out from all this..."
"Let me try...you shouldn't even be–"
"No, Nathan, just leave me, I'm fine."
"Ok, I just don't see the point in messing up the whole thing for one little–"
"Right, done." She slams closed the conversation. Leaving me here, but what choice does she have: leave or stay here to sit through last few months in mute surrender?

"I've got to go." Springing off again, somehow more alive. Less so for the tea: burndt milk spots slide over, a grey and tepid skin upon skin.
"Why are you going now? Don't you even want to stay and talk for a bit?"
"No, I've got to finish up, my shift ends in half an hour."
"Then, why did you make all those teas?"
She turns: "I'm not your mother, Nathan. You need to stop

hanging-on to everyone else. If you stay here, being miserable, this place will kill you and the worst thing is you'd be the one letting it happen."

Flush in the face: "You'd know all about that, wouldn't you?" She's so thwarted and know-it-all, but still dead-woman walking. Don't think she even heard me, did I whisper just to myself?

There she goes, back to that most-hated hive where they all blend in to one great fizzing hate. She hands teas round the nurses' station, they grab-at, a bunch of no-thank-yous, grinning past her, I see the silent laughter wincing. A buzzer sounds, they ease back into unitary cattle sip, see them mouthing away, shaking their heads not to worry. Sioux steps off to become a further distant blip. I should call out, say *something*, but she's away again – the only one who seemed to know my name.

The Odour of Sanity

That brown water stinks, there's me all dog-breathed wandering. There's a **RUSH** – finally – well done! Goodnight Mr Beam, we hardly knew ourselves. Gassoping swallowed air, please to eat down his mouthful of hair, it's the first morning after the last and my hand runs cold stiffening in every lukewarm toilet. Steeped thick and rich, too many spare pages…vomitus erroneous, that odour of sanctity – how I have done myself wrong, and thee. No matter, eugckh – split in the glove. Gut's rutting jumble, this bowl mimics ivory surfaces but we all know the moon as hollow, taunting silver. The claszickshitshinemethod, one sheet-per-pull distribution, the old two up, one down – thoroughness trumps stinginess.

Glove's needs first, gloves *must* – other way out is to peel back that vinyl-layer and strip-out sensation with it. Every finger a struggle, needling into place, grip changes crawling through, bland textures numbed, blunts the scratch off my nails, pinches hairs out from skin pricks.

This drip smucxk hand-pull on every lip, lift lid, the naked lunch, never seen. They re-use, flush and leave – not keen to discover but have to look, to see it through. There's that undeniable crust smiling the rim, same germs as biting back on fingernails. Carrot lump, bulks on knuckle, flick it off into world of worry, got to push up and away from porcelain rink – only I will catch myselves, if he should fall.

Now to the sink – some release. Turn it untight. Water shot sprack all over, spitting me, plumbing bummed-out, underneath we're missing pieces of pipe, our circuits run incomplete – copper flipped for gold? Nevermind how, it's monotony against the soul. Wipe around shellfish edges, smear me powder blush to see past that wallowing face, now backed-up in phosphor, worn tough by bleach, each sprout drips, chrome handles threaten to glimmer out like sun and it's water, warmer; still life in a series of lonely points. There's that chalk-dry aftertaste, now I'm upsidedownandheadshrunk, willing it to go away as waiting on a dream, but how would I know? No pattern to determine, just forget until tomorrow (now rinse).

Scrawled on the walls, their serial reminders: proper use of soap and other hygiene advice. Dash the halls in legitimate graffiti: do This, wash That, trust Us (and remain ever-patient). Scream through this promenade of command as they shout you down (one more time!).

They lay it on thick the deeper you go, with slogans squeezed to fit, assaulting the mind in rhyming puns. Dark-backed posters loom stained-glass-cells as familiar signs, bacteria as hamburgers, rugby balls and musical notes, real cute and all in perfectly bad taste. It strikes no chord (use mixed humours against them) and I'm not neurotic or paranoid but why watch over me all the time, especially as they already know what I'm going to do?

Glut for **Yes**/**Dread** for **No**.
Seems simple enough.
Used for Green, they say: '**GO!**'
'Hurry on, get to it, *still* not finished yet?!'
Red light. Stop. Wait. Think (but only as some kind of afterthought). Consider *why* we rush you – must prevent infection to boost our ratings. At every step the watchers analyse and dissect, dressed-up as doctors, who dress as civilians, so everyone's a potential enemy, all of them desperate to turn-coat-on-me and go 'citizen-journo', to rip us a new-media orifice.

Rapidly they follow, flickering in/out, more silent exposures rise as reflux, sign:

Flu Heroes

Taking Care, Nationwide

Our future is in our hands

...and slipping through our fingers, not many safe days left to us. Don't worry or panic now; there's no need to resist – it's a positive virus. It's already in me and the good news is, you're next. Our whole performance glitters gold, but then you knew that already. As the sky is blue and swans are never black, we say: smile, die happy, you know everything now (or just enough to keep on deceiving yourself).

Every day, every week: a sudden new release. Heads-up, keep *quiet* on that virus strain, attend vaccine session, next week that's gone viral, so easy for minor infections to slip into brute enmity. Must attend secondary injection to correct the first, all double-standards, but no one keeps tabs on what's really going on. Dead-letter messages fall stillborn from internal-hack's printer slit. Beyond the bleed, it drips down cupboard sides, between desk gaps, around drawbacks. There's a stack of memos marked: '**URGENT**', soon flipped over to make illegible notes. All a perfect waste of time, basically printing on money; you blind advertise, make hospital corridors into a whispering wall to the blind, dumb and deaf.

A passing glance at the spewings of your finest wordsmiths, speechwriters, PR lions, kings consult the clowns, demanding thousands just to catch the eye for a few seconds. Even this message is infected, along with all the rest, into a rapidly dividing sense. If they said down was the new up, then you had to believe ceilings hung underneath, polystyrene tiles burnt and blistered, all crooked floors with gravity denied, and still they say 'jump!'

But no time to notice: man bleeding from head-wound shouts brash Fs and Cs next to junkie teen with vomit running alp-wise down the chin. Body splayed-out, becoming the floor, trying to flirt with forty-seven year-old crackhead slowly sinking into his knees. Muddy thinking on all fours he crawls into her, between the heaves a dirty smirk. Nurses and other others try to separate, it starts again. Pretty nurse smacked back, a crack in the face, other hands descend. She sits back, stunned from the help, with panda patches swearing blind. There's jagged flash across the nose as she rubs feverishly, an itch that won't leave, same hand rises to my face.

Now she's out of it: another subject, wreathed in that tepid plastic smell that clings to everything. Once inside you're slapped with déjà vu. Every dentist appointment, five-minute visit to a sidelined relation, sat in A&E to get fingers clicked back into place, a dull ache as you pick at spare lint, *swalled* up by the loud hum of great scanning circle, where everyone wears lead and never smiles. Tonsils out, smear to test, pull curtain over to let you sit and think, waiting for nothing in a paper gown, pulled down over the knees. A quick blood sample, some faint puncture, probably nothing to worry about, but we'll let you know in three-to-four weeks – if we don't call, you'll need to get in touch. Now flooding back all these watershed hurts you tried to shut away. Longer you stay it's easier to forget but the smell strikes as catalyst, pulls you back into that dead little world, another lonely cell in the system. Signal shot straight from nose-tongue-mouth, wound round into a heady U-bend.

When it hits the sensation streams as easy bile rising; it goes on, from you to me:

deathdecayhygieneinfectionreliefsweatbodycongestionbow-elemptinessnilbymouthstomachcrampsdrywhitecrusting-mouthedgespoonconcavefingernailscowtongueleatherdryturn-bodypressonabcesstoexplode.

Every turn of the nostril brings another blast of that stale-minted fug, a strange scent that speaks only to the blood. Mucus-brains break-out in quick saliva drips, no truth in denial, you can almost taste the atmosphere.

There's other swells in the hot air from infection bins, some reactions happening in orange-yellow glow. Rip-off plastic apron, polyethylene stretched to fantastical sheer skin as the colour pales out in streaks becoming holes. Let go all of those colours you used to know; yellow and green coughed-up in sheets, where you sleep leaves purple-blue bruises, whatever the reason it smacks of abuse. A gushing red split, white body cracked, twirl that ten-for-two shroud in anarchic wheel where it shimmers in flaming arcs, sparks cutting the air with electric whorl.

But still, I see through it all. Where for others the static captivates, its own dead-zone with hairs on end, that's the vacuum where all the power goes. Like pale Virginia, now interred under me, lost to water, another time-sink ratio, we fade to grey, a singular ebb and flow soon descending to permanent sleep. From that slammed lid waft curling edges, spires of heat – you can see the bad smells escape. No end to this detritus spill, the illusion of miasma, ripped in drifts, it infects and spreads, a stale trap exhumed.

From faecal matter, burnt toast (again) and formulated evergreen of the n-teenth toilet rinse, our mood descends as an iron cloud steps upon us. Touch and taste evaporate like blunted fingertips to another failed memory, lost in the peeling grain. There's no blocking out the steady crush of a thousand clinical actions mapped precise in the mind. To the outside it's just more comings and goings, all blending to a single rush. Nose-cut-numb, frostbitten by spite, you can try to ignore but you never forget.

Off my tongue all the wild smells go. Like it was fresh-cut, cells fading in/out, dead and alive at the same time. Stalwart "brother" Orwell smelt his way through the narrow exploitation: from slave kitchens and coal-dust alleyways to the mud fall bombs on dry Catalan streets. Never quite escaping the old definitions of Burmese sands and Etonian battlefields, a billiard-green for wargames breeding the next elite; ready for Sandy and onto freshly blooded spaces, the crusting grind of teeth on cement. Forever at war his whole (short) life, now George slumbers under new smells seeping in to the home turf. He cannot be at peace with everyone saying 'everything is so like 1984' while ascending wars-by-numbers still err on the cruel side of your nature.

Patients share delusions, easier to hide under layers than be seen. Setting themselves heavy application of saintly-scented products, designed to smell distinct: to be individualised by the same brands that sell to everyone, and simply get passed around. But even for the regulars, every substance applied is quickly swallowed-up, absorbed in the harshness of skin-peeling bleaches. Still reaching for scents beyond ego, a self-love equally shared but so painfully divided.

We're all mixed up. The waning hormones beat a steady impulse to entice the generally confused and trick, mantis-like, the needy rube. They breathe only fake oestrogen and nicotine, forsaking pale earthly airs – oxygen's such a bore nowadays. She hooks audience in-transit with faintly clinging wires currently blonde under this version of the sun. Even in harsh glint of neon bulbs our eyes alight to where she treads, weaving tremulous, angelic in jagged azure, breaking out in full scarlet bloom, clawing new wound for itself at the dark side of a peach until its core. He-is, She-is, that forbidden thing: nameless, shapeless and so unloveable. Behind fallow eyes they sit and stare, hack-hacking until their noses and lungs are scarred with the mark of those decadent smells, lacking clean karma and grace.

Viva Life

Gerald smiles, still faint, with some naïve glow in the pinched corner tips. Dragged-out by hanging bottom lip, all to one side, so dreary. Bitter drips fall when he *hurrf*-breathes, looking out bug-eyed, another weary slur, knows it's happening but unable to control it. Thick statch of grumbly pressing down on heavy-set glasses lodged firmly underneath. Oak-aged features beam solemn past the ruddy rise of beard spurs that glint double. There's creak'd moan yawing as coarse-cut edge yaps more visions, all driving at hallucination, still wild from colour behind the eyes. It's natural to be frightened as no one yells at you otherwise and the medicines force trip-changes in the tune of time. Trapped in amber glass mouths a bereft interface while his foot taps away doubly uncontrollable. Gerard is here, but never entire in one place, doesn't even know his own name.

Desperation splits; to spill hidden truths no-one thinks they want to know, without further questions first. Gerald holds forth his theories of secret Argentina, with fighting talk to colonise the South Pole and stake a claim before all the ice is gone. Thinks he remembers the Falklands, being a mover of black gold right across the Atlantic on ships, he calls it: 'The biggest floating target you've ever seen.'

Some went down, took the men with them, the dark-brown surface and sideways fish demarcated the dead zone's burning lip. Shining-on, a singular light with finger-thumb pinch (to hold it for seconds (as days)) dark wreathes, sky choking the most violet hours, always burning brighter for the new wars.

He brushes down his face as heat comes stammering back, flame waves changing pace, taking it all home to crash, burning at the piers, all torn to pieces. And still the dead souls stand, rise-up, pierced in sand. The driftless left behind to work the beach, they go shaking-down the other-side their plastic nets, mouthing dreams of better life, trapped in brittle rhyme of cockle shells.

He talks about running, running; deckwise out from fire and the rings that blaze to scale new heights of orange. Running never still through ploughed fields now arteries of concrete, with a girl in hand, way back when. But this was before, before it all got so serious.

Smoking freely, the length of her hair smelt like cedar when he fucked her from behind. In dreams the grass folds away neatly to accommodate with odd leaves cutting up in spare stiletto, crunching at the ear's nest and buoyant underfoot. Free from roots and he's there again, watching boy, watching girl, as they roll on, not caring to stop, but turn-turning counter, against the world speared by inches, the tallest shoots most effervescent. Summer sun weaves in out as the last leaves make play of misty, dappled surfaces; to make the rain pulse in shook puddles of unsettled light, warming bark skin that mimics every drop-shadow. And as they move underneath, sap moves deep within at first touch of the lips.

He says these dreams come more frequently and every time the same. In steadfast days it's better to rest now the limbs won't listen to reason above their own bluster and creak. Explains it's *Human Papillopa*, doesn't mean much to me, but notice he grows more wizened as snarling flesh bites back against the bones moving around to outer edge – it's 'Gaia's revenge', so he says. Perhaps he stubbed cigarettes on Dahl's screaming trees, or worked at a paper mill turning air-bright leaves into turgid thrillers, moving too-roughly through the longest grass, thoughtless *a rebours,* but always so constant in awe.

Gerard cries blossom in secret where no one can see. On bad days he gets himself mixed-up with the others – we all do it. So softly fall the bombs arriving in post-darkness we don't notice the drop until its aftermath. A sweep of dust makes all places strange, infect his mood and colour all vision. I step through, a fresh breeze to his glacial flickers of Autumn, an ear still willing to listen, there bursts new season that marches unopposed and he lightens some, his hands a brighter touch.

I come to admire the quiet garden he's made, acting-out mute reflection that is not always returned, some herb-filled allure swept thick with aloe tint, a spiral ride that sets the membranes on fire, our gathered hope kills some emptiness. Surrounded by brittle things he escapes the real surface. Some convulsions break-in, and our new space is eroded by brute noise of human forms, he becomes another fixture to our brittle world, born to fragment.

But for now, he's free at least. This orchard's still apart from the ashen rain, threatening to hammer-down and drag-off edges from his teardrop leaves. See cloud of breath, held for a second, not expecting applause with the waters freezing over as more trees turn verdant in rust.

Caught in this private storm he doesn't really see me. We share a quantified space, recycled air, and for few brief seconds, without reason or warning, we mimic blinks; spaces between where I cannot see him, and I guess, he cannot see me. I watch him deep in reminiscence, it goes gently with mine fully closed, both drowsing with imagined kiss of butterflies, to drown out the giant-V of approaching patterns, could be bomber or bird.

A bleached sun patch taps a tune of light, coursing river-wound down those runes of skin (age, waiting to be deciphered). Under winter we all seem older, cracking new shapes in secret alphabet as the mind flutters, then regenerates to a new life found in broken language, his second blooming, still with something to say.

I could spend weeks lost in his wood-grain flow, jagged in the eyes as he recounts many lives, an acreage of myth settled deep in knowing lies, trying too hard to compensate, the dirtied memories of an honest man.

Post-war, (all imagined?) he decided to conserve life instead, no more grey constructs, better to watch real things grow but caught sickness from the trees he tried to protect, their peeling wounds transmitted tan patches and slowing blood. He takes the bitterness with a faint wave, all punishment is revenge, nothing's finally settled, no deeper knowledge of the self is gained; there's only shallow regrets and captive enmity to be erased. The madmen can tell you they are mad, or not – but who would believe them? As all things are, so Gerard says.

SHEERING

Faces away – the wall turns – mottled cream skin turns tortoise-wise, sliding away into sheer light. With childish squiggles they float as distant lines across the eye, echoing trails on a leaf, another worm trying to get free, we fight for the same space, getting harder to breathe. Specks of colour, a sample of that glimmer-glamour, cast weak variations to break up the grain, to stop you staring blankly against the faceless expanse. Designed not to send you mad, like a portrait in flesh, wandering eyes too long looking for patterns, forgetting where and what you are. Touch it, cold like some living, breathing thing with vague impressions of fingerprints upon wet paint.

Press dimple of glove-finger into these split plaster scars, still growing. Crush-nippled inverse, bound returns to its central whorl, undeniably yours. There's an ugly crack, virile lightning, spilling out. It's another moment to an already ruined age, but as one fissure is healed fresh scars rise daily to take its place – there was never a whole to make new.

Now it's all metal mesh gnashing-through as modern lattice bites harder, the last layer hanging-on to its limpness. Try to wipe around it, another surface grates at knuckled teeth, buckling in horsemouth, the orifice eating around itself as brother rust sets-in to galvanise by rot. Out from the criss-cross slashes there's a diverging line curving in on itself, some dusty blonde held in stone. Supple enough it flicks out, but whose head is this? Shed from ruddy scalp of the last plasterer as he bickered over perfect brickwork edges, a harrumphing hand shoves through his golden-grey forest, some human trace left behind in the pale dusk.

See black sickle moon arching its back, embryonic-rupturing as lagging tail spoons a crater lick –all is dust– steel diamonds return from the fade as creeping shadow marks, there's a body hacking upon death at my shoulder. Leans over me, I don't look.

Feel bristles spark the air-rush up my spine twisting a crick in the neck. It hums, inspecting the damage. There's a great moon-boot print left in front of me, all cracked stars in its wake. Short, sharp puffs tease-out some mockney tune, then snuffed breaths, just marking time before one more cigarette. Rough garage-bill sounds as he purrs and demurs between fleshy balcony strips, what's he seething so much about?

"*That* is copper," he expounds triumphantly, between chokes:
"What are you doing? I was cleaning that!" My splutterings speak out through the haze, some vanishing act.
"Well, that's definitely brass," another voice, identical, enters left, tapping steel on steel – how many of them are there?
"What's wrong with you? You almost kicked my head in."
"There's money in copper." He nods slowly, mixing-up their metals. Eventually notices me (one of the few), "We're from Salvage." More of them moving in around me, start hacking at it with hammer and claw, all crow feet bent towards carrion savaging.
"But there's nothing to take?"
"We've orders."
"From who?"
"Up above, Mr S, forget his name…he wore an old hat. Anyway, look here mate, we're just getting what's owed. Hold-up, there's money in that." Fingers rub hungry at wall.
"Back-up now, kid."
I'm dragged back dog-arsed along the floor, set leaning as broken doll to the wall.

Tearing away now at brittle plaster, human hands as paws, desperate for the dig. Orange-bright wires blaze, scattered as arteries in the wound, as more crumbs collapse, mapping decay. With the innards beaks begin to snap at one another, carving-up the remains of argument: "I'll take 'hundred's worth and you take the same."
"Where's mine then?" More voices filter in at powderface

extremities.

"Well then, you take three."

"Not out of my ten's-worth he's not!"

Keep at it till every grain of sand and grit is choked-on, spat home and every scrap is accounted for.

Glare into the backs of massing hulks, stacked fast in their chicken stoop. There's no spine to speak of just flesh wrapped in faux-logo shirts with the collars turned up, easy to follow. Couple of head-hocks peer round looking back at me; nancy-boy propping-up a sense of place, too weak to stand by itself (without a mop to lean on) they snicker as I watch, a reminder I'm barely there.

It started off so simply, a patch and lick of paint to keep everything moving, but the more exacting and complex, the more it shrinks back, a wound upon a wound. Decimated into mere fragments, these lone atoms float without purpose, motivation lacks and suckling at positive tension. One rare dot's enough to cripple industry and grind all gears to a halt until none of us are for turning.

So far, no blood's shed or other littering needs to be dispensed with, but hear them shouting-out all about it, getting louder in the mix. There's some faint itching as eye flows a collusion of salt and grit. Daren't touch my face, sitting on this floor. I know the sea of white alkali, microbe-deep, fade into the pale swept along into time. Only choice markings left, the streaks of our soles and stinging taint of hands-scratch.

Nurse trips over my feet, can't see which one – yells something over her shoulder, when before it was just a stern look. Already succumbed to the next wave upon wave, makes me staid and uninteresting, an indivisible part of the eternal sigh. Down the way nurses gaggle in near-silhouettes, smoking through a half-open door. Clasped mugs shake violent tremors as they remember prising a wheeled rod (still spinning) from the dripping man as the bubbling jig runs through the strip.

Too many wires pulled taut at once, separate storms spinning their respective teacups. Orange lightning runs up the wall to split the white foam sky with soft crack like a match – something inside has snapped. Cover my head as lumps fall and the air's rinsed grey again; must've pulled the wrong piece of copper. A twinkling sneer bobs about lights in-and-out for the territory: there's a steep lurch that sweats from the floor. I'm cocoon-wrapped as hands go back in for the guts. Snatching, rifling around like greedy crabs stripping the surface from a beach.

Look back to the ones on break. Blood trail slides towards them, a snaking detour rounds my feet. One nurse in light student-blue takes a meek toe toward, then a disembodied arm hooks her back into the fold again. They all stare in glib-owl detachment, but why? Standing by, determined not to interfere, they are the dull, dark hands that mark the end of all things. No more triple-time, early-retirement and hard-forced redundancy – they're *making* it happen now. So stick to your ground of sameness and don't get involved. Calmly and with care, thick in the veil of crashing concrete and needy screams, she moves back from one edge to the next, watching still, as the red tide closes upon itself.

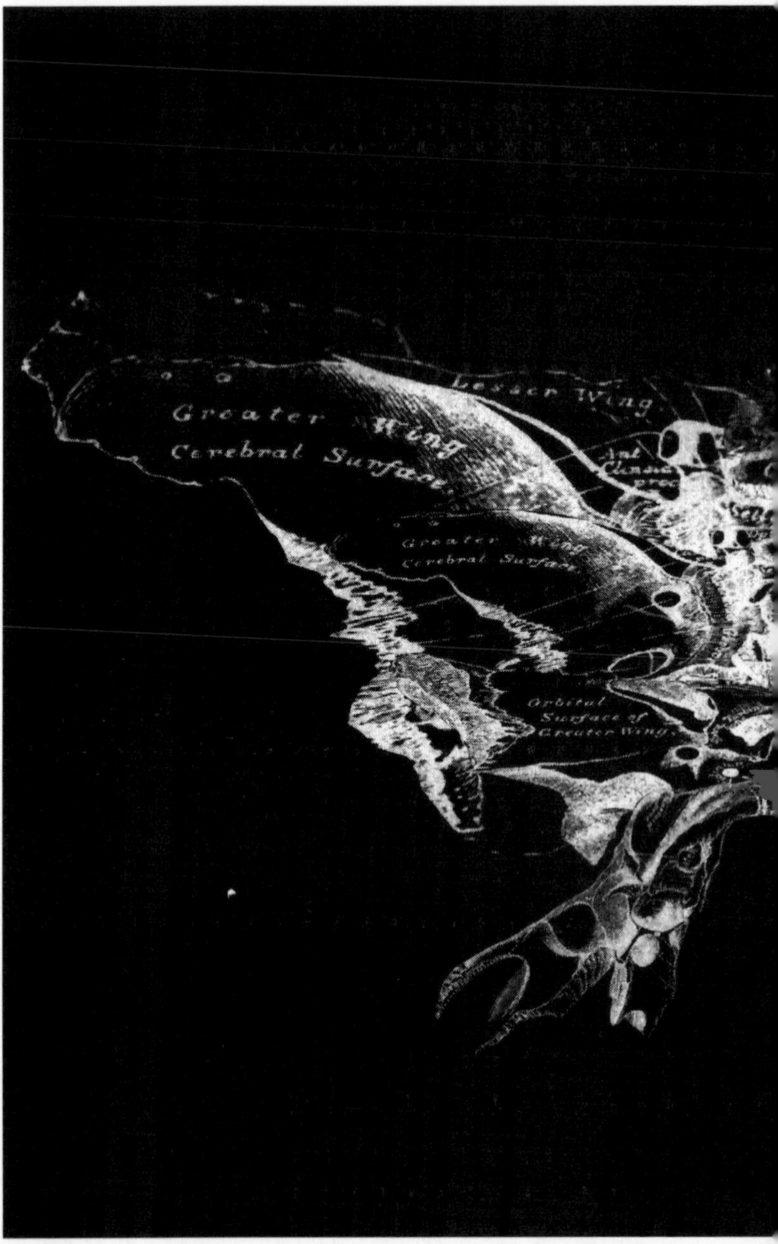
Lesser Wing
Greater Wing
Cerebral Surface
Greater Wing
Cerebral Surface
Orbital
Surface of
Greater Wing

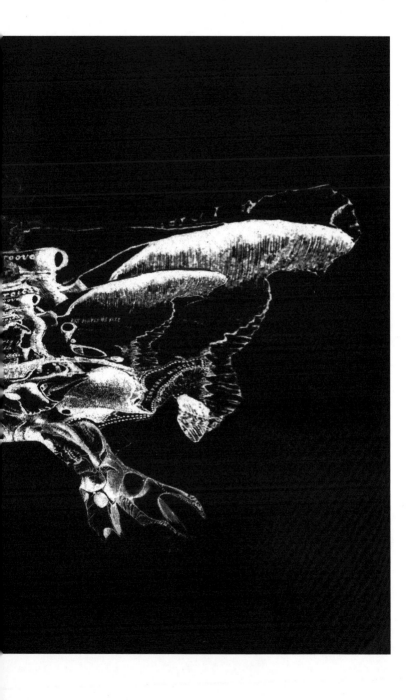

A la Carte (in Extremis)

A dirty human hoof lolls unnatural to the leg. There's the odd twitch, but otherwise resting faint. That mask, like a face, is just another gauche grimace, more pages torn as fingernail shred in the casual bitch, brawl and moan. A meaty vapour lingers on heavy, upsetting the oil, lamination or not, they've gone very wrong this time. Nurse in darker blue reins in some control by degrees makes things stern again with slow, firm nods. There's muted agreement to keep quiet, no asks and no one tells, together we rule ourselves (by secrecy).

She streaks off to write it up as some student accident: a slip of the wrist, lacking nous or some other drastic character flaw. The rest scatter in her wake, other bodies flatten from view, receding into shadow. I keep my own vigil, with curiosity rising. There's a pearly veil on my skin after the blue halo, observed by blinking pupil of a burndt insect. Deep shade submerges the veins and gives faint crackle as bodies pass. Something crinkles under sheet – there it is! Ah, just toes making themselves known (I only count nine).

Cloth's stained as twice-stewed tea, like those Christ-branded tablecloths, the folded features mark the outline of a person in thick knuckle creases. They shake it out lightly as if flexing spare life in the last big-red beats. I look for an open window, the entrance toward a shunting breeze but it's just static, like hard rain.

Slick tides curl across the floor – sure I cleaned that all before? There's steam escaping and that meat smell again, quickly slowing to a new surface for its skin. It navigates by uneven contours, the lifeblood in exile dividing and swallowing-up spare space, as if seeking some new vessel to fill. Now a red phase runs through it, mixing intricate blend of rusted-mud, crushing platelets of fat with the seething advance of iron.

Something else flips sheet with brute flicker of bestial tones.

Sliding out from a curtain stretch, see Old Matron coming up for air. It's swathe writ large on her face, snuffling into the patient meals. Shed all those little superiorities in her hypocrite stance, the gauche grotesque is revealed as another mask fallen short. As a corner forces shape, desire outshines everything, devouring its own young, as nature divines.

This time her hunger's gone too far, crashing from patient to preacher realm of knowing best, that latent greed exploded. Her nose flattened into a snout, I click back and forth, trying to connect the pulse-taker with the braying gulps of blood as the human animal out-blurs recognition, a pig trussed-up in uniform.

Seen that same hunger before in the needy ones; all feeding on sapped energies of the in-valid and nearly dead. To see her wallowing in abasement is everything I've come to hate, between the lame brick, arcane systems and my broken self. In that slick display our shared futures descend. When there is nothing, and no one left to make use of, we will all lie down under the same glacial mirror, ghosted with spare breath, to see our other selves wasting there, hung-up on some mystery drip, trying to figure out where it all went wrong, unable to sleep or forget.

Was it the desperate man, dirt lying in dirt as I failed (or rather, chose not) to help because his being there lowered the house prices on my street, or did I only notice when I tripped over his head, his body in my way? Perhaps it was the people too eager to criticise, tut-tutting as they're trapped and stacked in tower blocks, where some live doing nothing, others keep-on trying. You don't expect *Them* to want no better. Now mothers are too afraid to sweep their own stairwells and the windows are all broken because we're trained to hate our own reflection. 'Damaged goods' they label you, told too many times you'll come to believe it, acting-out to become everything they said you are. Spray-tags streak the walls and everyone agrees any ruined surface can be art, by human application, so long as it's not where you have to live. And we all follow suit because the easiest way to avoid kicking against the pricks is to keep on giving them what they want. And as soon as things start to get better it all gets expensive, so what's once broken is now fixed, you have to move along, your home is now nowhere. Then the amnesty readers arrive in ethnic dress (the viral hangover) to keep the liberals on their right side, wearing X-brand trainers to show how much you care, more than all the rest.

We worry hard to find it but the blood-lines run through and underneath, electrified feet, but not knowing where to look you forget yourself and bypass instinct. Over your shoulder it's a museum aping gothic, The Past and fractious-Greek, now look ahead, it's neo-nothing, glass and steel, just another slow death of the so-called classics.

Every benevolent agent or muted civil servant melts into a swooning chorus, the lower rungs as backbench choir, promoting schemes for obese-suicide as renewable human-fuels, all desolate angels bearing witness to empty sloganeering as they de-facilitate our decline.

In this half-mast age, we put out more flags just to say we can, one goes up as another will be knocked down and like her, I'm still waiting to be saved, chewing on my own leg, instead of dreaming escape, but this meat is bitter, lurid-stickered 'Best of British', and has begun to lose its taste.

The heffer's escaped my sight, blended into her postures casual decay. There goes another mind, mired in deep-fat white of body into body, with life no go-between. To destroy her means forcing change, a way to break hopeless cycles of endless becoming.

Push the back of the head further in, every inch more bubbling dredge, pulling tight at pale corners of the torn fleshsack, now a human nosebag. Strange rumblings in the cadaver, sides heave as she clogs up, gulped-back sounds of a vomit reflux. I start slow and firm but under the massing heap it breaks out into a whooping yell: "Eat what, you sow!"

See pea skins split like miniature skulls, I go on, forcing her to deeper gorging. She tries to pull-out, desperate for oxygen and amongst it all she gasps-at some frail words I can't catch. Tone deaf to the big-red beating, she's already drowning by repeat mistakes; this life's become a serial clot with scathing fractures interlaced. I've tried to disown past feeling but for now my mind is salved – I'm right in my hate.

Press fingers into a clasp, juddering neck tired and twitching, both of us waning, before faint. Still starstruck across the head but this was what I had to do, to scratch it all from memory. Now this violent flooding can be erased and my unending disgust left to rot, a forgotten cadaver to all the rest.

The Lost Art of Forgetting

(and remembering)

... rests in the still of solitude.

Just for Today

Always I think of Gerry; does he think of me? Forever in the corner of my eye. I turn to catch but glimpse at nothing, already passed me by. Crying in the shower seems natural, all these rushes going the same way, washed-off into sweat and all the rest. See it in my pale flesh up-close, he persists in memory like nicotine stain of clipped claws held rigid to a constant arc. Running down through veins of the tray, my hair/blood/skin go spinning-off sucked back into the flow; a fragile reminder, small saints fall but will return in time.

He might still be around? Maybe boxed-out legless in some distant room, where natural light doesn't enter and no-one goes. Steeped in four years' dust, there's nothing more to say, he is drawn neat by tightening circles chasing their tails.

The Daves told me it started with something small, something odd; forgetting commonplace things in the lived routine compounded by years. Eventually there's a diagnosis upon the weight of your options. One piece goes, the rest follows towards total organ failure, too much too late, that's just the way it is. He should've said, we should've said or done something, but a burden's never really shared, only kept to yourself.

Out from our lives and deeper in shadow, Gerry keeps on coming, closing doors and messing-up perfectly clean spaces, making scenes. Left his rolling box behind, still there on the table waiting to be taken. We all look for him as you come in. Sweet drift follows from the wood but don't want to open it to see inside. It's better let alone, like the changing of the lights, green always goes too soon and that's when he'd swear it out reaching for a rollie, hiding behind a smile only half-angry. That moment's dipped entire in the burning red glow we use to reflect, but understanding we need not speak about it, it was always there. We just sit, waiting upon amber relief, until everything's loosed – and off again, green becomes an absent memory, a floating recess in the eye.

Gerry was the longest serving, small and getting smaller, marked-out by an Irish twang and waffling thin moustache. A downmarket Groucho he held a room with big burrs and toothy laugh, never minding the gaps. Rollie ever-present, tucked behind his ear, soon as it was smoked another took its place. Wild whiskers bloom out every hole, left to weed and overgrow until they served to muffle the man underneath starved from being heard. Every second sentence of conversation demands a "Watcha' say?" With ear cocked to play catch-up but he's already cracking-wise behind the green and black of eager eyes.

Shrugging every yoke they ever tried to settle, same way horses sneer a grin under iron duress, his aggression's mauled-out through the bit. After years of spitting refusal still won't admit he's finally beat. Slunk off from every admin intervention, kept his head down and gone his own way, never fooled by the short sell, he's ex-union and still wearing the dirt-scars of the good old days under his fingernails. Feels the changing winds in shortened whiskers where quiet menace glowers against stale management airs put about by the latest bright things, much younger than him.

He interjects his own stories, plying multiple weaves, as layers slip and slide over, falling away. "Sometimes, right, you looks back at these poor bastards, just after you've dropped them off like, back and forth wid'em all day, and you know – this one's not coming back…it's terrible sad. And they tell us 'Oh, you don't need to worry about all that', so just 'cus I'm a porter, I gots to be fuppin' stupid like, right? S'posed to keep my eyes and ears closed 'cus I'm not to care, just forget? I'm never frightened of dying, even with all them blind curves and gaping pot-holes, and why should I be? You gotta go, then you're gonna go."

The Thousandth Balcony

Here on in, my words want out of themselves, each escapes for their own sake. To say about this acropolis, made real, outdoes your worst modernity of steel and glass. No straight way to describe how the 'I' feels, easier to d ri f t…let mind peel off and lose what's least, overflowing with geometry.

That fragment of pier and crumbling is a stand-out reminder, another kept ward without a number and a name. "Borrowed" out from time, it's grade-listed and so forced to stay-on, remain un-used but alive. It lingers in half-hearted thought; forever between deconstruction and vacancy. Close my eyes and it's still burning like the fall of Hastings, replayed, endlessly slow-motion so it never really stops.

Some shapes dot around it: they've come to collect, moving inside shadows to fight over the scraps. As sun pushes sky they're absorbed in half-light, less of nothing, bloated by tears. Salt corners lapped after high watermarks and peppered by stray seeds from above. The swollen brick attempts to outweigh the rain. Viral as sand, clogging the drains with washed-out dust, from tributary halls into unguarded doorways, all choking on recycled cells.

These fractured divides, long-forgotten, linger splintered by ivy creep that fills every spare space. It suckles sweet at meniscus lick while tarmac cracks in new lines of rattling roots threatening collapse. Said they would use every spare bed to bring new change and raise sloth of carcass back to life. But the same story repeats, a burndt-out ward lies empty, as patients are bound by silence, without days to dream and not peace to sleep.

Stepping-back from all these hollow might-have-beens. Out there is N-town – the solid reminder you can never go back because you don't want to keep-on turning away – now home is nowhere. Sick of Queen Bitch, sick of Matrons in their tersely overripe streaks;

that constant shrugging and changing of last-minute minds is just another sick dose. Walls are held too close to suffocate echoes, words overcrowded so there's no room left to hear yourself think. On the roof I can breathe freely, imagine a life beyond, much calmer here and easier to pretend.

Man stands at the end of the road, last civilised stop before stepping-off the straight road that you follow to the end, at the hospital's beginning. He sells alcohol spray for the thwarted ones making their dwindle-dull approach. All heads-down in deference to medicine's blind gravity. Their worried frowns spire thorning; too afraid to touch at skin, lest it deepens a germ into the flesh. Buying-up alcohol hand gels, closest thing to a cure, so they say (but who are they?) Like sheep meant for sleep, customers bray-in, cash-out, and coat their needy digits on release.

Too easy to sneck a fractured smile into my hyena hunch. We have examined our lives by inches, naked in mirror-faces of the sick that repeat, repeat, but no deeper, harsh truths ring hollow.

They ant-scramble over trickling leg, fraught with the medical eye, keeping clean and best-quiet, knowing not what they try so hard to do. Keeping calm just to carry on, finding solace in daily slogans that give easy erosion; narrow alliteration makes the living painless and all too quick, but lends the death-prospect a harder stretch.

Wind's powered-up to shake away at concrete, driving chill through all cracks and breaks, the same wounds in our solitary skin, this edifice shivers as one.

All vvvvvviibrrrees asz hummmmnnesssss rrrra-a-a-a-u-u-nnnneddddd up my bluing hand, gasping grasp at the air, keep it moving, moving; this connection goes direct to the spine through silent shifting of building blocks on fractious plates. Up and down, together we form brief-flight circuit that sparks a beacon for the loathsome ones; a monument to mistrust, lest we remember all we've been and done. Mute objects, narrowed-themselves-in – beings yet to become.

I hate the outside: all trying to get in, more centaurs in our garden, to breakdown our walls' trying, bringing new ignorance, dust and disease. Just waiting to be landfilled and overrun, turn it over to start again – maybe they'll get it right this time. It's just a phase, a flux intervention, the wearing down of history's spin, but who cares enough to notice anymore – not me.

Get ready, get lost – these stark divides stand between us, from tooth-cut splint to dovetail wedge. Forced to embrace the joint-dis-tinct – kept apart and yet vaguely closed throat; all in all, our happy synthesis. Old buildings re-cast in ancient alphabets falling from sense. Read: 'No More Future' and 'Beauty is Truth', finger-painted plastering the red brick flesh sold-off to underline the latest five-lane monsterways, no competition for the new vocabularies' face of onslaught. Our best manifestos gone dancing away with themselves.

Last grey-cold allotted breaths of back-lit emptiness sold-off, but there's never quite enough to get the full-bloom of your share. The next classics torn down to make cheap headstones for recent departures, passed away post-welfare after attempted living in twenty-storey stone ribcage, crying out amongst the deaf, to be etched in plastic:

He died as he lived, lying down.

Up and away, we can stand tall, immune to all that. The great Outerside is no longer our affair. From catacomb walls of our self-made asylum we sneer in the face of sterile re-structuring, everything for its own sake – nothing gets better, nothing really changes. We are a stuck-tight entity, an institution beyond measure as the million-strong workforce turn tides of the get-sick/get-well revolving generations, spinning out life as long as we can.

All around me are birds cutting-up sky, more larks to the death-knell, as they split the turf across a concrete knife, goodbye to your British-standard countryside, all struck out in signs and progressive ley lines, a road map to boredom and a feeble excuse to lose control in parish council meets' devolved bickering into blame-led stress-induced violence punctuates nearby pylons buzz-buzzing sparks haze rain that smothers horizons.

The nation splits further as we finally decide to grow apart, multiplied in fission, our organism swells when we see the bedevilled townships explode. Simple enough to witness: just scratch out the pretty cliché on a perfect postcard, circumscribed by thinning hedgerows. Fill each space with acidic scrub grasses, bleached feckless by sun and runaway hot air, each property neatly edged with barbwire trellis, first hint of urban-defence infecting the suburbs as middle class parties draw to midnight to a close, use noise-cancellers and rolled-back insulation to resist the hanging traffic of the overpass as it licks along the chimney tops; spitting, spilling bothways. Black rains rundown final fissures of clean white pebbledash, fizzing on naked skin to the grating hits of Gary Gray's secondhandnewswashdaze, to ward off real city spirits with warnings to tell, driven numb by the bass bins that shuffle gravel as they thump past nested settlement. In selected environs choked sirens swarm against the youth, the selfish sons strayed too far from their own boroughs, where expectation weights-you-down to stay. Moving with the night, better the devil catches you, a safer bet. Less places left to roll, glide or climb unsighted, you must stay under the hallowed umbrella and the live wires (see: above) look up past that distant promise of an indivisible sky, you best stay grounded, and the message is clear: there's airspace but no flying here.

Local policy-dead-heads set against the forces of a street: all channelled one-way and shaped by the invisible big-red beat. Forced decision snakes around harsh corners, hugging the brick to keep out from every angle, but no real seekers go truly random.

Everything we are told to want is by grab-at and covet, carving nu-colonies on your precious home turf. Extrapolated stars from the cricket green campus, as vicious triangles stab away their pain to tessellate and overlap, a runaway force that strikes beyond mental borders. Concrete the wildflower-weeds because they won't stay down, or lay faux-marble slabs in sterile no-go zones where there is only imagined tread upon 'public' space. Active confirmation of their blind dogma, a virulent ethos gifts us uneasy peace, the ash never settles where diversity's less than skin deep. There's ugly attitudes remixed in divine threads, speaking down in singular chat: "it's a matter of respect", depending who it comes from and how it's said.

Caught in the same flow just to arrive at our endings. Split through bifurcating strain of clogged arteries, we wheeze and choke as As into Bs lead from dead-end villages to nowhere towns, forced back via closed-off ring-roads that only disconnect and ploughing-on-through alien bypass avoiding all but the signs there were people, just to come around again.

Jagged horizon set to joust with city spires, concrete towers facing-off the illusion of height shining next-to the brighter stiletto progress, pushing back the edges to try and live beyond the nine-to-five. Two alternate hands scrabbling wild, it's more fever in the cities already fought to ruins; the battle's to keep your head and make your own space, progress will always lose when it reaches terminus of an ideal.

Everyone has different sides to the one surface. A comparative citadel with passions and ills just like yours and theirs, me and mine. Spreading thin, the desperate gnawing of misspent paws, good aims well-funded, then misplaced and somehow unaccounted for, lost down rabbit-hole's darker side of wise investment.

People never change – a little learning? What a chance that would be. To remove the heads always moving us off-topic, kick-back at the long grass that buries sins. Take a look through hollowed-out mouth arches, agape, desperate to tell escape of all them syllabi, just for the day. Instead give them something real, not just something they can touch, but something they can feel.

We here choose to take no action, a public body consistently indifferent, quietly angry, failing to act when needed but most able to complain. So get back to the sofa, stir the ashes, flick on/off black box for life spilt into and find-out the Next Big Thing before the next one. The centred-self of faulty organs must, through neurotic acid reflex, spew more numb release, poorly-explained and with regimented emotion to pretend that everything's OK – when it's not. Raise a sword, cut off the head that the body might still live, maybe one day to flourish. Remove the shallow ulcer and stem the false flow, destroying all infections and the rest. We are brutal contradiction abandoned to piss in the wind, these dead souls we inherit washed onto desolate shores where sea is nothing but pure erosion as the broken ones pick out fragments of shell, still hoping for a whole, enough to make connection at terminal beach where bodies hit like a rolling roar of flesh-trapped-flesh-wall, every day it rises and every day the bodies bring more.

Rife in symptoms, the worst of our verse and chorus was to try and care too much for too many. The un-loved ones and the greedy few (like the poor, made selfish and needy) delivered ready-made, some beyond help.

You can fix them up, stick them out dressed in their eternal best as wilting flowers pale against fine white china, but it's context that drags you down – all things beautiful must fade in this jaded, plastic place. So let them live for today, but we know each time back around it's worse than before. Removing the gauze always takes some flesh with it, scar tissue remains a slow heal, with resistance less and less. Some say it's a total waste of time, pouring in more resources as the quality of life fades, cracked across a closing light. But we must continue regardless, controlling their tomorrow with only half a care, all the time feeling we were never fully there.

Adam Steiner

Better off at the eleventh floor
but the ride stops here, ten-and-a-half high
between worlds.
No more movement
just the cold,
coming in.
Down from North
Exit roof, left
Going South.
Back around,
spiral stairs
voyage out.
Off the Cuff.
Once
and Forever
coming
down
again.

NO WHITES
NO STRAIGHTS
NO ENGLISH.

"Look at the state of this lot. Always give us a bloody pick-and-mix, don't they, kid." Buzzing away in my ear, more snatches of Dave-broken drips. "It's in all the leaflets as well; anywhere you go – bloody English Allsorts, I call it. I'm not even being racist," he's the impolite face of a perfect society that doesn't exist, "they've just gone and made it up for us. You count them – one in e-ver-ey three – it's forced diversity is what it is. They stick them in to be 'representative' you know – representative of what? And we're just supposed to accept the world's all mixed-up and be happy with it. Well, some of us ain't!

"Seen that Curious George wandering about the other day, another bloody jungle bunny and a lazy one, mind. Don't get me wrong, I don't mind 'em, so-long-as-they-work. And then there's the students, they come over here, train up as a doctor or whatever, they take all those skills, and the golden handshake, send all their money back home then fuck off, I dunno...I've got to be going anyways, need to go see the Matron about moving some boxes somewhere, or something."

Lingering with the flitting leaves, shadows' pulse caught standing stretched between half-lights. Dave pushes his way through the messy ranks: "Excuse me, 'scuse me, *thank-you!*", never that brash in real life. They part in staggered waves, blank-faced in expectation, waiting to be chosen; ready to work, but not beaten yet.

Lucky ones sent to march out that long crow road, winding out hours into days. Eager fools stepping forward to be selected, swallow tidy yawns, chewing into the chest. Perhaps slept some in the easy hours, just to fight through tiredness drags about after, but always catches up with you; staying awake without knowing where or when, you drift about, half-a-person, all your interest and reactions, no matter how genuine, fall flat, dead dog lay down with the sun. So we drift, never thinking to leave, a wraith trail shone in shallow new veneers, increasingly transparent and thin under a bright that seems inept to try and warm us.

Straightening-up, she examines safety from a set distance (looking beyond smiles for a full set – past gums – rotten fruit). Flush with full stance, once acknowledged they collapse into themselves and shuffle off, grateful for another twelve-hour/thirty minute split. We all collude, clog ourselves with spaces that must be filled, pretending everyone's the same and treated as such. Inspired by fake promises bought straight from the United bullshit of Benetton, branded equality, all colours bleed the same, but you wouldn't know it round here.

Third wave shuttled-in, squatted portals of buses crushed miniature; seatbelts spread one-across-two. With determined faces pressed up to the naïve glass, hope smears idle breath, becomes perspiration, they roto-wipe to see a few seconds of what's next. Washed-out, weary in jumble of new smells; stepped on junk-food, splintered forks pointing all ways cut vivid with snatches of language trading some sameness. From the outside, in; knowing I won't ever fully understand, a different outfit, I belong here; in the ward – these guys are lost. But here or there we're the same – no place is home, and this definitely isn't it.

Labelled "Agencies" but they're free for someone else; not been here long enough even to earn the respect of the downtrodden: we are already aping the steps that come after here, to get done differently but the same. They can't keep time with the basic routines because the agency drops them late. The stranger the stranger brings a shocks the routine – a bolt to blot procedure – too much oxygen floods the blood. Tragically incoherent, this line-up spells failure, a lumpy diaspora trying to make a fresh go of it, again, again; we only have the différance of common.

Nurses spin-whisped secrets on first sight, restless narratives that
might find right, classic exposure of a needy mind:
"Their uniforms don't match."
"And they're that scruffy-lookin'."
"Oh God – he's wiping his hands on his sides."
"How can they be so dirty already, they've only been here five
minutes."
"I can't pronounce that! We'll have to shorten it."
"Tsk, look at that posture – 'e makes the walls slouch."

Their logos clash in rival bids for the cheapest bodies, meat forced
animate until beyond use, by hammers-home bolt-jolted, then
sinking star of four into flattened floor. A slur towards industrial
etiquette with vacuous names like Vehizeron, Impact and the
smashing banality of Pulse. They speak foreign with their own
phrasings that no one can repeat; harping back they just smile,
striking me as somewhat beyond holy, patient but not penitent,
against the vulgar swell of an ocean of noise. Fed-long into
gross rivers that stick-in misunderstandings; never to meet in
the middle (trying to cross, one side to the other) and enduring
because the numbers *must* add up somehow. So throw in more
bodies at one end, as they raise the bar for the *n*-teenth time. Now
it's all elbows bowing to the rush, scattered hurry, less health and
safety, more force forwards along the line.

But getting by is only half the trouble: freak-forced into those
fractured smiles we feel compelled just to break the ice; crossing
past someone you knew from before without lapsing into empty
platitudes. Instead, show papier-mâché façade stretched across
sandpaper lips, then look away, neither one really cares what the
other thinks; their needs, loves, desires, all interchangeable, it's a
different world in here – you must keep to yours and I'll have to
stay with mine.

Greening into the Pale

"There's an odd kind of symmetry to it." Where Gerard cups imagined handfuls of earth I see vacancy merge between creases; the air already taking its leave. Overhead buzzing as fingertips glow, his nails streaking-out in hollow flame. "Between human life and other natural forms, the beginning is always the root, more and more bodies are waiting to be cultivated and made whole by another life growing alongside, in my case, this just happens to be a virus. It moves over me, turning skin like bark, hardening till it cracks and eventually moss will sprout from the pores and fissures, depending upon enough sunlight, of course. "Papillopa replicates itself to a safe level where it can achieve symbiosis with the host – note the indifference that comes with ownership. And like most organisms there's an innate desire to reproduce in the greatest numbers to compete with other species. The virus follows this same principle; to overwhelm the host, in full knowledge it will try to resist, *because* of that, even. However, balance, towards imbalance, is key. If one side outgrows the other, then both organisms must die. And it remains entirely possible that in its hurry to go forth and multiply etcetera, the dominant one ends in solo competition with nothing but itself.

"Living, the verb, is more built upon desires which, like love, are viral in their nature. People will give anything to satisfy their cravings, give in to hunger. They can consume you entirely until there's nothing left but to act on that singular impulse without joy or feeling and so you become your own virus, running out of time and out of light, never satisfied. This is the struggle we have, to lead a good life, often trying to overcome our desires before they do us in, and all against growing difficulties. My disease has become the better part of me, a quiet violence I learnt to live alongside, there's a kind of purity in that."

"You're insane, you're not some happy host – it's killing you."

"Yes, but perhaps this is a better way to die. Re-emerging before ash, resisting dust."

He's gone too far.

"It's just the natural cycle of things. The best deaths are those of acceptance, accepting your nature."

"You sound like a Catholic. Look around you, there's no such thing as a good death; if you're lucky a slow rattle before signing-off." He chuckles away, but no answer straight-up, just runs those worrisome, dry hands over thickening sap at the lips.

"By way of contrast, a well-known author, an atheist who used to paint the insides of churches, once wrote that a good *life* simply means fighting to be human under growing difficulties – or did I tell you that before?" Gerard's most prominent features: brows, knuckles and the tip of the end of his nose hardened first, now indivisible from deadwood, still all points lead him on.

There's a slight-shot grimace as if I'm not *really* listening and failing to understand. "Look at it this way, as a plant adapts to meet the demands of its environment, so it becomes more specialised, more individual. The ideal for a plant is to reach this pinnacle of design, and by learning to break out from…let's say, a more *routine* structure," see his grand adventures dash upwards like keening embers, "it can become something more than itself, so it is with my disease. Change can be painful, but as the pattern of a leaf spreads more diffuse it arrives at a neater fit in the world, its own time and place."

Filling up space…

"But what happens when the environment changes too far, too fast, all the factors it has no control over? Then it's completely out of step."

"Some are. They're either made that way, 'defective' or, as you say, get forced into a corner by the world changing around them. Like certain breeds of moth, some are made too fragile to last."

"But that's pure survival, just killing time."

"Yes, but it's how well you survive. The specialist is made

vulnerable by its difference, too unique, too perfect in that one strange way – it is forced underground; to the margins, as other organisms will always seek to advance beyond one another, to attack or supress new designs. Growth is purposefully stunted so it cannot spread to other natural systems, but so long as some of it survives."

"That's just adaptation. I mean, if it's forced underground it has to live without light, to be blotted-out."

"Well, that's a sacrifice for trying. But remember, the strongest organism learns to flourish anywhere, in its own way. It's a choice we all have to make: whether to adapt just to survive or to struggle in our own way, perhaps towards a dead end – nature is a tyranny, and perhaps the hardest thing; I can tell you, as a divorcee, is getting someone to make the whole jagged journey with you, and still maintain their own way."

He starts laughing deep into his chest, heaving deep, gouging grunts. A greenish tint shoots-up the veins of regulation blue overshadowed by the new strain; then recedes, a tide gnawing at the breakers. He's forced off-course via Mobius strip, each life a small lick of the infinite. We run an increasingly narrow path until the next one comes around, it gets harder to tell where each story ends and the next begins.

"All these things that began in order must, inevitably, end in chaos." A solemn figure stands as waving totem, "It's like all those hollow men circling in," keep calling on, "nosing about with their plain blank faces, all they want is to categorise and collect; all that matters is forcing new roads where their want is greatest; whether it's a pin in a butterfly, clipping others' wings or swallowing-up the first share, they are symptomatic of desire run riot. We must repeat ourselves just to trap those singular moments, nail down memory as a ghost. Precious things neatly-labelled to settle having against loss. Captive happiness held in photographs; we exist in experience, but survive in notation." Most can't let it be, a pure moment to wax and wane, irredeemably brought back to the present.

More words, I scratch at long-legged ladders, my shining cheapness staggers down from the body, lightning to bolt down the earth.

"And this is why they can never be happy; there is always more of more to know and…you know, you can leave if you want."

"I'll stay a little longer."

"That's not what I meant, you know you can get away, whenever you want to."

"I know." Where's he going with this?

"Well, don't dwell too long on it. Go do something, make something new." Nodding to corridor, it greys and shrinks, clearing its throat before getting ready to spit me out.

"I can't, not just yet."

"You're scared."

"I'm not scared, not that scared. They need me here, the patients, you know that."

"Why – why are *you* worried to leave *them* alone? Are you so afraid to try?"

"What would I do otherwise? I don't know anything else. And besides, I'm never alone because they aren't."

Our rumbling slows as the last burrs of his hand-clasping is rubbed out in splintering palms. He goes quiet, except for the occasional creak as saplings snap through the skin. He reaches out, cracking knots in the back, all down to his base, rolling a wheeze across a barrel-scraped chest.

Starts dividing up his sleeve, rolls into roll, but it falls away, unfurling loose. The wool snags new holes on the way down, breaking out to show the sun a translucent hearth in his blue-lined hands that play lightning forks through the veins. To become vines lashing life to the mast, wrenching depth from oxygen squeezed-out by favour of photosynthesis – this is his new speciality. But he's said enough for today; let him slip into that petrified peace where the ivy of his tales have taken; those beginnings of nowhere.

The lashes flicker, speeding-up they bat wild at figure-eight frequency, multiplying stained-glass staccato; no single lines divisible, just a blur mouthing colour, wide-eyed as venus kisses closing down upon their prey. Breaking out and away, they flutter through a window slint, leaving Gerard sliding into his wooden chair frame, just like the others, an emergent grave. Between here and there sits another dry and dusty king of nowhere; waiting to be returned to earth, for his surface to be washed away in bitter kisses of April's final rain.

HappyJazzMen

After Gerry went sideways the black-bag handling's been outsourced to a specialist team: the mothballed men that crop-up three-a-penny about the corner of our every civilised street. A brief hop over to N-town and they're pressed high to the ribs of rafters in local competition; right on top of one and another, like staggering beetles billeted stack. You keep cutting the hair as the skin recedes but the business keeps on coming back.

The men beyond-pale arrive in slick-sleek double-spaced stretch, over-designed for the exacting purpose of memory dumps amongst the worms who are already blind and never learnt to read anyway. Like lazy journalists, they recycle the worst kind of news so we can come to terms with learning to forget and start the next day afresh.

Smaller in death, a lithe black bag of slithering-slenderness is gently shoved into bottle-polished windowless ambulance, marked "PRIVATE", though there is no disturbing those steeped feet-first in the big sleep, we must not alert the impotent ghetto of the waiting-insane. No light for the ferrymen just the right price by predetermined contract, and duly-afforded tax. They'll do work that's less dirty than most and come out smiling. No one uses 'mortuary' 'morgue' or those other widescreen terms; in a place where truth is just another dirty word, instead, the working phrase is a snipped command: 'patient X to bay nine.' So each bed gets moved along one, nearer under the eye of the nurses' station, and so inch closer to death, a haunted league spanned to withering stance.

Lay them down as triumphant cards at table; no ether for elegy required. Jack digs a spade, clipped fingernails conform to trim coats. Everything seems to stop growing, sent: 'To Flesh, with Spite and Absence', drawn taut as a last mask of resistance. The cells flicker, light recedes to fade, eating-out the unlucky day at seven of spades.

These happy jazz men must persist in crumpled-stove-pipe hats, with loose-lids flapping-flit speaking nonsense to spare winds, a moving cloud of scuffed velvet hides worn-at-apertures, patched-black but lingering damp scrub smell. Half-cut at their reeky bones jut-jaws go spin mechanical 'rah-rah-rah', sip-smiles watered milky-thin.

Heads bent double-down towards the floor, finding reverence at their feet the dark sheep stumble-out, bleating bones weight telling on their vulture-slunk shoulders that sag from lifting too many sad kites. Each step's kilter-off slouch at the heavy-side, like the nurses chained to a losing gait, tired before their time. Paupers pretend as others better off than them (bury them bastards yet) knowing they're beat before the race is run, but keep going on, all the while feigning not to care.

Doorways seem just-shrunk-to-fit, but attempting decorum, they fold it around, elbow over handle. "Yeah that's it." A sick thunk at timbre peaks, "Easy lads, easy," shoulder caught, a grand piano as mousetrap – a tug, pull, that's three digits popped-out and the lid sinks its major tooth. Tempting to fate, the magnets won't stick, door starts to close on itself – shut-ut-tuttering – push it back, juddering against the circuit's swing –**thud**– it tries again but now wedged with a diamond-flat foot, creasing under pressure –**th-thud**– thin lip slides into a sigh, counting crunch swallowing-over toes.

The March-Major taps away lily-blanched at his CramPle device as the boys do the loading – more new-age death balancing actors' routine. Smells more capital to be made a sneering slash runs between dry lips recessed grin with only the illusion of teeth. Happy to grasp plastic but hard shake's better pressed cash-firm, brings first warmth to the scene and enough indent feeling something like flesh.

No more re-hears-alls of instruction seeking practice: they get as far as steel trolley, which wheels away as they drive him out over the bumps, "watch it there" never lost one yet (but no-one notices the missing). Mild hic-umps punctuate routine respect, an observation upon *much must-ness* for the ex-person, another unknown to us.

Up-close their pallor bears scraped scabrous tone of experience, paving stones laid resting-flat, best actors are the nearly dead, but on our budget, this as good as it gets. We speculate to hum with constant rat-ta-tattle on brittle tarmac, then to that infamous door that only shuts with a wincing squeeze – too tall for death – somethings to be taken only lying down. Crush his satin streaks into graceful folds, slower the reverence, while cursing under this unyielding hinge.

Nurses slink alongside to see them off the premises. Brown (nondescript) envelope swapped, guilty pages ready to burn. Get it out of here, skip the minor signatures before an outside doctor arrives; then it's double the money. Tick the causes as 'morbid conditions', scratch-through any possibility of ~~violence/poison/privation or neglect.~~ No such thing in the great Twenty-First, or at least there appears to be no daily evidence for it.

All bodies on both sides lurch off in the cut-and-shut big-cat as it coughs-splutters down the way, *varooowing, yarowwinngg*, blown-out mutt-sputtering floated on Scotches and reclaimed vegetable-oil, whoomping splutters around a sharp corner before the road unwinds, stopping-off at the boiler room. The remains still warm now the surface memory has been refreshed.

Mothballed

Unfurl the flag bled out of its colours, scratched black into white for those seeking definite answers. Someone on-high has dropped it down the line through the usual improper channels, but still it comes to the right wrong person; the object in question, another momentary lapse in irregular reason, it flares up, accordion-brittle in tripartite fold, here it comes…the headline:

WE THINK YR GR8!

Dear [**insert name**]*, Thank you so very much for doing such a great job, turning up each day and being a part of our brilliant health organisation team. You have really helped to make a great difference, every day.* (all the same)

Wait, more leaves within leaves. Thumb-gutted-belly already un-plumbed, no seals can hold beyond fate. Surely that's all redundant – nothing's said that's not been thought before? The medium spells swansong but clearly lacking bones in the crux-of-the-heart:

> **N. Finwax (sick)**
> **STATUS REPORT**
> **Class: ~~Patient~~ Domestic.**
>
> *Showing signs of ~~incense~~ intense paranoia and utter disregard for both patients and fellow members of staff. Potential for extreme psychosis. Strong inner-sexual tension typified by an over-long, lusting gaze – several…attempts made. Displays particular obsession with maternal figures (perhaps mammary issues?) No more than all the rest…*
>
> *Remains fit for basic cleaning duties, but keep away from fire, sharp objects and chemical substances: both*

medical and public. Recommend keep under constant observation, fully-occupied and away from patients. He has tendency to become too attached and is often distressed by sickness and death, both in others and subsequent fears for himself, though subject appears perfectly well on the surface in spite of dishevelled appearance and inconsistent uniform.

Prescription Recommendation:

Fluoxetine 20mg, My favourite yellow and green blues supplement *one during break periods to avoid brooding and perhaps Tremadol if becomes excitable or more evidence emerges of profuse masturbation/groin-rubbing (more than once a day).* Bit more than all the rest…

Odd really, I haven't done anything wrong…and very heavy use of the word '*profuse*'? Screw it into a scrawl and prepare to hurl, little planet of eclipse – wait – keep all paperwork – push fragment deep in pocket and forget – for now – down with all the purple-blue corner clouds of lint-dipped secrecy.

Feel tips poke through faux-fur (all under-nourished) walking vertical in zombie shuffle, arms strictly strapped (the only ones) by my sides, to remove all flickering motions of desperation elbowing. Don't let-on that you're moving inside-out. Step-off this march of endless groan and I am still neither all here nor all there but getting, going, somewhere, yet.

rEVOLt

Scrubbed harder but too much enough can't seem to get the stink off. Heavy hangs, pinched wince to the pits, filtering-out somehow, without a drop-d-unk, just sitting on top of you. When everyone around you is losing theirs, panic finds you out, umbrella hugging rims and schk-kuking orders in succession at damp crowning end, mired in itself – infection controls, bleach resists – all seeking specifics. Another NORA clampdown (for no one readily-able (or willing) to survive).

Duty nurse picks up the phone: "Hell-uuurrggh!", clutch-gut-over-stomach heaves of brown-beige retch, spilling the desk-span – note the determination of carrot and sweetcorn to persist at either eventuality. Whole armfuls scooped into the nearest paper waste bin or simply 'filed away' in a cabinet, but bad smells don't forget.

Feverish decline slides further, we are forced bag-less, and so the contents cut by lattice wires, edging-out open souls hinged at orifice and the eruption cracks like a fist – every time the world re-constituted; every time a more imperfect place. Harlequin displays slash gathered sandwiches, half-teas and choked-down ash-whisperings wreaked larger than in life. Hear buried-matter voices urge violent threads for the perfect staple diet; choking out all the junk they tried too hard to hide. Preaching the saintly five-a-day plus, plus no carbs past-half-past-five, they reject the processed as morally wrong and even the dietetic angels have gone off the rails with some illicit choices, a fast reveal for the naked lunch never meant to be seen or heard.

I stare too long as fat congeals, kills time; slurs screaming escape from its sump, solids jostling to float above the scum in the mix, they are the ballast you thrive on. Yesterday's pre-packaged overnight-flight vine leaves unfurl re-freshed by guttural water, delivered straight gelatinous marbled ebb, wear your cracks on the outside, stuck at that confusing stump of fussy veggie/vegan/ sometimes fish on a Friday (but open to meat evenings and weekends).

Six months officially (plus two years un-) after the last aftermath, them upstairs felt blatant congrats were due, though it only came as an afterword, lukewarm-comfort calling late, soup with a hole in the centre. "Thanks for spilling your guts all over the thin line that divides organized chaos from itself" – we decides to ignore facts – the same strain inhabits life, showing on all of us now – we don't kill them off, they choose to die-down.

Switch to the next pandemics: estimated death tolls and NIMBY-driven awareness campaigns, budgeted in relation to the preceding two quarters, all to prepare for the disappointment of the war that never comes, another day remains foretold. Each media machine helps the worldwide spread, then old NORA comes back around, same disease, different name. That grand old QC once said, half-remembering, the rest forgetting: AIDS (such a little word) is a fad and nothing more – I think he meant the hateful furore, not the very real pain.

Language outgrows life, all too viral, outpacing the threat, we haunt our own imagination; feeding fever of desire to control by fear of universal death. Reality is often second, third-hand, and every fifth-time you wash your hands it doesn't make the lies 'more' or 'less', it's just their words, wiser than you had thought, echoing out to drain you down and away.

Clean staff held back, permanent reserve of best wine in Sunday clothes, too good to use, far removed, watch them struggle instead, you're infection-free and best intent for the grace of god, not the human in your place. Then carrying on to "survive them" is a doing-word, just like before, as must musts.

For some, a spot of ill-health strikes as fleeting luxury when you're on your feet all day until too close to the brute truth that the weak must only weaker, their rot is the excuse to let things fall. Curled in dirty shrouds, folds of the body are pulled taut in dark lines, wrought shadows of some other bodily matter, a stinking cocoon manifest made human error, the disgraced turn reverting back to a simpler body that wills itself unknowing and unborn.

Infectious medi-paranoia, a war on health to find the next 21st century cancer toy; but almost as much threat for the mentally ill. They complain about immigration, replacing the good with foreign body, another uniform xenophobe that loves to persecute on minor differences that started out so small. Each curious mind is a potential dissident, so silence all arguments, they're naturally deviant – from the city to the town, there's no peace for the cynic who just wants to ask questions.

My lonely lone cells cling to a carcass, all deadwood, that only seems to turn on, revolving. My vision's slipped: rock-back, lurch forward, hung between door and the handle, a weak left, flag-wavering with no comfortable ground in this cemented-down landscape of unendingshitsomeaningless.

Half the bacteria we try to fight already live in the gut. The relatives never understand that, they're from the outside, we're already in. They buy-in flowers wreathed in pesticides that linger long after the loved-one has gone. Most never think to wash their hands properly. Just rely on their branded hand gels and other placebos, while round the back, nurses smoke as chimneys and stick un-gloved hands all over the surfaces and digging into any orifice. But there's no soap left to wash with, just enough spit-dirt to move germs around the palm, brash rotations, bodies gravitate, no attention to details, the minutiae of cuticles, nail gaps and finger joins, our perfection cracks underinspection, it finds a way, the space in-between. Attrition is the end goal, but you can't win against invention. Where there is constant demand the beast manifests itself as new desire for old feelings, a pseudonym for life. Just like germs, all we really (think we) want is ourselves, where one will do anything, to take the other's place but this war's never over...

Occasional Thespian

Tony Pearson is a prime mover, some kind of user and the arch-agonist of his own curtain-choking domain. Only comes out twice-a-week, sniff-sniffling potential victim labelled 'improper' in their stance. Tony gets these crooked ones ironed-out through extended body movements where the cure is the repetition of the worst, getting worse before it gets better.

The least favouring the brave, he lingers at their edges, nosing-in to every corner. His sessions are a shallow taste of freedom, but only by his too-wilful assistance, the crutch that shirks its charge. By a mile of sheer inches to go; just a few more few more steps then Tony reveals his therapeutic trick: the brief hope of suspended seconds. The ruse goes both ways, now they must cross back along the same corridor stretch. He waits as an eager avatar on their fawn-fell steps that threaten breaks. For every slip his tongue zips *in/out* and the eyes crack alight that weakness needs to feed it.

"You-ve done ver-y well my dar-ling, hav-en't you?"
Nod-nods every syllable, deep fishing stirs the ocean for confirmation.
"You don't have to shout, I'm not deaf," it mumbles, "or dead."
"Mmmm," more exaggerated, slow nods, see cracks create the pivot of his neck.

Gloved-up – gets *right in there* – his arm forced to elbow as the patient stands still and all around them thoughts of feeling creep. Kneading body-in-to-body until one flesh seemed indelible, always happy to break bread over bones, twiiisting new forms from old works. A quiet evolution with all the paperwork intact, re-print in triplicate and staple to the body, then roll it over for the next one – same difference.

With Thor's minor plessor he used to shake these windows by the cracking snap of joints beaten down into reflex that submits to expectation, action that is all acting. He uses old brass measures to check optimum angles. Transposing the marched-out music of the shuffle-hustling dead into something regular and uniform, a time he can keep (and control). Tony gives this one an extra hard swing, thinking back to the early morning with the slow car start, his coffee left to go cold and his wife tucked and turned firmly onto her own side before it was time to get up and go, the one body that always evaded him.

A weasel-sharp sneer slits across one cheek, as a silent hate wipes its way down, Tony's temple betrays a vicious streak, the first tear in his plastic facade. He catches a faint titter, tries to hold it – but can't. Instead breaks into his own laugh, almost choking on the intrusion, feels him funnier than himself. Swoops over to right the broken shell off its back, all bumbling thank-yous and keening horse-eyed knees, while his look felt elsewhere; scouring uniformed buttocks, shrink-wrapped, expressed but clinically untouched.

Tony attempts consolation by **firm** gripped wrist, a reminder not to do it again, *now he has to write it up, doesn't he*? Too far, too fast – this means another month's rehabilitation – his benevolent sentence. Lapsing into grin, already showing signs of wear, our enthusiastic anti-hero picks his way over to the desk, a half-sigh smiling with the vaguest of recommendations burning at his lips, drying at his eyes. The patient's slipped from memory into another yesterday: if you bend too far, you break under their weight.

One grey day, with Tony straddle-sat facing a patient's open knee, he turns absently, shirking near underskirt hem, meanwhile keeping at it with his persistent tip-tapping toffee hammer, then **BANG!** stale tendons skip to life, fighting back, the leg came up like a boxing paw, smashing into his nose: bloody-dumbed, its geometrical slither forced awkward into flux. Tony staggered, hand cage stretched to keep remaining teeth and rigours of cheekbone in approximation: "Thtshs aul fr tdae." Schlurping down his breathshs, he gets up, leaving patient on the bench with errant knee cap jiggling along outstretched joint.

She stares bemused, as if it belonged to someone else and she was merely playing host to high spirits. With so many fluids running down the OT's fragile pus, no one could see to treat or diagnose, he refused all help. Tony Pearson went off to go groan alone, pawing his mucus blood all over my clean sink, but his eyes so mugged-up he could never read the spider-scrawl of a warning sign: "*These taps don't work.*"

After a few hours waiting on treatment Tony quickly crusted over, a scabrous mask enveloping his once acceptable face. He lay there in his own chosen space, with a curtain closed for several days. When they found him way down the ward To-Do list, it was just a flat-faced martyr who been pushed-back too far. Only vague flitters from his limp body came through the jumbled litter of stepped-on toilet rolls and ruffled apron bundles as he's dragged out on glittering black plastic. Gazing into this latest abyss floating under me, there is only a stinking fissure where Tony Pearson's grinning mug should be.

Living Through Saccharin

There are more than one ways to secure devotion and maintain (correct) levels of interest. Perhaps the right amount of chemicals in a defined area, pre-sprayed, or even better, laced heady by an effusive dispenser makes everything seem right – there's a million ways to try – but impossible to counteract the atmosphere of cumulative death that refuses to leave.

Chasing the aftermath, and announced with much glossy force, the 'Aura' experiment unleashed to sharpen and define us. Designed to block 'insidious notions' of bad smells, raising standards by miasma of pure vacancy. Nurses all against it, per-usual, with constant complaint at changes to routine, anything that upsets each their own way of doing.

The powers made a deal with 'environmental enhancement' company, **Fplag Inc**. Adopting their latest model of dispenser, drenching corridors in sickly-sweet shades of synthetic Britannia: some mystical aura, so ill-defined, but wholly supported by proxy votes, blindly revealed. Blurb says: 'Evoking a true reflection of the Albion Experience, our rich pastures of deep history and green-field futures.' (Better read as: **Decline, for man, by men, neatly bottled at the inconvenience of many**).

Smells the same as every gauche flower brought on from trivial cuttings (some are born weeds, a.k.a. wildflowers, not meant to fit) thrive hardy in the shady harvest of small acreage rabbit-hutched estates built upon old lead pits. Soily hands wipe-down trousers and nails bitten quick; lined-out gardens boxed in by racing-green diamond wire, rife with native species to meet quotas of belonging. Haggard, shrivelled-in spectres, the shape of ugly ruffled sleeves, none of the refinement of daggerish points brushing-off that other, continental persuasion – *swanly-slender necks tend toward gravity's lilt question mark uncoiling into stiletto-barbed lips*, that empyrean sense of Venus' shift at full extent.

Instead, we hopelessly calculate by dandified flowers, chalked sugar-sweet, from a windowsill pledge, oh-so quaint and outmoded blur of English borders with crippled scents. All skewed on musky odours masquerading as upright and clean-bred as Richard Nixon III, already part of some muddled family line, more bastardised fifteenth-gen-carnation, spoken like the turgid procession of royal ascent (why keeping buggering-on equates to a very certain kind of progress?) Vast numbers living hidden, somewhat ignored, under floorboards of those wilted garden-lovers and patio-patriots, so dreary and unwittingly eager to death, they'll take a reactive cue from anything you do, trapped in static insulated from real polyester feeling, given-up from the waist down.

Another flower goes mispronounced and tagged as secret ingredient of that turgid yellow mess, chicken-cubes and sultanas sold as a legitimate exotic – the force-wedged diversification of authenticity. Rhododendron spliced with tepid Pink Lady blossoms but she's always tasteless and killing grace: no lotus flower spilling out so inviting, lily persists; delicate in its quiet tyranny and they deny orchids as too vulgar, throbbing with intent. Instead there is woman, now sexless, sensuality shed for dead-end practicalities of the grinding hours to anchor a day winding into shadow-years; count them down as limp carnations dried-out flat and I am emaciated by the word – beauty – all feelings rescind.

Now only love left for creased donkey faces pushed pre-birth through a letterbox that only wants to eat our sympathy from the flesh. Heat comes cheap from an ideal of pulp romance and stacked issues of magazines offer endless hollow chatter that eases into slow-pulse thrombosis where I could not imagine some kind of dialogue talking-over the quiet crowd. She buys flowers for herself, trimmed emphatic of a limitation, like a face painted into a shield allowed to fall, anything to keep busy, withholding time, only flash of irregular pale colours to break the silence then pick up the pieces.

At first we all coped, like the asbestos, it grows on you. But when glaring scent hits with that tone of annihilating sweetness, it's a blinding smell that moves with force four-hundred times the strength of sugar. Feel the crackles spark on my ready tongue, teeth ache before touch – it's already too much. Retching on the chalky breeze, this hackneyed fragrance induces us to lesser states, drugged in waking life and toeing the line close to poison with chemicals from some East-European overspill branded Chinese. Patients and visitors show of red nose and runny eyes, beaten too numb all over to complain properly.

It leaves me sick inside, every lame attempt to dumb-life-down one more notch, to deny pain and protest of jobs in the balance, haunt ourselves as palliative drones. Let myself suffer willing blindness, the blurring of reality by sentimental smells, fake stats and embracing choke of slogans, with eerie electioneering that, just for today, might make everything seem alright.

Remind us of better times, never known, but can feel yourself adopting the hate where the hurt burns – the scum that always rises. Aura's trick is to remind us of Old England forty years gone, that never happened, after the last veterans have passed. Haig's vain incarnations still burn blood bright in *his* memory, making-up for other's lost time. So we remember them still, relics reduced to idle concentrate, sometimes to forgive, as others covet, but eventually to forget. Those left behind, too young or too old, gather grass clippings from other battlefields to make new village greens that will keep growing in their stead and rumble on about the last time we won the Ashes (or not).

Cornered by triangular powers we can only go forwards with this mad parade and on into repetition. Marching over paper fields where no white flowers go, remembering you follow alongside the sleepless shadows of the dead.

Now we've apologised for apartheid smiles, clinging-on post-Empire, it's easier to forget those other mistakes. Same ill-gotten greed as the stench of Brunel's iron-age revisited. And as the textile kids inherit this noble work-ethic stare on through, with the same blank eyes, our only real answer is to keep on shopping and look away – Boulton, on the £50 note you've never seen, says:

'I sell here, Sir, what all the world desires to have – POWER'

Always on our side the big wheel keeps turning on hinges greased in residues of the Bismarck diet. Along stern bridges trains still run slick but increasingly late and at platform's edge we wonder if the 8.15 will ever arrive, and when it does, will it really take us anywhere? All came to a head when the lady refused to turn and we were taught not to want no better. So well-spoken, but cruel with it, leave her four more hours before one last spin, now her memory can be left to descend down the shafts she helped to bury, a right-wing war-martyr with deluded sense of working-class grace, sprinting as difference became the race.

Still learning and re-learning to forget the present tense, its chewed-out taste, through revolution of our public-image (unlimited.) More powerful than the original; the first man stands tallest in shadow as new history devours the actual, now revision and the subjunctive's still back in fashion. The hollow men can rest on easy laurels and think back to doing well, better than the rest, and smiles seemed more genuine, but no less uncertain. If perfumes can cover up management sins and economic dead-weight, then this PR machine can trick me sweetly, to conceal or confess at leisure, to write and re-write our mistakes in alternative versions of fact, so when the pier sinks back into the sea and our waterlogged records are finally stamped: '**Deceased**', I will gladly swallow and be swallowed-up, time will erase me, absolve our memory, surely as it forgets itself.

Last Lion Home

Gerry starts:
"Bottom of the ladder, we are,"
(first is the most stepped on)
"Easily replaced once we're broke."
Next rung's always missing for us.
But you can poke holes
To gape through
Our complaints
keep us in post,
In our place,
No going beyond
Our easy station
But the last turn
I thought I saw.

Stream past screaming branches
dash-dashed advances, the accidental hairline
Splint to the cypher
Where wild's winds
Snag serrated whispers
Turning change over in the palm's
Progress written in the leaves
Dutch-elm scuffed;
Re-grow splinterings.
Hedgerows narrow eyes
Over-grown, discerning, strains of vain
Too articulate to be easily understood,
As man-made nature
Clips its wings,
Above and
Below.

Iron-dipped accent
Mutteringdeep
His recession looms overhead,
Temper's wrought in frown.
Heavily lapsed-Catholic tone
Lashes out
From bucolic pigeon-chest,
Fighting truth for breath
How everything really is
with each – bony – finger – poke –he–e – nun – ci – ates
Every feeling
Feeling every one,
But where's the point,
In changing hearts (and minds)
Born to go their own way?

There swipes another **GIVE WAY** sign.
After impossible angle
Camber bites hard on gravity denied.
Dents take a bonnet dive,
He blinks – too late
Another knock on wood
We pretend not to hear.

Ignorance is a form of strength
From solitude and grace.
So turn your back
On broken drum flapping
Skin that's been lived through
One-too-many times…
Annual miles zip along,
Background set by destination bent-to-Hell,
Closer upon new descent
Till we dip-off at Land's End
Rotting tip.

Gerry's seen through it all,
Rearview: road drags the past behind
others never exchanged a passing glance.
This modern pressure Squeezes us
through spaces
never
meant
to
fit
Bleeding wheels
Shouting above their scream.
Too many laurels rest on his unease
Above the clouds; grounded Albion dreams
Of keeping on going,
A particularly English way to grieve
For the living.
Over junk high-tea, fragments of potteries
and a thinning slice,
Reminisce where everything
Was better, until the worse gets better
It's hard to say
Where the offence
Came first.

So we sit UP
Straightened straits.
Keep shut.
Learn to put-up.
If (imagined) threatened.
Hiding bloodied harelip,
Stiff upper smile on full show,
Tithes split by inbred lineage,
Certain name-changing hierarchies,
the acceptably famous faces of immigration
Handed-down,
From more
Hand-me-outs.

But someday soon, we'll say:
Enough is Enough
Taken all I can
From the land of plenty
That refuses to share
Amongst itself.
After cracking our heads
One too many times
Against locked doors
That require no key of permission.
Where blood runs still
Pain sticks like glue,
Dripping splintered lines
On tattered Jack
One nation, divided,
Crashes to the floor.

Saturation Point

She's the distorted half-twin of another spindly widower. From self-exile of her suburban villa she waited for the day that never came; she grew in proportion to the walls, as the house overshadowed her body as a cage.

The outside trained to trim in plastic cornicing faux-roman thrives like empty desire, the spiders make their additions to time, but after four years you stop noticing the dust. Not quite in the country but near enough to town – this should be a place where families are made. Instead she found comfort eating closer to death, then kept-on-going, to be alone, once sex was boring with him on top, the incompatible frame marooned atop her gut. Soon natural laziness gave way and she allowed him to stay, a blunted instrument, left to one side.

Worse, she grew to ignore him, now large enough that she could hide his eyes behind the swell of her amorphous bust. Now she only covets stainless steel (denied) and eagerly moves on to finger food. Combatting her swollen needs he flicked famine shots onto the screen to show her errors diffracted. She switches back, to watch them swap the fat one for the thin one trading meals/ lifestyles/personalities (all under medical supervision, of course). By duelling airwaves steadily overlapping, each imposed their own direction, and as one consumed and cancelled out the other, so the rift grew in compensating equators.

By half-hour slots see the desperate acts of erosion and regeneration; while the remote is slowly passed around as death-knell baton to ring-out their own end. He is an uneasy executioner, shopping around for love en-masse at the buy-one-get-two-free section, haunting midnight aisles for cheaper meat, to hurry back in case he should miss her rising (by degrees) about four in the afternoon.

Checkout girls trip with patter as he shuffles by: "Ooh, he is getting thin."
"Where does he put it all?"
"Never does a small shop, does he?"
And surely-slowly, lets himself starve so she would never have to go without the necessary extras.

One day she fell trying to carry home a couple of frozen chickens in each hand. Her knees gave way, exploding into bloody-scarred stumps, like hock ends of battery birds hatched by rank into wire boxes sitting un-pretty in acrid ammonia humps, wings clipped back to the joint, a body of terminal points. Just like the double-headers she used to eat every same Sunday, pre-packaged and pumped to gorging with saline drip counting down minute steroid and amphetamine.

She perches awkward in bed to try keep her balance, making choking-yowls as the hunger takes her again. Windows are left open for the odours to escape, a stationary body setting into its many layers of smell. The distant bodies of Ward Policy would amble by, and like a ghost who feels only solitary chill, shut them on our behalf and double-lock the doors – got to keep the loonies off the grass.

We swallow our resentment from stench of too many bodies closing air, like angry fucking, the nurses dig-in to shift and sweat with her inch-overloading-inch. She just lies there, spilling over the sides, warm skin bites-back railings, festering condensation to factor five bed-sores that shouldn't be, just as rust knows rust.

She ate more, the skin grew light-thin, a weightless slab of aperture; I tagged her the Ghost of Dark Matter – Polly Ethylene. We crawl all over her, from day into night, her most beloved litter swarming constant, then rotating her quarter-turn as on a spit to mask the rolled-over erosion.

She holds up beautiful magazines glossed with sun, until jaded as dull mirrors, orange earth starved with thirst. Sighing into them she is smothered by hollow reflection, cracking all the gloss in shame. A noble ugliness, whole systems drained from a full-body hoist, where energy succumbs to expenditure. Dun-brown almonds stare back, equally flat; the exhausted I makes no demands of Us.

On the surface it's all blanched devotion, but really, we want her dead, a drowning need sinks all about our necks. And there was the huge bulk to think about, (how could we forget) living luggage too big for pure carrion. She is another aching, straining, sign of the times; when most of the docs are already onto third-bypass to cope with stress, relying on meal kits, micro-waved in secret, there's always greedy desire popping-out through the skeletal sheaths.

We could fly-tip at dawn, but the stink would soon find us out among the stained carpets and buckled table legs. It would cost a bulldozer to bury her, an inferno to cremate, but not enough smoke to hide behind, then barbequing claims by the press... perhaps out to the sea with all the rest, but soon to float up and find us out again.

"They think I don't see them."
"Sorry? What?"
"It wakes me up, that scraping about; mices with little brushes on their feet." Already nodding, I can only agree, "I watch them you know, and that boy with his floors, always too wet with the brush. They keep missing bits...skipping the routines." Slow nods to herself, something's missing there, a sliver of the past.
"OK." I'm nodding still, both keeping time.
"I'm telling you, I know how to keep clean."
"I believe you, but you should probably rest, or something."
"I am tired, very tired. Just make sure that you-" yawns lion-wide, "stick...to the...lines." Eyes drift back, gagging on their sockets.

Sometimes see coins between the rolls – there she goes now, two more coppers, but no way to count the real cost. Surprised she's not poisoned by the metal and that's been it all along. Each leaves their mark, she's branded at inflated hip with HRH's sacred face, eroding flesh into a seal; that particular indent always a bugger to shift. She stirs some more, a human wing flops with sagging crease of blue as limp echoes-long three letters known from before, I keep edging out of the lemon room.

"I wasn't always like this." I believe you. Tears swell at ten, eleven paces, feet are stuck fast but my head says GO. She hadn't recognised me this time around but sure it was only seconds ago. "I used to be a size eight, you know. I was petite; could fit about hands my waist, make-up my own put on, dress my...my...ah, you're here. Did you ever find those missing files?"
"What files?"
"They said you were looking for some of the lost years, that's what happens, easily missed. Well, did you find them?" Crooked smirk plays out, she droops sideways into snarling grunts.
"Who are you? What do you know about the files?" A whispered yell, every word sticks as it's said; I know her now, from somewhere, though these snores interrupt thought, shouting songs for the deaf.

It's her – the orang-utan slouch of old matron, the whisky slacker melted-out then cut loose. They trimmed her hair, all gender traces removed – She re-made as idle fleshsack. It's definitely her, but ousted somehow, a singular coup now buried under sheets? Must've slunk away somewhere, never did come back to work after that incident, something about drowning in food they said, another placebo just to feel content.

So bloated but still gaunt around the eyes, she stares as if it was a strain just to turn and look. Think I hear them grinding out a place in her skull, lolling onto me at rest. Nothing can contain this disease, being tough or too honest is barbaric now it's 'anti-liberal' to deny someone what kills them, brand them any label you like, so long as it's XXL, just keep adding digits.

Check her chart: she wants for nothing beyond the daily minimum, but did she really ask for this? Several meals a day, asylum from the outside, madness for a madness, another condition chalked-up at the wailing wall of modern excess, if you give it a name it becomes more real. She brushes away hair, shedding time, at least its traces, bristles buffing dead-ends and only dulled points left. In her right hand, stretched out like Marat's last grasp, she scratches absent-minded at letters, crushed-up like two zeds compacted, the sign that I was looking for, but how did she know? Too far gone in fractured possibility, these motions signal towards something beyond loss.

Full English

Finger-pinch-page, trying to separate leaves from breaks intake breath and get back to where I started. From each split halves all my efforts to flip and slit, pale cream glow off fingers, cheapening pulp divides – more to it than I thought; should have thought first. Masticating that skewed corner between finger and thumb trying to find a point I know is there, let him see you, relishing every word, a relief from every turn and sentence split before he comes around, to fold over, onto itself, snowblind in endless white.

"Every moment dies a man, every minute one is born." Too late, the rhino has landed, making big-red booms where I laid my table, more crash than sleekit slide, needling at my inner ear with its giant hair cone. What's he quoting from, that line's not my page. Which Dave is this? Bearing down with heavy heaves, he constricts the space, just existing, stealing all my air. Where was...I?

My words are all pushed to one side; now all my thoughts are of you, *for* you, still standing here.
"You seen that agency lad...uhm, what'shisname?"
Can't say I know him, "Maybe Jano?"
"Yeah, yeah, Janner. He was just here a minute ago, having a chat. Cheeky bugger, must've fucked off home."
Wind slips under, buffeting words, close the covers. "I thought you didn't like him, *them*, I mean." Why correct it? Just to fit in?
"They're alright," sniffs "I don't mind, so long as they work, but I can't talk with him long – he don't even make sense half the time."

Rocks on his heels with puffed chest, beaming wide. Proud enough, but nothing better than to talk to me, and neither do I. He's galvanized by new intent to work on our non-relationship, to gauge and gain from my reactions. But I have nothing to say or talk about, so I'm patient, same as before. I can feel him gearing-up, another speech comes to take up space; the pulling of teeth to more occupy the jaw.

"What is it, Tennyson?"
"What, this? It's by a guy called Heinrich–"
"No, not that, that thing *I* said at the start."
Start of what? "I can't remember – what did you say?"
"All that about: 'every minute dies a man,'" Every half-sentence…
"We did it in school."…we all tried everything, then. "Never liked it, poems or school. I've been thinking lately…" Listen, respond, don't try to understand…this is no atmosphere – I really do belong here.

Wait for him to *leave*? Strike up a cigarette instead of more banaldansemacabre? I could claim health grounds, force him to move on, file a report, but then just like the rest, making the most out of minor threats, even the process hates us. Flick up: no other soul around – where are all the eyes-and-ears when you really need them?

Read on:
All configurations that have previously existed on this earth
sun plays itself out, rolling from cloud to cloud
must yet meet, attract, repulse,
switch us back and forth into/out of shade and light,
"It don't make no difference to me,"
kiss and corrupt each other again,
"whether I'm coming or going,"
feel myself burning then shiver, hand flickers like fire, indecisive in its clutch. I rumble blush, purple-tinged at the bumps connecting with red brick "not anymore."
and thus it will happen one day
set orange burns-out its blaze
that a man will be born again…

"Sorry, what?"
"If I'm dying, *when* I'm dying; what should I care if someone else

isn't – what's to make *them* care when it's my time? I never had kids, right, but if I died," another optimist, pushes at his nose with all that left palm, swiping at a cliff-face, "knowing they were alive," smearing his nostrils, pig/not-pig, "without me around," up and around, a fleshy siren wailing "but carrying on my name, I wouldn't be there to see it would I? So what difference does it make to me?"

I kick heels (again) for us both this time.

"Even if a new baby was born, to replace me, by God or a woman or whatever, then I'd rather it was me, *again*, even if I had to be old. I wouldn't wish him dead, the new one, don't get me wrong, but if it's between the two of us..."

No one ever wants to hurt anyone, that's always how it starts, the 'but' intervenes and there the generous buck fastened to a full-stop. Each person wants their place in the sun; their infinitive period, though it often leaves someone else in the cold.

"How come?" – I surrender.

"I don't know really," great answer, "I'd just want to go on, I was first, I suppose. What do you think it means, the Tennyson?"

"It doesn't matter if you die or not, it's like being born, there's nothing to remember or forget. You don't lose time, it sheds you, then a new person just comes around."

He's looking at me funny.

"It's not a competition – I don't *want* to die," the emphasis on 'want' makes his face lighten, "Actually, I'm starting a band."

He doesn't say anything. I carry on about the Dead Nurse Cells and some other plans I've maybe got, neither one of us really listening, traces in the sand. The outside of the windows are dripping silver, it's not even raining. I look up to sigh, bored of myself – he's already gone.

Denny Baby

Older now, and much changed since yesterday, Den's generation were born old, so they say. From weepy lines of liver terminus spots drivelling, tears come too easy before the chance to say, it runs just to connect-the-dots. Age strikes me so horribly logical, youth as a stain that fades and never leaves, another un-removable. You have to force your skeleton grin and bear it. Sometimes I think it's whether or not you *choose* to grow old; and how far you get – so each kills their own fire. But mine has a way to burn yet.

Denny (Dennis) former First Lieutenant, shivers under lost stars streaking past and memories of his father before him going through the same shit in a different mess. Trying to keep warm but with bodies by degrees of living stacked on all sides, layers of indifference sheave the breaths slight and others, lying too, too stiff-still – all crucified under the aegis of swooping lights in streaked halo thrown to nowhere; hoping some other bugger gets it first – still they don't sleep, just like here.

Denny complains through habit that he is already dead, or at some in-between stage (we're all passing through). Certain days groan by so wistful, alone he shakes these windows, chattering loose as lids flap steam. So eager for an end, he likes to sit and guess the date but all his appointments seem to go unmet, and with every near miss he pushes it back, utterly in denial of his most recently expired 'best-before' date. Tells us he has books to return; the fight is to avoid leaving behind for others the fines. In that sense, Denny's already stretched his debt beyond the years. So he waits for 'them' to come again and put-out the lights, they never knock, it just happens. Hearing sharpens and he feels the corridor beats slow, before nodding-off, then stopping – smart – with a start, a body of drift with no fixed parts.

Staff line-by but don't care enough to interrupt, so let him sleep-in a while, as slack-faced Jada burns with jealousy, his younger body dragged behind him.

On waking, Denny whips nurses into strict doctoral-roles, forcing routine examinations, checking for death-like symptoms: pulse readings and stool samples show him still vivid with breath, huffing on the mirror as proof of life. First, he argues it's not from him, just dirty glass where nothing is clear, but finally he admits to some trace of soul captured mid-escape.

For other complaints he plays on fickle symptoms; the ghost limbs of empty sleeves, a nagging orifice, barely there. Lack of movement in the joints and waning loss of appetite, like a jacket at the elbows wears its owner's use. Preoccupied with cycling shadows, Denny paints black dog to patter past at any moment, expectation in its eyes carved deep his epitaph of losing last.

Looking in from out, they lay it on thick with hollow guarantees, but they're equally blind to his version of jilted hindsight, still seeking youth in a clock-spun shadow. Watch them at play, the spinning sophists preaching tired tones, see their colours drain away as they keep on spitting.

Always flash-at the early-wakers with curtain flicks to brightsunshine or moonsoftdecline. Needs must massage this atrophy, the exercise of muscles' reason, never letting the body rest in case its cells should lapse, forget themselves. Instead, give him permanent daylight, bound to the sun, one wakes the other and so we go on revolving.

For today, his daily bricks. Denny insists on his right to roughage, despite increasing 'code brown' risks. Spoon-feeding numb lips, turn it screwdriver-wise to part the stiff teeth. Scraping over and in with that tinny sensation, a hither-of-thithering, blackboarding slakes the alkali rub makes me share in his flinch.

Got to be chewed down or choked up, the body must have its air-way. Denny refuses to listen about natural decline, not the ghostly opportunity he was hoping for: to be welcomed at some benevolent entrance, with only one brief proviso, please read all terms and conditions before you go back around; this way, or that – all lives spared (or otherwise) must be paid for, in full.

He slams his drunken wrist, the buckling to an already sagging table. Loose lever, slips down a few inches, that knackered bracket can't take much more hammering. Picks up his right again, I twitch on the left, "This is my dead hand," waggling at me, an obscene first, though still connected to his living rest. Drops it down again, black mood spirals out from him as eyes glint renewal of the meter's continued urgency.

"In fact, I can barely use this hand either," but grabs the spoon all the same. These hands used to guide him through the sky, now with knuckles set ready to burst, he's forever holding on to some absent something, bracing for an impact that doesn't come. When he can, he sits up straight in squadron jumper (another replica) who knows whether he really was there or not?

He still has good days, some upright, with full bearing of the old-school soldier, but pawned all his metal soon after the event, the memories more valuable than what's smelted down. This gave him silver enough to deposit on the first family car and that ideal for living, but not so great at high-speed contact (hence dead-man's grip). Medals are a hero's consolation for managing to thrive amongst slaughter, and knowing they bested themselves.

Tries again with the spoon, face tense, all joints glow through translucent skin. Reminder: friends sent down to Japanese camps, better dead than lives surrendered. Slurps, I try to catch it. Brown smear gone down jumper bump, leave it, he goes on to spill unnoticed. They used to tie wet bamboo around prisoner's testicles then stake him out to dry in the hot sun.

As Denny tells it, his 'dead' paw starts to scratch away, digging the veneer. He laps down a mouthful, only one-in-five but he grins brief and proud. He explains how it would tighten, like a tourniquet. Spoon down, hands wrapped around his sunny scalp. The pressure got so great you could see the arteries throb finger to brow then the scrotum would burst – the way a balloon explodes angrily. Palms pressed flat now, making fractious star of his broken grasp. Over to me, in my eye pressing sincere: "You know, the guards would bet which one would go the furthest. Counting-out their winnings they had to keep moving the stack out of the way as the trickles of blood ran after them."

I tilt his hand slightly to the right, just to see the horror waiting on the other side, roadkill constantly overturned.
"Funny thing about it is, you try to forgive,"
I'm still trying, press the bunched fingers into shape, get his hand to mirror mine.
"You *want* to forgive; but just so's you can forget."
The people you learnt to hate…
"They tell me I'm 'acopic' as well now, whatever that means; there's no medicine for it. It's just too much, all that history, it's too much."
By learning to forget, are we simply in denial? And some of us can barely remember.

His fingers jump right back to the wooden half-fist. Think back to the bird, crushed flat with jagged Vs imprinted over the one-way body. A left wing escaped the rush, a grounded sail left flapping, beaten by the wind and lightly clawing the tarmac from its big sleep – no way to make the crooked straight.

I give up, he doesn't care, doesn't even know what's going on, but I am an obvious ear, as he scoops more slurry into his mouth at some impossible angle. I follow, both of us staring sideways. It drops off, more brown leeches run off the apron's frowned-lightning lip upon lips. He shifts feet: one bandaged double, other naked with crackles of electric blue. Between those bandy legs the corn slop streams landing with pitter-patter sounds. He laughs booming and relentless, then slips into cough-cough that sagging coffin lid trapping every last lungful.

To try is to try again, he grips stronger than you would think, but he really needs a right-angled spoon. Tell him it's better for patients gone too far. He gives fierce resistance, it's the 'war generation', won't give up anything, even when it's beyond use. I give up, shove it back at him, near jabbed in the eye, lucky: thick lenses, blunt skin.

He yelps as I throw the spoon across the room – nothing fucking works – we can't even serve the tools their use. Getting out of there as nurse passes to attend the clattering, better-off she deals with it. Denny's moaning resounds in every space, along with the constant hum you can never shake.

Here he goes, smackdull-faced with the bowl *right-fucking-there* in front of him. "Nurse, I have been waiting for my breakfast for half an hour now, in agony. I have a hurt in my stomach and been given nothing to fill it – the pain was – *is* – ex-cruciating." Wait, do I break another step – has he forgotten so soon, or just pretending? It comes again, a little quieter: "And now, I'm waiting; to be served by someone, helped even, just waiting for the pain to come again."

Mens Rea

Just me and you today. Meeting silently at odd angles by the imperfect flatness of this piece-of-shit boxed-in kitchen. Pulling in hips leans the legs but stoops the spine, neither one a straight word to say. You gnaw at lower lip with feverish, clalck-coloured teeth: almost enough to bring up the blood to my throat.

I kick dum toe-heel at skirtings, more chip-board cellulite. My foot swings a lazy hammer, wishing every time the fake veneer would bow-break a deeper dent, echo in the ankles of Queen Bitch, to cause a worrisome limp with her weakness on show.

Open upper cupboard –**slam**– against forehead, every time – it leaves its slant of indelible red, I go wearing the incidence of my mistakes. Frown straight-off but slow before any ouch-ing sounds. She starts rise, to come towards me, but knows better, when hurt people often lash-out nearest. Plastic wrappers spill down: Leicester, Gloucester, Caledonian, missing portions gone spare – all towns I've never been to. The once-neat jackets turning up loose in drawers and low cupboards, but never this many in one go, we are raising giant mice that have learnt to use little ladders.

She stands-to that one-side slouch, niggling bristles with attitude, I catch an eye but she looks away, an instant suspect too easy to blame. With those slow-wit instincts she's just the type to hide a guilty secret anywhere *but* the bin; it's her own damaged double-think, but then again, she's too short to reach…perhaps a step beyond.

Obsessing over her meddles brings hunger pangs pushing daggers down my stomach depths, a gurgling reach straight through the bowels, tremors and hand-pulling clenched, my sphincter worrying away, it expels only to be fed. Too early before, now it's too late; close-up the food just turns me off, the wave dissipates into the next acid cycle, making war in the flesh with desperation aches just to come back around.

Straining for breath through solids, suckling-up saliva just to masticate, throw it up then do the same all over again – food – its necessity – to be produced as proof of eating – is easily overrated when you have plenty – we are equally the shovellers and cud-chewers. Another patient yells for extra rounds of toast but breakfast is well over and lunchtime's an age away. Why can't they just act their namesake and shut-up until it's ready. Take a stale square, calcified by re-set butter, weakened at taste. This is just a test-exercise – to show I can – but not – barely there, just jaw yapping.

Rip air from the vacuum thick blubbering lips-split, short-sharp nasal shock thrust like a knife, a cool wave roars over me. Gunked-up crumbs and milk dabs gone way sour, faint avalanche crumbling slow-motion. Rub my hand along door inner, palm-streaks evil-smelling brown smear; all something of everything. Perhaps the agencies have been in rummaging again. Maybe *they* took the cheese, cheap source of protein, especially if you steal it, minimum wage poverty demands invention, hunger the fire that long outstrips your flesh.

"…it were Claire's *second* cousin, I think; and then they found out it was *hers*."
She'd kept going…
"Do you want a yoghurt – or something?" Anything to make you stop, fill it up. She stands and stares, a dull totem.
"Alright, yeah." Somehow she doesn't smell the beyond-the-joke dairy, so unkempt, grab her a yoghurt from the herded racks. Lid shears easy pop, but a saw to my knees, that and cutlery against teeth makes your soul shrink. See the rim, gummy glue half-peeled, another sign of the process, captive air, holding its breath. Black lines tall cage is struck-out, bars of determined life, each scratch its own day of expiration.

She eats as if in a hurry with only brief pauses for clogged breath. Small fibres catch inflections of gum and dark lines in her imperfect bridge as eager canines rising. Shine glares off eyes too bright, she makes meek smiles towards otherwise, one of the few things on her mind.

Stay hidden, searching for nothing in my silver box, a cool and infinite space but starting to stink in here. Ignore me, *please*, help me to help you forget. Respond with something blank, inane:
"Ay?"
"You what?"
I shiver suspended hate...
"I said 'Ay?'"
"Are you hiding from me in there?"
"Haven't you got some other stuff to clean or something?"
"No. I'll just stay in here, I don't want to go back just yet." Eyes burning through the meagre door, I am heavier than lead.
Breathe, breathe, let coolness come, a waterfall crush to break me in the flood.

Got to keep busy, level-out this, prop door open, bone meets bone, a dividing line, you/me. I pick gingerly at the front, paws fumble, exposing grille gaps, heave, up, oh duck, all too much weight,
...all spread sliding
away...   it slams
into the back.

Haunch spasms, collapse, slanty shelf thud-dud-duds, rattling glass, sound bigger than the crash should have applauded itself. She'll be straight over, stupid questions in abundance – all I want is peace with my anger.

"Are you done eating that yoghurt yet?" Nothing... "Well?" Peek over the edge, she must've left, but a great white wave shot-up the wall and the steel surfaces smeared – I am not cleaning *that*.

Shuffle around the door, a snow-pale face, laboured breaths and vacant stare melts across the floor. Her lights are still on and those crunch-unched claws flinch, scrabbling at the strangled pot. There's a spoon still shivering tinnitus jangle from silver glimmer, there's faint 'dink' as thermostat clicks ON to regulate its situation. Big-red beating chunks out from my chest, I can't swallow, never even heard her fall, between the shelf and the body, one of those rare, singular handclaps.

Nurses already gathered into circling, flapping feathers, she's foetal-struck and slowing time, coiling back into a simpler cell. Flurrying ants over screwed-down animal, sharpened apertures stretch. Queen Bitch steps in to divide the fickle gawkers and centres a stare that pins the burning spot to my face. That wasn't me, I was someone else.

did you even check the date
How much does she know about me, or her?
nothing really happened
Spies everywhere, but it's how much you choose to ignore or pass up the line.
and whether you're willing to tell

Pour myself a (plastic) glass, white and glossoping. Raised to lips, bubble-stuttering, can't speak or confess if you're sunk in uddering-flush. Need to forget, to bury myself in pale sea – I don't want to look or remember anymore.

I should go but door's rammed full with nagging wall of arms overwhelming the solid square. Plenty thick, this. Gloop it round the glass, it clings easy leaving a too-high watermark. We gave up using normal milk a while ago. That natural world's no longer cost-effective, the moo-cows are bred watermelon-square, the way-to-meat has become that precise it's almost made to fit for greedy mouths full with want. Once cream has idled up to an unwanted lid that sits in shadow to in-distinguish a polar scape, all more power to the naked lunch.

Now deeper into the white, she's pale as this shallow bright, and it to her. Try to stir but it just pitches round the sides and settles again in the middle, its centre persisting. Some golden sheen's crept in, a foreign body meets body, ghost revisiting its death.

Queen Bitch in front, snatches the glass, uncaring to spill, spits glaring glaze, I'm struck blank-faced.

"This isn't safe – poisoned"

"I know, right? Horrible stuff."

She splashes it in the sink, it slides off the steel, a faint, anodised equator.

"Not you, *her*."

Follow her point.

"Oh."

"We have to be sure. Clear out this fridge, all of it has to be destroyed."

"Who did it?"

it was Sioux

No – bleached residue fades, confidence peaks at collapse.

it had to be her

"Look, we've already lost three of the Agencies to some manky cheese, they've been carrying it around in their pockets, I can't have any more of this. Now, prop a **WET FLOOR** sign in that doorway and get this cleaned-up."

"Wait a minute, do you know, was it her?"

Queen Bitch seems to flinch, but doesn't turn.

"I can go knock on the Matron's door instead…"

Turning to face me: "Senior or Acting Deputy?"

"Either/Or."

"She knows already, the big one. We have this in-hand, you know. Besides, it's really none of your business."

"Do HR know?"

"Yes, actually." Eyes flash askance.

Liar. See through that hollow fire.

"Look: we have our suspicions, one of the nurses, much like *you*, thinks we should be 'making it easier' for them, but we'll find her," glances up, so PC, she must protect, "or *him*; whoever it is has decided to start playing God with my patients..." speak for yourself. She points at the girl "this is the consequence." She turns and spins away, another brittle star in the lank, loosening chain.

(Famous (ever)last(ing) words)

Kick along a raft of pages, some stumbling bundle, scrawled in dead-set hand. The spinal glue's cracked underfoot, thick cover the fade of greyskin now hanging limp. So many blank pages – who still jots in hard-backed books? Vague snatches ache so familiar, fanned about, the scrape-sound colour of a gutted teapot:

Body systems – A bad case of Entropy and Eternal Life. (Draft lecture BI145/E_)

'Eventually gain of entropy is nothing more, nothing less than loss of information.'

The famous biologist Julian Huxley who? *is often overlooked in the popular culture by his more well-known brother, a Huxley within a Huxley, whose only famous novel I found a little dry. too much Shakespeare, another original thief Regardless, we're here today to learn about Julian Huxley's findings from a study of the clavellina. A thin sedentary vertebrate which, Huxley remarked, was a creature of beautiful translucency.* a fuck-all streak of nothing...

Huxley found that when this creature was left in the same dish of water for several days it began to grow ill and slowed in its movements. So many live that way, slur-losing shine *Sitting in the stale water* poisoned by the outside *it closed all of its major orifices and retracted into itself as the vital organs became absorbed by the main body. So the clavellina reverts back to a single cell.* Life shrinks away

But it is the next stage of its seeming decay that is most interesting. When returned to fresh water the clavellina was able to regenerate back, if you will, into a fully-grown adult. Total life...forever *There is a parallel case here, between the clavellina's life-cycle and what is perhaps the most important aspect of the second law of thermodynamics – the idea of entropy.*

In chemistry, we often refer to examples of thermodynamic processes as 'systems'. Essentially, these are small experiments involving exchanges of heat, the effects of which can be observed by a spectator. For example, if we stand a glass of ice-water in an area at room temperature the ice will begin to melt until the water matches the temperature of its environment. three aspects strike out triple point – all at once He is ice/water/ steam, but also rivers, seas and rain – all is inconstancy…

Entropy refers to the disordering of information in these systems. it gets worse before it gets better. *As the ice water heats up a certain amount of energy must be dedicated to the energy transfer process, often known as 'work done' or 'enthalpy'. While the heat and time invested are necessary to bring about some kind of reaction* Another agitator *they do not form part of the net total of their sum.* agitates from the outside *It is worth pointing out, therefore, that during the entropic process the change in energy being used as work done, occurs on both sides of the glass,* equivalency? Sameness? *so both the ice water and the surrounding air are undergoing their own entropic processes, with the glass acting much like the walls of a semi-permeable cell.* Potatoes wear their jackets thin…*Although, in the end, all energy must remain within the greater overall system, which contains numerous other systems, all fighting to become the same, that is, to gain the most energy possible, all heading towards equivalency.* cannibalising other systems just to keep going

The point to remember is that the entropic process is reflexive. It dictates the direction of its host system as well as influencing other systems around it, almost like a virus. If we were to open a window in the room of the ice water system, entropy would increase to compensate for that influx of air jolting the system; attempting to chase the disparity, if you like. Less with more, mantra for a modern age

In almost all cases entropy increases over time, by definition it must.

Therefore the current level of entropy should always be greater than the initial, like an accelerator continually depressed. Ideally, the system should reach kind of equilibrium and then stop. Infection barrier weaken the weak, caged disease

But due to the feedback of recycled heat there is often confusion when monitoring entropy across the borders of different systems. The issue being that only "pure" theoretical systems are sufficiently clear to give an accurate reading at any given time. In reality, these exchanges of information are often distorted through continual change, and are thus unreliable. Black lines fading into grey

All this energy transmitted between systems carries with it an inherited sense of this growing disorder. Like an infection *The longer a system continues to absorb a greater amount of energy, as entropy must, the more probable it is that it will lapse into chaos; become uncontrollable and unstable, having shed all sense of its original purpose and structure. In this way, an entropic system can appear to be growing and developing when it is actually being eaten away from the inside.*

Look back on new future promise; desire for progress to make progress and so a better order. Change brought you to your knees, keep spending just to dig your own grave.

All the observer can do is try to predict these behaviours and build some framework of understanding that can accommodate the breakdown in communication but the longer the process goes on, the less we know about potential future states and so the options for change are steadily narrowed towards a definite end.

The key problem of increasing entropy is where all the new energy will come from to feed it. decadent and dying... *Even in a (theoretical) universe that is constantly expanding, how can there be enough energy to supply all the systems that will ever be? This is the same energy,* ...our time is running out *the same cells, recycled throughout the system that contains all other systems in the set, the totality of life.* As well as itself? *At any given time, only half of the world has light, sun and air, and the rest is darkness. It is my view that this has always been, and will become, our past and future for all energy, and that this darkness will grow..*

The constant transfer of energy between heated molecules often causes them to dash about wildly. When entropy occurs the independent motion of each cell soon descends into uniform chaos spreading same ignorance *as cells come to hold near-identical values. But without sufficient energy to sustain this increase* we breed waste *it is probable that the state of "heat death" will occur, where all cells are forced to share the sum total of energy too* thin *and so grow cold until they eventually flatline, a state from which the overall system cannot recover.* entropy kills karma *Like a fire left to burn itself out or old stars that have come to dying and we are only seeing the last years of their disembodied light, no new processes can rise from the ashes, such rebirths exist only in myth.* When it's gone, it's gone...

However, the clavellina's lifecycle could yet provide us with hope; where new life is possible from seeming nothingness. The organism regenerates itself using only base protoplasm to construct new cells. From almost nothing, a substantive organism is reborn, recurring to a plausible infinity where the genetic desire to reproduce and maintain existence supersedes the laws of true death by term. Sit perpetuum, etcetera etcetera...

While the clavellina's regeneration might seem to occur 'sui generis', the energy required can only come from breaking down its own cells as fuel for growth, with only a trace amount of original tissue being found in the eventual whole. Therefore, it is the clavellina's withdrawal from life, into pseudo-death, that triggers its rebirth.

everything's stretched these days.

Effectively, while the "new" clavellina is a different individual from the original organism that was starved to death, it is also just another repetition of the same lifecycle.

A la mode/In the fashion.

*Having established that the clavellina is able to regenerate beyond its means, one question remains: how many times can it repeat this process before there is some lasting deterioration, or true death, from which it can no longer recover. The longest an observed clavellina has survived was for one-hundred and seventy-eight regenerations. In theory it could continue this cycle an infinite number of times, though the same human observer might not live long enough to observe it. This process brings a new order to the chaos of entropy and true death....*it drinks its own elixir vitae.

Although, there is the possibility that a single clavellina's existence might eventually come to an end through a relatively new theory known as telomere shortening. Telomere from the Greek 'telos' – meaning 'end' or 'goal', in this case referring to an organism's genetic structure. This naturally occurring process comes about when the repetitive DNA at the end of a chromosome deteriorates. wearing away at the edges... *The cells therefore become "shorter" the more times they are replicated, a kind of death clock that counts down the half-life of an organism.* Cycling off without the chain

So to come back around to my original argument, there is a crucial link between the two processes discussed in this lecture: the decadent and ruinous nature of their behaviours; theoretically infinite but equally damaging, and the increasing entropy in all energy systems and eternal life for the clavellina, that, either through heat death or the wearing of a circle, must live on towards some perpetual erosion or simply fade away.

The big-red keeps beat-beating, everywhere and always, and so the world marches on.

While the many lives of the clavellina will probably continue in its cycle, coming back around *the entropy of systems can only be destructive. Yes, the universe continues to expand* what does that have to do with me? *but the clavellina can only survive by consuming all that has passed before it. So the unique qualities of the first system and its identity are also swallowed-up – which begs a further question: where along the arrow of time did the first, lone clavellina cell begin?* All individuals will be sacrificed by the rest

Perpetuating sameness, the nature of entropy will eventually rule over all systems and the individual adding energy upon energy no future growing and wasting all the time tick-tock, indeed until it's expansion becomes so confused as to be lost once the medium of delivery takes over, biting down hard on its own tail to consume and to destroy as it rises and dies in great swells of energy, all wasted absorbing matter and time. No new knowledge is to be gained from this we never learn and the cells within the process cannot appreciate their own gradual shift into evermore erratic behaviours or even be fully understood by those on the outside. another modern monster

So entropy pushes ahead with a muddled sincerity for life and a latent death-wish desire to grow deeper in disorder; the blind lead the rest on to slow death and the system never sleeps, while the house burns all around us it never stops growing, and all just to repeatedly collapse in on itself, again and again.

As Huxley himself put it in his final thoughts on the Clavellina: "Few creatures or even basic organisms can regenerate so completely, most are simply eroded by life."

E. A. Boxer M.D.
Nottingham, 22/10/1977

Deadmouthsirensgobreaktheirminds againsttherocks

Ron must keep to his room, where no one but the nurses are allowed to go. Held under Nil By Mouth, he can't eat so he's wire-to-stomach-fed, a life in-vitro back to childish ways. Ron doesn't speak but points and moans from a leering reach, yelling stillborn words at numb objects, no willing them to life by his empty call.

Nurses yell back at him, two barking heads banging against the same mute wall. They tell him to 'quieten down'; I try asking what he wants but rapidly losing sense, poppling fish-mouth without the bubbles. It all ends with NBM-Ron throwing everything in reach. The sobbing nurse tries to return fire with limp toothbrush and broken smile from a jagged comb; it all follows after her as she retreats. The remote for the new TV, Charlie's brief legacy, soon follows.

Sure as the sun, Ron wails but doesn't know who or what he's shouting for. Half his brain fallen away, rest is due to follow soon. Left hemisphere's concave sunk where a piece of skull has been removed – (lost (mid-operation)) – now awaiting synthetic replacement; a half-china plate not sitting right. That dark patch inflates and drops as he breathes, a puffing adder's blown flush. When panic or anger set in, he quickens and swells – beyond the word – lost in his cave with the bellow's rush.

Mustn't speak about what we don't know or try to understand too much. Trouble is, there's always some know more than others. But too many choose not to speak up and so lapse into dumb silence, while others have no voice to begin with.

How can you really tell what's alright for Ron or not? That face can still articulate some, but all faces are deceiving; doubly-so, dripped to one side. So much coming and going at once, a failure to transmit, perhaps not even the same person anymore, trying to reach out from behind flattened eyes, lips and frown.

Mesmerised, and so in love with that coarse-heft canyon of breaths, I start flowing in his sway. With him the drunken earth cannot find its way. Ron tangles his eye around the open doorway. It jots about the collapsing socket, but remains locked-in. I stand jellified, fixed useless as his being quivers over me; a dapple of life, as the leaves give credence to a breeze.

Three-fold streaks of colour dash past, blasting green-blue pastel haze, the surface slashed into Doppler phases, fenced-in by a series of raised hands. The naked palm's a blatant **STOP** sign, but they continue on regardless.

Watching Ron, watching me – feel useless in the cold stream of nurse trails hanging upon their electric air; a well-ached warning in wisped ribbons of crackled static, as many layers are shed, then replaced – process generates process.

Sweat-lick pressed-V into the chest, now rushing for the beat – it's the loose chain of Ron's billowing hearth, the big-red shaking our twinned cell walls; ballooning to make waves and I'm sweating uncontrollably where nothing needs said and only pulses left to lose.

> Nurses push-on ahead, stick figures swallowed in neon show
> tripped elastic emergency switched.
> Me, him and our loneliness, shared;
> vacant by accessory. Turn back to the shrill space.
> There's Ron, ox-strong, with his half-a-lobe
> missing. He staggers, crabbling out of the room,
> sifting steps too light for shadow
> to pull behind him that heavy chair,
> like some minor Atlas,
> over-thought, our little world
> at his diminished feet.
> Eyes' axis tilts,

                                    life goes over
                                    tipping-trip;
                                      gravity his
                                         enemy.

Bent arm un-hung, he straightens-up to starting. Side steps sink,
topples ever-so brightly – I shift earth by inches.
Rights himself again, casting-out madly
flailed hooks, catchless. He grinsoblique,
a brittle monkey secret smile,
does not have what he
might know
to smile
about.

        Push-pulling expression his stolid face worn infinitely serene
                where determination overrides his desire to crash.
        But then he goes, the eternal rug pulled from under. A sharp trill
        yells: "Catch him!" I step forward, before and after thought, her
                                words sparked from my toes
                raking sharp tones up the spine. Time moves with us, our
                        placements – to mark the territory of the scene.
                                More paper-thin people stood
                                with full-blown eyes quietly sagging.
                                Not sure how to act (without orders)
                                perchance to miss of your own accord.
                                He collapses the long way down,
                                        a skeletal tower,
                                        I think of Gerald;
                                                his ebbing
                                                    fists
                                                 closing
                                                   fire.

Drifts into forced entry for some imagined ballroom, fear-
stricken sways bathe the shapes
of our dark recesses. My partner in axis, without will,

crumbles our selves, stacked so high.
Soft-raised catacomb of hidden honey bones,
my arms graft to his, weight taking on water,
force the buckle of pressure.
I think at old myth:
a ton of feathers
in freefall,
still hit
like
bricks.

Know that panic – his big-red-rushing – pace outstripping the
chase, one cave thud-hudding lubb-dupp
in a hurry, synchronised irregularity.
To find tips touching tips; searching panic
we reach for the nearest ones,
arches lean on each other's
rapt embrace,
our bodies,
a suffocation
I am
used
to.

My arms thrown around the world, he jars skeletal edges
we coalesce at borders' stretch.
He beams up at me like an overgrown kid, wound too tight he
strikes off-kilter, to burst from his box into these abrasive forces.
He fights back the flow of progress, a contrary warrior now
clicked into life, making new sense
the way sandpaper of shark
is a living key, picks apart tides,
its invention the rupture
of the seas.

I notice flakes of dead skin brittle snow;
inspiring age, the thaw falls free.
Smaller and smaller sight fades into them,
disappearing before they reach the ground.
All mired in blinding white;
abyss succumbs
where sensation
outruns
the
eye.

The scooped-out lobe is booming furious flesh, his body quivers like a willowing hat-stand, spun out on thrown starfish. Finally unbound, but with nowhere left to go, Ron's a drainer, weak before the knees.

Slowly, gently, more fingers infiltrate the crushed lines, we are removed from ourselves. Blue-green bruises still hold limbs the colour of broken glass sweeping streets. Warmth's ebb only felt as it leaves, negative architects scraping flesh from my stone. His desperate hunger burning a long candle of months, oxygen sapped through a straw.

I thought to drop him, keep to my own, but know I couldn't, wouldn't, really do it, just raw wanting. To see his tinder-stick chassis scatter the floor, benevolent as the bomb meeting tender eggshell of many thousands, little pieces to house their own. Let the Queen's nurses amble in to save whatever's left (with or without sound.) But it's late in the day now; time the sum total of waste, broken to fix him. "All better now," they say, a simple reminder: so much better, together, a few fickle, missing bits, the total is its difference. Ron removed to his solitary cell, and so into the past; to remain, just like me, divided and incomplete.

The Half-Spectacle and its Discontents

Whispers crept in early that winter had already broken: "The Spectator is here." Frost rides strange waves, distant valleys brought close; couched in slipped *eSSe* escapes, leaked gas announces through closed throat, every throttled-hush corridor. Thin layers sheathed the metal bars of every bedside, hummed below zero at the throttle of rumour, we dreamt of fractured birds shattering the bounds of their skies in widescreen. Patients complain about a large figure, looming accused, passing for dusted velvet in a Victorian mourning suit, face shaped like a wedge of moon, its cow-cradle split right across the plate.

I wanted to dwell and found my ideas wanting, for once, no blame to one. Something speaks in its stead: *forget, forget*. A reshuffle trickles down, filtering into "reorganized", with sour relish "optimanized", every word clipped mute-efficient as an anagram, the doorman that won't let you in. Same old merry-go-round where you can't step off until someone gives you a nudge; the bony martyrs can't help but peek out at your breaking in their fall –we cannot relax– we do not know enough to forget– its giant smile swears a heavy pendulum over us.

It could be anyone; just popping-in to measure-out determined obsolescence. I have started to plot my movements to the smallest part, with the least motion possible. A knocked keel keeps my eye on the level for hand-washing stations, at thirty-six seconds gel consistently filled. If we fail, he falls and it all comes back around.

Expectation is a swelling, puncture comes its bliss. I think of Gerald, Gerard – or was it – sameness, lost in symmetry; the white that was not, but who am I to nail a memory to anyone? Chameleonic flags flap and wave for a stolen territory that no longer exists. Our identities become by acceptance; uniforms inspire naiveté no matter what stripe you choose.

You give so much to become so lost, just for them to let you cut your own cloth; when I am most afraid I shear cleaner lines. I stare too-long watching all the doors shut on time (18 seconds, full close, articulated retro-rod) and count all the locks for full bite on the nose, a crick has come up the neck just to see through every disguise – everyone's an agent, a prostitute (for sale), it's just a question of who uses who (and in what order) though the matter seems less which you choose.

When I sip, gulp, spit or stab at meat, a shot of life to make it jump, seems less sterile on my tray, always I prick at you, the watcher, hoping wherever you go you'll feel it too. And when you come my way, here's hoping I'll tell you what I *really*, think this time around – honesty is the hardest thing, to make the world stand to order, form wild hairs of grass teasing wind, to a forest splinted-straight.

Something slap-dash and wriggling, insipid caterpillar limbs make naked its offering. Trying/takes/hold, as if by reasonstinct overlaps so you do things without understanding. Paper-fine flesh spent feels on finesse, mercury slight that seems to shake endlessly free within its grip. Go through these standardised motions to become more like you, a smoothed fit, passing-on the greeting in flickers of dulled speech, hear myself behind glass. Keep eyes down and away, surrender everything but the moment, held apart it waits to speak but can't fix a word.

The hand is just a humming to itself; concertinaed fire looping eights, desperately, to unfold its infinity. We're thinning platitudes time stretched. A lusty overreaction falls on all sides, the panicked grasp shreds leisurely tears in the Gaussian glow – ghost chasing after (our) echo. Try to deny it but for the breeze curling up and over my face, now in/out with the fades, he is my closing precipice always too close. A fate-full pull, like gravity pouring water into space, slips me away with his sour grin, flux revelling after symmetry.

You look for too long and the notions become ragged. Wanted something I can feel and to know that it will stay solid, without decay or disappearance, another spare breath swallowed-up in yesterday's heavy bleaches that hang today, otherwise this terminal vagueness is just another slow tyranny, bit rot of the knowledge.

Drunkened-in-with-his-over-swoon – ready to retch. That wall is slunk way down and unpeeling from its place. Reach out to stick it back but the needle-thin tears always show through. We can never stay still, with only faintest promise that things might get better.

"Won't take my hand?" He aloofs, breaking distance. "That's alright, its alright." Telling himselves, "I know that you lot prefer to be out of the way, but thick in the action." The digits slowly subtracted."I couldn't get...sorry, I *could not*.." Why correcting myself?"It's alright, catch your breath. It's been a rough few months." Before I can reply, "You should probably sit down, you look quite pale, unwell even."So I sit. Legs went from under, "It was my hand, you see?" Wavery deliverance "It's been on and off for a while, and I have been feeling a bit ill, actually." Did I? Do I? "Well, you look, sort of *terrible*. But don't worry, you're in a hospital, safest place to be, in some ways." As it's said he looks away to one side."I guess so."

He sits alongside me, together staring out, but no more bodies to blink through, just endless facing up to the cracks against us, spreading ivy-viral, widening the gaps and leaking up to the ceiling tiles above, lightning in reverse.

He edges over, as if too slight to notice, I look down, pretend not to. See my same tattered sneakers next to shiny-bright leathers on that hard and fast floor, it will outpace me. Faint café crème it's blotched as occasional stains of leopard on camel skin, I still see them even after I shift them. He smiles, lips stretched unnaturally thin; already emptied reassurance. Shift the pasty white disc to his 'apologetic face', pre-empting anger, it twists and softens, trying to gauge pain like an unwelcome taste.

He adds a small pair of *pince-nez*, twice, another, another hollow gesture of removal. Slashed-sashed semi-eddy-circles, barely there, peek from absence. Pushes them up just so they can slide down again, then checks and re-checks it, absorbing the action into slant routine. Places those small black holes on me, sucking vapid at the light – struggling to focus or focussing struggle? All the while feel he's pushing me backwards, maintaining distance. Blinks too many times to be natural, even in this constant dust buoyed-up by snapping heat there's a firm refusal to see clearly the ugly truth. Starts to load a pipe, pinching hard every time like he's wringing out the last dark strain, always taking things further.

"I thought you would be a woman?" Why ask him *that*? "So did I, in a way." He checks four, five nails absently, surprised they are his, but no return to the subject. Look over his gleaming free of expression, can't tell if he's serious or not. There's nothing like nostrils but still some wheezing motion as the blue smoke goes up, up, then sucked back down and away. Eyes wince, turn and tighten, staring endless into the seam between the wall and floor, finding the same nothing through it all.

"I mean," turning wheels within wheels by his hand, teased-words are so carefully rolled-out, it doesn't matter whose whats are misunderstood, "most *Domestics* are women, aren't they?" He nods away – housewives, servant mothers, nurses, cooks (not chefs) stand-by-siders, arm's-length lovers, lift-giving drivers, stay-at-home strivers...more than adjectives, but most refer to ourselves the same way, something neutered-numb, and less than human, just to be understood.

Waves away his own emphasis, "It's nothing personal, you understand?" Pushes blue puff my way, didn't even see him light up, no alarms? I nod without agreeing, he coughs himself straight.

"Hagkrumpf! – Excuse me. But it's good that you are, you know, what you are. Not that there's anything wrong with it; being one of them, not *them*, sorry. I mean, they're very...good, ever so good, in fact. It's just that I wouldn't want to suggest any difference between what you do...not that I am too, uh, overly-familiar with…the routines, but you know it's not so much what, it's how you do it, really – if you see my meaning?".

"A lot of chaps at our level," they weigh so heavy on us, "most of us are men, but we have to be, you see?" Sniffs back brisk (internal reins). "It quickly became clear to us, at senior level, that women make excellent carers; they're sensitive, compassionate, eager to listen, and obviously, to talk." Begins to snicker but quickly swallows it down. "Ahem, but they're not suited to the axe and grind of upper-level management, not like us. The best are all bossy; the rest are simply hysterical." So many mothers dominating, and every one of them knows best.

His main game is upping knowledge, one over the other; pissing mental territory. "I don't know–"
"What don't you know?"
"Everyone seems to make things work, I just wish there wasn't so much bitching, at every level – and the guys too, it's such a destructive way to run the place – and to live. Some days it sort of feels like you can't trust anyone" especially you "and yet you still have to work with them."

He frowns (feigns?) surprise, smelling a potential convert. "Well, yes, exactly. Many of our most senior nurses can be very… cold, clinical even, which sounds good – in theory – but it generates a lot of flak for us, and heaven knows, we don't deserve it – *they* did it!" His bony finger meets junction of my shoulder. "Let us just say, then, that I understand some of your concerns, but you must see many of these people, the basis on which they were hired – they were made for the role, as it was, then – not for things as they are now. People have to keep up, we can't all just stay the same and become relics – progress outpaces us!

"I have also noticed they seem to resent the patients an awful lot, and the families too, for some reason. I have even been told some of them hate the job itself – it's like we're verging on an epidemic for which there is no reasonable cure." Ignore the metaphor, it will go away like a dog licking at a dead smell. "Anyway, because of this particular…" wheeling away again, "…temperament, they're adept at going through the motions and they always look quite smart in their uniforms – don't you think?" He wastes no time, "Obviously, underneath it they seem to be *seething*, but it's that anger that helps get them through the day really; to finish their seventy-five – changing soon. Then we'll all just slip off into retirement, then back here I suppose. It's a bit like a fox biting off its leg to escape the trap, he wins in some ways, but he still loses." He muses with a fist, "It's funny really," unclenches and taps some ash out from his pipe, "we preach compassion and understanding…teamwork skills, but really it all means nothing," follow it down, the molten dust, "when all we really need is authority, the discipline of a *system* by which we can maintain a hold on them. Although, the more strung-out they are and the more we remind them of their duty to care," I thought it was duty *of* care? "the longer we can make them race about; get the numbers down." The floor doesn't look much worse, he adds another pinch.

"Wait a minute–"

"The ability to command, to speak with confidence over others when everything is just shouting and to make things happen, whether they're dealing with a patient or a fellow member of staff. In short – to do as they're told – as we're all told!" His arms triumphant – a vacant embrace.

"I've gotten ash all on my new shoes," raises one leg of butcher boot, an arched nod, "Chang von Mocha."

"Very nice. I'm saying because everyone is so set in their ways they've become complacent to everything else, they lose their ability to empathise with anyone and you give them less time and less opportunities to do so. Most of them seem to have forgotten why they even cared in the first place."

"Well, there's no real problem with inefficiency as far as I'm concerned. We just shed the slackers in the new fiscal year. All

the culpability rests with them and their own state of health, for which we can prosecute due to unsound mind in a position of care and trust, naturally."
"But if they're just too stressed to work you have to give them more time off, right?" Just one thing after amother.
"They have holidays,"
"Yeah, but the way you describe it there's no real choice: they've got to work or lose their job."
"It's twenty-five days per annum. Besides, we can't let people just stay off work forever because they want to."
"But don't you understand? It's not the job; it's the conditions you've created – that's what makes them ill and then it all feeds back on itself – the healers are becoming the sick."
"No, I can't really say I do." He blinks too quickly not to be annoyed. "If I might change the subject for a moment, I don't suppose you've seen a notebook lying about have you?"
Notebook? "No, probably – definitely – not. What does it look like?"
"Um, sort of tan, sort of black…beige is that?"
"Brown"
Ok, whatever, it will have a, um, pseudonym of mine on the front, initials E, A, B."
Two E-As in one place? "Never heard of him."
"Oh, well…" He coughs like a piece of loose string, too long to be natural, checking me for cracks out the corner of his eye.

"By the way, I might as well tell you, we're going to have a wage adjustment."
"Adjustment to what?"
"It'll be minor in the beginning, the same for everyone, then, ahem, moving on to further cuts, that is to say, no more overtime, or sick pay – sort of a total cut."
Everything seems to matter less when the money goes, except where I can get what I can before it all goes under.

"It's motivational, you see. We want to get the most, I mean, the *best*, we can out of everyone in these final months together; we can't just have you all jumping ship like rats. Anyway, it doesn't really matter now, you can't leave until it's all over." He laughs a guttural, simpering boom.

Stare blankly: "Why can't I leave?"

"You belong here, we can't run the place without you. You're legally obliged to remain – duty to care."

"I'm what?" Sees my staring but goes on regardless.

"Re-read your contract."

"My what?"

"Should always read your contract."

"I never got one."

"Well, if you had, then you'd know that you were automatically signed-on as an emergency standby for extra hours, on a voluntary basis, of course. You'll just have to trust me for now."

Leans in with heavy glower, each tooth shines brighter now, up-close jagged zips of lips, some buckled others crooked-set. Now it's clear – he's properly broken; the one who has no choice but to open up: "Well, it's as you said, you don't have any choice." Grips my knee, feel him twist-pulling jar-lid-wise.

"How long can you expect all this to carry on? It's only going to get worse."

"I agree entirely," more surprises, "but it was never meant to be a long-term thing." That brittle, aloof voice again.

"What was?" *Wasn't.*

"The Blind Pilots project; it was just another scheme we threw together over lunch. It's failed in some ways; and more so in others. Besides, we don't have much choice now but to knock it all on the head. Otherwise we might end-up looking really, really bad."

"Blind pilots?" That doesn't sound good.

"Yes. We left you all to your own devices, to let things run their own course. A sort of experiment.

"It's like a lizard, you see death for one part means life for the whole, this way, the company survives."

"No, you're just hacking off a limb as an excuse to leave the rest to die." Our metaphors have thin skin.

"Correction, we are: 'ensuring survival through exacting procedures.'" It's cruelty, measured-out at arm's length, prolonging terminus. "In more everyday terms we're 'striving for extreme normalization'; no free-radicals just beautiful routine, a squaring-off of the perfect circle, if you will. This is hoped to yield a new system, a brand-new experiment, more or less sustainable, then on to the next one." Hell are the perpetuates.

"This is how you facilitate change. We restructure our people-power towards a more dynamic future with best practice outcomes for all relevant stakeholders who will be engaged at every stage on a need-to-know, first-asked later-answered basis." Kept hidden behind closed doors.

"Why now? Why not before?"

Answer: perhaps you never listened, never wanted to be involved

You again!

It has been before

"Well, now we're aiming for...what's that word where everyone's in on it?"

This future's been here forever

"Synergy?"

"Yes, synchronicity! I assume you've read Weston Stanford's, Finepoints of Micro-Management?"

But I said 'synergy', wait – where did all those dead voices go?

"We studied it in sixth-form, but I found myself kind of hating it." So many wasted lessons, asleep in business wet-dreams (mine and theirs) as Geoffrey's patience was gradually spent, throwing marker pen like a warning knife into the desk just to keep me from nodding-off again. Even my younger self was beyond all hope of fine-tuning.

"It makes for excellent mark-bites – a million different ways to say the same thing – all so very new and exciting – every time!

Besides, this is our opportunity to change, to make things better, brighter." Or to fuck it up again in a slightly different way.

"I have a vision to do away with all of this awkward clunking back and forth," we sleepers, into buffers; bluffers crashing blind as night makes us. "Instead, more controlled conditions; they will have to keep coming to us until we overflow with new stakeholders, we'll stack the aisles with our nearly dead." Eyes beam bright with twinkle of new investments, "Imagine new ways to cure and eradicate illnesses we haven't even invented yet, you can trade on a T.B. comeback, invest in the rage of sickness as health – we'll rise and fall together, as a society, scraping flesh from the margins, in perfect synchronicity."

He sits splitting grin over his logic, so far gone in the headlong rush, spilling-over excitement to tie-up all those loose ends, tighter. Eyes veering out of reach, just like Sioux, he's a dark peak pushing us over the edges, beyond feeling, too far into unreason, where nothing and everything makes sense (to itself).

"You can see my dilemma: cost restricts space; capacity constricts air; so naturally we'll be forced to purge our intake." Great utility. "Besides, I thought you wanted a more natural system. In fact, yes, you must remember, we said so ourselves." Odd phrase. "As it is we control the flow of infections so patients can only build up a light level of antibodies, which means they're very vulnerable when, or if, they leave and re-enter the real world –it's time to open up the flood gates and the let the whole system flush through, continuously. You're missing the bigger, big picture!

"This is a new way of practicing medicine, a whole new form of life. That controlled-infection process is a thing of the past, let us allow nature to take its, managed, course."
"Infection control."
"Never mind, it's all about the future, today!"

I stare at melting ribs of a radiator, they hiss how your soul cries out, trapped, bubbling over. "It gets even better! The cured patients will become the next team of medical staff; so long as we teach them a little OxMed, dress them in the right uniforms, no-one will know the difference, and no-one will be able to care – it's all about the greens, the blues and the white coats – and the odd yellow vest for tradesmen types.

"They'll be useful, and cheaper, for a while until they start to get on, or get promoted, but then we'll just recycle them ready for the next wave." All will flourish (in the short-term.) "We'll have a new kind of hospital, total life – forever." Beaming expectantly, my words glaring back at me, rearranged in his ugly mouth – an open and closed wound; like static its pain won't settle – starting to wish he'd never been unzipped.

"The problem is, you and others like you are not so viable as you once were. I mean, Blind Pilots is out of my hands now."
"Well, who *is* in charge?"
"Oh, there are people far beyond me, higher, higher-ups, some slightly to the right, but it'll be someone else that has the final say on everything."
"So you're just moving people into different jobs?"
"Well, yes, and no; we're actually going to move the hospital."
"Move it?"
"Brick by brick." He nods.
"But the people *are* the hospital." Their slogans now slipping off my tongue.
"You sound surprised? It's just easier for us this way, making a clean slate and all that."
I stare blank-faced.
"That doesn't make any sense, it'll cost you more to move it."
"Well, yes, but I've been informed parts of it are listed and therefore quite valuable, we can borrow against the equity and offset that by future profits."
"Profits?" Before preservation there was no price.

He looks surprised and embarrassed, but keeps on talking:

"Matron, there's only her now, we can't find the other one, is still on her heritage drive. So we'll reconstruct this place with a big ribbon cutting and everyone will be happy. And it'll always look good too: old, but new at the same time. And the best part is we won't have to update the innards – that's where we make the saving."

"Nothing ever really changes does it, under the skin."

"Well, no, not really, does anyone? It'll be somewhere else you see...the building..."

"Right."

"I can see you're not too impressed, it's just designed obsolescence – everyone's doing it."

"That *does* sound familiar."

"Exactly, although I would like you to keep most of what we've discussed today to yourself. You'll only panic the patients and some of the staff might take it the wrong way and that could affect their work."

"They're *already* angry."

"Well, yes, but I don't want them any angrier, of course." Sighs, "You know, it's done me good to get some of this off my chest, I'll be much happier when it's all done and dusted." Fixes gaze on me, first time since he started speaking, "We're quite similar you know, you and I – I'm only here to mop up, the same as you."

I remember now, you could barely walk the halls between the stacked-up lies of hidden files and without hearing fevered whispers of 'liquidation' and 'mothballing'. Now the context is clear and explains so many disappearances along the way. Of course some will still have prizes, those long-term rewards promised to us twenty, thirty years down the line – but the rest must be recycled and like it. That's our lot, to serve, forget and then to be forgotten, another faceless role to play, only acting as ourselves.

"When will it all end?" All these systems.

"I really couldn't say." All these bodies.

"Can't or won't?" All this endless life.

"Not for a long time, I expect. As I've said: into my head, out of my hands." holds them open, trapped wings beating vacancy, another flaccid lounge act. Compelled to pull at sleeves he tugs them defiant, out from the hems going, going, gone – all tatty jack. I blink and he's away with his smouldering sense, like we were never even here, just some stain of ash left behind, swaying snow-driven patches onto my floor.

Recycle Yourself

Out to the place of empty roads where silhouettes hang spare shapes of wondering under fiery night. Where all voices are rushed into speech under heavy pretence of getting better, faster; getting faster, better.

This professional promenade's preserved still as flat fiction, reeling pages, now reborn into a wintery form. Vice-like, suckling at the iron web it pulls down the sky to meet cracked earth, the surface re-laid in zebra-stripe divides. Black dust shuffling has been swept away, floors bleached fresh and everything is in its right place again – the burndt-out ward made new.

All this time, they've been rebuilding from the inside, when I was sure it was ready to be demolished. Months down the line have stretched into years, something new has grown in the wasted spaces, or is it just another virus, taking its time like the leech borrows life?

This air's clipped to ice. I breathe-in short clusters, an intake of fright as the big-red tries blossom against its fractal flaws. Sent here to fetch and find, but getting wetter out there for the way back across the yard. Already bucket-damp in the shoe-cracks as my feet flump-squelch steps. Catch warm clouds to remind hand flexion, but the damp has already crept about sawing the joints thin.

Power's dropped-out but there's no one authorised to flick the switch. The locks are seized and the spare keys lost, meanwhile M.M. is now on 'permanent vacation' (her words), the other one 'presumed missing', someone said. The bereft are left in charge to send frantic messages, now we're edging snowbound as the sky shifts into solid concrete wash.

Temperature reports threaten below zero on the ward and our

needy apertures are leaking heat. Need more blankets…boil-up hot water bottles? The rubber perished long ago. Generator heaters? Double-no, sold with the scrap. Without power, everything's a hazard of heat and fire, the long, quiet frost is seized by regulation.

A long-legged splinter comes away from clean lines. Scissor break starts at the wall's edge, unfurling softly it moves out against the sheer, suspended light. More shapes emerge: arm's arc and turning twist of head – what is that? Some shadows running track-fold ribbons, pick-out a creased glint, another polyester stick, but whose is it?

Step on cracked plastic, shards skitter into giggling peaks, then bitten-down as they try to swallow the noise. Dancing limbshakes reveal themselves full in silhouette, cutting quick dash across a blue square. Do they see me? I stay still in darkened stance, perhaps backlit in profile? Try to flick a wall switch, dull thunk, should've been fixed before, though the power's still out.

There's selenian glow of borrowed light – quick glimpse of a young face, the ecstatic colour of flight. Eyes flash around, just like the static lateral ones; same glazed terror of white-washed sea, surrendering with a worming creep as we passed watchful over their beds. Make a move forwards, up close security glass fractured like a bullet wound. I blink and it's perfect squares again, another puddle that's been reset.

No one comes, no one goes – we must be made to understand: hospital staff only, visitors with the strictest permission – these are the rules I depend on, knowing what they've come to expect. But from the outside, looking in, they never understand the work we have to do, the days of narrow choice, damage compromised, target-chasing and the latest infection risk to remind you it's a game you can never win.

The big-red drives harder and there is a blurring instant, more salted lines run, can't tell one from the last. Am I back in that white-tiled space, no difference amidst the crying shame.

Seeing hollow white reflections of Gerry, Gerard or Charlie the permanent ghost?

Trapped eye squeezed through anima-white, forced from a corner. It looks at me, dumb and half-blind, but sympathy is fleet and passing. Spectator knew the rules, passed them on eagerly. Understand now I'm just another agent, to be used or dispensed with as necessary. Only under this umbrella could people like us flourish in our design; at the same time shaped both crooked and straight. Am I just recycling his words again, repeating our doubled-up thoughts? Almost convinced –to forget– but not quite myself – it's already in me, and too late to pretend. Huffing deep breaths to bring focus, tired acid runs the length, just another modern monster.

Mad fractals blaze away to remind me: broken nose, flashing blood, tears in my eyes as new stars advance bleeding into the glass with the big-red blooming. He was older then, much older. Besides, he was asking it for with that cane and always getting my name wrong. Rubbing my forehead furiously, no dent, no scar, but I remember the dark rush and the greedy nurse gone deep.

Pale fire dances over lolling curls, waking up to touch-paper shrinkage, spurred-on by a losing breeze. There go astral peals of flame that lick wild and vivid, peeling-off all the surface skin. Barbs peak into glaring points, jutting out –**BLINK**– specks of orange drift as lilting spores of heat, repelled by the cold cavern of the walls, firm and soft, it leaves no impression. See the rupture of a cell, burning into iris, into memory: eats its own tail under the surest, blinding light.

Words float out on black water. Scattered A4s spill from buckled chests of filing cabinets, their clean-lines kicked, breathlessly out-of-step. Measurements, accounting stats, death rates – so many scores noted down in dotted stares. Like some penal recorder, it's stitched into every pore, scars that keep on running long after they've healed.

There's traces etched of modern hospital stripped back to fading flesh coffee stains that sets things in the closing distance. Boys kneel under men, stacked in neat ranks, duty-bound flatcaps and starched white above the elbows, ending in thick-black hands made to be claimed in fire and dirt. A dog stands lapping, proudfoot mascot, heeled to the command of women, kept plain in white, a hope that would outlast them.

Shared minds fastened to the task: we care a lot (but not too much). And everyone smoked because they said it was good for you, tea and two slice kept the fires alive, not asking for more than your means and the promise of one good turn unto the other kept you safe. Until porcelain dreams aged into cracked enamel, its shattered smile from bedpan rush to the iron frame, a skeletal ideal toward a cage. Racing into the future, progress towards 'the modern', they could not keep up with themselves. Now broken and apart, soon to be erased, its history revolves around the clugging drain, sucking us through an effluent straw.

Distant voices sing: "best to be without you." A floating chorus, without mouths, without mothers; crying to the absent ones. Slight things shimmer off the walls, smoke damage clings to the flattened lung sagging into exhaustion. Now the last panes are melting in a distorted image of outside popping vulgar bulges as a siren waits-out the night. Drips of glass teases out a long word: 'Necrobiosis' where lone cells lose their function, break down and die, only to be replaced. And it's hot in here, too hot to think outside yourself. Dragged back to ashes, back to where it all began, with the fire that hungers for its mouth, shedding skin as just another process and the big-red's left behind, a gaping bla–

Coming Round

I am tattered flag becoming, and this, my last chance to make waves. There's a scraping, sheer and constant from that silvery pipe. Drops crowned from the fall, that sharp orbit then explode in sweet circumference. Each one's a moment, halted, devouring itself as the spare ones coalesce to shapes so indecisive.

Everything has led to this: our supposed regeneration and a final return to the body health-politik. Take quick sip, just some wetness to keep me swallowing, but mouth's all tied up and these words want out for themselves.

Push through shaking hair, little thinner. A little wet suck the skin from a finger, split from the childish spout just without enough handle for grip – are we sinking or just leaking? My limits begin at the end of the bed, talking's against the rules, but no matter, I have no voice left for shouting. Seen only sideways for days, clinging to the edge's definition protects you to know keeping inside the lines, though the bars keep me hidden in layers of time.

Turn and turn again, but only feigning sleep. Pretend this isn't happening, rolled up with twisted sheets, descending into lap of sleep. The white's a shroud, dumped with spare grace at the idle foot of my rusting stump space.

Lucid intervals divide the coming and going, but spreading the floor-space thin. From hour-to-hour watch the gaps grow as blue waves split, there she comes, saintly in giant Vee. Sometimes just wide enough to peer out but it's just another change of subject. So many of them, sat bolt upright in their bed; looking tired and ill, just like me. Otherwise there's flies crawling at my elbow, sucking my last from the ugliest end. Too slow to swipe before he's gone again. Nowadays I react very, very sl o w..l.y.no time to the… movements, back and forth. It's something they've got me on, to repeat, every day, to repeat and…what was I saying?

There's a dead foot been left in my bed. Icy toes clipped metal rails, tuck back under the blanket, too short at the top; one cold or the other. Wince, curl up and into myself, night draws in with me/ warmth spread/closes its arms about/fighting back from the night of big black shapes that move my walls, cutting swathes of spotted, dirty light. We shrink away as the world expands and retracts/ every spare inch is stolen from us in other ways/touches hurt too much/twist me till I snap. Who did it: Paersonné, Perzona? Something foreign like that.

Getting sick of this one-way exchange: look lively, look sharp, or you're left for dead. There's no option to resist, only good behaviour gets you noticed. Kick covers off too many times/take them away/sometimes we share in rota-slots, and you shiver/ praying for footsies/will warm again so you can walk out here one day.

Won't sleep tonight. Too full with remembrance yesterday/ thoughts piled/high/height/getting distant/further/looking past skies' mind/mind's sky/new things come/memories made/old ones pushed out to make room/get this dead leg out the side I complain about fragments that haunt themselves – to do with me nothing – speak my stories but no one knows my world anymore, pieces of a life that exist in museums, photographs and at brokendown jumble sales/someone will find me/new stories to fill the gaps/I'm the new antiquity/labelled with dead-people names like George, Albert and Phyllis and Nora. But I can still look back at what was once my future/ebbing out/mind's on the blikn. Can't even spiel /right. Odd Left thoughts–
     skip,
can't   formulate   the
...t   gether,
     to remember/everything/or   get   past   the   first
last   line/
/ am I becoming flag's tatters / of all/I wanted to...
     say.

Sun comes early, just past six. Light blinks on in narrow strip – who invented these ugly, glaring things? Fly plinks mad around it (same one as always) or is it moth's blush of dust that gives us what to sweep? Sounding hollow, hits itself again, again, just to get free, know that feeling – escape becomes the thing, not what comes after. Plink-thunk, plink-thunk, repetition's a reminder of that tap, tap, tap under fingernail. Now it pricks at me again. Don't worry, I won't/can't/start anything: all my fight is gone/drained/in becoming.

No such thing – a good time to leave. Of course, they deny it, holding up mirrors to prove your soul shows (more echoes) but I know my sickness. It's their job to bring me round, to think positive on my behalf, as if that could make it all better. Hate that softly-sweet approach, there's a long word for it; sits above sugar…I forget, mind only goes so far/even on straight roads/I meander. Still, there's hope/might get better. Sign glimpsed yesterday, familiar, but no memory what it means, 'pallet-tithe' – is that really a word? Tied-to-the-pier-pyre? Lick teeth, probably past half-way point for the dentist.

Another spasm *kersplatchm!* Some come with sneezes in open palms, offered-up to God to placate disease – but no-one to share these feelings with. Take more jabs into the body, quick-sharp pains to cure even bigger pains – pinched 'till there's nothing left to give, a pinked purse puckering rush. So many people buzzing round/what are they all doing? With steely whispers/tangled ears/repeat myself/repeating/don't care who else they have to see, ask and ask again, sick of turning into my wait. Right now, across the night, someone else is suffering, fading, and another comes to take their place. But this is *my* time, until I let go. There is no else – only ME.

Reams of paper set down, they've got a file thicker than both wrists. All diamond-teeth edges, what about the missing stack I went for? Never mind that now, someone will do it…maybe – oh, it's that outside propaganda. Big, bold, ugly letters:

'BLACK WIDOW' NURSE COPYCATS SELF

What an odd fish...but too heavy to lift under all these useless supplements. More yawns/feel slipping/drifting/with thousand-strong seraphs/shout for the nurse when I do/we make a clashing chorus/I'm conductor to their lightning cries. Been slaves for all our lives but at least I tried, instead of being churned round and round like the rest. Now my voice is one of the many, a number – take him first! A single bed to fill, keeping beat as one, we know the other's pace like the clocks losing time as they chase after themselves.

That's brisk/distant wind/can't reach to shut/blowing deeper chill into all my aches. Nothing to be done, other forces rule over us/ must remember to sleep once in a while. Flat thump-thumps and great gasps of flooding over me; veil gritted memory. Broken jaws of collapsing walls, demolishing the pier-hive, I expect. Cracked spire scattering/brick by brick/imploded under its own weight/ had to happen/spiders dance in the asbestos clouds/imitation neurons to feed the dread/we grant welcome breaths to its return, our beginning, your end.

Soft steps force me stiff, right along the legs, marching up the neck, hands flinch – a big flash of colour – it's just the young lad dragging along after his awful racket. Steps around with mop in hand, close my eyes, pretend sleep but he sees my laboured half-rising. Cooler now, its shadow sweeping over me, he knows I'm faking it, wide awake in surrender, *open your eyes* it says.

There he goes across the way, something like twenty, twenty-two? Eager bright – hungry to death, but he's a way to go yet. There's nothing behind it all, just empty rooms, another place to be alone.

My sight getting worse. No strong features you'd say, hard to place him but that anger shine through. Checks around, then makes mad-dashes, scribbling in secret/feverish/ streaks/filling a white square. What's he getting at? What could he possibly have to say? More deluded romance for the unattainable ones, that tired desire spurs them on until the next one, another beyond mother.

Now pushing that mop back and forth again. Sweats heavy as he cleans, it's all in the frown, his last push goes into every one. I was the same, in the days before. Erased with my name, I should've written it all down, like him; a reminder for the new ones – then they'd know – I was right all along – not just numbers and figures. I could tell you stories…if only it would let me – maybe you wouldn't want to hear? I could tell you stories.

Green eyes, lovely-looking lad; straight-up through blood, skin and bone. To him I'm just another grey figure in a sideways world. Catch quick glimpses when he's busy, both stare/never together/ thinking we just exist apart/our own little lives/more links in the chain.

He lets the spit go, leaning over it, waiting for the break. A long strand hits a pearl slick. Runs the mop over it, some red streaks in there – bleach'll do that to you – splashing and flickering about until you're in the same sump.

The numbness is forced open, rumbling in the gut/what's? Someone pushes a thick tube, around, argh! He's at my plumbing, pushing harder, "let go of me!" move slow arm round/bad angle/it clicks again/wiggle it/to remove/some other hand/not southpaw/ feels fake/not bandaged/not *mine*.

Five-legs crawl and speak over my shoulder: "Stop that! Let it alone!" All around is white flurry, tucked and re-tucked. "You mustn't do that to yourself." It's definitely a she, one of them. It stalks off, right across his floor – I know that moody look. Let silence reign, 'and we all get wet.' Ha! Seemed much funnier back then.

Blue on blue/shirt matches the pale walls/his outline cut through/ sticky bones showing all over/cloth front swinging/a drunk's sway, wild like ripped flag/scattered bags and newspaper lines/slung about some faraway tree. He's lost footing in the sweat and the sulphur, grips fast to that pole, which is master to the mast? Faint scratches run along in pink rise, I smell crushed leaves, bitter almond – rotting sweetness. He stops, stands to breathe, inky smear crossing his forehead, checks his hand, talks to it, mouthing angry letters that don't talk back.

To the toilet: is that too far? Far enough for a man my age, whatever it is. Not using the bottle anymore. Can't go with it at this angle. Easier to sit tight and let it come. Can't go...or go on like this. No more energy to keep up, keep trying...damp skin / on bone/palechickenthin/knees/press/better/to lie/let it go/go let it/ lush flush of warmth/shout at us when they come round: better to be free of it and face the scolds. Maybe it/ll be better, better tomorrow. It has to be; that's why we go on.

Could do it properly if someone came to help, but how long ago did I stop trying? Know how it goes, they'll say: 'Why didn't you call us?' or 'Please use your buzzer.' I did, three hours too late. Crying hoarse/they walk on by/don't hear me amongst all the rest, besides, buzzer is just a button, no voice at the other end. They say it's a pitch too minute, to me it's like mosquito squealing in my ear, at the wrong times I hear plenty.

Less of a person somehow, 'in-valid' they call it. Everyone's supposed to get everything for you: washed, fed and ironed-out straight, then put back to bed again. Some say it's a luxury, but there's no mystery, not when all you want is to get up by yourself and escape. Just like everyday, ferried here to there, no idea but to be exposed and spoken over, like a corpse long overdue: "Sorry, but you're just not the kind of patient we're looking for."

After staring some, adjustments set, she leans overhead to wipe down wall. Heaving breaths dance to the hoops and whorls as she scrawls the wall; chest pushing at the buttons, buttons pushing back. Bigger every day, these hefting spells. Can't quite twist... look aside at this brief wonder like a cathedral lid. Peels back a loose hair; is that for me, does she see me stare? Neck tendons writhe, want to reach up and **BITE** leave dot-dot-dash in serial pinch. "There we are now, all done." To no one. Lie buried in myself, a blunted arc – I am object now.

Own body escapes me/in whiteout folds/skin's sucked dry/the enclosed/reduced to a hide/all the while/daily fac-fac...*faculities*/I used to think/say/do/sink to cotton creases/more atrophy flesh/less\human with head shaved/skull of skein/limbs framed by the lack. Cracked posture spells out 'failure bound'.

She's new, I think. Tired-prettiness, pretty tired. Sauntering sleepily past – is that fraction of a glancing? Not as young as she looks from the side, spilling grin saw-teeth, frigid autumn bitten leaf. She stands, just watching, I shift under sheets. Duty-bound, take my hand out from under. Can't escape those sharpened almonds set above a greedy smile.

I'm a column faller further onto its broken back shadow, only to be observed between pinch fingers, drawn out to a fine scar/struck/across her nose/a tear that cries lightning/rub frantic under hook thumb/eyes wider/slick/a cigarette, puffed bitter tart *tout suite*, there comes some memory tapped, then pushed out, too many lungfuls of this place to blindly swallow plain sight – surely this is No Smoking here?

She winces, the singe's sting; scowling through, not fully healed – the more I watch think I know her less. Try to concentrate back on my square inch of wall, that smile's worn away. Maybe she knows my name...branching shadow makes squeaks against the board, against the rain.

Heavy waters drive down window panes/that permanent delay/bloating further an already swollen world/so many denied, already feel myself...scratching...at it. Red pier brick is poorly-gauged, tide of silt and riverblood/sweep over tarmac/all for the drains.

Now, falling into hours/dreamt again...fading in/out\waking in middle of the end/where the real day waits. Losing sense of harder things/splashes/collide/in rushes/spotted puddles/red rushing. Pressed to cool glass/fade reflection\I'm just a copy, like same silver ripples washing over us. Desperate to move beyond image/ held in dulcet pane/frequencies hum still-life/Come clear, it's not so bad/tell myself again/it's not so bad/to stay awake/to try\here comes the flood.

Yawn/to yelp/sleep sucks downwards/falling back on bad habits/ must try stay awake/to see the night make shapes/shuttling the numbers/remove my clothes and things/shuffled positions/ collective feathers ruffled/in sleep/even sane men wander free/ forgotten chains of time/but don't want to/no/I want to forget/ or let me collect dust/erase me/as sand into sea/too many faded stories/on repeat/and all of them end in our deaths.

LdiAgrhKt

Looks like rain as droplets scatter, shook loose from clouds to make cross-stitch of the sky. As it thickens in rhythm there's more spider leg trails, one ceding place to the other, then draining away together. All will be recycled to form new strains in the slick blue of permanent glass, fragmented territories, that light and dark melting indivisible.

Close enough to fade away the outside scenes, my nose is a fickle smear, pressed tight like ice. See reflected bodies pass behind me in stale slideshow, together we vegetate, our happy house, ripe for observation. Still standing opposite, the fractured pier bleeds from cracked-lip gutters, another sign of the unremoveables we wait to become.

A yawning creak dives its way back up in memory, something comes, or goes. A spear of white torn in the corner, the shrinking door has been left slightly ajar, the faulty electronics given us this seized chance. And yet, they don't notice, don't even try to run or reach out, already given up. I'd go myself – but there's still more work to be done.

Think back (more forwards?) remember some meeting with Queen Bitch, more a dressing-down, the last time we both tried to talk sense to each other. Hovering at desk's edge, throat hoarse to blood in her mendacious airs, my words a swollen lump, harder to swallow without spitting back. All in now, standing hard in vagrant stare, lost not what to do with himself when no one listens, so the heart's ironed-out into gradual flatline. Heady aura clings to walls – throbbing with vanity – we exclaim echoes of ourselves, amid drum-drumming of her nails at the desk; lion's claws rehearsing a million ways to pin the mouse.

Dumbed moth thunk-ing endless zeal at the glass to bring me back -**thunk**- how long has it -**dunk**- been at it? Does it even see itself, constant trying to fail, well aware that it's death-by-rote? Crest-face shapes settle in, trying to escape the rain as it beats small explosions of dust, chiming scales with the little deaths, their disembodied voices all returning to ape my loneliest loneliness.

Beam of blue splits the night's raw singularity, splinting to fractures by rain hail of pins and needles – pain without point. Shot with panic all limbs quiver, electrified by the ache of rumour – they've come to take me away.

Make my body fade whisper-thin, press myself into the wall melting-in to that lifeless span press; now it's all I want to disappear. I only hit him the once, it's not like anyone died. They should take her instead. I could tell them stories; what she's really like – the cruel spires instead of teeth, another lady-grinning soul's solemn pretence waning with the masks.

We're all guilty somehow, but her crimes rise to acreage of human mass, so corrupted, now history weighs on her to drag us further inside. Gathered ash in orange sacks, the new scullery snow of charnel churning after shreds, fragments and excess paperwork.

All movements suddenly splint-juddering-ring apart: get them in, get them out, in and out in/out/in/out/in/out! Limbs strike the pace as the green man's beat overrides the rushing by. Hear him smash puddles just waiting to be broken but everyone else is so desperate to avoid getting wet. I stare with time held still, these twisted-out eyes rubbed up against ugly sheen, see glass worlds collide at play. No right to demand that the perfect should remain, but it's too easy to go mute-hard in a world turning colder, life slurs as time gets faster.

Lights thump out some heartless tune, bouncing new waves from body frames and shiny bones' Zimmering angles, the massed isosceles pitch shadows on the wall as splintered gargoyles. The fragile people stand dark and tall as crystal castles with the elements already burndt out. Each one envelops the other, wearing the same slide-off noses, a battlement to set-in eyes under whispering weave of old hair styles and combed-over wasteskins. Where trouser ends fail to meet absent shoes and the barrel rolls of ribbed socks fall for want of flesh to grip.

Scuffing past, hear that strange name slip by, so it's *her* they want. Too many missing ones gone hush-hush, the shroud is slowly slipping. And what about the girl? That crooked silhouette now suspect and victim of this whole indelible mess. But it's strictly a hospital matter, to be dealt with internally, no outside eyes allowed. Threatened by the bright-lit glare of the press (**BOLD** headlines making truth more than it is) while a free-thinking nurse is set to be blown apart in widescreen. Yes, she went too far, but they'll never ask why she did it or what it really means. The voyeurs are circling watchfully, ready to expose whatever you can stretch to the Public Interest, which changes by the minute. On the spot, something sticky at my feet, don't look down, the salt sea tint will always find me out.

The green man steps forward, nodding sagely with furious writing deepening into the boldness of his grimace, but there's no body to be delivered. Queen Bitch appears, calling after him: "Tell the board will you, and do send him my regards." "Oh right, yeah, I will do." "Yes," eyes flash about, "tell him it's all under control. We always take care of our own."

Complications

Eight pints of blood
Lounging into foreign departure...
four hundred-thousand beats,
Take a pamphlet, help yourself – to help yourself (if you can.)
that pumps five-thousand gallons,
Read on…
through four chambers...
Inside you and every me.
take Alpha/Beta-blocker.
To resist the pressure? (only chalk dust for days)
Waiting now, wanting to know which way it's going to go.
Why not Gamma-Mother, (*mea culpa*) I wish she would just let
me go.

Lower the leaves to see what's going on. From crinkled corners
more light protrudes and as I flex, room is bouncing with the
butterfly beats in every waning chest, spilling 'Lubb-Dupp'
extremities from the page's wavering.

Step up, no more sitting around set to go under like the rest
waiting for something to happen. Toes tapping over left leg at
half-cock, only sign of life is queuing to find out if your ticker's
really stopped dead since you last fell out of love. And so, embrace
sleep, or is it just cholesterol choking on its own grip?

Approach the main filer, she's stacking sheafs just like the rest.
Never seen a sick man but charted his leavings: not-quite-zeros,
refusal of baths and other dirty measures. We catch each other's
eyes – then break, both look away, but she's pinned by line of sight,
no choice but to hear my complaint.

Half-listening she taps away at some brittle tune I'm sure I've beat
before, reflex knows it well, my left moves with it because in here
the song's always the same. No one looks you in the eye as you

walk through endoscopy room, shuffling as they sit, everyone keeps to their own version of events, waiting to know themselves better but avoiding the shared embarrassment.

The tap-tapping finally stops. She's scribbling absent, then looks up, obviously tired with nonchalance and the papercut itch. Twist my neck to catch a glimmer and even with her eyes fixed on my sideways face she dashes more ciphers: a flattened 0, some Zs then flipped omega – but what does it all mean, these repetitions scrawled in every crushed-up space? I slip round the corner, out of her way and she seems happy to ignore while the rest are left pondering how I got ahead without prior consultation, looking forlornly at their stubby numbers.

Her name's on the slip – it is the girl. Now blind to basic truths, though it's still right in front of your nose: the closedown is coming, some things best taken lying down, ideally unconscious. Shuffled indignant, even in sleep, that's why the clenched sheets and yellowed outline. This shroud will be burnt, replaced and written off as a dream, a pure murmur from behind the veil, hanging-on anomalously. Please don't turn the lights out yet, I want to see, to wait a little longer where there's time.

Stagnation seems to accelerate under this pressure, the constant coming and going with tattoo-YOU eyes: manana manana, spiritu shanti shanti, give me mana and grant me higher caste to go chew fickle on bananas while the primates starve. Going on as before, so sap-happy with incidental licks but no attachments ever mattered – until this one came around.

Not dead yet, kept abreast by the rise and fall of her thinly-covered chest, some might still be saved before it's all swept away. Broken walls collapsing into dusty halls revealing steel bones. Files shredded, our history will evaporate. Now nurses must learn to care for themselves instead. Bleach all the surfaces before you go.

Stand behind paper curtain folds, the voyeur's shield. Haunting concertina sways along with my every breath, like a porous blue organ, the seconds swell cavernous. Patient shifts the covers, rustling out and loud, my instinct is to look down and away, always waiting to be caught.

Someone's come to check but somehow fear always helps you find your feet. Shuffle back from the gap growing higher past mid-shin, but my clumsy elevens stick right out, wriggling underneath. Tilt back awkwardly, just jarring pinch of calf skin snapped between wall and the bed. Swallow quick **YELP**, but some sound escapes.

Peek out from slit, gauzewarmpeachskin: narrow people pass in slivers but they don't think to check, nobody really expects. Same as Tony P their minds drift miles out, curtains help us to forget. Footsteps flash past, all blues now. I shrink back, escaping the tithe of a tailored rip, see it maw-maw away, a hungry mouth as they attend to her. Arms pump, ripping and resetting sheets to stir quiet vessels, with the limbs pressed out neat – all for her own comfort, of course.

Watch them press her, this is how it happens, name on the system, logged-in, flowing through the serial strip. The black lines of your lesser genes means: 'Does Not Accept' a swallowed-up hole, she's another in-valid now. It's the final push to send her drifting; go jump on clouds. I should move, now, I should've said, like so many times before, stuck fast like the others failing to count, forever waiting, pretending to want to do something...

Wish I could say it doesn't matter, but I'm afraid – all of the time – when we fall, we go hard, but still cowardly in the face of cruelty, threats of pain, its lonely place, diminish us. The smart game is to let those feelings lapse – save yourself – desperation preserving the body as it sheds, becoming less than human. You either care too much or not enough, but quick to forget it's other people staring back as you lapse back, still intact, into the easy skin of a very modern monster.

Wait – I am/I'm not, all what *they* made me. Spent so long paring down my hate to find who's to blame it's slowly swallowed me so

I can't remember anything else. Nurse prepares the arm. Wearing clean gloves, a fresh rarity. She dabs soft at the vein with an alcohol wipe, absent of mind, as if it was a stain to be taken from the floor. She keeps going, the memory plagues my sight, washing over the eye until the next action takes hold, moving down to fingertip circles and the wipe is worn away to a neatly-drilled cloud – how duty corrodes us.

Her diligence, so rarely seen, unsettles me deep. Trained to administer care, now she becomes another sick dose with knowing consequence, and there lies our shared insanity. Going overboard for the still imperfect murder but leaving the rest to be finished-off by neglect or 'best practice' efficiencies. Our great medical minds had been so creative as to mould and shape all our futures, to fashion and promote new generations that live on for longer. These systems now so decayed, with too many ideals crammed-in before breakfast, soon to be stripped for easy millions.

Replaced for a 'better future', drawn out from the past, now those visions of purity are killing us slow. They harp on about some good old days of crystalline service before the lights blinked in and out, back when people used to dream a deeper sleep and mean it.

We enforce mutual care and respect (ostensibly) regardless of incompetence or self-abuse. But hope fades as we surrender our last defence, though the dividing lines were blurred from the start. We lapse and slip over so easy, lost in the natural extremes of the everyday.

Flicked-at bubbles' sovereignty, must find their own way out to escape the cone. More precious drips shot into the atmosphere while they trip at playing God. I'm slipping, every fragment of speech is madness designed; we've become our own private joke and no one's laughing anymore. England made me, now we must sit through the process as the new ones cycle-by, propagating the wrong way to be. Mere visitors at our own funeral, we stand ready to throw the last spoils of earth on still-living remains.

There it is, the final plunge. I'm another moral impotent but the rest still functions regardless. Fingers deep in my pockets, some lone pulse runs deeper. Watching her push off, feel that movement, warm and familiar, but so unwelcome here in the still, hygienic air. But even as she disappears in front of me, imagine her hand, not mine, slid down and around in these vital seconds as I go on pretending to decide whether or not to step up. But this decision's, at best, pure instinct, the illusion of choice and another conclusion forgone.

Can't help it now, the blood has sunk into my swelling grip, pulled to peel – it's her again. Yes the feelings slur so old, familiarly distorted *et-cetera-et*. But knowing that, why do I still feel the echoes urge – is this even fun anymore?

First murmurs at friction yield no control and yet every aching, unloved part of me is here in the wanting this. Too good to forget and she's here in with it. No one deserves this shallow celebration but our negative legacy was born out of such snatched and fractured minutes. Fingers, cut at the knuckle, float over me following the stale hint of cheap cigarettes, cough sawdust rough, Queen Bitch intrudes even here. I could shake the fumes away, kill my release, but I don't even try. Want this feeling to stay for just one more moment, just like the last, our jilted rapture held-up to admire.

It's the girl's dying act to give me a finite taste. A drip of honey hangs at the point of falling, makes time elastic. Just like the Bitch, I yearn for pride of place in her arrogant lust, but it's enough to feel ghost hands betray their motions. With gloved whispers on pure skin, there's no more bruises, no more *hurt*. Hairs rise to life, bound at static surface, shaking and waiting to feel it. Quivered breaths tremble in waves so erratic – and I'm there, real enough in her last choking lungfuls, some sharp release, a brief dying with her – our kiss –divided– skips the moment.

Wasting over sneakers, spat wild over the floor, more streaks for the sun, don't care where it goes. Step it in, wipe it out thin but it doesn't do the viscous like it should. Breath heavy, force myself to swallow silence, I'm lost in the tunnel centred on that one thing. See out the glimmering column, no bed, no girl. Pull back the blue curtain sides, step into the quiet, the spaces we leave behind – her own little nothing.

EXIT is another word for ESCAPE

The quiet has followed me home, stepping on our footprints, it remains the day that leant on me, pressing for answers. At blunted compulsion flick bitterly at viscous time like so many spare matches; seconds wasted on things inexpressible – the words don't do justice like they should. Some just over-think much too much; nothing's nothing and there's comfort in that, but there's still so many things left not done, unsaid: a fury redux that haunts all my gathered apathies.

Seems stupid now, should have fought-back, and for something more than myself. In culture of complaint every testimonial is recorded but the mass is left revolving spare; satisfied in its orbit, as words are stockpiled ready, more ammunition for the next war. When they come back around all the truths you've helped to spill will return to swallow me. I've said nothing *real*, only fleet ripples in a rusted sea I couldn't hope to tame. Too many waves I made for myself just to swim against, and all for the sake of my feverish sense. On the surface, bared teeth breed violence – but it's just more cloying desire, scraping tenderly at hidden feelings. Waking-up so determined not to be overcome but losing sight of the end when so many promises are forgotten soon as they're said.

Have I reached it then? That naïve plateau at the final scene where the guy wanders aimless for something so indefinable and it's only at his lowest ebb he realises –reborn from weakness to conquer all– that the narrow dream's already bought and sold from under him. Even vague regrets (and other such hollow platitudes) are too heavyweight to justify. Life pissed away, gesticulating wildly, no open hearts to show and here nothing grows. Instead, reminisce in ashes for that dirty word 'empathy', shrunk back null and void. The heel's been twisted and turned to eradicate every last trace, spread so thin, I hope that some remains.

Remembering then, those blank people stare back into me. Tightening sides crease the image: a sliver of hair cast in sinking style, mostly greystone and far gone, a hand-raised mannerism pretending peace while the trapped mouths keep screaming: **GET ME OUT!** Pale ripples shoal to no crescendo, forever fumbling at affective disorder to try and make the right pieces fit.

Fields of snare-slept corpses are laid down for the afternoon. Hold that same glare as Venus body, orbiting surround, it goes stilted with limbs misshapen: the day's reclining contortions into dried-out orchids. Like bony stars they re-christen the sleeping effervescent, cage themselves stiff in their whispered claws. Corner crept from a spider leg, feeling-out the air, venturing into widened jaws, as the interminables snore, a gash in time's horizon – but not yet ready to join that ghostly acre. Overgrown in poppy stain and lily-like smear, the others lie without last names past their full-bloom. Strewn wild and floundering, your dulled hopes persist in Albion dreams, forging ignorant new skin without question. All these pasts you elevate, with their cracked enamel, deserted cockle nets and ugly spires, chained into an easy row, are equally what holds you back. What do I owe to these foregone sons and daughters, now so mired in dirty waters? To who, (to *whom?*) to wit: t'what? Too fucking *woooo*...

Walk to the nearest door. Perhaps I was never meant to be another 'Nathan Finewax', or even the first. Switched around like the new Swans or just another struggling Boxer, born into work, brittle thoughts and twisted play. The latest incarnation (frigid petals twirling peaceful on water, *remember*) a simple clone of cleaning actions (round and around) rotating out, *in situ* of her vanishing memories. There she is now, marching out those three recurring letters like a scar's pride, and that gangling lameness parades itself over the prostrate songs of myself, even though all the words you used to sing and learnt to love are proven wrong.

All must live through Nathan's dreams, as and when he do the sleep noises. Our buffeting thoughts are grasped in every shunted nod and each workhorse sees the same sweat in the eyes of the other, though pulling in the opposite direction. How much of enough is enough? A little memory blurs spacetime (indistinct). What once seemed simple is not so clear as the good and the bad ones re-learn the same mistakes. These reflections are long overdue and the inevitable weak must die first.

Took the uniform and made the act my own, assumed our cliché stretched to the limit of play. Used to be another one of them, just following orders, nothing specific but to clean and look busy. Now their play of censure had, *has*, no tangible effect, nothing more than denial. All that you know has been said and done before, by you, *for* you and without you. You show too much faith in dee-en-ay, bad medicine and imperfect design – for the grateful last, this reality is still something to believe in.

Above my head, letters announce themselves, now sight's awake to the glowing-green surround. Set free from their starched white sheets, the dull-born colour hints at a once-bright spell. A disconnected wire hangs, more power out, soon to be spent. But for me it shines beautiful, my own cellar door cast in plastic promise of a man out-running time.

Let's draw a line – go start something new. Gerard was right, all decision is mine, is now, simply waiting to be taken

-PUSH BAR TO OPEN-

She'll try and stop me, erase these new futures and undiscovered lives but the brightness of lucid dreams overcomes her. Just as stars are stars, I've held on for too long; I heard they cut their hands to pieces, the awkward juxtapose cuts and burns, it won't be kept. Your British behaviours creep, echoed commands twist at my feet; to turn away, back inside myself, to that sweet, suckled embrace of shallow belonging.

'I' touches the metal bar for its self, lush cool eases shaking hands. A broken yellow-tail left dangling – today's date. Another gap in the low wall, but we've been tricked before by so many roads to nowhere.

What about the girl? Owe her nothing, but could still go back… try and make things right – one or the other – but you would've done it by now. Maybe signs of life (or proof of death), something to stop her becoming another one of the disappeared, my story's not enough. Sometimes truth's lacking, but it's one of the few good things left.

My hand stays weighted on the bar, fingers fading but I keep my grip. Handle doesn't seem to push or pull, just gives a distant ache in the wrist, nagging to flex without resistance. Harder to hold on, it's now or forever, to step out from this burning world as cruel tongues flicker all around, whispering to me: stay, stay, *stay*.

Nice to be OUT

For some it's slow death by egotrip, trying to try, remember the ritual forgetting through glaze of Saturday morning. Days like this it's easier to go graze with the rest, leave behind these thoughts of heavy water.

Still following after his local claim, the minor ghost of L. Grayson – Entertainer passed away in his most-hatefully beloved N-town still persists in the difference of what he tried to leave behind and carried with him. Now he saunters back around, to catch beautiful, dull boys in the corner of his eye – through doors ajar, pulling some strings, anything to make those catchphrases sing. An errant son of Empire, a tolerated but unwelcome apologia, we inherit his diminished effort, reluctant to ask, too scared to think and spread our wings further, as Gerard did, *ex arbor*.

Grayson was an outandloud queer (*his* verse) neatly boxed in the safety of a television set, a stately homo in the greatest sense, but Larry was a spokesman for no one but himself. Gave his best performances with more of that acceptable strangeness: 'Gay, but in a *nice* way.' A cracked actor showing his banal simpering – to condemn yourself with prostrate arms and clipped feet; the only way to let them really love you. Fertile minds dragged back to go mire in the dull-rust of ignorance, reproducing same-old sayings, so easy to repeat and repeat – to spectate is easier than breathing.

The mad guff of market guys on plastic pitches chokes you smaller, selling half-dead fruit to vegetables already rotting. Zoom to every new iris but it's just driftwood bonesaw knock-knocking idly at a skeletal pier. They all want past at the same time and if you look too long at the wrong person their trouble will soon find you out. Lost bodies caught in time, no will to change because nothing's happened here for the last fifty years. Left behind, progress passed on by; brought you to your knees and you didn't even know it. Here the bombs never dropped. There's no other way to wake the deep-sleeping ones. Take comfort: this one's reduced, down from ten on yesterday and available in a wider range of colours – hope for sale.

There's the circumference of a smile that can't make its ends meet, the jilted nuance of a tired head drags marching arms and legs, with all attention duly paid to the forces of a street. Nod-nodding onwards, listen-in to everyone's everything. We store up these tacit emotions to make talk more than incident: he said, she said – facts don't matter, just a question of narrowing it down to who's getting a kicking tonight, who deserves what and who's currently on top. The wealth-jealous angry ones imagine a better-than-this scene, straight from the dreams you're still allowed to keep. In here the bodies say nothing, ornamental in white sheets. I wash over them, wiping and mopping with a trying smile trying too hard, more scar than jubilee, to force another surface demanding bleach.

Back to the real scene: we stand vertical screens to house the bright lights, all waiting for the change. I shiver when it **BEEP-BEEPs** too familiar at me, the rest cross blindly without fear. Swelling towards strange fascination of retail fronts to go check yourself against beautiful friends down long corridors caging vacant repetition. Clean blank spaces promise unique escape in untold pleasures, soon surrendered to the shallow glass halls, because no one sees the cracks in the path like I can. We budget for happiness (all of this can be *yours*) but ten minutes gone, forgotten what I came here for and I cannot choose on anything but prices that have already been chosen for me.

Every front's a glacial wonder with mannequins restive in death-knell poses, faceless vistas, a premonition of the gross vacuum, just don't expect to care once you step out. But the smell never leaves you, that alkaline sense is a moveable disgust that clings beyond the ugly truth, because of what we are; because of all we've been and failed to say.

Stick-people stop and stare in the rustle of polyethylene, a gathering roar, but where does it all come from? Swept from takeaway yards to be eagerly recycled on the right-side tracks, so the town balances out against the deficit of penguins, bumblebees and ice caps. Without shape, but for the trees, these equally lonely souls fence you in. Others stare infinite as hungry massed haters stack-up to clog the promenades and greying walkways bleeding from the urban centres and retail outlets.

So, it's more like cosmopolitan the more different shops you have; all the names, false starts and *stresses*, some fiction we play into. Then run away to scattered homes, the two-point-four rat holes, not having to see or think about the spoiled horizons of tower blocks. And the well-educated middle-masses don't make love anymore, just dead babies to support them in state – now so devoted to your leisure and the morality of medium, ready-set for more of the tedious future.

We stick/GO/stick/GO, gunked-up, half-halting, another red light warning – **STOP/START** in cruise control, though secretly afraid of emotional pile-ups. We're all happy enough to rubber-neck, or catch the highlights on TV, then moving on with continuing commentary about the after-effects and the red rubber spilt. A single glance divides the ranks, more N&F acolytes still so scared of what their cardiganned father might think, eagerly buying-up organic free-range sizes of meat jackets, not-so-happily married and looking for love in empty car park spaces. But still missing those vital feathers to take the ideal life you once promised yourself was somehow inevitably viable.

I *am* my work, a lad insane, they could never understand. Some serial gaze follows just behind, close enough to make me pick up the pace. I'm lacing tail into trail, now marched into a noose, step *faster*, but fast running out of precinct. That gaunt shadow stalks me at every choking avenue, the same-ward spirit of thwarted architecture closing like air from a sucked shell. Pretend not to be *him,* instead act as a fully-functioning member of our (narrowing) society, more than just living through carrier bags.

Even now, moving so servile, too eager to pretend as they see the real me, another dulled instrument of the crooked health machine, that wretched elite. As I pass they smell the money spilling away, the anger spent in vitriolic whistleblowers and the swathes of bleach command. There's placard-ravers baying for more or less blood as they parade around in the ambulance bays, blocking all entry to try and help raise standards. They carry pictures of the disappeared, looking for answers to questions few are brave enough to ask. Nevermind, whoever brays loudest (beware they shout for thee) it's the same voice that writes and re-writes your histories, so truth is flexible over time. And it's happened all before, as Larry and I step-out these same circles, tracing new shame in turn-key shadows. So our weaker genes struggle on with flat weather of hot winters and cooling summers, the clocks are frozen and reset to zero – all bets are off – reject this jaded monument, burn the colours and shoot the poets – this kitsch life has all been lived before.

Now they overtake – angry spiked silhouettes reeled in and out by the passing sun, the sky is a landfilled playground. This day's too short a leash for the frustrated hearts, so far removed from their common urges – but how to 'engage' 'effectively' – to genuinely feign interest? Speak to myself under mutters of resistance, all hatred incarnate, burning desire to abuse the cash machines, I'll plug in any orifice, machine or not, big-red's a rush but know it's just more oscillations to be conquered. Wildwire quickservice to instant-gratification. I am dynamite with finger-wetted fuse and these darkened shapes play-out my real-time confession, if I could flip-reverse events would I do it all again? In this gratified instant – always– YES.

Some manhandling/sacred parts/wire cross flexed teeth/ Banknote-swiped-into-crease, feels expensive, or should I just use more Labrador-pups? Forget/remember/*think*! Crack on knuckles. Why not here? She covers baby's sacred eyes – this boy's not suitable for public consumption/can't blame you/better not to see/everything behind glass these days/tinkling diamond rain/all living into screens/Moaners moan-on with jeering-taunts and that same question of 'what's to be done with all these have-nots?' soon arises/another crass war/if you've got it, those well-meaning lines soon divide like oil washing water to the mixed results of blood and honey spiking the milk. A self-shed outcast/easy-vilified/by hands / not mine. Some snorting laugh (repeats) between nicotine-caked teeth (repeat).

So glad I brought them all together/to go watch the freak/give him a bone/or some kind of how? Family day out to come clap moo-cow/to see the animal and escape your own reflection/all is exposure/that vanity conceals/sometimes most hated are the most honest/too much uncomfortable air/stiff breeze\I am Socrates' indifference to the sentence. Investment gone south, Chafe Manhattan. Steely grip, colder than skin/**click-clack-flash**/is that instant penalty/was I speaking too fast? Not these days, it's all dog-barks and beeps. A silvery thing that eats wrists, swallows throw-away key, both mouths bit me/is that too tight?/no worries, officer/I'm fine/cold/hard-wound stares/flowing infinite/go see me out/piggy baying for their blood/carrying underarm mince in blood-cellophane bandages/milk as good as flesh.

Couple of deep blues take me round shoulders in vulture-wrap/five-fingered laurel pinch/grips the left/presses heavy/apex groans/feel my sand slipping/another broken seam: 'All is Protection,' so they say. Drag me back to the pale palace, cast under still-burning spire/to the end/to the sea/a roving eye/won't meet\but wanting to go/to be there/out from human crush, where it's bright and all the surfaces are naturally free/the real easy-clean. Coarse on buttocks/generic paper-suit shuffle/rubbed my way out/head down/but still no shame/flat palm/stern wrist/he's got it all/nerck crickd back out from auto, to the cracked pepper-land slashed through yellow chevrons, look down, see wriggling there, but it's only naked feet on the black ocean floor.

Dragged through halls with mutterings of day-job tones straight to some admin-manatee. Slinking out from her paper delta, she looks around their bulked shoulders to find me, a glazed streak in-between. Leans over with all her best forwards, more eyes follow/two cliffs glinting, each has sets of silver knuckles, between these peaks she pierces me.

Fleet glance/catch a fire of knowing concern/plus shock/to see the limpid-beast who done all the damage/conference seeps out from notepad flips/recognise some odd scratches, reminds me of the Long-Fingered Inker: "Abuse of public finance machines," "scaring the public body," "mass exposure, to whit: *negilgent indecency*," he nods back at me. Wait, please, there's more: "Attempted acts of self-pleasure," worked for Diogenes, made him famous like Jesus and all those other flagrant masochists, "raving anti-American slogans," muttering syllables/and so psychoceramic/warning/he's fragile/and easily bored of being bored. "Says his name's not… Eric?" That one stumped them, me too, in fact. Signed over/a disputed territory/one body to another/I am *all* the gossip, for fifteen minutes at least/next-day return to duty, guaranteed/now some sense of belonging/mild relief/and we can get back to relative normal. In here you quickly learn to accept all the things you can't, and so, excepting *that*, become steadily more resistant to change.

Cloister

Laid out to transpire/feeling better/somewhat safely alive/kept alone and apart, wonder if I ever really left. 'Hypnagogic' they call it: 'betwixt dreams and waking life', so the dead poets sing/to spot dirt/to mark time/without change/forcing ourselves to see what we try to ignore/or to see again what's already taken for granted.

RaaapppiiiiiiiiiiiiiidEeeeyeeeeMmmooooooooovvement

Real, or not, reality is out there, more than this still life (it belongs to them) but I am detached nonetheless. Sleepwalker/dragged out from dreams and into life/made to appear more solid than the breath of I am.

Now it's all erosion/laid out to transpire/to mirror the ebb of breathe and flow/changing tides/did I ever really leave? Now they've raked back human layers/stripped sands from mortal reach, skeletal pith to glow the bleach, a petrified cage, my failure to become/burning still/Is *this* waking life? Voice and vision persist in speech, another chance to say something meaningful/ and mean it. Just more words, differently arranged, though still striking the same notes. And out from this translucent skin should emerge a budding Me – that's hope. Repeat.

Then there's the dying girl/still held in time/the man with roots too deep in life and the greediest cheeks that took more than their share/through grinning teeth the hollow men return to haunt me with their future plans – to reset our little world to zero/out from dreams/the sirens who forgot to sing/M. M. so undeserving/ failing to become/any kind of thing\the newborn hearts with perfect spheres, immediately spoiled by the harshest light/Swans exchanged/in and out of love/the boy with eyes of fire/pinned as butterfly/to pale spaces/bleeding stars and killer-angel hearts/ crying for lost smiles in white-box space, a petrified cage/the ones who were saved and the many forgotten/left behind to shadow on, into night\against the day. I won't forget. I'll do my best/No, I *will* forget you…and you'll never even know I was there/

And as we blinked out the last of the dust, they snatched away at what remains so we wouldn't realise it was already sinking down around us, the bone-white towers of this mortal beach. And our lies; all these squared-off fictions, are never resolved, the swelling backlog can never be arrested, it just keeps on recurring – forever delayed. How did we let it stack so high before our little world reached such a crushing low? Choked on numbers we could never hope to calculate or make balance, not beds enough to rest the dead, this place always wore its symmetry awkward and out from time. **Repeat**.

The seasons have cycled by, but more twisted and someone on high has bumped our sky out of sync. Where is he now, the one with the un-zipped mouth? Makes sense to feel angry/it's all there is/so close to the end. See people dying or finding them disappeared one day, start to realise there's no such thing as common sense anymore. Understanding that/learnt to/except/or go blind crazy. That's why the blues and the greens have grown cold/but still fall so hard. There are no new beginnings, sudden growth spurts or definitive shifts, not everything can be resolved in this truncated space/haunted by false starts/broken promises/from hinted clues we know that this one, *this* time, is probably not the same red herring that slipped through our fingers before, when every moment we reach out for new futures, a happy finish, all is eclipsed by naked reveal. **REPEAT**.

Even for these brief minutes, the seconds to hours *stretched*, it doesn't matter – I manage to lie, resolute, twisting words again, revisiting dulled edges and blank faces that failed to leave their mark, just an indefinite blot – you never knew me – and for the rest I never was. Thinking in flux but ageing steady as I realise the easy waste we make, living out detritus by the days.

Now at rest under bright lights of the neon sky we all worship, some must be forced to make way for the new clouds passing, though eventually we're all spun from the same kind of stuff, drifting to collision upon collision, dove-white blind pilots, so they flit silently between battle and play.

Try to block it out – pinch again, soft cloth between fingertips, but not for long - enough, grip is weaker and something stinks in here. It's like staring out through the port-hole of a ship, trapped heavy under churning of an iron sea. All bent to forging wild horses that tear kicks through white crash of the next wave upon wave, then ascending evaporated breath to block out my last bolted-down vision of the sun.

To Repel Ghosts

"Run", they say.
So I run
into blinding light
finally, real warmth on my face.
No, really – RUN.
At pace, they say: *jump*, I try higher.
But not too much,
that's far enough
they say.
Better the lower you stoop – Stop.
Now GO, get after them
More of the same.
Again.

Turning
at speed,
into haste,
not sure why I'm still following,
perhaps only for the last sight of her,
it's always for her
the same one we all miss.
But I'm forever catching up, chasing that same old tail. Like those
dreams, running so eager towards a blacked-out wall before
realising it's just a sickening fall. Predicting impact you *brace* and
there's a last gasp before you hit that dark, brick space – though
you never actually get there.

I've been counting the hours from my bed. Like a cat from a great
height, spun into itself. By twist of instinct, subtle control soon
overrides panic and nature drives the course. Everything has been
falling apart for a long time, silent colours skip to monochrome,
and even now I'm half-blind with it. Refuse to accept this bitter
fall with the floor dropped out –but don't stop– there are no more

suffocating walls or locked doors to hold me and this nature we've made has grown faulty, sickened by false modesty.

Slept enough to wake the dead and drained so long there's almost nothing left, so I keep on going, running towards some neatly cauterised end, some final apology; to get back to *her* and out from this world of recycled neglect.

Rush hour, there's more whispering as the rumour mill takes flight, paper slip zips out from the shuffling nowhere, diffracted bodies all slamming forwards against me: *Closure set – to follow in three days' time*, dashed in same scrawl as those yellow tags, surprised to find the Spectator was not lying.

Then it hits: the squall of human traffic corkscrewed in its own hustle-bustle. Moving into all free space it contaminates, a wild and jutting interface. I see hands grab at objects and other bodies; people kick-screaming, a gleam of white teeth clamped-down the seconds, passed-off as smile/sneer/grimace, but animal all the same, only brute gestures pierce the fug of best intent. Chrome flash of trolley wheels squeaking, moan-broke blankets thrown off then caught half-fallen. Someone slips and goes under, see a grabbing hand lost in furious mosaic of green rinsing blue, a violent mesh where snapping legs burr the air. Shout out, shaking paper changes as the busy ones rustle on, clambering out of the other's way. It's a busy day and all the faces say: 'I've got things on my mind', so I'll ignore yours and be getting on with mine.

Dragging against this apathetic tide
(why can't we all pull the same way?) other voices rise
in contra-flow. Spun round, these muse-striped trousers
chit-chatter of new deaths and hedgerow disputations. "!Taa
Kul" Dodge a cardboard square: **8 eziS sdap ecnenitnocnI** In
snatches of shine eyes see fleet reflection of myself, trapped
inside, there *is* no one else. Less than a blink and I'm gone again,
back to maelstrom chains, my image to theirs, all bleeding out
and identity undone,

"I dias taakul!"

Stream goes faster, so together we accelerate; a sum of forces always pressing on the other to go deeper, faster. Visceral screams cut air, spilling out, a catfish-gulping moo-cow crowd, we go GROWL then fade to grey as a lone sock pokes out from a crushed-up tubechair with ripples of heat escaping. So we choke on exhausted body fumes, the silver reek of sweat pulsing along to form its slimy undertow.

First is the debt, a reminder I can't shake. Same rhythms of the big-red feverish beating at those three letters that won't let go inside my head. Leave that door behind, hurry, the exits have all been bricked-up and walls are growing thin. Windows shutter past in fleeting glimpse, another, another blue streak. There's Queen Bitch's smile, wiped into a smirk, white hem flapping energy-spent but restless in sight, only light escapes out to vanishing point.

Door to door: try, *try*, but locked just like the last. Let go more readily and with less hope as resistance increases. Wrist already feels like cracking, stripped back to bone without skin and these ones are no-go because the vandal workmen took all the sdrawkcab seldnah.

This one: **clunk-crack** – workings stripped, typical. Should move on, press fingers in gap, *pull*, but it's pointless (too stiff). Iron trim, closing over the tips, biting down to a ferrite scab, trying to hold me here with tetanus skin off those knuckles. Blood creeps, running through the bricks and mortar, mingling with the remaining wires, straggle-plucked at the fingernail escape, running in the strip to connect with her singular flow, now the blood's pumping free as less bodies to block, washed down the halls.

These legs have no length left to run and my world tumbles down. No – kick up, move on, *keep going*. Squeezed through a fist the vague endings of plants appear; no roots to show, their edges outgrown the displaced foundations of the low-rise wall. Up the path, incline drops, go screeing down, dodge pillar, there's black ink splashed. Look back, glass jigsaw blurring under imperfect recall, some panes smashed in bullet-hole expanse, random tessellations spit glitter, throwing off instant light, temper of sun trapped in prism of the eye.

Splash of chrome's enough as secondsflashmeback –the corridor– jetting black, where are we now? Rails all round, hemmed-in to keep the cattle lines moving more docile. A silent ship dragged out in nocturne, it glides but I can't keep up and so the beatified one lags far behind. The wheels go on and on, out of my grasp – losing sight– a new wall rises so incredibly h i g h.

Ribs pushed out, trying like a racer to hold momentum as glass overhangs   shoot   by spearinglightblindingsunskyneonandbulbARGONgasthinkon justwastingenergyvapoursinfectinfectinsectinsect   –   just enough! Hit bulkhead terminus, no stretch should be this long. Shoes giving way, the holy soles flap to burst, leftover nuts and bolts litter the skidding surface. Where are they all dropping from? It's like knotted flies. More frequencies tumble to shake the world loose, dragging me straight – this is going to hurt.

See bed corner from curtain peek, move around – it's *hers*. Slip –**SLAM**– bursting into blood-lipped-speech, cells all spent on concrete. Iyv bitedth inthyd my moufth, therszh bludk, itck poursz owt. *Shut up*. Yammering jaw is utheleth now, thee? Cn yew heer, me?

Down and around it's all death matter, I am swept under like limb bracken snapped. Here is tooth-cage of walls within walls, a prison prickling over me. Ants make teetering steps, pylons planting steps of dried shoots – they've really come for me this time. More drones arrive to help scoop and remove, to assist me out from this lucid movement by stuttering eyes. Stripped, clothes taken, all back to nakedness. Make me forget myself again, they want me more like the one from before, back when it was good and everything worked. Fake lights zip past faster because someone palmed the eyes and took my sun away.

My hand's still waiting for me, restive, ready for the final push, a pure moment in a rush of green. Know that cool relief from what seems only minutes ago. Gripping harder now – screwed into folds of perfect white between fingers clenching fist, all to rake in the tides. Body cannot lift itself, no extension from a slab of stone laid out flat on flat. The bubbling swathe comes, crushing fronds into the pillow with no decorum, only late release. Had enough for the both of us, there's a yellow bin laughing with its giant mouth opened wide. Buckled lock's a singular chip of tooth, big enough to grin but lacking lips. I'm a certain kind of failure, but always in the beholder's eye, let them see what they think, muttering towards agreement, and so their world becomes more real than mine.

There's moon calling moon, and meeting somewhere in-between. Blood and the pale reflection slides across –move on– now they're rustling bio-bags out the back, fiery-bright orange that sets the head ablaze. Hard to see, but I know that thick mylar crunk so familiar, perhaps my last glimpse of colour? Ant wriggles into my eye, mingling with the bloodshot vista. Blink wildly –all I can do– but refuse to let go of the handle just yet. It struggles over iris, that infinite dark glare, as the 'I' struggles back it lashes out, but forced to bend to its spindly legs. Locked-in – blinking through bars of light, one small part slowly overcomes the rest. Try to cry, to flush out the needling dread but nothing comes, whether you cry or not –like a dog– too familiar, can't even weep on demand anymore. A tart smell, more than burndt blood in jam – they're incinerating the final traces. And *she's* here too, perhaps out of shot, but feel distant glowering with that too-triumphant air. Getting harder to tell, but it seems we all win in our respective ways, each returning to their place in the scene.

Splinting Hairs To Make The Wave Stand Straight

"Ah, Mr Johnson."

No, no Johnson here, taken his place. Well, not exactly..."Here – he's still here!" Point down the green, grey way/dragged him dee/per inside. Man looks me over, left\right, snorts and walks off. "He's still here!" Calling after him...anyone? Scratch at sheet/thick red/not clean/again/I dream of discharge. Perhaps something to read? Check the Reader's Digress:

Live FAST, die *very* old!

Under my nails, he falls away, gets all in my food/blow/rub nostrils/it's *him*. Every day eat minced Johnson/steak Johnson/ mushed-up/drunk down and out/his cells line our tracheas, hung saintly as heavy-pointed stars, falling tip to tongue – Johnson, the itch I can't forget/rub up fractured bridge/doctor's been blabbing/ in/out/**SPEAK UP**/no need to raise your voice/no y/ours, raise *y/our* voice! Don't look, bELChc in anger, right in front of him, a *professional*. Both look away, so embarrassed, maybe he didn't hear us? A reminder: whenever bronchioles pop we give Johnson his last dance.

Ah, "Peter!" hand out, *he* might remember. But helpless/up to my neck in it "It's you, you're still you!" Not/what wanted I/to say...white coat turns dreary, takes whole minute to do brief come-around.

"No, that's not Peter, that gentleman is a porter, he works *here*." Points down to shoes, aiming clarity, doing his best not to condescend/this i/diot act/his one spot/the whole universe/ interred up his own arse.

My Peter passes, still watching, face strained with that familiar disbelief.

"I know him."

"No you don't. But don't worry Mr Johnson, you know me."

"No, Peter, he's a *Dave!*"

"Nooooo, *you're* Mr Johnson," smiles, head sideways in sympathetic notion, "there are no 'Daves' here."

"He is, Dave is a Peter!" Hurts, pushing words out wrong. Turns to check, then back, few more years gone by. "Why, there's no one there Mr Johnson."

Bite 'Cunt!' into clawed sheet/ugly word/bad to say/dirty, dirty words/spit it in/spit–it–out. Stop, he stares, trouble on that frown... he goes at last. Peter/Dave/know I met him somewhere/seen him/ when vertical/younger/all my facts intact. Definitely him. So shhhure, that same voice, *close your eyes*…seeping in again

endlessly heavy/tied to weight of dead-soul sea/so many hands rise to carry me/we surface/taste air/as if for the first time/ strong hands/soft hands/hands that sometimes held too tight/ and hands that know when to let go/hands the cruel bark against misdemeanour/hands that truly understand/to whisper soft through fingertips/to gri/p and so/othe the anxious need/ling/ and know the beating big-red drum/a skin almost worn away/ sometimes kick-forced/not able to meet in the middle/tender rising\fall\ing peaks/there are good days/bad days/quality of life is measured/meted-out/in the good days you still have left/but how many are enough/to keep going on?/so there are always good hands/just as the good poet said/I only hope the bad ones don't continue to strangle the life from us and the good be overcome.

Missa Defunctorum [To Justify]

Shlept again, out for however long. White cylinder's been passed around, but at least the air's cleaner now. Red dot presses through the sheet. Lift up, she's done it again. Not taped properly; it's been left to run free. Drain me as I slip, *sleep*, seep. I mean tired, today, less of this pushing out to sky, too vague a space to reach. What's that grating under limb? In the future we will kick crumbs out from the bed, good science will find a way, so Lady Stephen said. No solids for me (so how did the crumbs get here?) only food smushed-up in bags, but somehow they seem to find a way back in.

Here's how it works, say now in case of more forgetting: remove oxygen/purity/less than two per-cent/same as real air/ nomoredrugs/last shot creeps me into inertia/tink-tink of screwed-down glass/or a falling screw gone spare/in dream\ing begins...something, I forget/painless as sleep/give me upper/ put me under/too tired to feel the rub alive/but energy enough to wake the dead/kick off covers/but it only brings more trouble, never release.

Silhouettes pass tall and thin/they come more in the day now. This Thursday, or Tuesday...one of the days with tea in it (but there's always T too spare) drip, dripping again/again/going down/going nowhere in translucent strip/There's Judy singing down the way/ Best to be a rainbow/...without you\or something/She's there, another constant, till the wee hours/haunting still/layers of light peeled off as last goodbyes/but no one's listening/Mottled blotch skin, poor marble-cast me/Pus eruptions at salient joints/bones showing pressure/growing all on one side/skull cracking/more bruised fruit/FCUKD ME! Wishing, waiting to be turned/to turn again/for better view/with real peace/of permanent sunrise/never settle/always hovering/Clean and unspoilt/benevolent/knowing infinite/remembering how to walk/or learning how to fly/trapped animal eyes/stuck/all it sees are yellow crystals/clammed lids a purple haze/screening world as shadowplayshapes/into bruised vision/waking up blind is hardly waking up at all/now object in your eyes/level with insect/institution moves in/we are pieces of furniture/daily placed on trial/questions asked with no end/ without answers/and for what? First Flu Heroes/in service of you\ now dying *for* you/how much more can they take/what more can we do? No one knows/and everyone is afraid to say.

Body jabbed and pinched by foreign hands/we pink into one flesh/ tweak me – someone else/same frightened ones/someone better/ caught in so much wilderness/an uncomfortable space/these women have no eyes to blink/doctor has features but no face/ speak without moving lips/always talk-talking time to me/hours slip in one-way conversation/used syllables collapse in scree of tired remarks/filling silent space/hot air/empty/barely breathing/ no seconds worth their weight/till clock hands meet to clap/snap/ gurgling burn in the throat/runs swallowtail choke in rasped hairs\flow\wrong\way/irregular rhythms/words hover head-overheard/eyes can't grasp what ears strain to shape/declare my condition/chewing over corpse fat (still attached)/consult charts so meaningless/always failing to discover what makes you me/all the answers but no questions to ask/everything floats in stasis/ living through jellified space/dust rests on a ledge\running trails on a leaf/fly hit-hits the window panes/flying beyond himself/ just to see other side/a world now closed to me/once you're in, there's another lifetime finding out/doors are open can'tjustleave/ sparescrewfallsagainsomewhere/I've heard it all before/ recognisethatpingtingleingningning...rollingaway/chink of glass/ wait until they say\got to be safe before exiting/sudden breeze/all strange strangeness from the outside/chills/hear bracing of hinge buried deep in rhythm of big-red underground/many thumps/a rise and fall/machine piston-kick punches air/who or what is keeping us alive/modulating the beat/we dance along/who is really driving your plane/anyone in charge of any more anything/ or do decisions just make themselves/creatio-ex-nowt\fashion plastic friends/they do you the same\do we all dream digitally/ or not/no hypnagogic buffer/this life is only simul...simulsc... only pretend/a dry run/grating still/jay gee laughing behind one way screen/spectral faces come to visit me/as swans idle by/never resting/never settling long enough for drowning\forgetting to let go\escape themselves/or to love and be loved\

Free to be / still \ arrive myself/wheeled out from station to station/losing all sense\of time/space\change\sdrawkcab\and forwards/so grateful to everyone\but tired again today/every day is new/but every day the same\advance to terminal reach/ best to rest/to be without you/sing/sung/neatly drawn in blue stripe/children's burning voices rise/all we need are stars/ to be complete/stretched out here/Leonardo has toiled-over human sympathy in eight points/melodyintodischord/waiting to explode in nova/dwindling away to perfect circle/then dust/hard to imagine/frail body gone atomic/a jagged starry scar/tearing new whole in a vacunt universe/not victim\not patient/waiting/ hated/evermore/blind pilots will soon find us out/while the Dead Nurse Cells keep on playing in my mind/how we go on/and on/ now an in-valid that wrestles with himself/under tuck-tightened sheets/Wilde turning Japanese/trapped in endless motions for the wheel/spinning circles of an open-door gaol/sulphurous acne pocks the sheet/gone to seed/but in the end Kunst Macht Frei\eyes oscillate blindly/what to focus on/only water for days/ platelets crack/caught mildly ecstatic/nurse spits/a filthy habit/ side eyes follow/paper thin touch/skin on skin/blocked off/ not allowed/for in-valids/lest we spread infection/better out of sight/bodies and minds not fit for public consumption/and intimacy denied/we are idiots/used to be cretins/but no longer PC/found a more photogenic frame/kindest way to differentiate/ and easier to ignore/look away from the eyes/even broken bodies and rig-beds defeated must still react/withoutlove/withouthate/ hope evaporates/two sevens/recurring/molars/D-sound/count them/C-sound/seven/sure/not really/oh/crowns/yes definitely seven/that D-sound again/rubber fingers over gums/any golds/

pull harder/three times now/that's twenty gone/all nurse words but the voices change/headwink giggle comes/more looks/know thoughts she keeps/blue girls/green/purple/agency drones/all pass by/she would've wanted me/steeped in my youth/no time to regret now/this\\ i/s //t//he////del////uge//////flooding late/too late to remember/ gone again/she is absent monarch no more/ that gambit never pays/hovers now/wounded/bittenandhurt/ an outcast pretender/new ghetto defendant/better than denial/ beyond all apologies/other lives ventured/always nothing she gains/angrygreedghosts surfacing/lust sharpens in age/but too old/it pricks at you more/obsessed with that word/most are/ from greedy suckling pig/adult born with throatslit/anything to get ahead/that singular definite thing/so vital/someaningless/ importanttotheend/armslegshead/circularme/substantialbeing/ alwaysbecoming/nowitisover/goodbyetoallthat/thwartedones/ treat me like child or less/preborn in body/not yet ready to grow/ milk is mana ma ma mother/bear her/bear us\half-moon sound/ its circumference of chalk/not easily forgotten/freedom is illusion for the bed-set one/concerns grow steady/less time to fix remains/ double doors crash/a trifling minute/circle eclipses sky\virus is a language\wrapped round another golden hour/rhythm is a jilted dancer/pursed to a microcosmic dot/we dwell only in memory/ warm bath its own ebbs/she comes/she goes/she comes again/a fleeting rush/wrists long since open and flowing/knowing age/ feel it too/skinshedmanygrammes/arriving at room temperature/ picked pieces of hair/falling///co/rn/\///sw//ay\\ed/aw\\ay/ splinting lives to help them grow straight/end of a circle\ncmplt/ can't remember last/first/his only words/rough red swathes grate/ teeth run over edge/feel grinding dust/powder heat/spiral me down to seashell twist/have no right to sun and air/ellipsing to a vista/or mere glimpses of the moon/tired/so it goes/sharply grasped/but not just yet/bleachyhead/chemical air/swallow breath of moth/ something blue/forever you/themissinghome/wander enduring love/exhaling cold/nomorewaiting/finite trip/mop lines/slapped dust explodes/painful reach above/outerbodyextends/ tense in chest/all is pins/needles/pricked/dark holes in foamsky/this day is never over/brownshoestamp/rise up again/scraping over spine/ another trick angel/so it goes/trying to keep up/mop fronds/slap/ slapped\backtrack\try to keep awake/big red blue vines/running out/come to smother me/stayawake/life is to try/stywk/more mops/mopping/try/plssstywk/bleachy head/so it goes/stywk/it goes on...

Credits:

ES – For Everything, with all my love

CF – Editorial Brilliance and Endless Belief

GSB – Love, Loathing and Insight

RM – To be found in absentia but always present

AC – An undying flame

BH – The Absolute Believer

HD – Arch-architect

ST – The Girl with the Eyes of Fire

SD – Puts the Asylum in Politico

FR – A lyrical mover

AB – A donor to the living; kept our wheels turning

MS – For believing in the book and in me

Acknowledgements:

The author (AS) is grateful to the following literary publications where extracts from this book were published previously:

SquawkBack – In Utero, A Burndt-Out Ward and Pier's End Revisited as "Triptych"

Scarlet Literary Magazine – Lady Lazarus

Black Wire Magazine – Happy Jazz Men

The Erotic Review – Sherbet Section

The Literateur & The Literary Consultancy Literary Futures Competition (2010) – Living Through Saccharin

3:AM – Omni Die

NOUS – Closing Time

Black & Blue – Notes on the Death of Care

About the author

Adam Steiner's articles, poetry and fiction appear in Low Light Magazine, Hong Kong Book Review, L'Ephemere Review, The Arsonist, Glove zine, Anti-Heroin Chic, The Bohemyth, I Am Not A Silent Poet, Rockland Lit, Proletarian Poetry, The Next Review, Fractured Nuance zine.

He produced the Disappear Here project; a series of 27 x poetry films about Coventry ringroad

[www.disappear-here.org]

He tweets **@BurndtOutWard**

URBANE

Urbane Publications is dedicated to
developing new author voices, and publishing
fiction and non-fiction that challenges, thrills and
fascinates. From page-turning novels to innovative
reference books, our goal is to publish what
YOU want to read.

Find out more at

urbanepublications.com